KU-739-441

Toni Morrison was born in Lorain, Ohio. She now divides her time between Rockland County, New York, and Princeton, New Jersey. She is Robert F. Goheen Professor, Council of Humanities, Princeton University. She is the author of five other novels, *The Bluest Eye*, *Sula*, *Song of Solomon*, which won the 1978 National Book Critics' Circle Award for fiction, *Beloved*, which won the 1988 Pulitzer Prize for fiction, and *Jazz*. Her most recent book is *Playing in the Dark: Whiteness and the Literary Imagination*. In 1993 she won the Nobel Prize for Literature.

Also by Toni Morrison in Picador

**The Bluest Eye**
**Sula**
**Song of Solomon**
**Beloved**
**Jazz**

**Playing in the Dark**

# Toni Morrison

# TAR
# BABY

**PICADOR**

*In association with Chatto & Windus*

First published in Great Britain 1981 by Chatto & Windus Ltd
First published in Picador 1991 by Pan Books Ltd
in association with Chatto & Windus Ltd

This edition published 1993 by Picador
a division of Pan Macmillan Publishers Limited
Cavaye Place, London SW10 9PG
and Basingstoke
in association with Chatto & Windus Ltd

Associated companies throughout the world

ISBN 0 330 33636 3

1 3 5 7 9 8 6 4 2

A CIP catalogue record for this book is available from
the British Library

Printed and bound in Great Britain by
Cox & Wyman Ltd, Reading, Berkshire

For

Mrs. Caroline Smith
Mrs. Millie McTyeire
Mrs. Ardelia Willis
Mrs. Ramah Wofford
Mrs. Lois Brooks
—and each of their sisters,
all of whom knew
their true and ancient
properties

For it hath been declared
unto me of you, my brethren, by them
which are of the house of
Chloe, that there are
contentions among you.

I CORINTHIANS 1:11

HE BELIEVED he was safe. He stood at the railing of H.M.S. *Stor Konigsgaarten* and sucked in great gulps of air, his heart pounding in sweet expectation as he stared at the harbour. Queen of France blushed a little in the lessening light and lowered her lashes before his gaze. Seven girlish white cruisers bobbed in the harbour but a mile or so down current was a deserted pier. Carefully casual, he went below to the quarters he shared with the others, who had gone on shore leave, and since he had no things to gather—no book of postage stamps, no razor blade or key to any door—he merely folded more tightly the blanket corners under the mattress of his bunk. He took off his shoes and knotted the laces of each one through the belt hoop of his pants. Then, after a leisurely look around, he ducked through the passageway and returned to the top deck. He swung one leg over the railing, hesitated and considered diving headfirst, but, trusting what his feet could tell him more than what his hands could, changed his mind and simply stepped away from the ship. The water was so soft and warm that it was up to his armpits before he realized he was in it. Quickly he brought his knees to his chest and shot forward. He swam well. At each fourth stroke he turned skyward and lifted his head to make sure his course was parallel to the shore but away. Although his skin blended well with the dark waters, he was careful not to lift his arms too high above the waves. He gained on the pier and was gratified that his shoes still knocked softly against his hips.

After a while he thought it was time to head inland—toward the pier. As he scissored his legs for the turn, a bracelet of water circled them and yanked him in-

1

to a wide, empty tunnel. He struggled to rise out of it and was turned three times. Just before the urge to breathe water became unmanageable, he was tossed up into the velvet air and laid smoothly down on the surface of the sea. He trod water for several minutes while he regulated his breathing, then he struck out once more for the pier. Again the bracelet tightened around his ankles and the wet throat swallowed him. He went down, down, and found himself not at the bottom of the sea, as he expected, but whirling in a vortex. He thought nothing except, I am going counterclockwise. No sooner had he completed the thought than the sea flattened and he was riding its top. Again he trod water, coughed, spat and shook his head to free his ears of water. When he'd rested he decided to swim butterfly and protect his feet from the sucking that had approached him both times from his right side. But when he tore open the water in front of him, he felt a gentle but firm pressure along his chest, stomach, and down his thighs. Like the hand of an insistent woman it pushed him. He fought hard to break through, but couldn't. The hand was forcing him away from the shore. The man turned his head to see what lay behind him. All he saw was water, bloodtinted by a sun sliding into it like a fresh heart. Far away to his right was *Stor Konigsgaarten*, lit fore and aft.

His strength was leaving him and he knew he should not waste it fighting the current. He decided to let it carry him for a while. Perhaps it would disappear. In any case, it would give him time to regain strength. He floated as best he could in water that heaved and pulsed in the ammonia-scented air and was getting darker all the time. He knew he was in a part of the world that had never known and would never know twilight and that very soon he might be zooming toward the horizon in a pitch-black sea. Queen of France was already showing lights scattered like teardrops from a sky pierced to weeping by the blade tip of an early star. Still the water-lady cupped him in the palm of her hand, and nudged him

2

out to sea. Suddenly he saw new lights—four of them—to his left. He could not judge the distance, but knew they had just been turned on aboard a small craft. Just as suddenly the water-lady removed her hand and the man swam toward the boat anchored in blue water and not the green.

As he neared it, he circled. He heard nothing and saw no one. Moving port side, he made out *Seabird II* and a three-foot rope ladder gently tapping the bow. He grabbed a rung and hoisted himself up and aboard. Panting lightly he padded across the deck. There was no trace of the sun and his canvas shoes were gone.

He sidled along the deck, his back against the walls of the wheelhouse, and looked into its curved windows. No one was there, but he heard music from below and smelled food cooked with a heavy dose of curry. He had nothing in mind to say if anyone suddenly appeared. It was better not to plan, not to have a ready-made story because, however tight, prepared stories sounded most like a lie. The sex, weight, the demeanour of whomever he encountered would inform and determine his tale.

He made his way aft and cautiously descended a short flight of stairs. The music was louder there and the smell of curry stronger. The farthest door stood ajar and from it came the light, the music and the curry. Nearer to him were two closed doors. He chose the first; it opened into a dark closet. The man stepped into it and closed the door softly after him. It smelled heavily of citrus and oil. Nothing was clear so he squatted where he was and listened to what seemed to be radio or record-player music. Slowly he moved his hand forward in the dark and felt nothing as far as his arm could reach. Moving it to the right he touched a wall. He duck-waddled closer to it and sank to the floor, his back against the wall.

He was determined to remain alert at all costs, but the water-lady brushed his eyelids with her knuckles. He dropped into sleep like a rock.

The engine did not wake him—he had slept with the

noise of heavier ones for years. Nor did the boat's list. Before the engines, was the forgotten sound of a woman's voice—so new and welcoming it broke his dream life apart. He woke thinking of a short street of yellow houses with white doors which women opened wide and called out, "Come on in here, you honey you," their laughter sprawling like a quilt over the command. But nothing sprawled in this woman's voice.

"I'm never lonely," it said. "Never."

The man's scalp tingled. He licked his lips and tasted the salt caked in his moustache.

"Never?" It was another woman's voice—lighter, half in doubt, half in awe.

"Not at all," said the first woman. Her voice seemed warm on the inside, cold at the edges. Or was it the other way around?

"I envy you," said the second voice, but it was farther away now, floating upward and accompanied by footsteps on stairs and the swish of cloth—corduroy against corduroy, or denim against denim—the sound only a woman's thighs could make. A delicious autumn invitation to come in out of the rain and curl up by the stove.

The man could not hear the rest of their talk—they were topside now. He listened awhile longer and then stood up slowly, carefully, and reached for the doorknob. The passageway was brightly lit—the music and curry smell gone. Through the space between doorjamb and door he saw a porthole and in it, deep night. Something crashed to the deck and a moment later rolled to the door saddle where it stopped in a finger of light at his foot. It was a bottle and he could just make out Bain de Soleil on the label. He did not move. His mind was blank but on call. He had not heard anyone descend, but now a woman's hand came into view. Beautifully shaped, pink nail polish, ivory fingers, wedding rings. She picked up the bottle and he could hear her soft grunt as she stooped. She stood and her hand disappeared. Her feet made no sound on the teak boards, but after a few

4

seconds had passed he heard a door—to the galley, perhaps—open and close.

He was the only man aboard. He felt it—a minus something, which eased him. The two or three—he didn't know how many—women who were handling the boat would soon dock at a private pier where there would be no customs inspector stamping passports and furrowing his brow with importance.

The light from the passage allowed him to examine the closet. It was a shelved storage room with a mixture of snorkelling and fishing gear and ship's supplies. A topless crate took up most of the room on the floor. In it were twelve miniature orange trees, all bearing fruit. The man pulled off one of the tiny oranges no bigger than a good-sized strawberry and ate it. The meat was soft, fibreless and bitter. He ate another. And another. And as he ate a wide surgical hunger opened up in him. He had not eaten since the night before, but the hunger that cut through him now was as unaccounted for as it was sudden.

The boat was under way and it did not take him long to realize that they were headed out, not for Queen of France after all. But not very far, he thought. Women with polished fingernails who needed suntan oil would not sail off into the night if they were going very far. So he chewed bitter oranges and waited on his haunches in the closet. When the boat finally drew along and the engine was cut, his hunger was no longer formal; it made him squeeze his fingers together to keep from bolting out of the closet toward the kitchen. But he waited—until the light footsteps were gone. Then he stepped into the passageway spotted in two places by moonlight. Topside he watched two figures moving behind the beam of a heavy-duty flashlight. And when he heard a car's engine start up, he went below. Quickly he found the galley, but because lights would not do, he patted counter surfaces for matches. There weren't any and the stove was electric. He opened a little refrigerator and discovered its bottled water and half a lime. Elsewhere, in refrigerator light, he located a jar of Dijon mustard, but nothing of the curry food. The dishes were rinsed and so was a white carton. The women had not *cooked* — they had warmed up carry-out food that they'd brought aboard. The man ran his finger deep into corners of the white carton and up its sides. Whatever had been left, they must have given to the gulls. He looked in the cupboards: glasses, cups, dishes, a blender, candles, plastic straws, multi-coloured toothpicks and at last a box of Norwegian flat bread. He covered the bread with mustard, ate it and drank all that was left of the bottled water before going back on deck. There he saw the stars and exchanged stares with the moon, but he could see very little of the land, which was just as well because he was gazing at the shore of an island that, three hundred years ago, had struck slaves blind the moment they saw it.

# 1

THE END of the world, as it turned out, was nothing more than a collection of magnificent winter houses on Isle des Chevaliers. When labourers imported from Haiti came to clear the land, clouds and fish were convinced that the world was over, that the sea-green green of the sea and the sky-blue sky of the sky were no longer permanent. Wild parrots that had escaped the stones of hungry children in Queen of France agreed and raised havoc as they flew away to look for yet another refuge. Only the champion daisy trees were serene. After all, they were part of a rain forest already two thousand years old and scheduled for eternity, so they ignored the men and continued to rock the diamondbacks that slept in their arms. It took the river to persuade them that indeed the world was altered. That never again would the rain be equal, and by the time they realized it and had run their roots deeper, clutching the earth like lost boys found, it was too late. The men had already folded the earth where there had been no fold and hollowed her where there had been no hollow, which explains what happened to the river. It crested, then lost it course, and finally its head. Evicted from the place where it had lived, and forced into unknown turf, it could not form its pools or waterfalls, and ran every which way. The clouds gathered together, stood still and watched the river scuttle around the forest floor, crash headlong into the haunches of hills with no notion of where it was going, until exhausted, ill and grieving, it slowed to a stop just twenty leagues short of the sea.

The clouds looked at each other, then broke apart in confusion. Fish heard their hooves as they raced off to carry the news of the scatterbrained river to the peaks of hills and the tops of the champion daisy trees. But it was too late. The men had gnawed through the daisy trees until, wild-eyed and yelling, they broke in two and hit the ground. In the huge silence that followed their fall, orchids spiralled down to join them.

When it was over, and houses instead grew in the hills, those trees that had been spared dreamed of their comrades for years afterward and their nightmare mutterings annoyed the diamondbacks who left them for the new growth that came to life in spaces the sun saw for the first time. Then the rain changed and was no longer equal. Now it rained not just for an hour every day at the same time, but in seasons, abusing the river even more. Poor insulted, brokenhearted river. Poor demented stream. Now it sat in one place like a grandmother and became a swamp the Haitians called Sein de Vieilles. And witch's tit it was: a shrivelled fogbound oval seeping with a thick black substance that even mosquitoes could not live near.

But high above it were hills and vales so bountiful it made visitors tired to look at them: bougainvillea, avocado, poinsettia, lime, banana, coconut and the last of the rain forest's champion trees. Of the houses built there, the oldest and most impressive was L'Arbe de la Croix. It had been designed by a brilliant Mexican architect, but the Haitian labourers had no union and therefore could not distinguish between craft and art, so while the panes did not fit their sashes, the windowsills and door saddles were carved lovingly to perfection. They sometimes forgot or ignored the determination of water to flow downhill so the toilets and bidets could not always produce a uniformly strong swirl of water. But the eaves were so wide and deep that the windows could be left open even in a storm and no rain could enter the rooms—only wind, scents and torn-away leaves. The floor planks were tongue-in-groove, but the hand-kilned tiles from Mexico, though beautiful to behold, loosened at a touch. Yet the doors were plumb and their knobs, hinges and locks secure as turtles.

It was a wonderful house. Wide, breezy and full of light. Built in the days when plaster was taken for granted and with the sun and the airstream in mind, it needed no air conditioning. Graceful landscaping kept the house just under a surfeit of beauty. Every effort had been made to keep it from looking "designed". Almost nothing was askew and the few things that were had charm: the little island touches here and there (a washhouse, a kitchen garden, for example) were practical. At least that was the judgment of discriminating visitors. They all agreed that except for the unfortunate choice of its name it was "the most handsomely articulated and blessedly unrhetorical house in the Caribbean". One or two had reservations—wondered whether all that interior sunlight wasn't a little too robust and hadn't the owner gone rather overboard with the recent addition of a greenhouse? Valerian Street was mindful of their criticism, but completely indifferent to it. His grey eyes drifted over the face of such guests like a four o'clock shadow on its way to twilight. They reminded him of the Philadelphia widows who, when they heard he was going to spend the whole first year of his retirement in his island house, said, "You'll be back. Six months and you will be bored out of your mind." That was four Decembers ago, and the only things he missed were hydrangeas and the postman. The new greenhouse made it possible to reproduce the hydrangea but the postman was lost to him forever. The rest of what he loved he brought with him: some records, garden shears, a sixty-four-bulb chandelier, a light blue tennis shirt and the Principal Beauty of Maine. Ferrara Brothers (Domestic and International) took care of the rest, and with the help of two servants, the Principal Beauty and mounds of careful correspondence he was finally installed for the year on a hill high enough to watch the sea from three sides. Not that he was interested. Beyond its providing the weather that

9

helped or prevented the steamers bringing mail, he never gave the sea a thought. And whatever he did think about, he thought it privately in his greenhouse. In the late afternoons, when the heat had to be taken seriously, and early in the morning, he was there. Long before the Principal Beauty had removed her sleeping mask, he turned the switch that brought the "Goldberg" Variations into the greenhouse. At first he'd experimented with Chopin and some of the Russians, but the Magnum Rex peonies, overwhelmed by all that passion, whined and curled their lips. He settled finally on Bach for germination, Haydn and Liszt for strong sprouting. After that all of the plants seemed content with Rampal's Rondo in D. By the time he sugared his breakfast coffee, the peonies, the anemones and all their kind had heard forty or fifty minutes of music which nourished them but set Sydney the butler's teeth on edge although he'd heard some variety of it every day for forty years. What made it bearable now was that the music was confined to the greenhouse and not swarming all through the house as it often did back in Philadelphia. He could hear it only thinly now as he wiped moisture beads from a glass of iced water with a white napkin. He set it near the cup and saucer and noticed how much the liver spots had faded on his employer's hand. Mr. Street thought it was the lotion he rubbed on nightly, but Sydney thought it was the natural tanning of the skin in this place they had all come to three years ago.

Except for the kitchen, which had a look of permanence, the rest of the house had a hotel feel about it — a kind of sooner or later leaving appearance: a painting or two hung in an all right place but none was actually stationed or properly lit; the really fine china was still boxed and waiting for a decision nobody was willing to make. It was hard to serve well in the tentativeness. No crystal available (it too was closed away in Philadelphia) so a few silver trays had to do for everything from fruit to petits fours. Every now and then, the Principal Beauty,

10

on one of her trips, brought back from the States another carton chock-full of something Sydney asked for: the blender, the carborundum stone, two more tablecloths. These items had to be carefully selected because they were exchanged for other items that she insisted on taking back to Philadelphia. It was her way of keeping intact the illusion that they still lived in the States but were wintering near Dominique. Her husband encouraged her fantasy by knotting every loose string of conversation with the observation "It can wait till we get home". Six months after they'd arrived Sydney told his wife that periodic airing of trunk luggage in the sunlight was more habit than intention. They would have to tear down that greenhouse to get him off the island because as long as it was there, he'd be there too. What the devil does he do in there, she had asked him.

"Relaxes a little, that's all. Drinks a bit, reads, listens to his records."

"Can't nobody spend every day in a shed for three years without being up to some devilment," she said.

"It's not a shed," said Sydney. "It's a greenhouse I keep telling you."

"Whatever you call it."

"He grows hydrangeas in there. And dahlias."

"If he wants hydrangeas he should go back home. He hauls everybody down to the equator to grow Northern flowers?"

"It's not just that. Remember how he liked his study back at the house? Well, it's like that, except it's a greenhouse kind of a study."

"Anybody build a greenhouse on the equator ought to be shame."

"This is not the equator."

"Could of fooled me."

"Nowhere near it."

"You mean there's some place on this planet hotter than this?"

"I thought you liked it here."

11

"Love it."

"Then stop complaining."

"It's because I do love it that I'm complaining. I'd like to know if it's permanent. Living like this you can't figure nothing. He might pack up any minute and trot off someplace else."

"He'll be here till he dies," Sydney told her. "Less that greenhouse burns up."

"Well, I'll pray nothing happens to it," she said, but she needn't have. Valerian took very good care of the greenhouse for it was a nice place to talk to his ghosts in peace while he transplanted, fed, air-layered, rooted, watered, dried and thinned his plants. He kept a small refrigerator of Blanc de Blancs and read seed catalogues while he sipped the wine. Sometimes he gazed through the little greenhouse panes at the washhouse. Other times he checked catalogues, brochures and entered into ringing correspondence with nurseries from Tokyo to New-burgh, New York. He read only mail these days, having given up books because the language in them had changed so much—stained with rivulets of disorder and meaninglessness. He loved the greenhouse and the island, but not his neighbours. Luckily there was a night, three years ago, after he'd first settled into tropic life, when he woke up with a toothache so brutal it lifted him out of bed and knocked him to his knees. He knelt on the floor clutching the Billy Blass sheets and thinking, This must be a stroke. No tooth could do this to me. Directly above the waves of pain his left eye was crying while his right went dry with rage. He crawled to the night table and pressed the button that called Sydney. When he arrived, Valerian insisted on being taken to Queen of France at once, but there was no way to get there. At that hour fishermen had not even begun to stir and the launch was twice a week. They owned no boat and even if they had neither Sydney nor anyone else could handle it. So the quick-witted butler telephoned the neighbours Valerian hated and got both the use of a fifty-six-foot Palaos called

12

*Seabird II* and the boat skills of the Filipino houseboy. After a daring jeep ride in the dark, an interminable boat ride and a taxi ride that was itself a memory, they arrived at Dr. Michelin's door at 2:00 a.m. Sydney banged while the Filipino chatted with the taxi driver. The dentist roared out the second floor window. He had been run out of Algeria and thought his door was being assaulted by local Blacks — whose teeth he would not repair. At last, Valerian, limp and craven, sat in the dentist's chair where he gave himself up to whatever the Frenchman had in mind. Dr. Michelin positioned a needle toward the roof of Valerian's mouth but seemed to change his mind at the last minute, for Valerian felt the needle shoot straight into his nostril on up to the pupil of his eye and out his left temple. He stretched his hand toward the doctor's trousers, hoping that his death grip — the one they always had to pry loose — would be found to contain the crushed balls of a D.D.S. But before he could get a grip under the plaid bathrobe, the pain disappeared and Valerian wept outright, grateful for the absence of all sensation in his head. Dr. Michelin didn't do another thing. He just sat down and poured himself a drink, eyeing his patient in silence.

This encounter, born in encouraged hatred, ended in affection. The good doctor let Valerian swallow a little of his brandy through a straw and against his better judgment, and Valerian recognized a man who took his medical oaths seriously. They got good and drunk together that night, and the combination of Novocain and brandy gave Valerian an expansiveness he had not felt in years. They visited each other occasionally and whenever Valerian thought of that first meeting he touched the place where the abscess had been and smiled. It had a comic book quality about it: two elderly men drunk and quarrelling about Pershing (whom Valerian had actually seen), neither one mentioning then or ever the subject of exile or advanced years which was what they had in common. Both felt as though they had been run out of their

13

homes. Robert Michelin expelled from Algeria; Valerian Street voluntarily exiled from Philadelphia.

Both had been married before and the long years of a second marriage had done nothing to make either forget his first. The memory of those years of grief in the wake of a termagant was still keen. Michelin had remarried within a year of his divorce, but Valerian stayed a bachelor for a long time and on purpose until he went out for an after lunch stroll on a wintry day in Maine, a stroll he hoped would get rid of the irritable boredom he'd felt among all those food industry appliance reps. His walk from the inn had taken him only two blocks to the main street when he found himself in the middle of a local Snow Carnival Parade. He saw the polar bear and then he saw her. The bear was standing on its hind feet, its front ones raised in benediction. A rosy-cheeked girl was holding on to one of the bear's forefeet like a bride. The plastic igloo behind them threw into dazzling relief her red velvet coat and the ermine muff she waved to the crowd. The moment he saw her something inside him knelt down.

Now he sat in the December sunlight watching his servant pour coffee into his cup.

"Has it come?"

"Sir?"

"The salve."

"Not yet." Sydney removed the lid from a tiny box of saccharin tablets and edged it toward his employer.

"They take their sweet time."

"Mail's cut back to twice a week I told you."

"It's been a month."

"Two weeks. Still botherin you?"

"Not right this minute, but they'll start up again." Valerian reached for the sugar cubes.

"You could be a little less hardheaded about those shoes. Sandals or a nice pair of huaraches all day would clear up every one of them bunions."

"They're not bunions. They're corns." Valerian

14

plopped the cubes into his cup.

"Corns too."

"When you get your medical degree call me. Ondine bake these?"

"No. Mrs. Street brought them back yesterday."

"She uses that boat like it's a bicycle. Back and forth; back and forth."

"Why don't you get one of your own? That thing's too big for her. Can't water-ski with it. Can't even dock it in the town. They have to leave it in one place and get in another little boat just to land."

"Why should I buy her a boat and let it sit ten months out of a year? If those nitwits don't mind her using theirs, it's fine with me."

"Maybe she'd stay the whole year if she had one."

"Not likely. And I prefer she should stay because her husband's here, not because a boat is. Anyway, tell Ondine not to serve them anymore."

"No good?"

"One of the worst things about being old is eating. First you have to find something you can eat and second you have to try not to drop it all over yourself."

"I wouldn't know about that."

"Of course not. You're fifteen minutes younger than I am. Nevertheless, tell Ondine no more of these. Too flaky. They fly all over no matter what you do."

"Croissant supposed to be flaky. That's as short a dough as you can make."

"Just tell her, Sydney."

"Yes, sir."

"And find out if the boy can straighten those bricks. They are popping up all over the place."

"He needs cement he said."

"No. No cement. He's to pack them down properly. The soil will hold them if he does it right."

"Yes, sir."

"Mrs. Street awake?"

"I believe so. Anything else special you going to want

15

for the holidays?"

"No. Just the geese. I won't be able to eat a bit of it, but I want to see it on the table anyway. And some more thalomide."

"You want Yardman to bring you thalomide? He can't even pronounce it."

"Write a note. Tell him to give it to Dr. Michelin."

"All right."

"And tell Ondine that half Postum and half coffee is revolting. Worse than Postum alone."

"Okay. Okay. She thought it would help."

"I know what she thought, but the help is worse than the problem."

"That might not be what the trouble is, you know."

"You are determined to make me have an ulcer. I don't have an ulcer. You have an ulcer. I have occasional irregularity."

"I *had* an ulcer. It's gone now and Postum helped it go."

"I'm delighted. Did you say she was awake?"

"She was. Could have gone back to sleep, though."

"What did she want?"

"Want?"

"Yes. Want. The only way you could know she was awake is if she rang you up there. What did she want?"

"Towels, fresh towels."

"Sydney."

"She did. Ondine forgot to—"

"What were the towels wrapped around?"

"Why you keep thinking that? Everything she drinks you see her drink. A little dinner wine, that's all and hardly more than a glass of that. She never was a drinker. You the one. Why you always trying to make her into one?"

"I'll speak to Jade."

"What could Jade know that I don't?"

"Nothing, but she's as honest as they come."

"Come on, now, Mr. Street. It's the truth."

Valerian held a pineapple quarter with his fork and

16

began cutting small regular pieces from it.

"All right," said Sydney, "I'll tell you. She wanted Yardman to stop by the airport before he comes Thursday."

"What for, pray?"

"A trunk. She's expecting a trunk. It's been shipped already, she said, and ought to be here by then."

"What an idiot."

"Sir?"

"Idiot. Idiot."

"Mrs. Street, sir?"

"Mrs. Street, Mr. Street, you, Ondine. Everybody. This is the first time in thirty years I've been able to enjoy this house. Really live in it. Not for a month or a weekend but for a while, and everybody is conspiring to ruin it for me. Coming and going, going and coming. It's beginning to feel like Thirtieth Street Station. Why can't everybody settle down, relax, have a nice simple Christmas. Not a throng, just a nice simple Christmas dinner."

"She gets a little bored, I guess. Got more time than she can use."

"Insane. Jade's here. They get on like schoolgirls, it seems to me. Am I wrong?"

"No, you're right. They get along fine, like each other's company, both of them."

"They don't like it enough to let it go at that. Apparently we are expecting *more* company, and since I am merely the owner and operator of this hotel, there is no reason to let me know about it."

"Can I get you some toast?"

"And you. You have finally surprised me. What else have you been keeping from me?"

"Eat your pineapple."

"I am eating it."

"I can't stand here all morning. You got corns—I got bunions."

"If you won't take my advice, bunions are the consequence."

"I know my work. I'm a first-rate butler and I can't be first-rate in slippers."

"You know your work, but I know your feet. Thom McAn will be the death of you."

"I never wore Thom McAns in my life. Never. In nineteen twenty-nine I didn't wear them."

"I distinctly recall at least four pairs of decent shoes I've given you."

"I prefer my bunions to your corns."

"Ballys don't cause corns. If anything they prevent them. It's the perspiration that causes them. When —"

"See? Gotcha. That's exactly what I been tellin you. Philadelphia shoes don't work in the tropics. Make your feet sweat. You need some nice huaraches. Make your feet feel good. Free em up, so they can breathe."

"The day I spend in huaraches is the day I spend in a straitjacket."

"You keep on hacking away at your toes with a razor and you'll beg for a straitjacket."

"Well, you won't know about it because your Thom McAn bunions are going to put you in a rocker for the rest of your life."

"Suit me fine."

"And me. Maybe then I could hire somebody who wouldn't keep things from me. Sneak Postum into a good pot of coffee, saccharin in the lime pie. And don't think I don't know about the phony salt."

"Health is the most important thing at our age, Mr. Street."

"Not at all. It's the least important. I have no intention of staying alive just so I can wake up and skip down the stairs to a cup of Postum in the morning. Look in the cabinet and get me a drop of medicine for this stuff."

"Cognac's not medicine." Sydney moved toward the sideboard and bent to open one of its doors.

"At seventy everything's medicine. Tell Ondine to quit it. It's not doing a thing for me."

"Sure don't help your disposition none."

18

"Exactly. Now. Very quietly and very quickly, tell me who this company is."

"No company, Mr. Street."

"Don't antagonize an old man reduced to Postum."

"It's your son. Michael's not company."

Valerian put his cup carefully onto the saucer. "She told you that? That Michael was coming?"

"No. Not exactly. But so Yardman would know what to look for she told me where the trunk was coming from and what colour it was."

"Then it's coming from California."

"It's coming from California."

"And it's red."

"And it's red. Fire red."

"With 'Dick Gregory for President' stickers pasted on the sides."

"And a bull's-eye painted on the lid."

"And a lock that only closes if you kick it, but opens with a hairpin and the key is . . ." Valerian stopped and looked up at Sydney. Sydney looked at Valerian. They said it together. ". . . at the top of Kilimanjaro."

"Some joke," said Valerian.

"Pretty good for a seven-year-old."

They were quiet for a while, Valerian chewing pineapple, Sydney leaning against the sideboard. Then Valerian said, "Why do you suppose he hangs on to it? A boy's camp footlocker."

"Keep his clothes in."

"Foolish. All of it. The trunk, him and this visit. Besides, he won't show."

"She thinks so this time."

"She's not thinking. She's dreaming, poor baby. Are you sure there was nothing between those towels?"

"Here comes the lady. Ask her yourself."

A light clicking of heels on Mexican tile was getting louder.

"When the boy goes to the airport," whispered Valerian, "tell him to pick up some Maalox on the way back." "Well," he said to his wife, "what have we here? Wonder Woman?"

"Please," she said, "it's too hot. Good morning, Sydney."

"Morning, Mrs. Street."

"Then what is that between your eyebrows?"

"Frownies."

"Beg pardon?"

"Frownies."

Sydney walked around the table, tilted the pot and poured coffee soundlessly into her cup.

"You have trouble frowning?" asked her husband.

"Yes."

"And that helps?"

"Supposed to." She held the cup in front of her lips and closed her eyes. The steam floated into her face while she inhaled.

"I am confused. Not senile, mind you. Just confused. Why would you want to frown?"

Margaret took another breath of coffee steam and opened her eyes very slowly. She looked at her husband with the complete dislike of a natural late-sleeper for a cheerful early-riser.

"I don't want to frown. Frownies don't make you frown. They erase the consequences of frowning."

Valerian opened his mouth but said nothing for a moment. Then: "But why don't you just stop frowning? Then you won't need to paste your face with little pieces of tape."

Margaret sipped more coffee and returned the cup to its saucer. Lifting the neckline of her dress away from her she blew gently into her bosom and looked at the pale wedges Sydney placed before her. Ondine had left the spiky skin on the underside deliberately—just to hurt and confuse her. "I thought we'd have . . . mangoes." Sydney removed the fruit and hurried to the swinging doors. "What gets into everybody? The same thing every morning?"

20

"I wanted pineapple. If you don't, tell Sydney at night what you'd like for breakfast the next morning. That way he can—"

"She knows I hate fresh pineapple. The threads get in my teeth. I like canned. Is that so terrible?"

"Yes. Terrible."

"They tell *us* what to eat. Who's working for who?"

"Whom. If you give Ondine menus for the whole week—that is exactly what she will prepare."

"Really? You've been doing that for thirty years and you can't even get her to fix you a cup of coffee. She makes you drink Postum."

"That's different."

"Sure."

Sydney returned with a bowl of crushed ice in which a mango stood. The peeling had been pulled back from the shiny fruit in perfect curls. The slits along the pulp were barely visible. Valerian yawned behind his fist, then said, "Sydney, can I or can I not order a cup of coffee and get it?"

"Yes, sir. 'Course you can." He put down the mango and filled Valerian's cup.

"See, Margaret. And there's your mango. Four hundred and twenty-five calories."

"What about your croissant?"

"One twenty-seven."

"God." Margaret closed her eyes, her blue-if-it's-a-boy blue eyes and put down her fork.

"Have a grapefruit."

"I don't want grapefruit. I want mango."

Valerian shrugged. "Slurp away. But you had three helpings of mousse last night."

"Two, I had two. Jade had three."

"Oh, well, only two . . ."

"Well, what do we have a cook for? Even I can slice grapefruit."

"To wash the dishes."

21

"Who needs dishes? According to you, all I need is a teaspoon."

"Well, someone has to wash your teaspoon."

"And your shovel."

"Funny. Very funny."

"It's true." Margaret held her breath and stuck her fork into the mango. She exhaled slowly as the section came away on the tines. She glanced at Valerian before putting the slice in her mouth. "I've never seen anyone eat as much as you and not gain an ounce—ever. I think she adds things to my food. Wheat germs or something. At night she sneaks in with one of those intravenous things and pumps me full of malts."

"Nobody pumps you full of anything."

"Or whipped cream maybe."

Sydney had left them discussing calories and now he was back with a silver tray on which wafer-thin slices of ham tucked into toast baskets held a poached egg. He went to the sideboard and lifted them onto plates. He laid stems of parsley on the right rim and two tomato slices to the left of each plate. He whisked away the fruit bowls, careful not to spill the water from the ice, and then leaned forward with the hot dish. Margaret frowned at the dish and waved it away. Sydney returned to the sideboard, put the rejected dish down and picked up the other. Valerian accepted it enthusiastically and Sydney edged the salt and pepper mill an inch or two out of his reach.

"I suppose you are decorating the house with guests for Christmas. Push that salt over here, will you?"

"Why would you suppose that?" Margaret stretched out a hand, a beautifully manicured hand, and passed him the salt and pepper. Her little victory with the mango strengthened her enough to concentrate on what her husband was saying.

"Because I asked you not to. It follows therefore that you would defy me."

"Have it your way. Let's just spend the holidays all

alone in the cellar."

"We haven't got a cellar, Margaret. You should take a look around this place. You might like it. Come to think of it, I don't believe you've seen the kitchen yet, have you? We've got two, two kitchens. One is—"

"Valerian. Please shut up."

"But this is exciting. We've been coming here for only thirty years and already you've discovered the dining room. That's three whole rooms. One every decade. First you found the bedroom. That is I assume you did. It's hard to tell when a wife sleeps separately from her mate. Then in nineteen sixty-five I think it was, you located the living room. Remember that? Those cocktail parties? Those were good times. Heights, I'd say. You not only knew the airport and the dock and the bedroom, but the living room as well."

"Yes. I am having guests for Christmas."

"Then the dining room. Speak of a find! Dinner for ten, twenty, thirty. Think what's before you in one kitchen, let alone two. We could entertain hundreds, thousands."

"Michael's coming."

"I wouldn't put it off any longer if I were you. If we hurry by the time I'm eighty we can invite Philadelphia."

"And a friend of his. That's all."

"He won't come."

"I've never had more than twelve people in this house at any one time."

"His friend will show and he won't. Again."

"And I am not a cook and I never have been. I don't want to see the kitchen. I don't like kitchens."

"Why work yourself up this way every year? You know he'll disappoint you."

"I was a child bride, remember? I hadn't time to learn to cook before you put me in a house that already had one plus a kitchen fifty miles from the front door."

"Seems to me you did once. You and Ondine giggling away in the kitchen is one of my clearest and fondest memories."

23

"Why do you say that? You always say that."

"It's true. I'd come home and you'd be—"

"Not that! About Michael, I mean. That he won't show up."

"Because he never has."

"He never has *here*. Down here in this jungle with nothing to do. No young people. No fun. No music . . ."

"No *music*?"

"I mean his kind of music."

"You surprise me."

"And so he won't be bored to death, I've invited a friend of his—" She stopped and pressed a finger to the frownie between her eyes. "I haven't invited anybody down here in years because of you. You hate everybody."

"I don't hate anybody."

"Three years it's been. What's the matter with you? Don't you want to see your son anymore? I know you don't want to see anybody else—but your own son. You pay more attention to that fat dentist than you do Michael. What are you trying to prove down here? Why do you cut yourself off from everybody, everything?"

"It's just that I'm undergoing this very big change in my life called dying."

"Retirement isn't death."

"A distinction without a difference."

"Well, I am not dying. I am living."

"A difference without distinction."

"And I'm going back with him."

"Sounds terminal."

"It might be."

"Christmas isn't the best time to make decisions like that, Margaret. It's a sentimental holiday full of foolish—"

"Look. I'm going."

"I don't advise it."

"I don't care."

"He's not a little boy anymore. The knapsack, I know, is confusing, but Margaret, he'll soon be thirty."

24

"So what?"

"So what makes you think he'll want you to live with him?"

"He will."

"You're going to travel with him? Go to snake dances?"

"I'm going to live near him. Not with him, near him."

"It won't work."

"Why not?"

Valerian put his palms down on either side of his plate. "He doesn't care all that much for us, Margaret."

"You," she said, "he doesn't care all that much for you."

"Whatever you say."

"Then I can go?"

"We'll see. When he gets here, ask him. Ask him if he wants his mother next door to the reservation in a condominium."

"He's through with that. The school closed. He's not with them anymore."

"Oh? He's done the Hopis? Gone on to the Choctaws, I suppose. No, wait a minute. C comes before H. Let me see, Navajos, right?"

"He's not with any tribe. He's studying."

"What, pray?"

"Environmental something. He wants to be an environmental lawyer."

"Does he now?"

"Yes."

"Well, why not? A band manager, shepherd, poet-in-residence, film producer, lifeguard ought to study law, the more environmental the better. An advantage really, since he's certainly had enough environments to choose from. And what will you do? Design no-nuke stickers?"

"You can't make me change my mind."

"It's not a matter of changing it. It's a matter of using it. Let him alone, Margaret. Let him be. You can't do it over. What you want is crazy."

"No. *This* is crazy. I live in airplanes now. Nowhere.

25

Not in Philadelphia where I at least have friends. Not here boiling under a palm tree with nobody to talk to. You keep saying next month, next month, next month. But you never do it. You never leave."

"But you do—whenever you like. Lots of people live in two places."

"I want to live in one—just one. In October you said after New Year's, you'll come back. Then when New Year's comes you'll say after carnival. If I want to live with you I have to do it your way—here. I can't keep flying back and forth across the ocean wondering where I left the Kotex. Anyway. I'm going back with Michael. For a while. Make a home for him."

"You'll have to eat corncakes. Three hundred and twenty-five per serving."

"I told you he's not there anymore. He's applied at U.C. Berkeley, I think."

"Marijuana cookies then. Two hundred—"

"You will not listen."

"Margaret, promise me something."

"What?"

"That you won't go unless he agrees to it."

"But—"

"Promise."

She studied him for a moment for she never knew if he was teasing her, patronizing her or simply lying. But now he looked deadly earnest so she nodded saying, "All right. All right. That's no risk."

"What about Jade, then?" asked Valerian.

"What about her? She can stay as long as she likes."

"She thinks she's working for you."

"Let her work for you while I'm gone."

"Oh dear."

"Or just relax. She wanted to spend the winter here is all. Why, I can't think."

"Getting over an affair, I thought."

"At her age it takes three days, not three months."

"You don't like her anymore?"

26

"I love her. But I'm not going to give up going back with Michael just to help her cool off for another month or two. Besides, look what she has to go back to."

"What?"

"Everything. Europe. The future. The world. Why are you frowning? Does she need money?"

"No. No. Not that I know of. She signed on with some agency or something in New York, or is about to."

"There. She doesn't need the pretence of working for me."

Valerian swallowed the last bit of egg and ham and tapped the toast basket with his fork. "Clever. Very clever."

"Jade?"

"No, Ondine. This is really good. I think she served something like this in the States."

"Talk about calories. You're eating like a horse already and the day has just started."

"Pique."

"Pique. Why?"

"The nursery, Stateside, sent a defective order. Completely ruined."

"Shame." Margaret reached toward a croissant, changed her mind and withdrew her hand.

"Have it," said her husband. "It wasn't four twenty-five, that mango. Not even a hundred."

"You liar. I should have known. I was going to ask Jade about that."

"She wants to open up a little shop of some sort," he said.

"You're mumbling."

"Shop. She wants to be a model a little longer, then open up a shop."

"Wonderful. She has a head. You'll help her, won't you? Won't you?"

"Of course."

"Well, why the long face?"

"I was thinking of Sydney and Ondine."

27

"As usual. What about them?"

"They like her here."

"We all do."

"She's their family. All they have of a family left."

"And you. You're as much family to them as she is. They've known you longer than they have her."

"It's not the same."

"What is it? What are you thinking?"

"Nothing."

"Something."

"Sydney's very excited about that shop idea," Valerian said. "Ondine too."

"Oh?"

"Nothing definite. At the dreaming stage still."

"Now who's worked up?"

"It's a possibility, that's all. An attractive one for them, I suppose."

"That's selfish, Valerian."

"Perhaps, but I don't think so. I don't think so."

"You're worrying about nothing. They won't leave you and the situation they have here to go into the retail business. At this time of life, never."

"Yes?"

"Of course yes. Look at you." She laughed. "You're scared. Scared Kingfish and Beulah won't take care of you."

"I have always taken care of them."

"And they will do the same for you. God knows they will. You couldn't pry them out of here. With or without Jade. They are yours for life."

"Don't snarl. Your frownie is coming loose."

"I'm not snarling. They're loyal people and they should be."

"I've never understood your jealousy."

"That's just like you to call it jealousy."

"When we were first married I used to have to pull you away from Ondine. Guests in the house and you'd prefer gossiping in the kitchen with her."

"Well, you sure put a stop to that, didn't you?"

"I put a stop to a hostess neglecting guests. I didn't put a stop to —"

"I was shy."

"But I didn't want you to turn around and be outright hateful to her. She would have quit even then if I hadn't —"

"I know. I know, and then Sydney the Precious would have left too. Don't dwell on it. They're here and they always will be. I can guarantee it."

"But you won't be."

"I said for a while."

"*If* Michael comes."

"He will."

"We'll see."

"Then it's all set? I can go?"

"Don't push me into my last and final hour, Margaret. Let me saunter toward it."

"You are sweet."

"Not sweet, helpless."

"You? Valerian Street, the Candy King? You've never been stronger, or more beautiful."

"Stop. You got your way."

"You *are* beautiful. Slim. Trim. Distingue."

"Forgive her, Larousse."

"Distingue?"

"Distingué."

"Joueaux Noël."

"Dear God."

"Joyoux Noël, Sydney."

"Ma'am?"

"Did you tell the boy about the trunk?"

"He hasn't come yet, ma'am. As soon as he does . . ."

"And turkey. Ondine will do a turkey. Sydney?"

"Ah, yes, ma'am, if you like."

"I like. I really like."

"I've ordered geese, Margaret."

"Geese?" She stared at Valerian for suddenly she could

29

not imagine it. Like a blank frame in a roll of film, she lost the picture that should have accompanied the word. Turkey she saw, but geese . . .. "We have to have turkey for Christmas. This is a family Christmas, an old-fashioned family Christmas, and Michael has to have turkey."

"If Tiny Tim could eat goose, Margaret, Michael can eat goose."

"Turkey!" she said. "Roast turkey with the legs sticking up and a shiny brown top." She was moving her hands to show them how it looked. "Little white socks on the feet."

"I'll mention it to Ondine, ma'am."

"You will not mention it! You will tell her!"

"Yes, ma'am."

"And apple pies."

"Apple, ma'am?"

"Apple. And pumpkin."

"We are in the Caribbean, Margaret."

"No! I said no! If we can't have turkey and apple pie for Christmas then maybe we shouldn't be here at all!"

"Hand me some of my medicine, Sydney."

"Yes, sir."

"Sydney?"

"Ma'am?"

"Will we have turkey and apple pies for Christmas dinner?"

"Yes, ma'am. I'll see to it."

"Thank you. Is Jade down yet?"

"Not yet, ma'am."

"When she is, tell her I'll be ready at ten."

"Yes, ma'am."

Margaret Lenore stood up so suddenly her chair careened for a brief moment before righting itself. Quickly she was gone.

"Everything all right, Mr. Street?"

"I am going to kill you, Sydney."

"Yes, sir."

30

BEYOND THE doors through which Sydney had been gliding all morning was the first kitchen. A large sunny room with two refrigerators, two steel sinks, one stove, rows of open cabinets and a solid oak table that seated six. Sydney sat down and immediately the place he took at the perfectly round table was its head. He looked out the windows and then at his wife's arm. The flesh trembled as she wire-whisked a bowl of eggs.

"Mango all right?" she asked without turning her head.

"She ate a mouthful," said Sydney.

"Contrary," murmured his wife. She poured the eggs into a shallow buttered pan, and stirred them slowly with a wooden spoon.

"It's all right, Ondine. Lucky you had one."

"I'll say. Even the coloured people down here don't eat mangoes."

"Sure they do." Sydney slipped a napkin from its ring. The pale blue linen complemented his mahogany hands.

"Yardman," said Ondine. "And beggars." She poured the eggs into a frying pan of chicken livers. She was seventeen years her husband's junior, but her hair, braided across the crown of her head, was completely white. Sydney's hair was not as black as it appeared, but certainly not snow white like Ondine's. She bent to check on the biscuits in the oven.

"What's the Principal Beauty hollering about?"

"Turkey."

Ondine looked at her husband over her shoulder. "Don't fool with me this morning."

"And apple pie."

"You better get me a plane ticket out of here." She straightened.

"Calm down, girl."

"She want it, she can come in here and cook it. After she swim on back up to New York and get the ingredients. Where she think she is?"

"It's for the boy."

"God help us."

"She wants an old-fashioned Christmas."

"Then she can bring her old-fashioned butt in here and cook it up."

"Pumpkin pie, too."

"Is any of this serious?"

"I told you. The boy is coming."

"He's always coming. Ain't got here yet."

"Then you know as much as I do. Every year the same. She'll walk on a hot tin roof till he wires saying he can't. Then look out!"

"You can't be serious about apples. Surely."

"I can't be certain, Ondine. Looks like he might make it this time. He's already shipped his trunk. That old red footlocker, remember? Yardman supposed to pick it up Thursday."

"She don't know that. He call her and say so? Ain't been no mail come in here from him, has it?"

"She called him, I believe. This morning. Making sure of the time difference."

"That's what she rang you up for?"

"I didn't have time to tell you."

"When's he due?"

"Soon, I reckon." Sydney dropped two sugar cubes into his Postum.

"I thought all he ate was sunflowers and molasses these days."

Sydney shrugged. "Last time I saw him he ate a mighty lot of steak."

"And fresh coconut cake. The whole cake as I recall."

"That's your fault. You spoiled him stupid."

"You can't spoil a child. Love and good food never spoiled nobody."

"Then maybe he'll fly in here for sure this time just to get some more of it."

"No way. Not down here, he won't. He hates this place, coconuts and all. Always did."

"Liked it when he was younger."

"Well, he's grown now and sees with grown-up eyes, like I do."

"I still say you ruined him. He can't fix his mind on nothing."

"I ain't ruined him. I gave him what any child is due."

"Uh-huh."

"You really believe that? That I ruined him?"

"Oh, I don't know, girl. Just talking. But between you and the Principal Beauty, he never wanted for affection."

"Bitch."

"You have to stop that, Ondine. Every time she comes down here you act out. I'm getting tired of refereeing everybody."

"The Principal Beauty of Maine is the main bitch of the prince."

"You worry me. Cut the fire out from under that pan and bring me my breakfast."

"I just want you to know I am not fooled by all that turkey and apple pie business. Fact is he don't want to be nowhere near her. And I can't say as I blame him, mother though she be."

"You making up a life that nobody is living. She sees him all the time in the States and he don't complain."

"Visits. Visits he can't do nothing about, but he never comes to see her."

"He writes her sweet letters."

"That's what he studied in school."

"Letters?"

"Poems."

"Don't think he don't love her. He does."

"I didn't say he didn't love her; I said he don't want to be near her. Sure he love her. That's only natural. He's not the one who's not natural. She is."

"You and Mr. Street just alike. Always thinking evil about that girl."

"When she get to be a girl?"

"She was a girl when I first saw her. Seventeen."

33

"So was I."

"Aw, the devil. Everybody's going crazy in this house. Everybody. Mr. Street hollering about Postum and putting cognac in his cup—she's hollering about mangoes and turkeys and I don't know what all and now you denying her her own son."

"I'm not denying her nothin. She can have him. He turned out to be a different breed of cat anyway after he went to all those schools. He was a sweet boy. Now I suppose he'll be wanting mangoes too. Well, he can have em if he'll stop coming in my kitchen to liberate me every minute."

"He means well, Ondine."

"What's this about the Postum?"

"He says no more diet stuff. Regular coffee, real salt, all such as that."

"He'll rue it."

"It's his life."

"Okay by me. It's bothersome trying to cook with all those concoctions. Fake this. Fake that. Tears up a meal if you ask me. That plus everything temporary like this. Seems like everything I need to cook with is back in Philadelphia. I was just going by what the doctor told him three years ago. He leave that liquor alone he could eat like regular people. Is he still constipated?"

"Nope. Other people get constipated. He gets occasional irregularity. But he wants some Maalox just in case. Tell Yardman to bring a bottle out next time."

"He the one should be eating mangoes. Open him right up. Other than for that, I can't think of a soul in this world eat mangoes for breakfast."

"I do."

They hadn't heard her come in. She stood before the swinging doors, hands on hips, toes pointing in, and smiling. Sydney and Ondine looked around, their faces bright with pleasure.

"Here she is!" said Sydney, and reached out a hand to hug her waist. She came forward and kissed his forehead.

Then Ondine's.

"Sleep well, sugar?"

"Well and late." She sat down and locked her arms over her head in a deep yawn. "The air. The night air is incredible. It's like food."

"You weren't serious, were you?" asked Ondine. "About wanting a mango?"

"No. Yes. I don't know." Jadine dug her fingernails into her hair and scratched.

"I've got some nice liver. Sautéed just right. With eggs."

"What kind of liver?"

"Chicken."

"The chicken's eggs and its liver? Is there anything inside a chicken we don't eat?"

"Jadine, we're still at the table," said Sydney. "Don't talk like that." He patted her knee.

"Pineapple," she said. "I'll have some pineapple."

"Well," said Ondine, "thank God somebody in this house got some sense. That hussy sure don't."

"Let up, woman. She's got something to deal with."

"So has he."

"Yeah, well, I've known him practically all his life and I'll tell you this: he gets his way. Even when he was a little boy, he got his way."

Jadine looked up. "Valerian was a little boy? You sure?"

"Hush up." Sydney wiped his mouth with the pale blue napkin. "You be around all day today?"

"Most of it. But I may have to take the boat back to town."

"What for? More Christmas shopping?"

"Yep."

"You sure you won't have some livers?"

"No, thanks, Nanadine, but could I have a cup of chocolate?"

"In this heat?" asked Sydney. He raised his eyebrows, but Ondine smiled. She loved it when her niece called her that—a child's effort to manage "Aunt Ondine". "Sure

35

you can," she said, and went immediately to the nickel-plated door that opened on a hallway. At the end, four steps descended to the second kitchen where supplies were kept and which was equipped like a restaurant kitchen.

Back in the first kitchen Sydney grumbled in the sunlight. "Air conditioning in the shed, but none in the house. I swear. All that money."

Jadine licked sweet wet juice from her fingertips. "I love it. Makes the nights so much better. As soon as the sun goes down it's cool anyway."

"I work in the daytime, girl."

"So do I."

"You still calling that work?"

"It is work."

Sydney sucked his teeth. "Exercising. Cutting pictures out of magazines. Going to the store."

"I type," she said. "And going to the store is a twenty-three-mile boat trip, *after* driving through jungle, swamp . . ."

"You better not let him hear you call anything on this island jungle."

"Well, what does he call it? The Tuileries?"

"You know what he calls it," said Sydney, digging in his vest pocket for a toothpick. "L'Arbe de la Croix."

"I hope he's wrong." Jadine laughed.

Ondine entered, limping a little from the few stairs and frowning. "There's something in this house that loves bittersweet chocolate. I had six eight-ounce boxes, now there's two."

"Rats?" asked Sydney. He looked concerned. Mr. Street and the other families had pooled money to have mongooses shipped to the island to get rid of snakes and rats.

"If rats fold wrappers, then yes, rats."

"Well, who then? Couldn't be over fifteen people on the whole island. The Watts are gone; so are the Broughtons," said Sydney.

36

"Maybe it's one of the new staff over at Deauville. All Filipinos again, I heard. Four of them."

"Come on, Nanadine. Why would they walk all the way over here to steal a piece of chocolate?" Her niece swirled a napkin ring on her finger.

Ondine poured a tiny bit of water into a saucepan and plopped a chocolate square into it. "Well, somebody is. And not just chocolate either. The Evian, too. Half a case."

"Must be Yardman," said Sydney, "or one of them Marys."

"Couldn't be. He don't step foot inside the house unless I'm behind him and I can't get them Marys further in than the screen door."

"You don't know that, Ondine," said Sydney. "You not in here every minute."

"I do know that and I know my kitchens. Better than I know my face."

Jadine loosened the straps of her halter and fanned her neck. "Well, let me tell you your face is prettier than your kitchens."

Ondine smiled. "Look who's talking. The girl who modelled for Karen."

"Caron, Nanadine. Not Karen."

"Whatever. My face wasn't in every magazine in Paris. Yours was. Prettiest thing I ever saw. Made those white girls disappear. Just disappear right off the page." She stirred milk into the chocolate paste and chuckled. "Your mother would have loved to see that."

"You think you'll ever do that again?" Sydney asked her.

"Maybe, but once is plenty. I want my own business now."

Once more they looked at her, pleasure shining in their faces. Ondine brought the chocolate and set it down. She touched Jadine's hair and said softly to her, "Don't you ever leave us, baby. You all we got."

"Whipped cream?" asked Jadine, smiling. "Any

whipped cream?"

Ondine looked in the refrigerator for cream while Sydney and Jadine turned to the window as they heard footsteps on the gravel. Yardman came alone on Saturdays, pulling his own oars in his own mud-coloured boat with *Prix de France* fading in blue on the prow. Today being Saturday and no dinner party or special work to be done, he did not bring a Mary who, according to Sydney, might be his wife, his mother, his daughter, his sister, his woman, his aunt or even a next-door neighbour. She looked a little different to the occupants of L'Arbe de la Croix each time, except for her Greta Garbo hat. They all referred to her as Mary and couldn't ever be wrong about it because all the baptized black women on the island had Mary among their names. Once in a while Yardman brought a small-boned girl too. Fourteen, perhaps, or twenty, depending on what she chose to do with her eyes.

Sydney would go down to the little dock then, in the Willys jeep, and return with the whole crew, driving through beautiful terrain, then through Sein de Veilles saying nothing for he preferred their instructions to come from his wife. Yardman sometimes ventured a comment or two, but the Mary and the small-boned girl never said anything at all. They just sat in the jeep quietly hiding their hair from the eyes of malevolent strangers. Sydney may have maintained a classy silence, but Ondine talked to them constantly. Yardman answered her but the Mary never did except for a quiet "Oui, madame" if she felt pressed. Ondine tried, unsuccessfully, for months to get a Mary who would work inside. With no explicit refusal or general explanation each Mary took the potatoes, the pot, the paper sack and the paring knife outdoors to the part of the courtyard the kitchen opened onto. It enraged Ondine because it gave the place a nasty, common look. But when, at her insistence, Yardman brought another Mary, she too took the pail of shrimp outside to shell and devein them. One of them even hauled the ironing board and the basket of Vera sheets out there. Ondine made her bring it all back and from then on they had the flat linen done in Queen of France along with the fine.

Yardman, however, was accommodating. Not only did he run errands for them in the town, he swept, mowed, trimmed, clipped, transplanted, moved stones, hauled twigs and leaves, sprayed and staked as well as washed windows, reset tiles, resurfaced the drive, fixed locks, caught rats—all manner of odd jobs. Twice a year a professional maintenance crew came. Four young men and an older one, all white, in a launch with machines. They cleaned draperies, waxed and polished floors, scrubbed walls and tile, checked the plumbing and the wiring, varnished and sealed the shutters, cleaned the gutters and down-spouts. The money they made from the fifteen families on the island alone was enough for a thriving business, but they worked other private and semiprivate islands year-round and were able to drive Mercedes and Yamahas all over Queen of France.

Now all three looked out the kitchen window at the old man as though they could discover with their eyes an uncontrolled craving for chocolate and bottled water in his. Yardman's face was nothing to enjoy, but his teeth were a treat. Stone-white and organized like a drugstore sample of what teeth ought to be.

Ondine sighed pointedly and walked to the door. She wished he could read, then she wouldn't have to recite a list of chores and errands three times over so he would not forget: a red foot-locker, a bottle of Maalox, the Christmas tree, thalomide, putting down bricks—but she'd be damned if she'd mention a turkey.

# 2

A HOUSE of sleeping humans is both closed and wide
open. Like an ear it resists easy penetration but cannot
brace for attack. Luckily in the Caribbean there is no
fear. The unsocketed eye that watches sleepers is not
threatening—it is merely alert, which anyone can tell
for it has no lid and cannot wax or wane. No one speaks
of a quarter or half moon in the Caribbean. It is always
full. Always adrift and curious. Unastonished but never
bored by the things it beholds: a pair of married
servants sleeping back to back. The man without
pajama tops in deference to the heat; his wife up to her
neck in percale to defy it. There is safety in those backs.
Each one feels it radiating from the other, knows that
the steady, able spine of its partner is a hip turn away.
Then their sleep is tranquil, earned, unlike the sleep of
the old man upstairs in cotton pajamas. He has napped
so frequently in his greenhouse during the day that
night sleep eludes him. Sometimes he needs a half
balloon of brandy to find it, and even then he chats the
night away, whispering first to his wrist, then to the
ceiling the messages he has received that need telling.
And when he has got it straight—the exact wording,
even the spelling of the crucial words—he is happy and
laughs lightly like a sweet boy. His wife, in another
room, has carefully climbed the steps to sleep and
arrived at its door with luggage packed and locked:
buffered nails, lightly oiled skin, hair pinned, teeth
brushed—all her tips in shining order. Her breathing is
still rapid, for she has just done twelve minutes of
Canadian Air Force exercises. Eventually it slows, and
under her sleeping mask two cotton balls soaked in

40

witch hazel nestle against peaceful eyelids. She is hopeful in sleep for this may be the night she will dream the dream she ought to. Next to her bedroom, adjacent to it with a connecting door (she is not in this house year-round and has chosen a guest room rather than the master bedroom as her own), a young woman barely twenty-five years old is wide-awake. Again. She fell asleep immediately when first she lay down, but after an hour she woke rigid and frightened from a dream of large hats. Large beautiful women's hats like Norma Shearer's and Mae West's and Jeanette MacDonald's although the dreamer is too young to have seen their movies or remembered them if she had. Feathers. Veils. Flowers. Brims flat, brims drooping, brims folded, and rounded. Hat after lovely sailing hat surrounding her until she is finger-snapped awake. She lay there under the eye of the moon wondering why the hats had shamed and repelled her so. As soon as she gave up looking for the centre of the fear, she was reminded of another picture that was not a dream. Two months ago, in Paris, the day she went grocery shopping. One of the happiest days of her life—full of such good weather and such good news she decided to throw a party to celebrate. She telephoned all the people she loved and some she did not and then drove all the way to the Supra Market in the 19$^{ème}$ arrondissement. Everything on her list was sure to be there, and no substitutes or compromises were necessary: Major Grey's chutney, real brown rice, fresh pimiento, tamarind rinds, coconut and the split breasts of two young lambs. There were Chinese mushrooms and arugula; palm hearts and Bertolli's Tuscany olive oil. If you had just been chosen for the cover of *Elle*, and there were three count three gorgeous and raucous men to telephone you or screech up to your door in Yugoslavian touring cars with Bordeaux Blanc and sandwiches and a little C, and when you have a letter from a charming old man saying your orals were satisfactory to the committee—well, then you go to the

41

Supra Market for your dinner ingredients and plan a rich and tacky menu of dishes Easterners thought up for Westerners in order to indispose them, but which were printed in *Vogue* and *Elle* in a manner impressive to a twenty-five-year-old who could look so much younger when she chose that she didn't even have to lie to the agencies, and they gave what they believed was a nineteen-year-old face the eyes and mouth of a woman of three decades.

Under such benevolent circumstances, knowing she was intelligent and lucky, everything on her list would of course be there. And when the vision materialized in a yellow dress Jadine was not sure it was not all part of her list — an addition to the coconut and tamarind, a kind of plus to go with the limes and pimiento. Another piece of her luck. The vision itself was a woman much too tall. Under her long canary yellow dress Jadine knew there was too much hip, too much bust. The agency would laugh her out of the lobby, so why was she and everybody else in the store transfixed? The height? The skin like tar against the canary yellow dress? The woman walked down the aisle as though her many-coloured sandals were pressing gold tracks on the floor. Two upside-down *V*'s were scored into each of her cheeks, her hair was wrapped in a gelée as yellow as her dress. The people in the aisles watched her without embarrassment, with full glances instead of sly ones. She had no arm basket or cart. Just her many-coloured sandals and her yellow robe. Jadine turned her cart around and went back down the aisle telling herself she wanted to re-examine the vegetables. The woman leaned into the dairy section and opened a carton from which she selected three eggs. Then she put her right elbow into the palm of her left hand and held the eggs aloft between earlobe and shoulder. She looked up then and they saw something in her eyes so powerful it had burnt away the eyelashes.

She strolled along the aisle, eggs on high, to the

42

cashier, who tried to tell her that eggs were sold by the dozen or half-dozen—not one or two or three or four—but she had to look up into those eyes too beautiful for lashes to say it. She swallowed and was about to try again when the woman reached into the pocket of her yellow dress and put a ten-louis piece on the counter and walked away, away, gold tracking the floor and leaving them all behind. Left arm folded over her waist, right hand holding three chalk-white eggs in the air, and what will she do with her hands when she reaches the door? they wondered. Take her elbow out of the palm of her hand and push it open? Turn around and ask for a paper bag? Drop the eggs in a pocket? Each one of them begged in his heart that it would not happen. That she would float through the glass the way a vision should. She did of course and they needn't have worried—the door always opened when you stepped on the mat before it, but they had forgotten that or had taken it for granted so long they had not really seen it until that woman approached it with the confidence of transcendent beauty and it flew open in silent obedience.

She would deny it now, but along with everybody else in the market, Jadine gasped. Just a little. Just a sudden intake of air. Just a quick snatch of breath before that woman's woman—that mother/sister/she; that unphotographable beauty—took it all away.

Jadine followed her profile, then her back as she passed the store window—followed her all the way to the edge of the world where the plate glass stopped. And there, just there—a moment before the cataclysm when all loveliness and life and breath in the world was about to disappear—the woman turned her head sharply around to the left and looked right at Jadine. Turned those eyes too beautiful for eyelashes on Jadine and, with a small parting of her lips, shot an arrow of saliva between her teeth down to the pavement and the hearts below. Actually it didn't matter. When you have fallen

43

in love, rage is superfluous; insult impossible. You mumble "bitch", but the hunger never moves, never closes. It is placed, open and always ready for another canary-yellow dress, other tar-black fingers holding three white eggs; or eyes whose force has burnt away their lashes.

Jadine's luck continued. The dinner party was memorable and nowhere had anything begun to spoil. Like the arugula leaf, life was green and nicely curved. Nothing was limp. There were no tears or brown spots. The items on her shopping list were always there. The handsome raucous men wanted to marry, live with, support, fund and promote her. Smart and beautiful women wanted to be her friend, confidante, lover, neighbour, guest, playmate, host, servant, student or simply near. A lucky girl—why leave the show? cable to old relatives? write a cheery request-type, offer-type letter to a rich old pushover and split to Dominique on whatever Air France had to offer when everything on her shopping list was right there in Paris? Nothing was absent, not even the spit of an African woman whose eyes had burnt away their lashes.

Jadine slipped out of bed and went to the window. She knelt on the floor, and, folding her arms on the sill, rested her head on the pane. She lifted the back of her hand to her mouth and squeezed the soft flesh with her teeth. She couldn't figure out why the woman's insulting gesture had derailed her—shaken her out of proportion to incident. Why she had wanted that woman to like and respect her. It had certainly taken the zing out of the magazine cover as well as her degree. Beyond the window etched against the light of a blazing moon she could see the hills at the other side of the island where one hundred horsemen rode one hundred horses, so Valerian said. That was how the island got its name. He had pointed the three humps of hills out to her, but Margaret, who had accompanied them on the tour of the grounds when Jadine first arrived, said no such

44

thing. One rider. Just one. Therefore Isle de *le* Chevalier. One French soldier on a horse, not a hundred. She'd gotten the story from a neighbour—the first family Valerian had sold to. Valerian stuck to his own story, which he preferred and felt was more accurate because he had heard it from Dr. Michelin, who lived in town and knew all about it. "They're still there," he said. "And you can see them if you go over there at night. But I don't suppose we'll ever meet. If they've been riding for as long as the story is old, they must be as tired as I am, and I don't want to meet anybody older or more tired than I am."

Maybe they're not old, Jadine thought, staring out the window. Maybe they're still young, still riding. One hundred men on one hundred horses. She tried to visualize them, wave after wave of chevaliers, but somehow that made her think of the woman in yellow who had run her out of Paris. She crawled back into bed and tried to fix the feeling that had troubled her.

The woman had made her feel lonely in a way. Lonely and inauthentic. Perhaps she was overreacting. The woman appeared simply at a time when she had a major decision to make: of the three raucous men, the one she most wanted to marry and who was desperate to marry her was exciting and smart and fun and sexy . . . so? I guess the person I want to marry is him, but I wonder if the person he wants to marry is me or a black girl? And if it isn't me he wants, but any black girl who looks like me, talks and acts like me, what will happen when he finds out that I hate ear hoops, that I don't have to straighten my hair, that Mingus puts me to sleep, that sometimes I want to get out of my skin and be only the person inside—not American—not black—just me? Suppose he sleeps with somebody else after we're married? Will I feel the way I did when he took Nina Fong away for the weekend? He was amazed, he said, at my reaction. Weren't we always to be honest with each other? He didn't want a relationship with lies.

45

Did I? And then we made up, set the date—no wedding, just a marriage—he got rid of his old mattress and bought a new one, a new one for us to grow old on, he said.

Then the magazine cover, and then her degree assured and then, the woman in yellow. And then she ran away because Ryk is white and the woman spit at her and she had to come to see her aunt and uncle to see what they would feel, think, say. White but European which was not as bad as white and American; they would understand that, or would they? Had they ever said? They liked her being in Paris, the schools she'd gone to, the friends she'd had there. They were always boasting about it. And it was not like she needed their views on anything. After her mother died they were her people—but she never lived with them except summers at Valerian's house when she was very young. Less and then never, after college. They were family; they had gotten Valerian to pay her tuition while they sent her the rest, having no one else to spend it on. Nanadine and Sydney mattered a lot to her but what they thought did not. She had sought them out to touch bases, to sort out things before going ahead with, with, with anything. So far she had been playful with them, had not said anything definite about her plans. When they asked her was she serious about this Ryk fellow who telephoned and who sent letters every week, she pretended it was nothing. That she was thinking of going back to Paris only to get her things. There was a small assignment in New York; she would take it and then she wanted to see about opening a business of her own, she'd told them, a gallery, or a boutique or a . . . she'd looked at their faces then . . . well, something they could all do together so they could live together like a family at last. They smiled generously, but their eyes made her know they were happy to play store with her, but nothing would pull them away from the jobs they had had for thirty years or more.

46

Jadine kicked off the sheet and buried her head under the pillow to keep the moonlight out of her eyes, and the woman in yellow out of her mind.

WHEN JADINE had gotten out of bed to stare at the hills, Valerian woke up. He had finished chatting to the ceiling and into his wrist the exact spelling of the message: *These iceboxes are brown broken perspective v-i-o-l-i-a-x is something more and can't be coal note.* He had sipped the brandy rather quickly, annoyed by the day's turn of events, and had lain for a while thinking how impossible it was that, unlike other men, he had been pushed into a presidency but had to fight for his retirement.

When he was thirty-nine he swore that he would quit at exactly sixty-five before he started spending his days travelling from the executive toilet back to his desk where the ballpoint pens mounted on marble had gone dry and his pencils were always long and sharp. That he would never permit himself to become the industrial nuisances his uncles had: stubborn, meddlesome, hanging on to their desks with their fingernails; flourishing once or twice a year when a crisis occurred with an old client or a new F.D.A. official that needed their familiarity or style or some other antiquated company charm. His uncles had been good to him. Their mother (Valerian's grandmother) had four sons each of whom had married a woman who had only girls. Except Valerian's mother who delivered one girl and one boy, who was the future of the family. When his father died and Valerian was seven, the uncles gathered to steady everybody and take over the education of their dead brother's son since it was, they said, "self-understood" that he would inherit the candy factory. And just to show how much they loved and anticipated him, they named a candy after him. *Valerians.* Red and white gumdrops in a red and white box (mint-flavoured, the

47

white ones; strawberry-flavoured, the red). Valerians turned out to be a slow but real flop, although not a painful one financially for it was made from the syrup sludge left over from their main confection — Teddy Boys.

"What's the matter with them?" asked the uncles.

"Faggoty," said the sales reps.

"Faggoty?"

"Yeah. Like Valentines. Can you see a kid sitting on a curb tossing those fairy candies in his mouth? Seasonal is all we can do. Valentine's Day. Give us something with nuts, why don't you?"

Nobody in the East or Midwest touched them. They sat in movie house display cases and on candy store shelves until they were hard as marbles and stuck together like grapes.

"But somebody's buying them," the uncles said.

"Jigs," said the salesmen. "Jigs buy 'em. Maryland, Florida, Mississippi. Close the line. Nobody can make a dollar selling faggot candy to jigs."

"But when they move north, don't they ask for what they got in Mississippi?"

"Hell, no. They're *leaving* the South. When they move out they want to leave that stuff behind. They don't want to be reminded. Alaga syrup is dead in New York. So is Gold Dust Soap and so are Valerians. Close it out."

But they didn't close it out. Not right away, at least. The uncles let the item sell itself in the South until the sugar shortage of the early forties and even then they fought endlessly to keep it on: they went to the bathroom, to lunch, read food industry literature and held caucuses among themselves about whether to manufacture a nickel box of Valerians in Mississippi where beet sugar was almost free and the labour too. "Ooooh. Valerian!!" said the box. And that was all. Not even a picture of the candy or a happy face eating it. Valerian appreciated their efforts but recognized them

48

as sentimental and not professional and swore again he would retire exactly at sixty-five if not before and would not let his ownership position keep him there making an ass of himself. After all he was the first partner with a college education and a love of other things. And it was because of these other things—music, books—that all the way through a nine-year childless marriage to a woman who disliked him; all the way through a hateful, shoddy, interminable divorce; all the way into and out of the military service, he could be firm. After the war he went to a convention of industrial food appliance sales in Maine and stepped out for a breath of winter air. There on a float with a polar bear he saw Miss Maine. She was so young and so unexpectedly pretty he swallowed air and had a coughing fit. She was all red and white, like the Valerians. So already at thirty-nine he was showing signs of the same sentimentality his uncles had. It made his resolve even firmer; out of respect for the company, the industry, he would do what they required the Swedes and Germans who worked for them to do—retire at sixty-five. After all, it was a family shop. They had taken a little bit of sugar and a little bit of cocoa and made a good living—for themselves and ninety others, and the people who lived in the factory's neighbourhood stayed there and loved it there largely because of the marvellous candy odour that greeted them in the morning and bid them goodnight. Smelling it was almost like having it and they could have it too, way back then, because damaged lots of Teddy Boys were regularly given to children and homeless men. And when the homeless men found themselves on a train in Oregon or a camp in Boulder, Colorado, they remembered the delicious smell of Philadelphia with far more pleasure than they remembered its women. The childhood of the children growing up in that candy air never quite left, and may have been why they never quite grew up. They moved to Dallas and Altoona and listened to other people's stories of childhood politely but without envy. They seldom tried to describe their own, because how could you make another person know what it was like? All you could say was "there was a candy factory in our neighbourhood and it smelled so good". So they kept it to themselves and kept their childhood longer than they should have in Dallas and Altoona and Newport News.

And the Street Brothers Candy Company never left the neighbourhood or forgot the workers. It expanded, but right on the block and behind the original building; they hired more salesmen and even when they bought machines to do what the Swedish and German women had done they kept them on in other capacities although it was clear they had no need for them—out of respect for Grandmother Stadt and out of respect for the industry. They had six good items by the time Valerian took over and all the women were dead but not the uncles and it was because of this same respect for the industry and its legendary place in the neighbourhood and the hearts of those who lived there that he was determined to retire at sixty-five—before he got foolish.

He married Miss Maine and when she had a baby boy he was as relieved as the uncles, but resisted the temptation to introduce a new confection named after his son. By that time they had reduced the size of the Teddy Boys' hats which nobody connected anymore to Theodore Roosevelt. (An error the uncles encouraged since the candy had been made first by their workaholic mother as a treat for Theodore, her youngest son, and later on to sell for pin money. Hers were big, chocolately things, like gingerbread boys, but when they went into business they were much smaller.) Now you couldn't even see the Teddy Boys' buttons. Through it all Valerian never swerved from his sixty-five timetable. He prepared for it. Bought an island in the Caribbean for almost nothing; built a house on a hill away from the mosquitoes and vacationed there when he could and when his wife did not throw a fit to go elsewhere. Over the years he sold off parts of it, provided the parcels were large and the buyers discreet, but he kept his distance and his dream of getting out of the way at sixty-five, and letting his son take over. But the son was not charmed by Teddy Boys or island retreats. Valerian's disappointment was real, so he agreed to the company's sale to one of the candy giants who could and did triple the volume in two years. Valerian turned his attention to refining the house, its grounds, mail service to the island, measuring French colonial taxes against American residential ones, killing off rats, snakes and other destructive animal life, adjusting the terrain for comfortable living. When he knew for certain that Michael would always be a stranger to him, he built the greenhouse as a place of controlled ever-flowering life to greet death in. It seemed a simple, modest enough wish to him. Normal, decent — like his life. Fair, generous — like his life. Nobody except Sydney and Ondine seemed to understand that. He had never abused himself, but he thought keeping fit inelegant somehow, and vain. His claims to decency were human: he had never cheated anybody. Had done the better thing whenever he had a choice and sometimes when he did not. He had never been miserly or a spendthrift, and his politics were always rational and often humane. He had played his share of tennis and golf but it was more for business reasons than pleasure. And he'd had countless discussions with friends and clients about the house he was building in the Caribbean, about land value, tax credit, architects, designers, space, line, colour, breeze, tamarind trees, hurricanes, cocoa, banana and *fleur de fuego*. There had been two or three girls who had helped him enter the fifties (lovely, lovely). Nothing to worry Margaret had she known. Merely life preservers in the post-fifty ocean, helping him make it to shore. There was a moment during the war when he thought some great event was in store for him, but it never happened. He was never sent with the message the world was waiting for. He knew the message was not his, that he had not thought it up, but he believed he was worthy of delivering it. Nothing of the sort befell him, so he returned to civilian life a bachelor, intact. Until he saw Miss Maine (whom a newspaper, published by the envious grandfather of a runner-up, called "a principal beauty of Maine"), looking like the candy that had his name. His youth lay in her red whiteness, a snowy Valentine Valerian. And Bride of Polar Bear became his bride. The disgust of the aunts at his marriage to a teenager from a family of nobodies dissolved with the almost immediate birth of his son. Valerian didn't need a youth then, the boy was that. Now the boy was a grown man, but perpetually childlike so Valerian wanted his own youth again and a place to spend it. His was taken from him when his father died and his mother and aunts all changed from hearty fun-loving big sisters to grave, *serioso mammas* who began their duties by trying to keep him from grieving over his father's death. Luckily a drunken woman did their laundry. And although he stayed on one year past sixty-five to make some changes and another year past that to make sure the changes held, he did manage to retire at sixty-eight to L'Arbe de la Croix and sleep the deep brandy sleep he deserved.

MARGARET was not dreaming nor was she quite asleep, although the moon looking at her face believed she was. She was experiencing the thing insomniacs dread—not being awake but the ticky-tacky thoughts that fill the space where sleep ought to be. Rags and swatches; draincloths and crumpled paper napkins. Old griefs and embarrassments; jealousies and offence. Just common ignoble scraps not deep enough for dreaming and not light enough to dismiss. Yet she was hopeful that sleep would come, that she would have the dream she ought to for maybe that would dispel the occasional forgetfulness that plagued her when she forgot the names and uses of things. It happened mostly at meals, and once, years ago, with the Princess telephone which she picked up with her car keys and address book and tried to stuff in her purse. They were rare moments, but dark and windy enough to last. After lunch with friends you could go to the powder room, twist the lipstick out of its tube and wonder suddenly if it was for licking or writing your name. And because you never knew when it would come back, a thin terror accompanied you always—except in sleep. So there was peace and hope on the face of this beautiful woman born to two ordinary-looking people, Joseph and Leonora Lordi, who had looked at their beautiful redheaded child with shock and amazement. Of course there was no thought of adultery (Leonora was sixty before she showed the world her two bare legs), but the hair bothered Joe—caught his eye at the dinner table and ruined his meals. He looked at little Margarette's skin as delicate as the shell of a robin's egg and almost as blue and stroked his thumb. Leonora shrugged and covered her head with lace older than Maine itself. She was as puzzled as her husband but not as alarmed, although it did look funny at the nine-thirty mass: Margarette's head glowing like an ember among the coal-dark heads of her other children. She couldn't explain it and didn't try, but Joe never left off stroking his thumb and staring at his little girl's blue-if-it's-a-boy blue eyes. He stroked his thumb and stroked his thumb until he smashed his temple with his fist having just remembered Buffalo. The Buffalo great-aunts Celestina and Alicia—twins with hair the colour of saffron and the white skin of the north. He roared and began to tell people about his Buffalo aunts whom he had not seen since he was six. And, although his brothers shouted yeah, yeah, when he reminded them, he thought he saw doubt in the eyes of his friends. Thus began a series of letters to Buffalo inviting the twins to South Suzanne. They were flattered by his letters, but could not understand the sudden affection from a great-nephew they did not remember. For a year they declined to pay a visit on account of advanced age, until Joe offered to pay their bus fare. "Where?" asked Leonora, "where will they sleep?" and Joe touched his fingers: Adolphe, Campi, Estella, Cesare, Nick, Nuzio, Mickelena or any of the other Lordis scattered around the county. Leonora looked at the ceiling, covered her head with lace older than Maine itself and went to mass to beg for sanity, Madre de Dio, if not for peace in her house.

The aunts came and when Joe picked them up at the bus station and saw that the saffron had turned to garlic he smashed his temple again. It turned out better than nothing however for he was able to regale them in the presence of company about losing their flaming hair, and they smiled and acknowledged that it had certainly been lost—which was proof enough for everyone that such hair and such skin had existed at one time and therefore could legitimately reappear four generations later on the tiny head of Margarette Lenore. Still it left its mark on her—being *that* pretty with *that* colouring. Joe and Leonora left her alone after the Buffalo aunts went home. Maybe her beauty scared them a little; maybe they just felt, well, at least she has that. She won't have to worry. And they stepped back and let her be. They gave her care, but they withdrew attention. Their strength they gave to the others who were not beautiful; their knowledge, what information they had they did not give to this single beautiful one. They saved it, distributed it instead to those whose characters had to be built. The rest of their energies they used on the problems of surviving in a county that did not want them there. During the months when the earth permitted it, Joe and his brothers dug a hole in the ground. They cinder-blocked it, topped it and put in a toilet and a gas line. Little by little the Lordis moved out of their trailer across the yard into the cinderblock basement. They lived huddled and quite warm there, considering what Maine winters were like. Then Joe started the first floor walls and by 1935 all six of them were in a seven-room house the Lordis brothers had built with their own hands. Leonora rented the trailer, but kept its back yard for peppers, corn, fat squash and the columbine she loved beyond reason. But Margarette always loved the trailer best for there the separateness she felt had less room to grow in. In the hand-built house, and later in the brick house on Chester Street, after her father and uncles bought two trucks and began Lordi Brothers, the loneliness was only partially the look in the eyes of the uncles and the nuns. Much of it was the inaccessibility of the minds (not the hearts) of Leonora and Joseph Lordi. So when she got married eight months out of high school, she did not have to leave home, she was already gone; she did not have to leave them; they had already left her. And other than money gifts to them and brief telephone calls, she was still gone. It was always like that: she was gone and other people were where they belonged. She was going up or down stairs; other people seemed to be settled somewhere. She was on the two concrete steps of the trailer; the six wooden steps of the hand-built house; the thirty-seven steps at the stadium when she was crowned; and a million wide steps in the house of Valerian Street. It was just her luck to fall in love with and marry a man who had a house bigger than her elementary school. A house of three stories with pearl-grey S's everywhere — on cups, saucers, glasses, silverware, and even in their bed. When she and Valerian lay snug in bed, facing each other and touching toes, the pearl-grey S on the sheet hems and pillow slips coiled at her and she stiffened like Joan Fontaine in *Rebecca* until she learned from her husband that his ex-wife had nothing to do with it. His grandmother had had some of the monograms done and his mother the rest. Margaret's relief was solid but it did nothing to keep her from feeling drowned when he was not there in the spaciousness of that house with only a coloured couple with unfriendly faces to save her. Alone in the house, peeping into a room, it looked all right, but the minute she turned her back she heard the after-boom, and whom could she tell that to? Not the coloureds. She was seventeen and couldn't even give them orders the way she was supposed to. It must be like room service, she thought, and she asked them to bring her things and they did but when she said thank you and sipped the Coca-Cola, they smiled a private smile she hated. The woman Ondine cooked and did the cleaning; the man too, and he also had morning chats with Valerian, brushed his clothes, sent some to the laundry, some to the cleaners, some disappeared altogether. There was nothing in that line for her to do but amuse herself in solitude and, awful as that was, the dinners with Valerian's friends were worse. There men talked about music and money and the Marshall Plan. She knew nothing about any of it, but she was never stupid enough to pretend she did or try to enter the conversation. The wives talked around the edge of such matters or dropped amusing bits into the conversations like the green specks in cannoli filling. Once a wife whom she showed to the downstairs powder room asked her where she had gone to school and she said South Suzanne. What's there? asked the woman. South Suzanne High School, said Margaret. The woman gave her a wide generous grin for a long time, then patted Margaret's stomach. "Get to work, fast, sweetheart."

Margaret lived for the concerts Valerian took her to, and the dinners for two at restaurants and even alone at home. Otherwise it was solitude with the coloured couple floating mysteriously through the house. In the fourth month of her marriage she sat on the screened porch listening to "Search for Tomorrow" when Ondine passed by with a can of linseed oil and said, "Excuse me. Did they arrest Joan Barron yet?" Margaret said No, but they must be about to. "Oo," said Ondine, and began to

56

fill her in on the cast of characters. Margaret was not a regular listener but she became one with Ondine and a maiden friendship flowered. Margaret was not afraid anymore (although it was some time before Sydney did not inspire her with awe). She looked forward to the chats with Ondine whose hair was black then and "dressed" as she called it, once a month. They talked about Valerian's family and South Suzanne and Baltimore, where Ondine was from. Ondine was just about to show her how to make crust (and Margaret by then knew the honour of the offer, since Ondine didn't like sharing recipes or kitchen space) when Valerian put a stop to it saying she should guide the servants, not consort with them. The next thing you know they'd be going to movies together, which hurt Margaret a lot because taking in a movie with Ondine was definitely on her mind. They quarrelled about it. Not because Margaret thought Valerian was wrong: she had never known him to be and doubted if he could be in error about anything. Not him, not with those calm eyes or that crisp quiet voice that reassured and poked fun at you at the same time. And although the theme of her defence in the argument was that Ondine (if not all coloured people) was just as good as they were, she didn't believe it, and besides that wasn't the point of the disagreement anyway. Valerian was never rude to Ondine or Sydney, in fact he pampered them. No. The point was not consorting with Negroes, the point was her ignorance and her origins. It was a nasty quarrel and their first in which they said regrettable things to each other that resulted in not touching toes in the night. It frightened Margaret—the possibility of losing him. And though she abandoned the movie idea, and still sneaked into Ondine's kitchen of an afternoon, she took the advice of the lady in the powder room and "got to work, fast". When the baby was born everything changed except the afterboom which got louder and louder and even when she carried her baby through the rooms it was there as soon as she turned her back. It had been a horror and a pleasure to teach little Michael how to count by walking him up those wide stairs flashing white like piano keys. One, two, three . . . his little hand in hers repeating the numbers as they mounted each tread. No one would believe that she loved him. That she was not one of those women in the *National Enquirer*. That she was never an overprotective or designing parent with unfulfilled dreams. Now that Michael was an adult, of all the people she knew in the world, he seemed to her the best. The smartest and the nicest. She liked his company, to talk to him, to be around him. Not because he is my son, she told herself, my only child, but because he is interesting and he thinks I am interesting too. I am special to him. Not as a mother, but as a person. Just as he is to me.

In wanting to live near him she was not behaving like a brood hen. Quite the contrary. She had cut the cord decisively and was enjoying her son as an individual. He was simply better society than her women friends. Younger, freer, more fun. And he was better company than the men of her acquaintance who either wanted to seduce, lecture or bore her to death. She felt natural, easy, unafraid with Michael. There was no competition with him, no winning, no preening, no need to be anybody but who she was, and in his presence she did not forget the names and uses of things. It wasn't always that way. When he was an infant he seemed to want everything of her, and she didn't know what to give. She loved him even then. But no one would believe it. They would think she was one of those mothers in the *National Enquirer*. And since she was not anything like them, she fell asleep finally, but did not have the dream she ought to.


DOWN BELOW, where the moon couldn't get to, in the servant's quarters, Sydney and Ondine made alternate trips to the bathroom and went quickly back to sleep. Ondine dreaming of sliding into water, frightened that her heavy legs and swollen ankles will sink her. But still asleep she turns over and touches her husband's back—the dream dissolves and with it the anxiety. He is in Baltimore now as usual and because it was always a red city in his mind—red brick, red sun, red necks and cardinals—his dream of it now was rust-coloured. Wagons, fruit stands, all rust-coloured. He had left that city to go to Philadelphia and there he became one of those industrious Philadelphia Negroes—the proudest people in the race. That was over fifty years ago, and still his most vivid dreams were the red rusty Baltimore of 1921. The fish, the trees, the music, the horses' harnesses. It was a tiny dream he had each night that he would never recollect from morning to morning. So he never knew what it was exactly that refreshed him.

They were all asleep now. Nothing disturbed them. Not the moon and certainly no footsteps in the dark.

# 3

FOG CAME to that place in wisps sometimes, like the hair of maiden aunts. Hair so thin and pale it went unnoticed until masses of it gathered around the house and threw back one's own reflection from the windows. The sixty-four bulbs in the dining-room chandelier were no more than a rhinestone clip in the hair of the maiden aunts. The grey of it, the soil and swirl of it, was right in the room, moistening the table linen and clouding the wine. Salt crystals clung to each other. Oysters uncurled their fringes and sank to the bottom of the tureen. Patience was difficult to come by in that fuzzy caul and breathing harder still. It was then that the word "island" had meaning.

Jadine and Margaret touched their cheeks and temples to dry the places the maiden aunts were kissing. Sydney (unbidden but right on time) circled the table with steps as felt as blackboard erasers. He kept his eyes on the platter, or the table setting, or his feet, or the hands of those he was serving, and never made eye contact with any of them, including his niece. With a practised side-long glance he caught Valerian pressing his thumb to the edge of the soup plate, pushing it an inch or so away. Instantly Sydney retraced his felt steps to clear the plates for the next course. Just before he reached Margaret, who had not yet touched anything, she dipped her spoon into the bisque and began to eat. Sydney hesitated and then stepped back.

"You're dawdling, Margaret," said Valerian.

"Sorry," she murmured. The maiden aunts stroked her cheek and she wiped away the dampness their fingers left.

"There is a rhythm to a meal. I've always told you that."

"I said sorry. I'm not a fast eater."

"Speed has nothing to do with it. Pace does," Valerian answered.

"So my pace is different from yours."

"It's the soufflé, Margaret," Jadine interrupted. "Valerian knows there's a soufflé tonight."

Margaret put her spoon down. It clicked against the china. Sydney floated to her elbow.

She was usually safe with soup, anything soft or liquid that required a spoon, but she was never sure when the confusion would return: when she would scrape her fork tines along the china trying to pick up the painted blossoms at its centre, or forget to unwrap the Amaretti cookie at the side of her plate and pop the whole thing into her mouth. Valerian would squint at her, but say nothing, convinced that she was stewed. Lobster, corn on the cob — all problematic. It came. It went. And when it left sometimes for a year, she couldn't believe how stupid it was. Still she was careful at table, watching other people handle their food — just to make sure that never again would she pick up the knife instead of the celery stalk or pour water from her glass over the prime ribs instead of the meat's own juices. Now it was coming back. Right after she managed to eat the correct part of the mango, in spite of the fact that Ondine tried to trick her by leaving the skin on and propping it up in ice, she had dug in her fork recklessly, and a slice came away. Right after that Sydney presented her with a plate of something shaped like a cardboard box. Now she had hesitated to see if the little white pebbles floating in her bowl were to be eaten or not. It came to her in a flash — oysterettes! — and she had dipped her spoon happily into the soup but had hardly begun when Valerian complained. Now Jade was announcing a new obstacle: soufflé. Margaret prayed she would recognize it.

61

"Mushroom?" she asked.

"I don't know," said Jadine. "I think so."

"I hate mushrooms."

"I'm not sure; maybe it's plain."

"I like it when it's hot, plain and fluffy," said Margaret.

"Well, let's hope that's what we get. Omelette's more likely in this weather." Valerian was fidgety and signalled for more wine. "The only thing I dislike about this island is the fog."

"It may not be good for eggs, but it's doing a good job of souffléing my hair," said Jadine. "I should have had it cut like yours, Margaret." She pressed her hair down with both palms, but as soon as she removed them her hair sprang back into a rain cloud.

"Oh, no. Mine's so stringy now," said Margaret.

"But it still looks okay. That's why that haircut's so popular, you know? Uncombed, even wet, it's got a shape that suits the face. This shaggy-dog style I wear has to be worked on, and I mean *worked* on."

Margaret laughed. "It's very becoming, Jade. It makes you look like what was her name in *Black Orpheus*? Eurydice."

"Chee, Margaret, chee," said Valerian. "Eurydi-chee."

"Remember her hair when she was hanging from the wires in that streetcar garage?" Margaret contined to address Jadine.

"You mean the hair in her armpits?" Jadine asked. She was uncomfortable with the way Margaret stirred her into blackening up or universalling out, always alluding to or ferreting out what she believed were racial characteristics. She ended by resisting both, but it kept her alert about things she did not wish to be alert about.

Margaret's blue-if-it's-a-boy blue eyes crinkled with laughter. "No, I mean the hair on her head. It was lovely. Who noticed her armpits?"

"I would like to stay well through dessert, ladies, if you please. Could we find another topic?"

"Valerian, could you for once, just once—"

"Say," Jadine broke in. "What about Christmas? That's a topic we need to talk about. We haven't even begun to plan. Any guests?" She picked up the salad utensils from the bowl of many-coloured greens Sydney held near her. "Oh, I meant to tell you, the von Brandts sent a note . . ."

"Brandt, Jade. Just plain Brandt. The 'von' is imaginary," Valerian said.

Margaret took hold of the long wooden handles poking out of the salad bowl that Sydney held toward her. Carefully she transferred the greens to her plate. Nothing spilled. She took another helping and it arrived safely also. She sighed and was about to tell Jade to decline the Brandts' invitation when Valerian shouted, "What the hell is the matter with you?"

Startled, Margaret looked around. He was glaring at her. Jade was looking at her plate while Sydney leaned near her wrist. "What?" she said. "What?"—looking down at her plate. It was all right, nothing spilled, nothing broken: lettuce, tomatoes, cucumber all there. Then Sydney set the bowl on the table and picked up the salad spoon and fork. She had left them on the table.

"Oh, I'm sorry," she whispered, but she was angry. What was so awful about that? They had looked at her as though she'd wet her pants. Then quickly they pretended it had not happened; Jadine was chirping again.

"Well anyway, they want you both for dinner. Small, she says. But the Hatchers are having a big weekend thing. And they want—" She paused for half a heartbeat. Their faces were closed, snapped shut like the lids of jewellery boxes. "They thought you'd like to come for the entire weekend. Christmas Eve, a dinner party; then breakfast, then some boating in the afternoon, then, then a cocktail party with dancing. The Journeymen from Queen of France are playing. Well, they're not really *from* there. New Jersey, I think, but they've been playing at Chez Marin—" She couldn't go on in that

63

silence. "What's the matter, Margaret?"

"Let's go back to armpits," Margaret said.

The maiden aunts smiled and tossed their maiden aunt hair.

"We'll do nothing of the sort. You were saying, Jade?" Valerian drained his wineglass.

Jadine shrugged. "Are you planning Christmas here—or where?"

"Here. Quietly. Although we may have a guest or two."

"Oh? Who?"

"Tell her, Margaret."

"Michael is coming. For Christmas." Margaret's smile was shy.

"But that's wonderful," said Jadine.

"Valerian thinks he won't. He will though, because I promised him this really terrific present."

"What? Can you tell me?"

"A poet," said Valerian. "She's giving him his favourite poet for Christmas. Isn't that so, love?"

"You make everything I do sound stupid."

"I thought I described it fairly."

"It's not the words; it's the tone." Margaret turned her head to Jadine. "I've invited B. J. Bridges for the holidays and he said he'd come. He used to be Michael's teacher."

"And Michael doesn't know?"

"Not exactly. But he'll guess. I gave him a hint—a big one—so he could. I used a line from one of Bridges's poems in my letter. 'And he glittered when he walked.' "

"Then you may as well have your nervous breakdown right now," said Valerian. "He won't come. You've misled him entirely."

"What are you talking about? He's on his way. His trunk's already been shipped."

"That is not a line from anything Bridges ever wrote. Michael will think you're dotty."

"It is. I have the poem right upstairs. I underlined it myself. It was the one Michael used to recite."

"Then Bridges is not only a mediocrity, he's a thief."

"Perhaps he was using it as a quotation, or an allusion—" Jadine fiddled with her hair.

"He'll think you're batty and . . ."

"Valerian, please."

" . . . and go snake dancing."

"Then I'll go with him."

"We've been all through this, Margaret."

"When will you know for sure?" Jadine's voice affected lightness.

"She already knows for sure. The rest is hope and a determination to irritate me."

"Irritating you doesn't have to be determined. All anybody has to do is breathe a slice of your air—"

"Must you always speak in food measurements? The depression is over. You are free to leave something on your plate. There's more. There really is more."

"I don't have to sit here and listen to this. You're trying to ruin it for me, but you're not going to. I tear my life apart and come down here for the winter and all I ask in return is a normal Christmas that includes my son. You won't come to us—we have to come to you and it's not fair. You know it's not. This whole thing is getting to be too much!"

"Is that a problem for you? Having too much?"

"That's not what I mean."

"I know what you mean, but is it a problem for you? Because if it is I can arrange for less. I could certainly do with less myself. Less hysteria, less shouting, less drama . . ."

Jadine, unable to think of anything to do or say, watched tomato seeds slide into the salad dressing, and set about applying the principles of a survey course in psychology. During the two months she'd been there, Valerian and Margaret frequently baited one another and each had a dictionary of complaints against the other, entries in which, from time to time, they showed her. Just a May and December marriage, she thought, at

65

its crucial stage. He's seventy; she's knocking fifty. He is waning, shutting up, closing in. She's blazing with the fire of a soon to be setting sun. Naturally they bickered and taunted one another. Naturally. Normally, even. For they were decent people. Over and above their personal generosity to her and their solicitude for her uncle and aunt, they seemed decent. Decent like Sydney and Nanadine were decent, and this house full of decent folk situated in the pure sea air was exactly where she wanted to be right now. This vacation with light but salaried work was what she needed to pull herself together. Listening to Margaret and Valerian fight was a welcome distraction, just as playing daughter to Sydney and Nanadine was.

But recently (a few days ago, last night, and again tonight) flecks of menace lay in these quarrels. They no longer seemed merely the tiffs of long-married people who alone knew the physics of their relationship. Who like two old cats clawed each other, used each other to display a quarrelsomeness neither took seriously, quarrelling because they thought it was expected of them, quarrelling simply to exchange roles now and then for their own private amusement: the heavy would appear abused in public, the aggressive and selfish one would appear the eye and heart of restraint before an audience. And most of the time, like now, the plain of their battle was a child, and the weapons public identification of human frailty. Still, this was a little darker than what she had come to expect from them. Bits of blood, tufts of hair seemed to stick on those worn claws. Maybe she had misread their rules. Or maybe (most likely) she wasn't an audience anymore. Maybe she was family now—or nobody. No, she thought, it must be this place. The island exaggerated everything. Too much light. Too much shadow. Too much rain. Too much foliage and much too much sleep. She'd never slept so deeply in her life. Such tranquillity in sleep made for wildness during the waking hours. That's what it was: the

wilderness creeping into Valerian and Margaret's sea-
soned and regulated arguments, subverting the rules so
that they looked at each other under the tender light of a
seventy-year-old chandelier, bought by Valerian's father
in celebration of his wife's first pregnancy, lifted their lips
and bared their teeth.

". . . she never liked me," Margaret was saying. "From
the very beginning she hated me."

"How could she hate you from the beginning? She
didn't even know you." Valerian lowered his voice in an
effort to calm her.

"That's what I'd like to know."

"She was perfectly polite and gracious to you in the
beginning."

"She was awful to me, Valerian. Awful!"

"That was later when you wouldn't let Michael visit
her."

"Wouldn't let? I couldn't make him go. He hated her;
he'd shrink at the very—"

"Margaret, stick to the facts, Michael was two or three.
He couldn't have hated anybody, let alone his aunt."

"He did, and if you had any feelings you would have
hated her too."

"My own sister?"

"Or at least told her off."

"For what, for God's sake. For having a private
wedding instead of a circus? You never invite them down
here and she's probably upset about it, that's all. And
this is her way of—"

"Dear God. You have screamed at me for years for
having too many people. Now you want me to invite Cissy
and Frank. I don't believe—"

"I didn't *say* that. I don't want her here any more than
you do. I am only trying to explain why they didn't let us
know about the wedding. From what I gather—"

"What do you mean *us*? She invited Michael! But not
me!"

"Stacey's idea."

67

"Do you think if Michael got married I would invite Stacey and not her parents?"

"Margaret, I don't give one goddamn—"

"She's always treated me that way. You know what she did to me the first day I met her."

"I suppose I should but I don't."

"You don't?"

"No. Sorry."

"What she said to me that first day?"

"It's been some time."

"About my cross?"

"Your what?"

"My cross. The cross I wore. My first communion present. She said for me to take it off. That only whores wore crosses."

Valerian laughed. "That sounds like her."

"You think it's funny."

"In a way."

"That your own sister . . . my God."

"Margaret, you didn't have to do it—take it off. Why didn't you tell her to go to hell?"

"Why didn't you?"

"I don't remember."

"Because you agreed with her, that's why."

"That my bride was a whore?"

"You know what I mean."

"All I know is that you let her get under your skin and she's still there after thirty years. You don't give a gnat's ass about the wedding. You just wanted to be anywhere Michael is. You can't stand for him to be wherever you're not."

"That's not true."

"You wanted to crash some fatheaded wedding because Michael was there. You are too stupid to live."

"I don't have to sit here and be called names!"

"Idiot. I married an idiot!"

"And I married an old fool!"

"Of course you did. Who else but an old fool would

68

marry a high school dropout off the back of a truck!"

"A *float*!" Margaret shouted, and when the wineglass bounced from the centrepiece of calla lilies and rolled toward him he didn't even look at it. He simply watched his wife's face crumple and her boy-blue eyes well up.

"Oh," said Jadine. "This is . . . maybe . . . Margaret? Would you like to . . ." But Margaret was gone, leaving the oak door swinging behind her and the maiden aunts cowering in the corners of the room.

Sydney (unbidden but right on time) removed the glass and placed a fresh white napkin over the wine spot. Then he collected the salad plates, replacing them with warm white china with a single band of gold around the edges. Each plate he handled with a spotlessly white napkin and was careful, as he slipped it from the blue quilted warmer, not to make a sound. When the plates were in position, he disappeared for a few seconds and returned with a smoking soufflé. He held it near Valerian a moment for inspection, and then proceeded to the sideboard to slice it into flawless, frothy wedges.

Jadine considered her soufflé while Valerian signalled for more wine. It seemed a long time before he murmured to her, "Sorry."

Jadine smiled or tried to and said, "You shouldn't tease her like that."

"No, I suppose not," he answered, but his voice held no conviction and his twilight gaze was muddy.

"Is it because she wants to go away?" asked Jadine.

"Of course not. Not at all."

"Michael?"

"Yes. Michael."

He said nothing more so Jadine decided to exit as quickly as she could manage it. She was folding her napkin when suddenly he spoke. "She's nervous. Afraid he won't show. I'm nervous. Afraid he will."

There was another silence as Jadine struggled to think of something purposeful—even relevant—to say. She couldn't think of a thing so she gave up and said the

69

obvious. "I remember Michael. He's . . . nice." She recalled an eighteen-year-old boy with red hair and cut-off jeans.

"Quite," said Valerian. "Quite nice."

"If he does come, as well as his friend, how can it hurt?"

"I don't know. It depends."

"On what?"

"Thing outside my control. I can't be responsible for things outside my control." He pushed away his plate and drank his wine.

Jadine sighed. She wanted to leave the table, but didn't know how. Does he want me to stay or doesn't he? she wondered. Does he want me to talk or doesn't he? All I can do is ask polite questions and urge him to talk if he feels like it. Maybe I should go to Margaret, or change the subject, or have my head examined for coming here. "No one asks you to be," she said softly.

"That's not the point, whether I'm asked or not. A lot of life *is* outside and frequently it's the part that most needs control." He covered his lips with his napkin for a while then uncovered them and said, "Margaret thinks this is some sort of long lazy vacation for me, designed to hurt her. In fact I'm doing just the opposite. I intend to go back at some point. I will go back but actually it's for Michael that I stay. His protection."

"You make him sound weak, the way you say that. I don't remember him that way at all."

"You did know him, didn't you?" Valerian looked at her with surprise.

"Well, not really *know* him. I met him twice. The last time when you invited me to spend the summer in Orange County. Remember?" Jadine perked up, animated by her own memory. "My first year at college? He was there and we used to talk. He was . . . oh . . . clearheaded—independent it seemed to me. Actually we didn't talk; we quarrelled. About why I was studying art history at that snotty school instead of—I don't know

70

what. Organizing or something. He said I was abandon-
ing my history. My people."

"Typical," said Valerian. "His idea of racial progress is
All Voodoo to the People."

"I think he wanted me to string cowrie beads or sell
Afro combs. The system was all fucked up he said and
only a return to handicraft and barter could change it.
That welfare mothers could do crafts, pottery, clothing
in their homes, like the lacemakers of Belgium and *voilà!*
dignity and no more welfare." Jadine smiled.

"That's exactly what the world is waiting for: two
billion African pots," said Valerian.

"His intentions were good."

"They were not good. He wanted a race of exotics
skipping around being picturesque for him. What were
those welfare mothers supposed to put in those pots? Did
he have any suggestions about that?"

"They'd trade them for other goods."

"Really? Two thousand calabashes for a week of
electricity? It's been tried. It was called the Dark Ages."

"Well, the pottery wasn't to be utilitarian." Jadine was
laughing. "It'd be art."

"Oh, I see. Not the Dark Ages, the Renaissance."

"It was a long time ago, Valerian. Eight years? Nine?
He was just a kid then. So was I."

"You've grown. He hasn't. His vocabulary, perhaps,
but not his mind. It's still in the grip of that quisling
*Little Prince*. Do you know it?"

"Know what?"

"That book. *The Little Prince*."

"No. I never read it."

"Saint-Exupéry. Read it some time. And pay attention
not to what it says, but what it means."

Jadine nodded. It seemed like a perfect exit line to her,
since she didn't know what he was talking about and
didn't want to pursue his thoughts if they were anything
like his eyes at this moment. Without melanin, they were
all reflection, like mirrors, chamber after chamber,

71

corridor after corridor of mirrors, each one taking its shape from the other and giving it back as its own until the final effect was colour where no colour existed at all. Once more she stirred to rise from the table and once more he stopped her, not irritably this time but with compassion.

"Did they trouble you—the things he said that summer?"

"For a while."

"You knew better?"

"I knew the life I was leaving. It wasn't like what he thought: all grits and natural grace. But he did make me want to apologize for what I was doing, what I felt. For liking 'Ave Maria' better than gospel music, I suppose."

Nothing on Sydney's face showed his disappointment that the soufflé had not been completely eaten up by either one of them. He collected the dishes with his look of alert serenity, and stepped through the hair of the maiden aunts with an easy silent tread. He was perfect at those dinners when his niece sat down with his employers, as perfect as he was when he served Mr. Street's friends. The silver tray of walnuts, the equally silver bowl of peaches he brought in, and a jiffy later, the coffee—all were exactly and surreptitiously placed on the table. One hardly knew if he left the room or stood in some shadowy corner of it.

Jadine leaned her cheek on her fist. "Picasso *is* better than an Itumba mask. The fact that he was intrigued by them is proof of *his* genius, not the mask-makers'. I wish it weren't so, but . . ." She gave a tiny shrug. Little matches of embarrassment burned even now in her face as she thought of all those black art shows mounted two or three times a year in the States. The junior high school sculpture, the illustration-type painting. Eighty percent ludicrous and ten percent derivative to the point of mimicry. But the American Blacks were at least honestly awful; the black artists in Europe were a scandal. The only thing more pitiful than their talent was their pre-

72

tensions. There was just one exception: a Stateside Black whose work towered over the weeds like a sequoia. But you could hardly find his stuff anywhere.

"You look sad," said Valerian. "He must really have made you suffer. You should have mentioned it to me. I wanted that summer to be an especially pleasant one for you."

"It was. Actually it was good he made me think about myself that way, at that place. He might have convinced me if we'd had that talk on Morgan Street. But in Orange County on a hundred and twenty acres of green velvet?" She laughed softly. "Can you believe it? He wanted us to go back to Morgan Street and be thrilling."

"Us? He was going with you?"

"Just to get us started. He meant us Blacks: Sydney, Ondine and me."

"*Sydney? a potter?*" Valerian turned his gaze toward his butler and laughed.

Jadine smiled but did not look at her uncle.

"You can see how much he knows about Sydney. And I haven't given you one-thousandth of what I gave him, of what I made available to him. And you have fifty times the sense he does, I don't mind telling you." Valerian's sentences changed tempo. They were slower, and it was taking him longer to blink his eyes. "Margaret did that. She made him think poetry was incompatible with property. She made a perpetual loser of one of the most beautiful, the brightest boy in the land." He held his forehead for a moment. To Jadine he seemed terribly close to tears and she was relieved when he merely repeated himself. "The most beautiful, the brightest boy in the land."

"He didn't turn out the way you wanted?"

"No."

"You want him to be something else?"

"I want him to be something at all."

"Maybe he is."

"Yes. An adolescent. A kitten. But not playful.

73

Complaining. A complaining kitten. Always mewing. Meow. Meow. Meow."

"You shouldn't hate him, though. He's your son."

Valerian took his hand from his forehead and stared deep into the peaches nestled in their silver bowl. "I don't hate him. I love him. Margaret thinks I don't. But I do. I think about him all the time. You know . . . this isn't going to sound right . . . but I never was convinced that she did. Perhaps she did. In her way. I don't know. But she wasn't ready for him. She just wasn't ready. Now, now she's ready. When it's over. Now she wants to bake him cookies. See him off to school. Tie his shoelaces. Take care of him. Now. Absurd. I don't believe it. I don't believe her. When he was just a little thing I came home one day and went into the bathroom. I was standing there and I heard this humming—sing-ing—coming from somewhere in the room. I looked around and then I found it. In the cabinet. Under the sink. He was crouched in there singing. That was the first time, but not the last. Every now and then I'd come home, he'd be under the sink. Humming to himself. When I'd pull him out, ask him what he was doing there, he'd say he liked the soft. He was two, I think, two years old, looking in the dark for something—soft. Now imagine how many soft, cuddly things he had in his room. Bunny rabbits, slippers, panda bears. I used to try to be it for him, but I wasn't there during the day. She was though. I sometimes had the feeling that she didn't talk to him very much, then it would go away. The feeling, I mean. She'd change, she'd get interested in him, read to him, take him to shows, parks. Months would pass. Then I'd come home and he'd be under the sink again, hum-ming that little, I can't tell you how lonely, *lonely* song. I wasn't imagining it; it was lonely. Well, he got older and she'd go hot and cold, in and out. But he seemed to miss her so, need her so that when she was attentive he was like a slave to her. Then she'd lose interest again. When he was twelve he went to boarding school and things were

74

better. Until he came to visit. She would do things—odd things—to get his attention and keep it. Anything to keep his eyes on her. She'd make up things, threats to herself, attacks, insults—anything to see him fly into a rage and show how willing he was to defend her. I watched, and tried to play it down or prove, *prove* she was making it up. I always checked, it was always nothing. All I ended up doing was making him angry with me. I thought another child—but she said no. Absolutely refused. I have until this day never understood that. When he left for college I was relieved. It was already too late, but I still hoped he'd get out from under her. In a way he has, I suppose. Never visits, seldom writes. Calls sometimes. Complains. About Indians. About water. About chemicals. Meow. Meow. Meow. But he is on his own, I guess. On his own. But now—" Valerian turned to Jadine and stared right at her chin. "Now she wants to get hold of him again. Tempting him with some fake poet. And she wants to go back with him, live near him. For a while she says. Know what that means? A 'while'? It means as soon as he trusts her again, needs her again, counts on her, she'll change her mind, leave him. I haven't seen him for three years, and the last couple of times I didn't like him, or even know him. But I loved him. Just like I loved the boy under the sink, humming. That beautiful boy. With a smile like . . . like Sunday."

The maiden aunts, huddled in the corners of the room, were smiling in their sleep. Jadine flared her nostrils in an effort not to yawn. Another cup of coffee, another glass of port—nothing could bring her alive to the memories of an old man. I ought to be saying something, she thought. I ought to be asking questions and making comments instead of smiling and nodding like a puppet. Hoping there was a residue of interest in her eyes, she held her chin toward him and continued to smile—but only a little—in case what he was remembering was poignant but not happy. Long ago she had given up trying to be deft or profound or anything in the company of people she was not interested in, who didn't thrill her. Gazing at her stem of crystal she knew that whatever he was saying, her response was going to miss the point entirely. Her mind was in automatic park. She played with the little bit of port, gently swirling it around the well of her glass. "Sunday," he was saying with the bell-full voice of ownership like "in the land" or "the whole of London" or "*tout* Paris". He had a smile like Sunday. His Sunday. She wondered what Sunday was to this tall, thin man with eyes like the gloaming. Light? Warmth? A drawing room full of flowers? He was pouring himself a fifth glass of wine, too morose, too preoccupied with Sundays to think of offering her more. The peaches and walnuts were quiet in their silver bowls. She took a cigarette from a crystal cigarette holder. Next to it lay a round matchbox patterned like an Indian carpet. Inside were tiny white matchsticks with speckled gold heads that exploded with a hiss when struck. Three months, no two, and the quiet to which the house succumbed at night still disturbed her. Sunset, three minutes of Titian blue, and deep night. And with it a solid earthbound silence. No crickets, no frogs, no mosquitoes up here. Only the sounds, heard or imagined, that humans made. The hiss of a gold-headed match; the short cascade of wine into a goblet; the faint, very faint, click and clatter of the kitchen being tidied, and now a scream so loud and full of terror it woke the maiden aunts from their sleep in the corners of the room. And when they saw those blue-if-it's-a-boy blue eyes gone white with fear, they fled, pulling their maiden hair behind them.

She stood in the doorway screaming, first at Valerian and then at Jadine, who rushed to her side.

"What? What? What is it?"

But she would not stop. She just balled her beautiful hands into fists and pummelled her own temples, screaming louder. Valerian stared through port-softened eyes at his wife as though he, not she, were in pain.

"What is it, Margaret?" Jadine put her arm around her

shoulders. Sydney and Ondine both burst through the other door.

"What's the matter?"

"I don't know."

"She hurt herself?"

"I don't *know*."

"Hold her hands or she will."

"What is it? What happened?"

Then Ondine, fed up, shouted, "Speak, woman!" and Margaret sank to her knees gasping for the breath with which to whisper the words: "In my closet. In my closet."

"Her what?"

"Her closet. Something's in her closet."

"What's in your closet?"

"Black," she whispered, her eyes shut tight.

Jadine dropped to her knees and leaned close to Margaret's face. "You mean it's dark in your closet?"

Margaret shook her head and put the back of her fist in her mouth.

Then Valerian spoke for the first time since she had come screaming into the room. "Margaret, this is not the Met. It's a simple house on a simple island. Michael's not even here yet . . ."

But she was screaming again and Jadine had to shout, "Tell me! Tell me!"

"In my things!" said Margaret. "In all my things!"

"What's she saying?"

"Go look in her closet."

"Take the gun, Sydney." Ondine was the ranking officer, barking instructions.

"Right!" he answered, and ran back through the door to the kitchen.

"And be careful!" Ondine shouted after him.

"Hadn't I better call the harbour, Valerian?" asked Jadine.

"Don't leave me!" shrieked Margaret.

"All right. All right. Nanadine, give her some of that wine."

77

"Maybe she's had enough of that."

"No. She drank hardly anything."

"I heard her slam up the stairs in the middle of my dinner," said Ondine. "Between then and now she could have killed a quart." Ondine spoke without moving her lips hoping it was enough to keep Valerian from hearing.

"He's in my things, Jade." Margaret was crying softly.

"Okay, okay."

"You have to believe me."

"I don't smell anything on her breath; maybe she just flipped." Ondine was mumbling again.

"Can't you get her to a chair?" asked Valerian. He hated seeing her bent over like that on the floor.

"Come on, honey. Let's sit here," said Jadine.

"What are you doing?" Margaret was screaming again and trying to stand. "Why are you acting like this? He's there. I saw him. Valerian, please. Somebody better . . . go, call the harbour!"

"Let's wait for Sydney before we call the police," said Ondine.

"She's drunk," said Valerian with the wisdom of the drunk, "and nobody's paid her any attention for a whole hour."

"Why don't you believe me?" She looked around at them all. They looked back at her, each thinking why, indeed, he didn't; and then they heard the footsteps of Sydney plus one. Into the light of the sixty-four-bulb chandelier came Sydney pointing a .32 calibre pistol at the shoulder blades of a black man with dreadlock hair.

"It's him!" Margaret screamed.

"Have mercy," said Ondine.

"You can call the harbour now, Mr. Street," said Sydney.

"I'll do it," said Ondine.

Jadine said nothing. She did not dare.

Valerian's mouth was open and he closed it before say-

78

ing in a voice made stentorian by port, "Good evening, sir. Would you care for a drink?"

The black man looked at Valerian and it seemed to Jadine that there was a lot of space around his eyes.

# 4

BEES HAVE no sting on Isle des Chevaliers, nor honey. They are fat and lazy, curious about nothing. Especially at noon. At noon parrots sleep and diamondbacks work down the trees toward the cooler undergrowth. At noon the water in the mouths of orchids left there by the breakfast rain is warm. Children stick their fingers in them and scream as though scalded. People in town go inside because the sky weighs too much at noon. They wait for hot food with lots of pepper so the day will feel cooler by comparison. They drink sweet drinks and swallow bitter coffee to distract their insides from the heat and weight of the sky. But the eaves of the house on Isle des Chevaliers were deep—the curtains light and lightfiltering. So the sky did not require the occupants to distract themselves. They were free to concentrate on whichever of their personal problems they wished: the wrapped and shelved ones—the ones they always meant to take down and open one day—or the ones they caressed every hour. Just as on beaches, in summer homes, in watering places, tourists the world over lay under the breeze behind their anti-sunglasses wondering and mulling. So mulled the occupants of L'Arbe de la Croix that noon the day after a man with living hair stayed for dinner. Outwardly everything looked the same. Only the emperor butterflies appeared excited about something. Such vigorous flapping in blazing heat was uncommon for them. They hovered near the bedroom windows but the shutters had remained closed all morning and none of them could see a thing. They knew, however, that the woman was in there. Her blue-if-it's-a-boy blue eyes red-rimmed with longing for a trailer softened by columbine and for her Ma. Leonora, the daily communicant; Leonora, whose head was covered at mass with lace older than Maine itself, who at sixty folded away her stockings and from then on wore white socks with her black Cuban-heeled oxfords. Sweet, darling socks out of which grew strong, wide legs that had never been crossed at the knees.

I have come full circle, Ma, thought Margaret. Now that the breakfast rain was over and cleaned light filtered through the shutters she was amazed to discover how much like the trailer it was. Full circle, she thought, I have come full circle. The trailer had been like this room. All economy and parallel lines. All secret storage and uncluttered surfaces. South Suzanne's idea of luxury back then had been the antique-stuffed houses of old Bangor families: blue bottles and white mouldings, soft yellow wallpaper and re-covered Federal chairs. But Margaret loved the trailer best and when she married the non-Catholic over the objections of her parents and moved to Philadelphia, it took years to get rid of the afterboom and now that she had, he'd left it and put her in this room that was "sculpted" he said, not decorated, that for all its Mies van der Rohe and Max whatever reminded her of the trailer in South Suzanne where she had been the envy of her girlfriends for the first dozen years of her life and was fourteen before she discovered that everybody in South Suzanne had not shared that envy. Did not think the little toilet was cute, or the way the tables folded down and beds became sofas was really neat like having your own dollhouse to live in. And when she did discover that most people thought living in a trailer was tacky, it might have crushed the life out of her except that she discovered at the same time that all of South Suzanne was overwhelmed by her astonishing good looks. She agreed, finally, with their evaluation, but it didn't help much because it meant she had to be extra nice to other girls to keep them from getting mad at her. It meant having teachers go fuzzy in her presence (the men with glee, the women with distrust), fighting off cousins in cars, dentists in chairs and feeling apologetic to every woman over thirty. Privately she neither valued it nor enjoyed it and before she could learn to use it properly, she met an older man who was never fuzzy in her presence. She knew that because almost the first thing he said to her was "You really *are* beautiful", as if it could have been fake like the float but wasn't. And she smiled because he seemed surprised. "Is that enough?" she asked, and it was the first honest response she had ever made to a male compliment. "Beauty is never enough," he said. "But you are." The safety she heard in his voice was in his nice square fingernails too. And it was that, not his money, that comforted her and made her feel of consequence under the beauty, back down beneath it where her Margaret-hood lay in the same cup it had always lain in—faceless, silent and trying like hell to please. And now she longed for her mother's trailer so far from Philadelphia and L'Arbe de la Croix but maybe not so far after all since the bedroom she had locked herself into was a high-class duplication, minus the cosiness, of the first.

Margaret Lenore stared into the spaces and thought desperately of coffee, but she did not want to ring up Sydney or Ondine, for that would begin the day she was not sure she wanted to participate in. She had had no sleep to speak of, and now, drained of panic, wavering between anger and sorrow, she lay in bed. Things were not getting better. She was not getting better. She could feel it and right smack in the middle of it, with Michael on his way, *this* had to happen: literally, literally a nigger in the woodpile. And of course Valerian had to think up something to shock everybody and actually ask him to dinner. A stranger who was found hiding in his own wife's closet, a bum that even Sydney wanted to shoot, he invited to dinner while she was shaking like a leaf on the floor. In her closet. The end, the living end, but as disgusting as that was, it wasn't as bad as Valerian's insult

82

that it was okay for him to be there. And if it wasn't for the fact that Michael was coming, she would pack up that very day and really leave him this time. Valerian knew it too, knew he could get away with it, because Michael's Christmas visit was so important to her and would keep her from leaving. Now he was playing that boring music in the greenhouse as though nothing had happened. She was so hungry and coffee-starved but she couldn't start things off just yet. And Jade hadn't knocked at all.

Usually when Margaret overslept Jade woke her with a smile, some funny piece of mail or an exciting advertisement. She would sink her cup of chocolate into Margaret's carpet (there were no end tables in the chic sparse sculpture) and they would begin the day with some high-spirited girlish nonsense.

"Look. Chloë has four new perfumes. Four."

"I think Mr. Broughton's lover has gone; you have been invited to dinner. You'd better go, 'cause I think *her* mistress is due to visit them soon. Have you seen the three of them eating together? Ondine says the cook over there said it makes her sick." Long ago when Jade used to come for holiday visits, Margaret found her awkward and pouty, but now that she was grown up, she was pretty and a lot of fun. All those colleges hadn't made her uppity and she was not at all the Mother Superior Ondine had become.

She didn't know how the dinner went. Did Jade stay? When did the man leave? She lifted her hand to press a button. Then changed her mind. Maybe the man killed everybody, and she alone escaped because she had run up to her room and locked herself in. No. If he had, the boring music would not be going. God. Maybe he will come back and do it later. And what could they do to stop him? All the neighbours would have to be told that a black man had been roaming around, and it could happen again. They would have to share security and keep in touch with each other. Each house could post one of the help so that around the clock someone was on guard. She wouldn't mention Valerian's feeding him dinner first and trying to make her stay there and watch him eat it. The neighbours would think he was crazy and blame him for whatever the burglar did. Maybe he was already in jail. He couldn't have gotten off the island last night but, early in the morning, she'd heard the jeep take off and return. Sydney probably drove him to the launch where harbour police shackled him. In any case, she wasn't going to pretend what Valerian did was okay by her. He hadn't even bothered to come in and explain, let alone apologize to her. Just as he never bothered to explain why he wouldn't go back to the States. He really expected her to steam in that jungle, knowing as he did what heat and sun and wind did to her skin. Knowing that after Maine, Philadelphia was the torrid zone for her. That her arms went pimiento with even a little sun and her back burst into pebbles. Still he stayed in this place she had never enjoyed except when Michael was younger and they all vacationed there. Now it was a boiling graveyard made bearable — just bearable — by Jade's company, shopping in Queen of France and lunches with the neighbours. She would never get through Christmas here without Michael. Never. Already the confusion was coming back. The salad things last night, for instance, and earlier at breakfast. But with Michael around she never forgot the names and uses of things.

Margaret Street closed her eyes and turned over on her stomach although she knew she would not sleep again. All night she'd been conscious of the closet door where she had gone to find the poem just to make sure Valerian was making fun of her and that there really was the line "and he glittered when he walked" in the poem Bridges had dedicated to Michael. It was a walk-in closet with dressing room separate from the wardrobe and a tiny storage niche at the very back where she kept things and in there right among all her most private stuff she saw him sitting on the floor as calm as you please and as filthy

84

as could be. He looked at her but never moved and it seemed like hours before she could back out and hours more before she could make sound come from her open mouth and how she got down the stairs she would never in this world know but when she did it was like a dream with them looking at her but not looking as though they believed her and Valerian was worst of all sitting there like some lord or priest who doubted her confession, the completeness of it, and let her know with his eyes that she'd left something important out like the salad things. She had lain there all night with the lights on thinking of her closet as a toilet now where something rotten had been and still was. Only at dawn did she slip into a light and unrefreshing sleep not dreaming something she was supposed to be dreaming. She was exhausted when she woke but, as night disappeared, so did her fear. Among the many things she felt, anger was the most consistent but even that kept sliding away as her thoughts, unharnessed, turned sorrowful and galloped back to Leonora and a trailer sunk in columbine.

It was getting unbearably hot but she would not toss aside the sheet. Her door was locked. Jade would come soon to see about her. Valerian could do what he wished. She herself would not budge. In her things. Actually in her things. Probably jerking off. Black sperm was sticking in clots to her French jeans or down in the toe of her Anne Klein shoes. Didn't men sometimes jerk off in women's shoes? She'd have the whole closetful cleaned. Or better still, she'd throw them all out and buy everything new—from scratch. What a louse Valerian was. What a first-class louse. Wait till Michael hears about it. Just wait. And then she was crying about the night she won the beauty contest in a strapless gown that her mother had to borrow money from Uncle Adolph for and a gold cross that she always wore until her sister-in-law told her only whores wore crosses. The bitch.

She lay there wiping teary cheeks with the top hem of a Vera sheet. There was nothing the cool sculptured spaces could do to keep her from forgetting the fact that she was almost fifty sitting on a hill in the middle of a jungle in the middle of the ocean where the temperature was on broil and not even a TV with anything on it she could understand and where her husband was punishing her for forgetting to put the salad things back and there was no one to talk to except Jade and where her sex life had become such a wreck it was downright interesting. And if that wasn't enough now this nigger he lets in this real live dope addict ape just to get back at her wanting to live near Michael. "We'll see about that," she said. "Just wait till Michael comes." She whispered so nobody would hear and nobody did, not even the emperor butterflies. They were clinging to the windows of another bedroom trying to see for themselves what the angel trumpets had described to them: the hides of ninety baby seals stitched together so nicely you could not tell what part had sheltered their cute little hearts and which had cushioned their skulls. They had not seen the coat at all but a few days ago a bunch of them had heard the woman called Jade telling the woman called Margaret all about it. The butterflies didn't believe it and went to see for themselves. Sure enough, there it was, swirling around the naked body of the woman called Jade, who opened the French windows and greeted the emperor butterflies with a smile, but the heavy one called Ondine said, "Shoo! Shoo!"

"Leave them alone, Nanadine. They don't bother anything."

"They die and have to be swept up. You should put some clothes on and cover yourself up. I thought you asked me to come up and see your coat, not your privates."

"This is the best way to feel it. Here. Feel."

"Well, it's nice enough, no question about that. Mr. Street see it yet?"

"No, just you and Margaret."

"What'd she say?"

86

"She loved it. Said it was prettier than hers."

"Does this mean you're going to marry him?"

Jadine dug her hands deep into the pockets and spun around. Her hair was as black and shiny as the coat. "Who knows?"

"He must mean business if he fly that out to you all the way from Paris. And he must expect you back there. Lord knows you don't need a sealskin coat down here."

"It's just a Christmas present, Nanadine."

"It's not *just* anything, honey. I could buy a house with what that cost."

"No, you couldn't."

"I'd lock it up somewhere if I were you."

"I have to find a cool place for it. Maybe Valerian will let me use the air-conditioned part of his greenhouse."

"You crazy? Don't you dare leave that coat out there."

"There you go again. Nothing's going to happen, I told you. He'll be out of here by tonight."

"He better be. I'm not going to spend another night underneath the same roof with him."

"Apparently you've spent several. We all have."

"Well, I didn't know it. Although why I didn't, I can't figure. Stuff has been missing for weeks—all my chocolate, the Evian. No telling what else. I'm going to take inventory. Me and Sydney—"

"What for? What he ate, just replace. He'll be out of here tomorrow."

"You said tonight."

"It's not my house, Nanadine. Valerian invited him to dinner."

"Crazy."

"So it's Valerian who has to tell him to go."

"Why'd he put him in the guest room though? Sydney almost had a stroke when Mr. Street told him to take him there."

"Well, if he didn't have a stroke when he said 'Hi' to him, he won't have one at all."

"He said 'Hi'? Sydney didn't tell me about that."

"*Un*believable."

"Well, I can't stay up here gawking at a coat. I have to get the breakfast things cleared up. Did you call Solange yet?"

"No. I'll do it now. How did you manage to place orders before I came?"

"It was a mess, believe me. I can't get my tongue right for that language."

"Three geese, then? And another quart of raspberries?"

"That should do it. I wish they'd tell me things. How can I cook if I don't know how many's eating?" Ondine walked over to Jadine's bed and straightened the sheets. "Now when is he due?"

"Christmas Eve, I think. Just after Michael gets here."

"You sure?"

"No, but if he's a Christmas present, he'll have to be here by Christmas, won't he?"

"I can't believe that. Giving your son a whole human being for a Christmas present."

"Michael worships him. Took all of his courses at college."

"Now he'll own him, I suspect. What money can't buy. I've got to go. I want to fix a nice lunch for Sydney. He's still shook."

"Tell him not to worry."

"I'll try, but you saw him at breakfast. Mean as a tampered rooster."

"It'll be all *right*, now. I'm telling you."

Ondine left, holding her hand to her neck, hoping Jadine was right and that Mr. Street was finished being funny and would get rid of that thieving Negro before it was too late. A crazy white man and a crazy Black is a shake too much, she thought. She glanced quickly down the hall to the door of the room where he had been put. It was closed. Still asleep, she guessed. A night prowler—sleeps all day, prowls all night.

Jadine took off the sealskin coat and wiped her damp

neck. She thought of another quick shower before she dressed but decided against it. Hot as it was, the seal-feel was too good to let go. She put the coat back on, sat down and dialled Solange. No response other than a light free-floating buzz. Everybody on Isle des Chevaliers seemed to live rather well without good telephone service. She and Margaret used it more than all the families combined. Since she had come, shopping had become a major part of Margaret's life as it had always been her own. She fondled the hides of ninety baby seals and went to the closet thinking she may as well begin wrapping her gifts.

There were a dozen shirts for Sydney, who loved fine cloth. And a stunning black chiffon dress for Ondine. A little overdone, but Ondine liked that. Zircons on the bodice and the waist, swirls of chiffon skirting. And (the best thing) black suede shoes with zircons studding the heels. Hooker shoes. Ondine wouldn't be able to walk long in them, but how she could reign from a sitting position. She had wanted to get her a tiara too but maybe that *was* pushing it. The dress she packed neatly in a box among layers of tissue paper. The zircon-studded shoes went into a red satin shoe bag. Perspiration was forming on her forehead as she finished, and she blotted it away without ever taking off the coat. Both Sydney's and Ondine's presents were too large for the wrapping paper she had, so she put them aside and wrapped Valerian's record album. Finally she had to admit she was stifling and took the coat off. Naked she walked to the window. The emperor butterflies were gone now. Not one had fallen dead on the Karastan. Only the bougainvillea saw her standing in the window, her head thrown back to catch all the breeze she could in the soft place under her chin. I'm all done, she thought, except for a half-hour or so of finishing Margaret's chain of gold coins. Unless, of course, she was expected to buy something for Michael. Should she? Should the—what?—social secretary buy a present for the son of her employer/patron? She could exchange gifts with the Streets because she had known them so long, and they were like family, almost, and had given her so much. But she wasn't sure if giving a gift to their son was not a presumption. If she were married to Ryk (coat and all) it would be all right. Her status would be unquestioned. But like this? She had seen him only twice. He was always at prep school or camp or some spa when she visited before. A gift would embarrass him, probably, because he wouldn't have gotten one for her. Or would he? What had Margaret told him about the household? Even so, would he be offended by a gift from her, however modest? No, of course not. He was a poet, presumably, and a Socialist, so social awkwardness wouldn't trouble him the way it would have his father. But if she did get him one, it would have to be something earthy and noncapitalistic. She smiled. A loaf of bread maybe?

Footsteps on the gravel interrupted her. That must be Yardman, come to mount the Christmas tree. Jadine stepped away from the window so Yardman shouldn't see her nakedness, wondering what he would think of the black man in the guest room. She went to the bed where the skins of the ninety baby seals sprawled. She lay on top of them and ran her fingertips through the fur. How black. How shiny. Smooth. She pressed her thighs deep into its dark luxury. Then she lifted herself up a little and let her nipples brush the black hairs, back and forth, back and forth. It had frightened Ondine, the coat. She spoke as though the marriage was all right, but Jadine knew Ondine would be heartsick. More and more Sydney and Ondine looked to her for solutions to their problems. They had been her parents since she was twelve and now she was required to parent them—guide them, do the small chores that put them in touch with the outside world, soothe them, allay their fears. Like with that wild man sleeping down the hall. She had to calm them and make them understand Valerian's whimsy. Style. All style. That was Valerian. He had once been mugged on a

90

trip to Miami. He stood there, his arms over his head, while the muggers, some black teenagers with rags around their heads, ran their fingers through his pockets. One of them looked at him and must have seen the disdain in Valerian's eyes. He sneered at Valerian and said, "You don't like us, do you?" "Gentlemen," Valerian had replied, "I don't *know* you." It must have been that same antique grace that made him look at a raggedy black man who had been hiding in his wife's closet (with rape, theft or murder on his mind) and say, "Good evening," and offer him a drink. Then tell Sydney to prepare another place for "our guest". Jadine smiled as she pushed her nipples into the baby seals' skin. You had to give it to him. He was marvellous. All while the man ate limp salad, flat soufflé, peaches and coffee, Valerian behaved as though it was the most ordinary of incidents. Margaret never left off shaking and would not stay at the table in spite of Valerian's insistence that she do so. (She locked her bedroom door and, according to Sydney, did not come down for breakfast—only Valerian was there with his robust morning appetite.) Jadine and Valerian held up the conversation, and it was Jadine who cautioned Sydney and Ondine with meaningful looks to help them get through the serving with composure. At one point, after the man was seated and when Sydney held the bowl of salad toward him, the man looked up and said, "Hi." For the first time in his life, Sydney had dropped something. He collected the salad greens and righted the bowl expertly, but his anger and frustration were too strong to hide. He tried his best to be no less dignified than his employer, but he barely made it to civility. Valerian, however, was splendid. As soon as the man sat down Valerian was sober. Jadine thought she may have imagined it, but she believed Valerian was comforted, made more secure, by her presence at the table. That she exercised some restraint on the man; that Valerian believed that in her presence the man might be kept manageable. At any rate he sipped his brandy as

91

though the man's odour wasn't there. He didn't even blink when the man poured his demitasse into the saucer and blew on it gently before sipping it through a lump of sugar. More than grace, she thought, Valerian had courage. He could not have known, could not know even now, what that nigger was up to. He didn't even know his real name.

"How long have you been with us, Mister —? I'm sorry, I don't know your name."

The man looked up from his plate. His mouth was full and he chewed silently and swallowed before he answered. "Five days. A week maybe."

"And before that?" asked Valerian.

The man removed the pit of a black olive from his mouth. "Swamp."

"Oh, yes. Sein de Veilles. It couldn't have been very comfortable for you there. The local people avoid it entirely. Spirits live there, I'm told."

The man didn't answer.

"Did you see any ghosts while you were there?" Jadine asked him.

He shook his head but did not look at her. "No, but I guess they saw me."

Valerian laughed heartily. "Are you a believer then?"

"Sometimes," said the man.

"Sometimes? You pick and choose when to believe and when not?"

"In a swamp, I believe," said the man.

"An excellent solution. Excellent." Valerian chuckled. He seemed to be enjoying himself thoroughly. "You're not local, are you? Your accent is American. Am I correct?"

"Yeah."

"Have you just left there?"

"No." The man sopped the salad dressing on his plate with a round of French bread, and gulped it down. Then he wiped his mouth with the back of his hand. "Jumped ship and tried to swim ashore. Couldn't make it so I climbed aboard this boat I thought was going to dock there, but it brought me here. I waited a few days for a way to get back. Nothing. So I came to the first house I saw. I was—" he glanced at Jadine—"good and hungry by then." He was exhausted it seemed, having said so much.

"Reasonable," said Valerian. "But I'm confused. Is there a pantry in my wife's bedroom?" He gazed at the man's profile.

"Huh?"

Valerian smiled, but did not repeat the question.

"He wants to know why you were in the bedroom," said Jadine. "If you were just feeding yourself, that is."

"Oh. I got tired sitting in one spot all day. I was just looking around. I heard footsteps and hid." He looked around at them as though his reply had finally solved everything, and he could now be sociable. "Nice pad you got here," he said smiling, and that was when Jadine felt the first bolt of fear. As long as he burrowed in his plate like an animal, grunting in monosyllables, but not daring to look up, she was without fear. But when he smiled she saw small dark dogs galloping on silver feet.

More to regain her confidence than to get information she asked him, "Why didn't you take the boat?"

"What?" He looked at her quickly and just as quickly looked away.

"You said you were waiting to get to Dominique. The *Seabird* is docked. If you've been to sea, you could have managed the boat."

He stared at his plate and said nothing.

"Boats are highly visible, dear," Valerian said to Jadine, "and call a great deal of attention to themselves." He smiled at the man and went on. "I'm sorry, but I don't know your name."

"That makes us even," said the man with a wide smile. "I don't know yours either."

And they still didn't, but Valerian instructed him to be put up in the guest room anyway. And Sydney's jawbones were still working back and forth the next morning as he told his wife and niece about putting silk pajamas out for him. Jadine laughed and said he would slide out of bed in them, but Sydney couldn't see any humour in that, and Ondine was too concerned about her husband to join the pretty careless girl in laughter.

ONDINE picked up an onion and pressed it for soft spots. Things went back to their natural state so quickly in that place. A layer of slippery skin gave way beneath her thumb, but the onion was firm underneath. At that moment, Yardman scratched the screen door and when Ondine turned to look she saw his bloody shirt first and then his foolish smile.

"Leave it." She turned back to her table and tossed the words over her shoulder. "Put some newspaper down out there."

He broadened his smile and nodded vigorously, but Ondine did not see that; she assumed it and, as an after-thought lest he think she had no manners at all, she said, "Thanks." She put down the onion and turned one eye of the gas range up high. In fact, the "thanks" was sincere for she felt guilty about letting him do what was once a marked skill of her own.

Can't do it anymore, she thought. Have to chase around too much. She didn't like asking Yardman to do it for her, but her feet were too tender and her ankles too swollen to manage, so when he brought four or five young hens tied in a crate, she told him she needed only one at a time—let the others pick around behind the washhouse and to "wring one of them for me while you're at it".

"Yes, madame," he said as he always said.

"Are they young? Tender?" she had asked him.

"Yes, madame."

"Don't look it. Look like brooders."

"No, madame. Pullet every one."

"We'll see," she answered him. "Mind how you go. I don't want to be scrubbing up blood all afternoon." But he was bloody anyway so she said, "Leave it," to let him know that he had killed it wrong and also to remind him that she did not want him in her kitchen. And there it was on the newspaper and wouldn't you know he had not plucked one single feather, heavenly Father? That'll take me forever.

She lifted her head to call him back, come right back here, she was going to say, but suddenly she was too tired. Too tired to fuss, too tired to even have to confront him with his sloppiness. She sighed, picked up the chicken and brought it into the kitchen.

She hoisted a large pot of water onto the burning eye and wondered what he did with the head and feet. When the water was hot enough she dropped the chicken in and held it down with a wooden ladle long enough to loosen the pins. Then she removed it from the hot water and with newspaper spread out, started to pluck. She was still nimble at it but slower than she would have been if she wasn't being careful about where the feathers went. A big nuisance to have to do it herself; it was going to make Sydney's lunch late, but she didn't feel up to seeing Yardman again, or giving him an order angrily, firmly or even sweetly. Yesterday everything was all right. The best it could be and exactly the way she had hoped it would be: a good man whom she trusted; a good and permanent job doing what she was good at for a boss who appreciated it; beautiful surroundings which included her own territory where she alone governed; and now with Jadine back, a "child" whom she could enjoy, indulge, protect and, since this "child" was a niece it was without the stress of a mother-daughter relationship. She was uneasy about the temporary nature of their stay on the island and Margaret's visits always annoyed her — but it was being there that made Jade want to stay with them for a longish spell. Otherwise their niece would light anywhere except back in Philadelphia. She hoped Mr.

95

Street would stay on in spite of his addled wife. Now here come this man upstairs in the guest room. Maybe Jadine was right, she thought, he would be gone today or, certainly. the next and they were making too much of it. Ondine stopped plucking and lifted her eyes slowly to the place where the window shutters did not quite close. A bit of the sky was unhidden by foliage. She thought she heard a small, smooth sound, like a well-oiled gear shifting. Not a sound really—more of an imagined impression, as though she were a dust mote watching an' eye blink. There would be the hurricane wind of eyelashes falling through the air and the weighty crash of lid on lid.

Slowly she returned to the white hen in her hands. She was down to the pinfeathers when Sydney walked in with a small basket of mail.

"Already?" she asked him.

"No. I just thought I'd finish it up in here."

"It'll be at least an hour. Maybe two."

"What are you doing that for?" He pointed at the pile of feathers on the floor.

"That's the way I got it."

"Call him. You want me to call him back here?"

"No. I'm just about finished now."

"He knows better than that. Where is he?" Sydney moved toward the door.

"Sit down, Sydney. Don't bother yourself."

"I'm already bothered. I can't run a house like this with everybody doing whatever comes to mind."

"Sit down, I say. Hen's done."

He sat at the table and began sorting letters, circulars, magazines, and putting them into piles.

"Maybe we should look for somebody else. I'll speak to Mr. Street."

"It's not worth the trouble, Sydney. Unless you can guarantee the next one won't be worse. On balance, he's still reliable and he does keep the place up, you got to give him his due."

"You don't sound like yourself, Ondine." He looked at her heavy white braids sitting on her head like a royal diadem.

"Oh, I'm fine, I guess," but her voice was flat, like a wide river without any undertow at all.

"I never heard you stand up for Yardman when he does something contrary to what you tell him."

"I'm not standing up for him. I just think he's a whole lot better than nobody and a little bit better than most."

"You the one doing the plucking. I'm trying to make it easier for you—not me."

"He *is* easier for me. I was just thinking how I used to be able to get my own yard hens. Not no more. If they tear loose from me, they free. I can't chase em anymore. I don't even know if I got the strength to wring their necks."

"Well, what you don't have the strength for, Yardman is supposed to do. I don't want you running all over the yard after chickens. Killing them neither. We long past that, Ondine. Long past that." He rested his hands on a letter for a minute as he recollected the bloody, long-legged girl in the back of Televettie Poultry sitting with three grown women, ankle deep in feathers among the squawks of crated fowl. At their feet two troughs of dead birds, one for the feathered ones, one for the newly plucked.

"I know, and we're going to stay past it, too."

"Not if you start changing up on me, we won't. Not if you start letting people run over you. Start changing the rules in the middle of the stream." He pushed the stack of magazines to one side.

Ondine laughed lightly. "You mean horse."

"What?"

"Horse. Horse in midstream. Never mind. You know as well as anybody that I can handle Yardman and you also know that I'm not changing up on you. That's not what you're going on about. You're edgy and I understand. That makes two of us. Three, I guess, since the

97

Principal Beauty locked herself in. She call you for anything yet?"

"No. Not a thing."

"Me neither."

"Why three? Jadine ain't bothered?"

"Not as far as I can see. She's laughing and swinging around in that coat."

"Damn."

"She says we're overdoing it. That Mr. Street'll have him out of here today."

"But what'd he do it for? She say anything about that? I been knowing him for fifty-one years and I never would have guessed—not in a million years—he do something like this. Where does he think he is? Main Line? Ain't no police out here. Ain't nobody hardly. He think that nigger came here and hid in his own wife's bedroom just to get a meal? He could have knocked on the back door and got something to eat. Nobody comes in a house and hides in it for days, weeks . . ."

Ondine looked at her husband. Talk about changing up, she hadn't seen him this riled since before they were married. "I know," she said, "I know that, but Jadine says it was a joke; he had too much liquor and him and her had an argument and . . ." she stopped.

". . . and what? Can't finish, can you? No, 'cause it don't make a bit of sense. Not one bit."

"There's no point in gnawing it, Sydney, like a dog with a bone. Swallow it or drop it."

"Can't do either one."

"You have to. It ain't your bone."

"You have taken leave of your senses, woman. It is my bone and right now it's stuck in my craw. I live here too. So do you and so does Jadine. My family lives here—not just his. If that nigger wants to steal something or kill somebody you think he's going to skip us, just 'cause we don't own it? Hell, no. I sat up in that chair all night, didn't I? Mr. Street slept like a log. He was snoring like a hound when I went in there this morning."

"He drank a lot, Jadine says." She reached in the oven and poked a baking potato.

"Ain't that much whiskey in the world make a man sleep with a wife-raper down the hall."

"He didn't rape anybody. Didn't even try."

"Oh? You know what's on his mind, do you?"

"I know he's been here long enough and quiet enough to rape, kill, steal—do whatever he wanted and all he did was eat."

"You amaze me. You really amaze me. All these years I thought I knew you."

"You're tired, honey. You didn't sleep hardly any at all with that gun in your lap, and carrying it around under your coat ain't making things better. You really ought to put it back where it belongs."

"Long as he's in this house, it belongs with me."

"Come on, now. It's barely noon. Mr. Street'll get rid of him just like Jadine said. Then everything will be just like it was."

"Like it was? Like it was, eh? Not by a long shot. When I brought him his coffee and rolls, he never said a word. Just 'More coffee, please'. Ondine, it's more than just being here, you know. I mean, Mr. Street had him stay in the guest room. The guest room. You understand me?"

"Well?"

"What do you mean, 'well'?"

"I don't know what you're driving at."

"Where do we sleep? Ondine?"

"Me and you?"

"You heard me."

"We sleep where we're supposed to."

"Where's that?"

"It's nice down there, Sydney. And you know it is: sitting room, *two* bedrooms, patio, bath . . ."

"But where is it?"

"Over there."

"Over where?"

"Up over the downstairs kitchen."

"Right. Up over the downstairs kitchen."

"Jadine sleeps up there. With them."

"Jadine? Now I am through. You comparing Jadine to a . . . a . . . stinking ignorant swamp nigger? To a wild-eyed pervert who hides in women's closets? Do you know what he said to me?"

" 'Hi'?"

"Before that. When I was bringing him down the stairs under the barrel of my gun?"

"No, what'd he say?"

"Could he take a leak."

"A leak?"

"A leak! I got him with his hands up and the safety off and he wants to stop and pee!"

"That's nerve all right."

"Nerve? He's crazy, that's what. You understand me? Crazy. Liable to do anything. And I have to show him to the guest room and lay him out some fresh pajamas. The guest room, right next to Jadine. I told her to keep that door locked and not to open it up for nobody."

"You should have left it at that. You didn't have to go creeping up there all night to make sure. Scared her to death."

"Wait a minute. Whose side you on?"

"Your side, naturally. Our side. I'm not arguing for him. I told you last night what I thought about it. I just want to calm you down. He's leaving, Sydney. But we're not, and I don't want no big rift between you and Mr. Street about where that Negro slept and why and so forth. I want us to stay here. Like we have been. That old man loves you. Loves us both. Look what he gives us at Christmas."

"I know all that."

"Stock. No slippers. No apron. Stock! And look what he did for Jadine, just because you asked him to. You going to break up with him, lose all that just because he got drunk and let a crazy hobo spend the night. We have a future here, as well as a past, and I tell you I can't pick

100

up and move in with some strange new white folks at my age. I can't do it."

"Nobody's talking about moving."

"If you keep working yourself up, you'll rile him, or do something rash, I don't know."

"If I stay on here, I have to know whether—"

"See there? If. Already you saying if. Keep on and you'll have us over in them shacks in Queen of France. You want me shucking crayfish on a porch like those Marys? Do you?"

"You know I don't."

"Then drop that bone. Drop it before it chokes you. You know your work. Just do what you're supposed to do. Here. Take him his potato. Finish the rest of the mail later. Just give Mr. Street his. He likes to read it while he eats, if you call that eating. And Sydney? Don't worry yourself. Remember, Jadine's here. Nothing can happen to us as long as she's here."


SYDNEY went out with the tray on which a steaming potato in a covered dish was situated to the left of an empty wineglass, a napkin and a stack of mail. As the kitchen door swung on its hinges, Ondine took a deep breath. She had surprised herself. Before Sydney came in she was as nervous as he was. Still tasting her breakfast, too confused to quarrel with Yardman about the un-plucked hen. She didn't put any stock in Jadine's assurances, but when Sydney looked like he was falling apart, she'd pulled herself together and talked sense. Good sense. That was what surprised her. She talked sense she didn't know she had about a situation that both frightened and disoriented her. But in talking to Sydney she knew what it was. The man was black. If he'd been a white bum in Mrs. Street's closet, well, she would have felt different. Sydney was right. It was his bone. Whether they liked it or not. But she was right, too. He had to drop it. The man upstairs wasn't a Negro—meaning one

101

of them. He was a stranger. (She had made Sydney understand that.) Mr. Street might keep him for two days, three, for his own amusement. And even if he didn't steal, he was nasty and ignorant and they would have to serve him anyway, if Mr. Street wanted it. Clean his tub, change his bed linen, bring his breakfast to his bed if he wanted it, collect his underwear (Jesus), call him sir, step aside if they met him in the hall, light his cigarettes, hold open his door, see to it there were fresh flowers in his room, books, a dish of mints.

"Shoot," she said aloud. "That nigger's not going nowhere. No matter what they say." Ondine picked up the chicken. Her fingers quickly found the joints they were searching for, and broke each one. Then she removed the wings from its back. The hen's little elbows held a dainty *V* as though protecting its armpits from the cold although it was noon and the water the breakfast rain had left in the mouths of the orchids was so hot it burned the children's fingers—or would have, if any children lived at L'Arbe de la Croix. But none did. So the stamens of the orchids went untickled and the occupants of the lovely breezy house with the perfectly bevelled cabinets heard no children's screams and no tramp of red soldier ants marching toward the greenhouse, past the washhouse where a woman sat rubbing the dirt from her feet with one of seventeen Billy Blass towels. Stacked before her in two wicker baskets were the other sixteen, some everyday table napkins and tablecloths, assorted underwear and T-shirts, four white uniforms, four white shirts, a corset, six pairs of black nylon socks and two thin cotton nightgowns. She was happy as she sat there cleaning her calluses. Her laundry load was getting smaller each week and the bundle of clothes that travelled by motorboat to Cecile's in Queen of France was getting bigger and bigger. She knew quite well that she was supposed to be insulted by that, and when the opportunity arose she managed a pout, but in her heart of hearts she was happy.

102

She put the black socks in a bucket to soak and dropped the corset in a basinful of soapy water and vinegar. She made the Billy Blass towels the first load for the washing machine since they took longest to dry. Once the machine began to agitate she could sit for a while and attend to her own thoughts while she waited for Gideon to come by her. From the pocket of her dress she pulled two wrinkled avocados and some smoked fish and placed them on a piece of newspaper and covered it all against flies with a stained Dior napkin. Then she disconnected the dryer, plugged in her hot plate and set an old drip-pot of coffee on to heat. She had no assigned lunch hour so she ate while the laundry washed itself. It was such a pleasure. Washing for these people was child's play compared to the way she did it on Place de Vent. But at least there she had the pleasure of gossip over the tubs; here there was mostly silence (unless you counted the music that came from the *serre chaude*), which is why she could hear the soldier ants so clearly and why she was so eager for Gideon to finish with the hens and join her on some pretext or other for if the heavy one with the braids crossed like two silver machetes on her head caught them chatting in the washhouse or in the garden behind, she would fly into a rage and her machetes would glitter and clang on her head. The silence was why she often brought Alma, and although the girl's chatter was so young it made her head ache, it was better than listening to soldier ants trying one more time to enter the greenhouse and being thwarted as usual by the muslin dipped in poison and taped to the doorsill.

She was sorry Alma could not come today. Gideon and she had a bet on how long the chocolate eater could last. Gideon said, "Long as he wants. Till New Year," while she said, "No. The chocolate eater's heart would betray him — not his mind or stomach." And as they rowed back to Queen of France she raised the bet to 150,000 francs instead of the 100,000 she began with. She laughed and spat in the sea as she raised him, so confident was she.

103

For she had seen evidence of the man who ate chocolate (in the washhouse, in the trees, in the gazebo, down by the pond, in the toolshed, near the greenhouse). And it was he who brought the soldier ants onto the property with his trail of foil paper containing flecks of chocolate that the ants loved and sought vigorously. She had seen him in a dream smiling at her as he rode away wet and naked on a stallion. So she knew he was in agreement with her and any day now he would be discovered or reveal himself. As soon as she got out of the jeep that very morning, she was convinced that today was the day.

A great rush of butterflies was what she noticed first and later, as she stood in the courtyard waiting for machete-hair to bring the baskets of clothes, she instantly saw that the machetes were not clanging now. They, like their owner, were subdued — by fear, she thought. The chocolate man would be the cause of that. She could think of nothing else — hurricane wind, or magic doll, diamond-back or monkey teeth — that would quiet those curved and clanging knives. Only the man who ate chocolate in the night and lived like a foraging animal and who was as silent as a star could have done it.

She had eaten the fish and one avocado and still Gideon had not come. She didn't want to start on the coffee, because it ran right through her and not having access to a toilet (she felt unwelcome even in the kitchen) she did not want to run off to the bushes behind the garden in the middle of his visit. She insisted she knew about the man before Gideon — although it was he who actually saw him first. She knew of his presence twelve days ago long before he left the trail of chocolate foil paper (which she mistook for a fabricated attack against herself made up by machete-hair who had asked her point-blank had she been taking chocolate and she had said, No, madame, over her shoulder to every query without allowing her eyes to see the heavy one). Before that mistakable trail, he left the unmistakable one of his smell. Like a beast who loses his animal smell after too

104

long a diet of cooked food, a man's smell is altered by a fast. She caught the scent twelve days ago: the smell of a fasting, or starving, as the case might be, human. It was the smell of human afterbirth that only humans could produce. A smell they reproduced when they were down to nothing for food. So a hungry man was on the grounds, or, as she said to Gideon, "Somebody's starving to death round here." And Gideon said, "Me, Thérèse," and she said, "No, not you. A really starving somebody." And later that day a bug-eyed Gideon crept over to her under the lime tree near the kitchen terrace and whispered that he'd seen a swamp woman dart out from behind some trees near the pond. Thérèse stopped scaling grouper fish and said that what he saw was what she smelled and it couldn't be a swamp woman because they had a pitchlike smell. What he saw must have been a rider. So she took to bringing two avocados instead of one and leaving the second one in the washhouse. But each third day when she returned it was still there, untouched by all but fruit flies. It was Gideon who had the solution: instead of fixing the sash on the window of the pantry as he was ordered, he removed one of its panes and told machete-hair he was having trouble getting another. The heavy one fumed and removed "perishables" and things that attracted flies into the other kitchen until he could repair the window. In the meanwhile, they hoped the horseman would have access to the food left there. And soon they saw bits of folded foil in funny places and they knew he had gotten from the pantry chocolate at the very least. Once Gideon saw an empty Evian bottle in the gazebo. Then they knew he had fresh water too.

Thérèse removed the coffee pot from the stove and put it back five times before she heard Gideon's footsteps. She poked her head out of the doorway, grinned and started to speak.

"Sh," he said, "sh." His finger touched his lips. But Thérèse could not restrain herself.

"Something's going on. I can tell." Then as he stepped

inside and came close she saw his shirt. "You slaughter the hen or the hen slaughter you?"

Gideon held up one hand to shush her and with the other pulled the door shut.

"Open the door, man," she complained. "Too hot in here."

Gideon stood fast. "Listen," he said. "He's in the house. *In* it! All out in the open! I saw him!"

"I knew it! I knew it!" Thérèse's whisper was close to a shout. Gideon went to the coffee pot. Two cups were sitting on top of the folding table and he filled them both.

"A little fridge out here wouldn't be a bad idea," he said. "Just one of them little ones, like he got out in the greenhouse. Plug it up right there . . ."

"Talk, man. Stop going on about a fridge."

"Wouldn't you like a little cold beer or chilled wine from time to time?"

"Cold beer?" She looked at him in amazement. "That country ruined you, man. Stop fooling with me. Where did you see him?"

"In the window. Her window." He took the chicken head and feet from his shirt and wrapped them in newspaper.

"Doing what?"

"Looking. Just looking. A sheet or something wrapped around him, but bare naked on top."

"Did he see you see him?"

"No. Don't think so. I pretended I was taking off my cap to scratch my head and looking off up in the trees."

"He didn't do anything? Move?"

"Nope. Just looked around. Then I turned and walked back away."

"Alone? Was she with him?"

"Can't say. But it was in her room. Get what I mean? And I saw her up there before naked as a worm when I was fixing to put up the tree. She jumped back, but didn't do no good. She don't know I got eyes in the top of

106

my head. Then next, about a hour or so later, there *he* was. Naked too, almost. Just a piece of white stuff around his waist. You reckon they got it on?" He had stopped trying to appear uninterested and was openly enjoying the possibilities.

"I told you!" said Thérèse. "He's a horseman come down here to get her. He was just skulking around waiting for his chance."

"Maybe. Maybe." Gideon looked at her milky eyes. "You damn near blind, but I have to hand it to you. Some things you see better than me. Otherwise why would a big strong-looking man be hiding round here like that? Why this house all the time? Why not over the other side, or up the road where those Filipinos are? He must have been looking for somebody specific."

"The chippy. The fast-ass," said Thérèse. "That's why he went straight up to her room. Because he knew she was here, he saw her from the hills. Maybe he'll run her out of here."

"Back to the States, eh?"

"Or France even. Where that big box came from. Maybe he's not a rider. Maybe he's an old boyfriend and he the one sent her the box, Gideon."

"Hold on. You going wild."

"And machete-hair she don't like it. Tried to keep them apart. But it didn't work. He find her, swim the whole ocean big, till he find her, eh? Make machete-hair too mad. Now she tell her bow-tie husband . . ." Thérèse sat on the wooden chair and rocked in the telling, pressing her fingers into Gideon's shoulder as each new sequence presented itself to her. "Bow-tie get mad very. 'Cause he lives near machete-hair's thumb . . ." The more she invented the more she rocked and the more she rocked the more her English crumbled till finally it became dust in her mouth stopping the flow of her imagination and she spat it out altogether and let the story shimmer through the clear cascade of the French of Dominique.

Gideon couldn't stop her, so he tried to gulp coffee while warding off the jabs to his shoulder. When she abandoned English he stopped listening for it was in French that she had tricked him into leaving the States after twenty years and coming back to Dominique to handle family property. So he shut his ears and tried to finish his coffee submitting to the shoulder jabs out of deference to her because she was his mother's baby sister and because of a grudging respect for her magic breasts and because she had been able to trick him (of all people) with thirty-four letters in fifteen years, begging him to come home and take care of the property by which she must have meant herself because when he got there that's all there was left: no land, no hills of coffee bush. Just Thérèse, two years his senior, and a cement house whose roof had to be put back on after every hurricane which meant four times a year. When he looked at the house—one of a dozen scattered over the emerald hill—and discovered that the 130 *arpents* he'd remembered from his childhood belonged, like the emerald hills, to the Frenchman who lived in Guadeloupe and that except for the kitchen garden and the village garden on the riverbank there was no land to care for, only this laughing, lying crone with a craving for apples, he wasn't even angry. Just amazed that he had believed those thirty-four letters written in perfect French by the priest at first and then by an acolyte describing the burden of managing so much property, too much for an old lady who nevertheless always thought of a way to get a ten-dollar money order out of him, and asking over and over again to make sure he brought apples when he came or to send them, and if he would let her know when that would be she would alert a friend at customs because apples were contraband and could not be imported into Dominique which was true because only French-grown fruit and vegetables could arrive at that port or be sold in the stores. And ships unloaded wilted lettuce, thin rusty beans and pithy carrots every month. A hardship for the

108

rich and the middle class, neither of whom would
consider working a kitchen garden (except, of course, the
American, who made it a hobby) and were dependent on
the market but it was of no consequence to the poor who
ate spendidly from their gardens, from the sea and from
the avocado trees that grew by the side of the road. Only
Thérèse had tasted apples once when she was seven and
again when she was thirty-five and had a craving for
them akin to hysteria. When Gideon appeared in 1973
with twelve apples hidden in the lining of his electric blue
leisure suit which Thérèse's friends at customs
noticed — but for two dollars U.S. ignored — her gratitude
was so complete he didn't get on the next plane back as
he threatened. After all he hadn't left much: just U.S.
citizenship, the advantage of which was the ability to
send an occasional ten-dollar money order, buy a leisure
suit and watch TV. Most of the friends of his youth had
emigrated to France, but the stories of their lives there
were so heartbreaking, he'd chosen Quebec instead
although he had to wait until he was twenty-two for a visa
and then he arrived in the coat pocket so to speak of a
Canadian farmer. And two years later, by much subter-
fuge (including marriage to an American Negro) got into
the States where money orders, leisure suits and TV
abounded. Now that he'd come back what was there to
do but build a new roof after each hurricane, find a little
work, and wait for carnival? At first he was ashamed
before his family and friends. Just as Thérèse had lied to
him, so had he lied to her about the wealth he had
accumulated in the States. Now there he was for all the
world to see building another temporary roof, looking for
tourist tips, eyeing women at the bars — just like before.
With no suitcase of American dollars. Just twelve apples
and a leisure suit. Humiliating. Who but an ass would go
back to Dominique with no more than what he had when
he left? Those who wished desperately to come back
(from France, Quebec, New York City or wherever)
could not, would not, unless they were accompanied by

the college certificates or money they had gone to find. He spoke English very well, however, and that could have been something of an asset on the island, but at his age with no certificate and out of touch with friends who could make a way for him he could not carry luggage at the airlines, or wait tables at the Old Queen. So he drifted to the docks for a few days' work or got a lucky day collecting fares for a taxi man until, finally, all of his forty years of immigrant labour paid off when an American who owned a house on Isle des Chevaliers came to stay and needed a regular handyman/gardener with boat skills, English and a manner less haughty than that of the local Blacks. For in spite of the fact that they built their houses four times a year the natives of Dominique did not hide the contempt they felt in their hearts for everybody but themselves.

Gideon got over the shame: the work at Isle des Chevaliers, which began for a season and had lasted three years, helped and so did the fact that the jokes and insults heaped on him by his family were nothing compared to the humiliations of immigrant life which U.S. citizenship did not change. Also the thought of being able to die in those coffee-growing hills rather than in those lonely Stateside places gave him so much happiness he could not hold a grudge or sustain anger for more than an hour. Unlike Thérèse whose hatreds were complex and passionate as exemplified by her refusal to speak to the American Negroes, and never even to acknowledge the presence of the white Americans in her world. To effect this she believed all she had to do was not look at them (or rather not look at them while they looked at her) so her face was always turned away when they addressed her and her glance (when it was not on her work) went to a distant point on the horizon which she could not have seen if her life depended on it. What they took for inattentiveness was a miracle of concentration.

"Hush, Thérèse," said Gideon. "They can hear you in the harbour. Finish making up your romance in your head. I have to go." He stood up and rubbed the abused shoulder. "But you forgetting one thing in your story. One important thing. I said I saw him in the house, in the open. Open. Get it? Now there are five people living there. Not three. And two of them is white and the same two is the boss of everything as well. While you making up your story about what this one thinks and this one feels, you have left out the white bosses. What do they feel about it? It's not important who this one loves and who this one hates and what bowtie do or what machete-hair don't do if you don't figure on the white ones and what they thinking about it all." He tapped her on the chest bone and left her sitting there with a half-finished plot on her tongue.

Thérése unplugged the hot plate and put the last of the Billy Blass towels in the dryer. Then she put all the white shirts and uniforms into the washing machine. The load was too tight and too much, but she had wasted time gossiping with Gideon so she left it that way. She sat down again on the chair and began sloshing the black socks of the bow-tie husband.

It was true, she thought. She had forgotten the white Americans. How would they fit into the story? She could not imagine them. In her story she knew who the others were: the chocolate-eating man was a lover, the fast-ass a coquette who had turned him down; the other two were the traditional hostile family. She understood that, but now she had to get a grasp of the tall thin American who played in the greenhouse whom she had never seen clearly and certainly never spoken to. And also the wife with the sunset hair and milk-white skin. What would they feel? She realized then that all her life she thought they felt nothing at all. Oh, well, yes, she knew they talked and laughed and died and had babies. But she had never attached any feeling to any of it. She thought of her priest, the shopkeepers, the gendarmes, the school-teachers Alma talked about, the two little French girls she took care of one day when the governess ran away,

111

and the hundreds of French babies who used to nurse at her magical breasts. What went on inside them? Inside.

Thérèse resented the problem and the necessity for solving it to get on with the story. "What difference does it make," she murmured. "I don't know what they would think about him, but I know for certain what they would do about him. Kill him. Kill the chocolate-eating black man. Kill him dead. Ah. Poor thing. Poor, poor thing. He dies and the fast-ass is brought low at last. Too late, bitch — too late you discover how wonderful he really was. How gentle, how kind. And you are full of remorse, but too late, cow, too too late; you will never have him now. And you machete-hair and you bow-tie you will think everything is all right now he's dead, but no! you will suffer too, because the fast-ass is grief-stricken and will blame you for his untimely death and hate you forever. So you can go back to the States the whole pack of you and choke to death on your big red apples."

THE SKIN of the baby seals sucked up the dampness of her own. Jadine closed her eyes and imagined the blackness she was sinking into. She lay spread-eagled on the fur, nestling herself into it. It made her tremble. She opened her lips and licked the fur. It made her tremble more. Ondine was right; there was something a little fearful about the coat. No, not fearful, seductive. After a few more moments of nestling she got up and made preparations to take another shower and to get dressed. The clock showed twelve-thirty and she still had to phone Solange, answer letters, and see about Margaret. She would need soothing. Maybe they would take their fruit and cold consommé down by the fish pond or farther up the hill to the gazebo. Because of Margaret's refusal to leave her bedroom, they had already missed their session of exercise and muscle-tightening calisthenics. Valerian would be in the greenhouse through lunch where he usually had a baked potato or some other single item. Only Ondine and Sydney ate a substantial lunch. Both had three very full meals a day and their menu was in no way related to what was served at Valerian's table.

Jadine came out of the shower as moist as she was when she went in, so she dressed as slowly as possible in order to prevent more perspiration.

The emperor butterflies were back now agitating the air. Jadine watched them languidly as she brushed her hair and bound it into a knot at the top of her head. Then she pulled a few strands over her ears and temples to soften the look. On impulse she put on her coat again and she was looking in a full-length mirror judging the effect when the smell hit her. She moved a little to her left to see what the mirror reflected behind her. There he stood in mauve silk pajamas, his skin as dark as a river-bed, his eyes as steady and clear as a thief's.

"Morning," he said, and smiled bringing once more into view the small dark dogs galloping on silver feet. Jadine could not find her tongue. She was staring into the mirror at his hair. Last night, sitting with Valerian in the soft light of the dining room, it had looked merely long and unkempt. Here, alone in her bedroom where there were no shadows, only glimmering unrelieved sunlight, his hair looked overpowering—physically overpowering, like bundles of long whips or lashes that could grab her and beat her to jelly. And would. Wild, aggressive, vicious hair that needed to be put in jail. Uncivilised, reform-school hair. Mau Mau, Attica, chain-gang hair.

"Good morning." He said it again.

She struggled to pull herself away from his image in the mirror and to yank her tongue from the roof of her mouth. She was sober now and the thought that she had not grasped fully the night before, the picture that only Margaret had seen clearly, was framed for her now in the fruitwood of the mirror: this man had been living among them (in their *things*) for days. And they had not known it. What had he seen or heard? What was he doing there?

113

"Hey. I was saying good morning to you."

She turned, freed at last from the image in the mirror.

"You could knock, you know."

"The door was open." He gestured to the door behind him.

"But it's still a door and can be knocked on."

He seemed to close his eyes to her without shutting the lids, and what was left of his smile disappeared into his beard and the river-bed darkness of his face.

This is wrong, she thought. I shouldn't make him angry.

"I'm sorry, but you startled me. Did you sleep well?"

He nodded but did not return the smile she dredged up to her own lips.

"The shower doesn't work," he said, glancing around the room.

"Oh." She laughed and, to hide her confusion, shed her sealskin coat, throwing it on the bed. "There's no handle. Just push the knob in the centre. It'll come on. It took me a while too, at first."

He looked past her to the sealskin coat sprawled on the bed. Jadine flushed as though he could see the print of her nipples and thighs in the pelts. He walked toward the coat and the bed. The pajamas they'd given him were too small—the sleeves ended somewhere between wrist and elbow and the pants leg came to just above his shins. As he stood looking at the coat she could not tell whether he or it was the blacker or the shinier, but she knew she did not want him to touch it.

"I'll get Sydney to get some clothes for you if you like." Then thinking of Sydney's response to that chore she added, "Or Yardman. Yardman can get some things for you."

"Who?" He turned away from the coat.

"Yardman. The gardener."

"That his name?"

"No." She smiled, searching for the leashes of the small dark dogs. "But he answers to it. Which is something, at least. Some people don't have a name of any kind."

He smiled too, moving away from the bed toward her. "What do you like? Billy? Paul? What about Rastus?"

"Don't be funny. What *is* your name?"

"What's yours?"

"Jade."

He shook his head as though he knew better.

"Okay. Jadine. Jadine Childs." She reached for a cigarette.

"Can I have one of those?"

"Sure." She gestured toward the escritoire for him to help himself. He pulled out a Gauloise filter, lit it and began to cough.

"Been a long time," he said, and for the first time looked vulnerable. Jadine grabbed the leashes.

"Keep the pack," she said. "There's plenty more if you want them."

He nodded and took another drag with a little more success.

"Who's the copper Venus?" he asked her.

Jadine dropped the leashes. "Where did you see that?"

"I didn't see it. I heard it."

"Where?" She could not find them, they were gone.

"The woman who comes to work here. She talks to herself out in the washhouse."

Now she had them again, safely back in her fingers. "Mary. It must have been Mary." Jadine laughed. "That was a publicity thing. When I was modelling they called me that. I wonder how Mary knows about it. I don't think she can even read."

"You were a model?" He narrowed his eyes with interest.

Jadine walked over to a large straw chest. As she left the Karastan her gold-thread slippers clicked on the tile. After rummaging awhile she pulled out a fashion magazine with her face on the cover. When she handed it to him he sat down at the desk and made a flute

115

sound between his teeth. And then another as his eyes travelled from the crown of her head to the six centimetres of cleavage supported (more or less) by silver lamé. Her hair in the picture was pressed flat to her head, pulled away from her brow revealing a neat hairline. Her eyes were the colour of mink and her lips wet and open. He continued the flute sounds and then opened the magazine. After flipping the pages for a few seconds he came to a four-page spread of her in other poses, other clothes, other hair, but always the same wet and open lips.

"Goddamn," he whispered. "Go-oddamn."

Jadine said nothing, but she held on tight to the leashes. The look on his face made her smile. He examined the pictures closely, whispering "shit" and "goddamn" softly to himself at intervals.

"What does it say?" He put the magazine flat on the desk, turned at an angle so she could read and translate the text.

"Oh, it's just stuff about me." She leaned on the edge of the desk facing him and the magazine. "Where I went to school. Things like that."

"Read it to me."

Jadine leaned over and translated rapidly the important parts of the copy. "Mademoiselle Childs . . . graduate of the Sorbonne . . . an accomplished student of art history . . . a degree in . . . is an expert on cloisonné, having visited and worked with the Master Nape . . . An American now living in Paris and Rome, where she had a small but brilliantly executed role in a film by . . . " She stopped. The man was tracing her blouse with his forefinger.

"This," he said, lifting his finger from the picture to point at the caption beneath, "what does this say?"

"That's just a description of the dress. Natural raw silk . . . honey-coloured . . ."

"Right here it says 'fast lane', What's that about?"

"Oh, they're trying to be hip. It says, 'If you travel as
116

Jade does in what the Americans call the fast lane, you need elegant but easy-to-pack frocks.' Then it goes on about the jewellery."

"What about the jewellery?" Now he traced the heaps of gold necklaces above the honey-coloured silk.

"The total worth of it is—" she calculated quickly from francs into dollars— "thirty-two thousand dollars."

"Thirty-two *thou*sand?"

"Um-hm."

"Shit. And the earrings? Do they talk about the earrings?" He was looking at a facing close-up of her, from the nose down to the first swell of her breasts, which featured earrings, a sculptured piece around her throat and again the wet and open lips.

"Lovely, aren't they? Antiques. They belonged to Catherine the Great."

"Catherine the Great. A queen, huh?"

"Empress. The Empress of all the Russias."

"She give them to you?"

"Stupid! She's been dead for almost two hundred years."

"Oh, yeah?"

"Yeah." She drew out the word and made it as flat and American as she could. But she was smiling at the same time.

"They must be worth a lot, then."

"Quite a lot. Priceless."

"Nothing's priceless. Everything has a price." He was tracing again, circling Catherine's earrings with his forefinger. Jadine felt her earlobes prickle as she watched him.

"Well, half a million, certainly."

"Half a million? Shit."

"Don't you have any other word to express awe?" She tilted her head and fastened her big minky eyes on him.

He nodded. "Goddamn."

She laughed then, and for the first time there was no tension in it at all. He merely smiled and continued

117

fingering the photograph. "Are these your clothes or did they just let you use them for the pictures?"

"They're mine. Some were given to me after I was photographed. A kind of payment."

"And the jewellery? They give you that too?"

"No. That was mine from before—except the earrings. They were on loan from the Russians. But the rest is part of my own collection."

"Collection, huh?"

"Why? Are you a thief?"

"I wish I was. Be a lot easier for me if I could steal."

"If? What do you call what you were doing in this house for days? Or were you planning to give Ondine back her chocolate?"

"You call that stealing?"

"You don't."

He shook his head. "No. I call it eating. If I wanted to steal I had plenty of time and plenty of opportunities."

"But no way to escape with what you took. So maybe there was no point in stealing. *Then*."

"You think there's a point in my stealing now?"

"There might be. It depends on what you want from us."

"Us? You call yourself 'us'?"

"Of course. I live here."

"But you . . . you're not a member of the family. I mean you don't belong to anybody here, do you?"

"I belong to me. But I live here. I work for Margaret Street. She and Valerian are my . . . patrons. Do you know what that means?"

"They take care of you. Feed you and all."

"They educated me. Paid for my travel, my lodgings, my clothes, my schools. My mother died when I was twelve; my father when I was two. I'm an orphan. Sydney and Ondine are all the family I have, and Valerian did what nobody else even offered to do."

The man was silent, still staring at the pictures.

118

Jadine examined his profile and made sure the leather was knotted tightly around her wrists.

"Why don't you look at me?" she asked him.

"I can't," he said.

"Why can't you?"

"The pictures are easier. They don't move."

Jadine felt a flash of pity. "You want me to be still? Will you look at me if I'm still?"

He didn't answer.

"Look," she said. "I'm still. Very still."

He lifted his head and looked at her. Her eyes were mink-coloured just like in the pictures, and her lips were like the pictures too. Not moist, but open a little, the way they were in sleep. The way they were when he used to slip into her room and wait hours, hardly breathing himself, for the pre-dawn light to bring her face out of the shadows and show him her sleeping mouth, and he had thought hard during those times in order to manipulate her dreams, to insert his own dreams into her so she would not wake or stir or turn on her stomach but would lie still and dream steadily the dreams he wanted her to have about yellow houses with white doors which women opened and shouted Come on in, you honey you! and the fat black ladies in white dresses minding the pie table in the basement of the church and white wet sheets flapping on a line, and the sound of a six-string guitar plucked after supper while children scooped walnuts up off the ground and handed them to her. Oh, he thought hard, very hard during those times to press his dreams of icehouses into hers, and to keep her still and dreaming steadily so that when she woke finally she would long as she had longed for nothing in her life for the sound of a nickel nickelodeon, but after a while he began to smell like an animal in that room with her and he was afraid his smell would waken her before the sun did and before he could adjust his breath to hers and breathe into her open mouth his final dream of the men in magenta slacks who stood on corners under sky-blue skies and sang "If I Didn't Care" like the Ink Spots, and he fought hard against the animal smell and fought hard to regulate his breathing to hers, but the animal smell got worse and her breathing was too light and shallow for his own lungs and the sun always eschewed a lingering dawn in that part of the world and strutted into the room like a gladiator so he barely had time to breathe into her the smell of tar and its shiny consistency before he crept away hoping that she would break wind or believe she had so the animal smell would not alarm her or disturb the dream he had placed there. But now she was not sleeping; now she was awake and even though she was being still he knew that at any moment she might talk back or, worse, press her dreams of gold and cloisonné and honey-coloured silk into him and then who would mind the pie table in the basement of the church?

"How much?" he asked her. "Was it a lot?" His voice was quiet.

"What are you talking about? How much what?"

"Dick. That you had to suck, I mean to get all that gold and be in the movies. Or was it pussy? I guess for models it's more pussy than cock." He wanted to go on and ask her was it true what the black whores always said, but she was hitting him in the face and on the top of his head with a badly formed fist and calling him an ignorant motherfucker with the accent on the syllable *ig*.

Jadine jumped away from the desk and leaned forward trying to kill him with her fists while her mind raced to places in the room where there might be a poker or a vase or a sharp pair of shears. He turned his head a little but did not raise his arms to protect himself. All he had to do was what he did: stand up and let his height put his face and head out of her easy reach. She stretched none the less trying to tear the whites from his eyes. He caught both her wrists and crossed them in front of her face. She spit full in his face but the saliva fell on the *C* of his pajama top. Her gold-thread slippers were no good for kicking but she kicked anyhow. He uncrossed her wrists and swung her around, holding her from behind in the vice of his arms. His chin was in her hair.

Jadine closed her eyes and pressed her knees together. "You smell," she said. "You smell worse than anything I have ever smelled in my life."

"Shh," he whispered in her hair, "before I throw you out the window."

"Valerian will kill you, ape. Sydney will chop you, slice you . . ."

"No, they won't."

"You rape me and they'll feed you to the alligators. Count on it, nigger. You good as dead right now."

"Rape? Why you little white girls always think somebody's trying to rape you?"

"White?" She was startled out of fury. "I'm not . . . you know I'm not white!"

"No? Then why don't you settle down and stop acting like it."

"Oh, God," she moaned. "Oh, good God, I think you better throw me out of the window because as soon as you let me loose I am going to kill you. For that alone. Just for that. For pulling that black-woman-white-woman shit on me. Never mind the rest. What you said before, that was nasty and mean, but if you think you can get away with telling me what a black woman is or ought to be . . ."

"I *can* tell you." He nestled his cheek in her hair as she struggled in his arms.

"You *can't*, you ugly barefoot baboon! Just because you're black you think you can come in here and give me orders? Sydney was right. He should have shot you on the spot. But no. A white man thought you were a human being and should be treated like one. He's civilized and made the mistake of thinking you might be too. That's because he didn't smell you. But I did and I know you're

121

an animal because I smell you."

He rubbed his chin in her hair and blew at the little strand over her ears. "I smell you too," he said, and pressed his loins as far as he could into the muted print of her Madeira skirt. "I smell you too."

His voice was soft, breathy and seemed to her to come from a great height. Someplace far far up, higher than the ceiling, higher than the ake trees even and it frightened her. "Let me go," she said, surprised at the steadiness of her own voice and even more surprised that he did it.

She stood with her back to him, rubbing her wrists. "I'll have to tell Valerian."

He didn't say anything so she turned to face him and repeated, "I'll have to tell Valerian."

He nodded. "Tell him," he said. "All of it or part of it. Whatever you like."

"I will," she said, and started walking toward the door, clicking her gold-thread slippers on the tile.

"Except for one thing," he said. "Leave out one thing. Don't tell him that I smelled you."

She walked out the door and down the hall. She meant to go to the downstairs powder room and clean him off her, but she didn't want to stop walking just yet, so she descended the staircase, crossed the front hall and opened the door. The gravel of the driveway hurt her feet in the little gold-thread slippers, but she went on, rubbing her wrists, feeling frightened and then angry, then frightened then angry again. When she got to the end of the drive, she stepped with relief onto the gravel-free macadam and continued until she came to a large stone by the side of the road. She sat down on it under the eyes of an avocado tree and lifted the hem of her skirt to wipe her face. She would tell Valerian to get rid of him that very afternoon. He would go and that would be that. A minor episode in an otherwise uneventful winter in the Caribbean. Something to chat about at supper, to elaborate on with friends, and laugh and laugh and say,

"Can you believe it? He was in the house all that time! And when we found him, we invited him to dinner where he sat down and poured the coffee into his saucer and said 'Hi' to the butler. Ha ha, you should have seen Sydney's face and Margaret was out of her mind, but Valerian was superb, as you might guess, you know Valerian, right? Totally unflappable. Totally! But I was about to wet my pants, right? . . . and later . . . " But no. She would not tell that part, although it was funny, especially about how he asked her did Catherine the Great give her those earrings (he actually believed it, that they had belonged to the empress), and how he kept fingering her pictures, but she couldn't tell about the question he asked her: how much did she have to suck. She would make it some other impudence so she could get to the part about smashing his face and his trying to rape her, and maybe she could say that he was so dumb and country he thought she was white probably because she had a bath that morning and didn't have any hoops in her ears, and that he didn't want to rape her after all, but was content just to smell her. No, she'd leave out the smelling part. She would not mention that part at all.

Jadine felt the fear again and another thing that wasn't fear. Something more like shame. Because he was holding my wrists so tight and pressing himself into my behind? God, what a nasty motherfucker. Really nasty. Stink nasty. Maybe that was it. His smell. Other men had done worse to her and tried worse but she was always able to talk about it and think about it with appropriate disgust and amusement. But not this. He had jangled something in her that was so repulsive, so awful, and he had managed to make her feel that the thing that repelled her was not in him, but in her. That was why she was ashamed. He was the one who smelled. Rife, ripe. But she was the one he wanted to smell. Like an animal. Treating her like another animal and both of them must have looked just like it in that room. One dog sniffing at

123

the hindquarters of another, and the female, her back to him, not moving, but letting herself be sniffed, letting him nuzzle her asshole as the man had nuzzled hers, the bitch never minding that the male never looked in her face or ran by her side or that he had just come up out of nowhere, smelled her ass and stuck his penis in, humping and jerking and grinding away while she stood there bearing, actually *bearing* his whole weight as he pummelled around inside her not even speaking, or barking, his eyes sliced and his mouth open and dripping with saliva, and other dogs too, waiting, circling until the engaged dog was through and then they would mount her also in the street in broad daylight no less, not even under a tree or behind a bush, but right there on Morgan Street in Baltimore with cars running by and children playing and the retired postman coming out of his house in his undershirt shouting get that bitch out of here. She's in heat. Lock that bitch up. Every goddamn dog in town'll be over here and he went back inside to get a mop handle to run the males off and crack the bitch over the back and send her home, she who had done nothing but be "in heat" which she couldn't help but which was her fault just the same so it was she who was beaten and cracked over the head and spine with the mop handle and made to run away and I felt sorry for her and went looking for her to see if she was hurt and when I found her she was behind the gas station standing very quietly while another dog sniffed her ass embarrassing me in the sunlight.

All around her it was like that: a fast crack on the head if you let the hunger show so she decided then and there at the age of twelve in Baltimore never to be broken in the hands of any man. Whatever it took—knife blades or screaming teeth—Never. And yes, she would tap dance, and yes, she would skate, but she would do it with a frown, pugnacious lips and scary eyes, because Never. And anybody who wanted nice from this little coloured girl would have to get it with pliers and chloroform, because Never. When her mother died and she went to Philadelphia and then away to school, she was so quick to learn, but no touchee, teacher, and no, I do not smile, because Never. It smoothed out a little as she grew older. The pugnacious lips became a seductive pout — eyes more heated than scary. But beneath the easy manners was a claw always ready to rein in the dogs, because Never.

"Tell him," he said. "Tell him anything but don't tell him I smelled you because then he would understand that there was something in you *to* smell and that I smelled it and if Valerian understands that then he will understand everything and even if he makes me go away he will still know that there is something in you to be smelled which I have discovered and smelled myself. And no sealskin coat or million-dollar earrings can disguise it."

You son of a bitch I need this like a wart. I came here to get some rest and have some peace and find out if I really wanted to kick my legs up on a runway and let buyers with Binaca breath lick my ears or if I wanted to roam around Europe instead, following soccer games for the rest of my life and looking for another Bezzi or if I should buy an Alfa and drive through Rome making the scene where producers and agents can see me and say *Cara mia* is it really you I have just the part!

I came here to do some serious thinking and the fact is that I *can* come here. I belong here. You, motherfucker, do not and you, motherfucker, are leaving now as soon as I tell Valerian what you did to me and the harbour police will be here and return you to the sharks where you belong. Damn Valerian, what does he think he's doing? Playing white people's games? Or what the hell is the matter with him? He sits there and complains about Margaret, practically breaks down thinking about his son and talks about how he loves them both and has sacrificed everything for their happiness and then watches her go crazy, she's so scared. And instead of protecting her or at least getting upset he invites the very

125

thing that scared the shit out of her to dinner and lets him sleep down the hall from us all. Doesn't he know the difference between one Black and another or does he think we're all . . . Some mess this is.

Jadine cupped her elbows in her palms and rocked back and forth on the stone trying hard to pull herself together before she went back to talk to Valerian, to tell him he and his joke had gone too far and might backfire. She sat for a long time, longer than necessary since she had already made up her mind. She started to stand several times, but each time something held her to the rock. Something very like embarrassment. Embarrassment at the possibility of overreacting, as she told her aunt and uncle they were doing. More awful than the fear of danger was the fear of looking foolish—of being excited when others were laid back—of being somehow manipulated, surprised or shook. Sensitive people went into therapy and stayed there when they felt out of control. Was this really a funny story she could tell later or was there real danger? But there was more. She felt a curious embarrassment in the picture of herself telling on a black man to a white man and then watching those red-necked gendarmes zoom him away in a boat. But he was going to rape her; maybe Margaret too, or worse. She couldn't wait for Valerian to get bored or sober or come to his senses and she couldn't risk hanging loose in this place where there was no one really to call on, where they were virtually alone. It would have to be done now, in the light of day. There was no betrayal in that. That nigger knew better and if he didn't he was crazy and needed to be hauled away.

Besides that fear and the fear of fear, there was another authentic loathing that she felt for the man. With him she was in strange waters. She had not seen a Black like him in ten years. Not since Morgan Street. After that in the college she attended the black men were either creeps or so rare and desirable they had every girl in a 150-mile radius at their feet. She was barely noticeable in (and never selected from) that stampede. Later when she travelled her society included Blacks and whites in profusion, but the black people she knew wanted what she wanted—either steadily and carefully like Sydney and Ondine or uproariously and flashily like theatre or media types. But whatever their scam, "making it" was on their minds and they played the game with house cards, each deck issued and dealt by the house. With white people the rules were even simpler. She needed only to be stunning, and to convince them she was not as smart as they were. Say the obvious, ask stupid questions, laugh with abandon, look interested, and light up at any display of their humanity if they showed it. Most of it required only charm—occasionally panache. None of it called for this . . . this . . .

"Oh, horseshit!" she said aloud. It couldn't be worth all this rumination, she thought, and stood up. The avocado tree standing by the side of the road heard her and, having really seen a horse's shit, thought she had probably misused the word. Jadine dusted off the back of her skirt and turned toward the house. The avocado tree watched her go then folded its leaves tightly over its fruit. When Jade got near the greenhouse she thought she saw two figures behind the translucent panes. One was gesticulating wildly. Her heart pounding, she raced to the open door and peeped in. There they were. Valerian and the man, both laughing to beat the band.

# 5

"LAUGHING?" Margaret could not believe her ears.

"I'm telling you! They were in there laughing! I was looking right at them when you called out the window."

"Good God. What's gotten into him?"

"I don't know."

"Are you scared?"

"Not really. Well, sort of."

"You don't know him, do you?"

"*Know* him? How would I know him?"

"I don't know. This is making me crazy. Maybe we should do something."

"What? We're the only women. And Ondine. Should I go to the Broughtons' and . . ." Jadine stopped and sat down on Margaret's bed. She shook her head. "This is too much."

"What did he say?" asked Margaret. "When you all had dinner? Did he say what he was doing here?"

"Oh, he said he was hiding. That he'd been looking for food after he jumped ship a few days ago. That he was trying to get something out of the kitchen and heard footsteps and ran up the stairs to hide. Apparently he didn't know what room he went into, he was just waiting for a chance to get back out."

"Do you believe him?"

"I believe some of it. I mean I don't believe he came here to rape you." (Me, maybe, she thought, but not you.)

"How did he get here?"

"He says he swam."

"That's impossible."

"It's what he said."

"Well, then he can swim back. Now. Today. I'm not going to sleep with him in this house. If I had known that I would have had a heart attack. All night I waited for that bastard Valerian to come up here and tell me what the hell was going on. He never showed."

"And Sydney was patrolling the halls with a gun. I thought he would have killed him by now."

"What does he think?"

"He's angry. Ondine's scared, I think."

"I'm going to have it out with Valerian. He's doing this just to ruin Christmas for me. Michael's coming and he knows I want everything right for him, and look what he does to get me upset. Instead of throwing that . . . that . . ."

"Nigger."

"Right, nigger, instead of throwing him right out of here."

"Maybe we're making something out of nothing."

"Jade. He was in my closet. He had my box of souvenirs in his lap."

"Open?"

"No. Not open. Just sitting there holding it. He must have picked them up from the floor. Oh, God, he scared the shit out of me. He looked like a gorilla!"

Jadine's neck prickled at the description. She had volunteered nigger—but not gorilla. "We were all scared, Margaret," she said calmly. "If he'd been white we would still have been scared."

"I know, I know."

"Look. Valerian let him in. Valerian has to get him out. I'm sure he will anyway but you talk to him and I will too. It will be all right. You want to calm down. Let's do the breathing exercises. Cool out."

"I don't want to breathe, we have to *do* something. We can't leave it up to Valerian. Listen, let's leave: take the boat to town and fly to Miami. We won't come back till he's gone. Oh, but Michael!" She touched her hair. "I'll telephone him. He can meet us in Miami and if

Valerian's got his senses back . . ."

"But it's the twenty-second. There isn't time. And what about Sydney and Ondine?"

"You don't think he'd go after Ondine, do you? Well, we'll start. We'll look like we're going and tell Valerian why. We can call the police ourselves when we get to town. Is the boy here?" Margaret asked.

"Yes, but—"

"Jade. Come on, now. You've got to help. There's nobody else."

"Let's see if Valerian will send him away."

"You said they were in there laughing."

"Let's wait and see. Pack just in case. I'll get reservations."

"All right. But I'm not going to leave this room until I know something definite."

"I'll bring you something to eat."

"Yes, and please hurry. I don't want to take a Valium on an empty stomach."

They stayed in their rooms all afternoon, and the next time they saw the stranger he was so beautiful they forgot all about their plans.

WHEN JADINE had clicked out of her bedroom in her gold-thread slippers, the man sat down in her chair and lit another cigarette. He listened to the four/four time of her clicking shoes, tapping it out on the little writing table. The seat was too small for him—like a grade school chair—even though he had lost the ship-food weight and now—after two weeks of scavenging—his body was as lean as a runner's. He glanced around him and was surprised at how uncomfortable-looking her room was. Not at all the way it appeared at dawn when he crouched there watching her sleep and trying to change her dreams. Then it looked mysterious but welcoming. Now in the noon light it looked fragile—like a dollhouse for an absent doll—except for the sealskin coat sprawled on her bed which looked more alive than seals themselves. He had seen them gliding like shadows in water off the coast of Greenland, moving like supple rocks on pebbly shores, and never had they looked so alive as they did now that their insides were gone: lambs, chickens, tuna, children— he had seen them all die by the ton. There was nothing like it in the world, except the slaughter of whole families in their sleep and he had seen that, too.

He took another cigarette and walked to a table to look at the presents she'd started to wrap. Two damp spots formed on the yoke of his pajamas. Still smoking, he left off, looking at the packages and walked into her bathroom. Peeping into the shower he saw a fixture exactly like the one in the bathroom down the hall. But her shower had curtains, not sliding doors. Heavy shiny curtains with pictures of old-fashioned ladies all over. Towel material was on the other side, still damp. Water glistened on the tub and wall tile. On the corner of the tub was a bottle of Neutrogena Rainbath Gel and a natural sponge, the same colour as her skin. He picked up the sponge and squeezed it. Water gushed from the cavities. Careless, he thought. She should wring it out thoroughly, otherwise it would rot. The sponge was so large he wondered how her small hands held it. He squeezed it again, but lightly this time, loving the juice it gave him. Unbuttoning his pajama top he rubbed it on his chest and under his arms. Then he took the pajamas off altogether and stepped into the shower.

"Pull," she had said. Tepid water hit him full in the face. He pushed the knob in and the water stopped. He adjusted the shower head, pulled again and water peppered his chest. After a moment he noticed that the shower head was removable and he lifted it from its clamps to let it play all over his skin. He never let go the sponge. When he was wet all over, he let the shower head dangle while he picked up the bath gel, pumping the spout above the sponge. He lathered himself generously and rinsed. The water that ran into the drain was

131

dark—charcoal grey. As black as the sea before sunrise.

His feet were impossible. A thick crust scalloped his heels and the balls of both feet. His fingernails were long and caked with dirt. He lathered and rinsed twice before he felt as though he'd accomplished anything. The sponge felt good. He had never used one before. Always he had bathed with his own hands. Now he pumped a dollop of bath gel into his palm and soaped his beard, massaging as best he could with his nails. The beard hair tangled and crackled like lightning. He turned his soapy face up and sprayed water on it. Too hard. He stopped, wiped his eyes and fiddled with the head until he got mist instead of buckshot. He soaped his face again and misted the lather away. Some of it got into his mouth and reminded him of a flavour he could not name. He sprayed more and swallowed it. It did not taste like water; it tasted like milk. He squirted it all around in his mouth before pressing the button to shut off the water.

He got out dripping and looking around for shampoo. He was about to give up, not seeing any medicine cabinets, when he accidentally touched a mirror that gave way to reveal shelf upon shelf of bottles among which were several of shampoo boasting placenta protein among their ingredients. The man chose one and stood before the mirror looking at his hair. It spread like layer upon layer of wings from his head, more alive than the sealskin. It made him doubt that hair was in fact dead cells. Black people's hair, in any case, was definitely alive. Left alone and untended it was like foliage and from a distance it looked like nothing less than the crown of a deciduous tree. He knew perfectly well what it was that had frightened her, paralysed her for a moment. He could still see those minky eyes frozen wide in the mirror. Now he stuck his head under the shower and wet the hair till it fell like a pelt over his ears and temples. Then he soaped and rinsed, soaped and rinsed until it was as metallic and springy as new wire. After he dried it, he found a toothbrush and brushed his teeth furiously.

132

Rinsing his mouth he noticed blood. He was bleeding from the gums of his perfect teeth. He unscrewed the cap from a bottle of Listerine with instructions in French on the label and gargled. Finally he wrapped a white towel around his waist. He noticed another door in the bathroom and opened it with the easy familiarity of someone who has been there before. It led to a dressing room within an alcove in which stood a table and a mirror circled by lights. Farther along were dresses, shelves of shoe boxes, luggage, and a narrow lingerie chest. On a tiny chair lay shorts and a white tennis visor. The smell of perfume nauseated him—he had not eaten since the gobbling of cold soufflé and peaches the night before. He picked a robe, returned to the bathroom and urinated. Then he stooped to pick up the pajamas, damp and bunched on the floor, but changed his mind, left them there and walked back through the bedroom. The breeze from the open window was sweet and he went to it and stood looking out.

They are frightened, he thought. All but the old man. The old man knows that whatever I jumped ship for it wasn't because I wanted to rape a woman. Women were not on his mind and however strange it looked, he had not followed the women. He didn't even see them properly. When the boat docked, he stayed in the closet. Their voices were as light as their feet pattering on the dock and when he went, at last, to look, all he saw were two slim-backed women floating behind the beam of a flashlight toward what looked like a jeep. They got in, turned on the lights, then the engine (in that order, just like women would) and were gone. It amused him that these tiny women had handled that big boat. Which one had thrown the rope? Who jumped onto the dock and secured the line? He had not seen them clearly at all: just the hand and left side of one as she picked a bottle off the deck, and now their slim backs disappearing into the darkness toward a jeep. He had not followed them. He didn't even know where they were off to. He waited until the sea, the fish, the waves all shut up and the only sound came from the island. When he had eaten mustard, flat bread and the last of the bottled water he too disembarked but not before he looked up at the sky holy with stars and inhaled the land smell sailors alway swear they love. Behind him to his right the dim lights of Queen of France. Before him a dark shore. Ahead, under the stars and above the black of the beach he could barely see the hilly outline of the island against the sky.

He walked along the dock and then over forty feet of sand past the shadow of something that looked like a gasoline pump to the road the jeep had taken. He stayed on it and hoped he wouldn't meet anybody, for, having lost his shoes, he was not willing to cut through the bush, fat and tangled, by the side of the road. At every step clouds of mosquitoes surrounded him biting through his shirt and on the back of his neck. An old dread of mines chilled him — stopped him dead and he had to remind himself several times that this was the Caribbean — there were no beautiful pygmies in the trees or spring mines in the road.

He had not followed the women. He didn't even know what they looked like or where they were going. He just walked for an hour on the only road there was and saw nothing to make him stop; nothing that appeared to offer rest. At some point during that hour a foul smell rose about him. But the mosquitoes left him and he supposed it was the fumes coming from a marsh or swamp that he imagined he was passing through. When he emerged from it he saw above him a house with lights in its upper and lower stories. He stopped and rested one hand against a tree. How cool and civilized the house looked. After that hot solitary walk through darkness lined by trees muttering in their sleep, how cool, clean and civilized it looked. They are drinking clear water in there, he thought, with ice cubes in it. He should have stayed on the boat for the night. But he'd been shipbound so long and the land smell was so good, so good.

134

"I'd better go back," he told himself. "Back to the boat where there is a refrigerator and ice cubes and a bunk." He drew his tongue across his lips and felt the cracks. Moving his hand an inch or two up the tree in preparation to go his fingers grazed a breast, the tight-to-breaking breasts of a pubescent girl three months pregnant. He snatched his hand away and turned to look. Then he let his breath out in a snort that was more relief than laughter. An avocado was hanging from the tree right at his fingertips and near his cheek. He parted the leaves and stroked it. Saved, he thought. It smelled like an avocado, felt like an avocado. But suppose it wasn't. Suppose it was a variety of ake, the fruit that contained both a pulp that was edible and a poison that killed. No, he thought, ake trees are bigger, taller and their fruit would not grow so close to the trunk. He strained to see the colour, but could not. He decided not to chance it and looked again at the house lights—the home lights—beaming like a safe port in front of him. Just then the wind, or perhaps it was the tree herself, lifted the leaves and, precisely as he had done a moment ago, parted wide the leaves. The avocado swung forward and touched his cheek. Why not? he thought, and placed three fingers on either side of the fruit and bit it where it hung. Under the tough bitter skin was the completely tasteless, wholly satisfying meat and it made him thirstier than he was before.

He had not followed the women. He had not even seen them clearly, only their slim backs. What he went toward the house for was a drink of water. To find an outside spigot; a well, a fountain, anything to quench a thirst brought on by mosquitoes, the hot night and the meat of a teenaged avocado.

He approached the house from its northern side, away from the gravel of the driveway and over where the grass was wet and silky under his feet. Through the first window he looked into he saw not the women (for he was not following the women) but the piano. Nothing like
135

Miss Tyler's, but still a piano. It made him tired, weak and tired, as though he had swum seven seas for seven years only to arrive at the place he had started from: thirsty, barefoot and alone. No water, no shipboard bunk, no ice cubes could fight the fatigue that overwhelmed him at the sight of the piano. He backed away, away from the light and the window into the protection of the trees that were still muttering in their sleep. He would have sunk where he stood and slept under the dreaming trees and the holy sky except for the part of him that never slept and which told him now what it always told him: to hide, to look for cover. So he obeyed the self that never blinked or yawned, and moved farther from the house looking for anything: a hutch, a toolshed, a cloister of shrubbery—and found a gazebo. He crawled under the circular bench where he could sleep safely. But sleep did not join him there at once. What came, what entered the gazebo, what floated through the screen, were the boys who laughed at first when he used to go to Miss Tyler's and teased him about fucking Andrew's auntie when all he was doing was playing her piano, because there wasn't another one in town except behind the altars of the A.M.E. Zion and Good Shepherd Baptist Church. Two churches for fewer than three hundred people. Drake, Soldier and Ernie Paul laughed and pointed their fingers. How it feel? Is she good? But he went anyway because she let him and because nothing else mattered. And after a while she said she would give him lessons if he would weed for her. And a year later Drake, Soldier and Ernie Paul weren't laughing; they were sitting on Miss Tyler's porch steps listening and waiting for him to come out. Cheyenne too listened while he played and waited out front for him. But that was much later and thank God she did not come into the gazebo with Drake, Soldier and Ernie Paul. They kept him up all night, practically, so he thought they were probably alive somewhere. Each of them had been afraid for something different: his balls, eyes, spine. He had been afraid for his hands. All

136

through the war he thought of sitting in a dark and smoky joint—a small place that couldn't pack a hundred and could make it with a steady crowd of thirty—and him hidden behind the piano, surrounded and protected by the bass the drum the brass—taking eight once in a while but mostly letting his hands get to the crowd softly pleasantly. His hands would be doing something nice and human for a change. After he was busted—discharged without honour or humour—he had done it but so badly only the pity of the owner and the absence of a rival kept him there, playing at night while Cheyenne slept at home—waiting.

He had not followed the women. He came to get a drink of water, tarried to bite an avocado, stayed because of the piano, slept all through the next day because Drake, Soldier and Ernie Paul kept him awake in the night. That's how he came to sleep in the day and wander the property at night contrary to common sense and all notions of self-preservation. And he stayed tired. Even at night when he walked around looking for food and trying to think of what his next step should be. To go back to the boat and wait for one of them to sail i⸱ again. To examine the island and maybe find a rowboat—something anonymous—and make it to town at night. Get a little work, enough to fly to Miami and then work his way back home? To knock on the door, ask for help and take the risk of being turned in. Each possibility seemed fine and each seemed stupid. But he was so tired in the day and so hungry at night, nothing was clear for days on end. Then he woke up, in a manner of speaking. The first night he entered the house was by accident. The broken pantry window where he was accustomed to look for food and bottled water was boarded up. He tried the door and found it unlocked. He walked in. There in the moonlight was a basket of pineapples, one of which he rammed into his shirt mindless of its prickers. He listened a moment before opening the refrigerator door a crack. Its light cut into the kitchen like a wand. He shielded the opening as

137

best he could while he reached inside. Three chicken wings were wrapped in wax paper. He took them all and closed the door. The silence was startling compared to the noisy night outside. He pushed the swinging doors and looked into a moonlit room with a big table in the middle and a chandelier overhead. It led to a hall which he entered and which led to the front door which he opened and he stepped back outside. The chicken was incredible. He hadn't tasted flesh since the day he went crazy with homesickness and jumped into the sea. He ate the bones even, and had to restrain himself from going right back and raiding the refrigerator again. Later. Wait till tomorrow night, he told himself. And he did. Each tomorrow night he entered the house and it was a week before he ventured upstairs and then it was out of curiosity as well as a sense of familiarity. The door of the first bedroom at the head of the stairs was open, the room itself, empty. The one to the left was not empty. A woman was sleeping in it. He meant to look but not to watch and not to stay because he had not followed the women. Had not even seen them clearly. So the first time he entered her room he stayed only a few seconds, watching her sleep. Anybody could have told him it was only the beginning. Considering the piano and Cheyenne and this sleeping woman he was bound to extend his stay until he was literally spending the night with her gratified beyond belief to be sitting on the floor, his back against the wall, his shirt full of fruit (and meat if he could find any), in the company of a woman asleep. His appetite for her so gargantuan it lost its focus and spread to his eyes, the oranges in his shirt, the curtains, the moonlight. Spread to everything everywhere around her, and let her be.

He spent some part of every night with her and grew to know the house well, for he sneaked out just before dawn when the kitchen came alive. And he had to admit now, standing in the sunlight, that he had liked living in the house that way. It became his, sort of. A nighttime

138

possession complete with a beautiful sleeping woman. Little by little he learned the people. And little by little he forgot that he had not followed the women. He thought he·had. Only now did he remember that it was the avocado, the thirst, the piano. And now here he was with the immediate plans of a newborn baby.

He didn't like to think too far in advance anyway, but he supposed he'd have to think up a story to tell them about who he was and what his name was. Oh, he had been alone so long, hiding and running so long. In eight years he'd had seven documented identities and before that a few undocumented ones, so he barely remembered his real original name himself. Actually the name most truly his wasn't on any of the Social Security cards, union dues cards, discharge papers, and everybody who knew it or remembered it in connection with him could very well be dead. Son. It was the name that called forth the true him. The him that he never lied to, the one he tucked in at night and the one he did not want to die. The other selves were like the words he spoke—fabrications of the moment, misinformation required to protect Son from harm and to secure that one reality at least.


THROUGH the window on the ground below he saw the back of a man stooping at some cutting or digging chore. It was the black man he had seen off and on around the grounds. He stared at his back. Yardman, she called him. That was Yardman's back. He knew backs, studied them because backs told it all. Not eyes, not hands, not mouths either, but backs because they were simply there, all open, unprotected and unmanipulable as Yardman's was, stretched like a smokehouse cot where hobos could spend the night. A back where the pain of every canker, every pinched neck nerve, every toothache, every missed train home, empty mailbox, closed bus depot, do-not-disturb and this-seat-taken sign since God made water came to rest. He watched the angle of the old man's spine and for no reason that he could think of tears stung his eyes. It astonished him, those unshed tears, for he knew well the area into which his heart was careening—an area as familiar as the knuckle of his thumb. Not the street of yellow houses with white doors, but the wide lawn places where little boys in Easter white shorts played tennis under their very own sun. A sun whose sole purpose was to light their way, golden their hair and reflect the perfection of their Easter white shorts. He had fingered that image hundreds of times before and it had never produced tears. But now watching Yardman—he was kneeling, chopping at the trunk of a small tree—while he himself was so spanking clean, clean from the roots of his hair to the crevices between his toes, having watched his personal dirt swirl down a drain, while he himself stood wrapped waist-to-thigh in an Easter white towel—now he was as near to crying as he'd been since he'd fled from home. You would have thought something was leaving him and all he could see was its back.

Slowly Yardman stood. He turned around toward the house and for less than a pulse beat glanced at the trees that grew at the edge of the courtyard. Then he lifted his cap, scratched his head with his ring and little finger, and pulled the cap back on. "Thanks," whispered Son. "One more second of your smokehouse cot might have brought me there at last."


WHILE MARGARET had been lying in her sculptured bedroom, fighting hunger, anger and fear, Valerian was in his greenhouse staring out of the one glass window imagining what was not so: that the woman in the wash-house was bending over a scrub board rubbing pillow slips with a bar of orange Octagon soap. He knew perfectly well that a washer and dryer were installed there (he couldn't hear the hum, for the music and the drone of the air conditioner in the greenhouse obliterated

140

it, but he could see the steam puffing from the exhaust pipe) but the scrub board, the pillow slips and the orange soap were major parts of what he wished to see: the back yard of the house of his childhood in Philadelphia; the hydrangea, fat and brown in the September heat. His father, knocked down by a horse-drawn milk truck, lay in bed, the house already funereal. Valerian went out back to the shed where a washerwoman did the family's laundry. She was thin, toothless and looked like a bird. Valerian sometimes visited her, or rather hung around her shed, asking questions and chattering. She was like a pet who would listen agreeably to him and not judge or give orders. The first time he came, she had said, by way of polite conversation—the pointless conversation of an adult without stature to a child who had some—"What your daddy doin today?" And he had answered that his daddy was away on a sales trip to Atlantic City. From then on she greeted him that way. He would wander to the shed door and she would ask, "What your daddy doin today?" and he would tell her, as a preliminary to the conversation, "He's at the factory today" or "He's in New York today." It was a delightful opener to him because she and his father had never laid eyes on each other. A sort of grown-up conversation followed the question that they both took seriously. On one of the Wednesdays she came to work, his father died without regaining consciousness. Valerian was fussed over by his mother and relatives and then left alone while they busied themselves with death arrangements. He wandered out to the washhouse that afternoon and when the woman said, "Hi. What your daddy doin today?" Valerian answered, "He's dead today," as though tomorrow he would be something else. The woman looked up at him and paused for an awkward silence in which he suddenly understood the awfulness of what had happened and that his father would also be dead the next day and the day after that as well. In that instant, while the birdlike coloured woman looked at him, he knew limitlessness. The infinity of days

141

in which the answer to her question would be the same. "He's dead today." And each day it would be so. It was too big, too deep, a bottomless bucket of time into which his little boy legs were sinking and his little boy hands were floundering.

Finally she blinked and pointed to a shelf behind him. "Hand me that soap," she said. And he did. "Now unwrap it and stand right over here. Up close. Closer." He did that too and she made him rub soap on the wet pillowcase that clung to the washboard. He scrubbed his heart out, crying all the while, pillowcase after pillowcase, rubbed and rubbed until his knuckles were cherry red and his arms limp with fatigue. And when he could not do another, she patted him on the head and said she would hire him any day. Later George, the butler they had before Sydney, found out about it (he had wondered about those cherry-red knuckles) and told him to stay out of there because that woman drank like a fish and he mustn't let her use him to do her work. Valerian told him to mind his own "beeswax", but they let the woman go and Valerian never again had to say, "He's dead today," but he said it anyway to himself until his little boy legs were strong enough to tread the black water in the bucket that had no bottom. So, inconvenient as it was, he had insisted on a separate washhouse when he built L'Arbe de la Croix, less for an island touch than for the remembrance of having once done something difficult and important while the world was zooming away from him. Now another washerwoman came. It wasn't quite the same. No Octagon soap, no wavy gleaming washboard, but he liked looking at it through his greenhouse window knowing there was a woman in there doing something difficult but useful in peace. A soothing thought to concentrate on while his own house was prickly with tension and unanswered questions.

He had rattled last night to Jade. And why he had ascribed his exile to the Caribbean to the relationship between Margaret and Michael, he couldn't imagine.

142

The fact was he'd become a stranger in his own city and chose not to spend his retirement there at exactly sixty-five (or close to) in order to avoid watching it grow away from him. Sidewalks and thoroughfares were populated by people he did not know; shops were run by keepers who did not know him; familiar houses were bought by bright couples who either updated them or returned them to some era that existed only in their minds. They tore out unfashionable shrubbery for decks and patios; they closed in the wide-open porches and enlarged windows that had been tiny, private and sweet. These new people privatized their houses by turning them backward away from the street, but publicized their lives and talked about wine as though it were a theology instead of a drink. The unending problem of growing old was not how he changed, but how things did. A condition bearable only so long as there were others like him to share that knowledge. But his wife, twenty-two years younger and from another place, did not remember, and his friends were dead and dying. In his heart he was still the thirty-nine-year-old Temple alumnus working in the candy factory about to assume from his uncles control of the company, and who had married a high school beauty queen he was determined to love in order to prove he was capable of it to his first wife—that unlovable shrew who was unlovable to this day. She had died a year before his retirement in South Carolina, where she had gone to live with her sister. When he heard about it, she was already in the ground. He began to miss her at precisely that point—terribly—and when he settled in the Caribbean she must have missed him too for she started visiting him in the greenhouse with the regularity of a passionate mistress. Funny. He couldn't remember her eyes, but when she came, flitting around his chair and gliding over his seed flats, he recognized her at once. In nine years of marriage she had had two abortions and all she wanted to talk about during these visits was how relieved she was that she'd had at least that foresight. He wished she felt

143

something else. You'd think in death, in the Beyond, she would have felt something else. Or nothing at all.

He was not alarmed by her visits; he knew he conjured them up himself, just as he conjured up old friends and childhood playmates who were clearer to him now than the last thirty years were, and nicer. But he was astonished to see—unconjured—his only living son in the dining room last night. Probably the consequence of describing the sink business to Jade. Michael seemed to be smiling at him last night but not the smile of derision he usually had in the flesh; this was a smile of reconciliation. And Valerian believed that was part of the reason he invited the black man to have a seat, the forepresence of Michael in the dining room. His face smiling at him from the bowl of peaches was both the winsome two-year-old under the sink and the thirty-year-old Socialist. The face in the peaches compelled him to dismiss Margaret's screaming entrance as the tantrum of a spoiled child, the deliberate creation of a scene, which both father and son understood as feminine dementia. Michael had been on his heart if not in his mind since Margaret had announced the certainty of his visit. He could not say to her that he hoped far more than she did that Michael would come. That maybe this time there would be that feeling of rescue between them as it had been when he had taken him from underneath the sink. Thus when the black man appeared, Valerian was already in complicity with an overripe peach, and took on its implicit dare. And he invited the intruder to have a drink. The Michael of the reservation and the Michael of the sink was both surprised and pleased.

It was easy not to believe in Margaret's hysteria; he had seen examples of it many times before and thought she was up to her old combo of masochism plus narcissism that he believed common to exceptionally beautiful women. But when, in a flash too speedy for reflex, he saw his entire household standing there, and in each of their faces disgust and horror, and all together triumphant,

144

and all together anticipating his command, already acting on it in fact, just waiting for the signal from him to
call the harbour police and thereby make him acknowledge his mistake in not taking Margaret seriously, having to admit that he was not capable of judgment in a
crisis, that he was wrong, that she was right, that his
house had been violated and he neither knew it or
believed it when it was discovered and it had been Sydney
who had the foresight to have a gun and the legs to ferret
out the intruder, when he saw Margaret's triumphant
face, Jade's frightened one, and Sydney and Ondine looking at the prisoner with faces as black as his but smug,
their manner struck him as what Michael meant when he
said "bourgeois" in that tone that Valerian always
thought meant unexciting, but now he thought meant
false, but last night he thought meant Uncle Tom-ish. He
had defended his servants vigorously to Michael then,
with aphorisms about loyalty and decency and with
shouts that the press was ruining with typical carelessness
the concept of honour for a people who had a hard
enough time achieving any. What he had said to Jade, he
believed: that Michael was a purveyor of exotics, a
typical anthropologist, a cultural orphan who sought
other cultures he could love without risk or pain.
Valerian hated them, not from any hatred of the
minority or alien culture, but because of what he saw to
be the falseness and fraudulence of the anthropological
position. The Indian problem, he told Michael, was
between Indians, their conscience and their own derring-
do. And all of his loving treks from ghetto to reservation
to barrio to migrant farm were searches for people in
whose company the Michaels could enjoy the sorrow they
were embarrassed to feel for themselves. And yet, in the
space of that flash he felt not only as Michael must have
when he urged Jade to do something for her people (no
matter how silly his instruction), but something more.
Disappointment nudging contempt for the outrage Jade
and Sydney and Ondine exhibited in defending property

and personnel that did not belong to them from a black man who was one of their own. As the evening progressed, Valerian thoroughly enjoyed the disarray that his invitation had thrown them into. Margaret ran from the room — foiled. Jade was at least sophisticated about it, but Sydney and Ondine were wrecked while the intruder himself didn't even look "caught". He walked in with his hands raised and clasped behind his head and looked neither right nor left — not at Jade or Ondine or Margaret, but straight at Valerian and in his eyes was neither a question nor a plea. And no threat whatsoever. Valerian was not afraid then and he was not afraid at noon the next day, when Sydney tapped quietly on his door and brought his mail and his baked potato. Valerian could sense the small waiting in Sydney, some expectation or hope that his employer would give him a hint of what had been in his head last night. Valerian felt a twinge of compassion for him, but since he could not tell him about faces that looked up out of peaches, he said nothing at all.

Actually he had no plans. He was curious about the man, but not all that much. He assumed he was what he'd said he was: a crewman jumping ship, and his roaming about the house and grounds, hiding in Margaret's closet, was more outrageous than threatening. He had looked into the man's eyes and had no fear.

Digesting his potato and sipping wine, he was rewarded for his serenity by an expansive "Howdy" followed by the entrance of the stranger wrapped in a woman's kimono, barefoot with gleaming wrought-iron hair.

Valerian let his eyes travel cautiously down from the hair to the robe to the naked feet. The man smiled broadly. He looked down at himself, back at Valerian and said, "But I don't do no windows."

Valerian laughed, shortly.

"Good morning, Mr. Sheek," said the man.

"Street. Valerian Street," said Valerian. "What did

you say your name was?"

"Green. William Green."

"Well, good morning, Willie. Sleep well?"

"Yes, sir. Best sleep I ever had. Your name really Valerian?"

"Yes." Valerian shrugged helplessly and smiled.

"I used to eat a candy called Valerians."

"Ours," said Valerian. "Our candy company made them."

"No kiddin? You named after a candy?"

"The candy was named after me. I was named after an emperor."

"Oh," said the man looking around the greenhouse. Its sudden coldness was delicious after the heat outside. Shady and cool with plants shooting from pots and boxes everywhere. "It's sho pretty in here," he said, still smiling.

"Tell me the truth," said Valerian, "before you get confused by what you see. What were you really doing in my wife's bedroom?"

The man stopped smiling. "The truth?" He looked down at the brick walk in some embarrassment. "The truth is I made a mistake. I thought it was the other one."

"What other one?"

"The other bedroom."

"Jade's?"

"Yes, sir. I uh thought I smelled oyster stew out back yesterday. And it got dark early, the fog I mean. They done left the kitchen and I thought I'd try to get me some, but before I knew it I heard them coming back. I couldn't run out the back door so I run through another one. It was a dinin room. I ran upstairs into the first room I seen. When I got in I seen it was a bedroom but thought it belonged to the one y'all call Jade. I aimed to hide there till I could get out, but then I heard somebody comin and I ducked into the closet. I was just as scared as your wife was when she opened that door and turned that light on me."

"You've been skulking around here for days. Why didn't you ask at the kitchen for something to eat?"

"Scared. I ain't got a passport, I told you. You going to turn me over to the police?"

"Well, not in that get-up certainly."

"Yeah." He glanced at his kimono again and laughed. "They'd give me life. I don't reckon you have an old suit to lend me? Then I can go to jail in style."

"In one of my suits they'd make you governor. I'll tell Sydney to find something for you. But don't be surprised if he bites your head off."

Suddenly the man jumped and stamped his feet on the bricks.

"What's the matter?"

"Ants," he said.

"Oh dear. You've let them in, and I'm out of thalomide." Valerian stood up. "Over there, that can. Spray the doorsill. It won't do much good, but it will help for a while, and tuck that muslin in tighter."

The man did as he was told and then said, "You ought to get mirrors."

"Mirrors for what?"

"Put outside the door. They won't come near a mirror."

"Really?"

"Yeah," he said, and sprayed some of the ant killer on his legs. His kimono came undone at the belt and fell away from his body. Valerian looked at his genitals and the skinny black thighs. "You can't go round like that in front of the ladies. Leave that alone, and go tell Sydney to give you some clothes. Tell him I said so."

The man looked up letting the kimono hang to his sides. "You ain't gonna turn me in?"

"I guess not. You didn't take anything, but we'll have to figure a way to get you some papers. Go on now. Get some clothes." Valerian took the ant spray and set it down near a heavy plant of many shades of green. Its leaves spread out healthily and long stems stood straight up

148

among them. Stems with closed buds. Valerian peered into the plant and frowned.

"What's the matter with it?" asked the man. "Looks sick."

Valerian turned the pot around for a different view. "I don't know. It's been in bud like that for I don't know how long. They won't open no matter what I do."

"Shake it," said the man. "They just need jacking up." And he walked over to the cyclamen and with thumb and middle finger flicked the stems hard as though they were naughty students.

"What the hell are you doing?" Valerian reached out to grab the man's hand.

"Don't worry. They'll be in bloom tomorrow morning."

"If they are I'll buy you a brand-new suit; if they die I'll have Sydney chase you back into the sea."

"Deal!" said the man. "I know all about plants. They like women, you have to jack them up every once in a while. Make em act nice, like they're supposed to." He finished flicking the cyclamen stems and smiled first to himself and then at Valerian. "Did you ever hear the one about the three coloured whores who went to heaven?"

"No," said Valerian. "Tell me." And he did and it was a good joke. Very funny and when Jadine ran to the greenhouse certain the noise coming from it was somebody murdering somebody she heard laughter to beat the band.


SYDNEY had put some of his boss's old clothes in the guest room for him, and Valerian sent him off with Gideon to get a haircut, because Sydney refused flat out to cut it. Valerian half expected the man would get into town and not return, since he had given him enough money to buy some underwear and some shoes that fit him better than his did. While Valerian had dinner alone that night served by a silent steeping butler, and while Margaret pouted in her room and Jadine ate with Ondine in the kitchen, Mr. Green alias Son drifted off with Gideon and Thérèse in the *Prix de France*. With country people's pride in a come-from-far guest, they paraded the American Negro through the streets of town like a king. Gideon even got one of his friends to give them a free taxi ride to the outskirts of town, and then they had to walk and walk and walk up into the hills to Place de Vent before they reached the powder pink house where he lived with Thérèse and, sometimes, Alma Estée.

Thérèse was in ecstasy and kept moving her head about the better to see him out of her broken eyes. As soon as they had got ashore she let it be known to every island Black she saw that they had a guest, a visitor from the States, and that he was going to spend the night. Her pride and her message ran all over the streets and up the hillside, and at various times during the evening, heads poked in her doorway, and neighbours dropped by on some pretence or other. Thérèse sent Alma Estée flying back down the hill to the market for a packet of brown sugar, and she went into the bag that hung by her side under her dress for money for goat meat and two onions. Then she brewed black thick coffee while she listened to the men talk and waited her turn. Gideon told her stories on Isle des Chevaliers, but here at home he did not socialize with her—he kept to himself or spent his free time with old cronies. Only at work on the island of the rich Americans did he entertain her. Now she was to be privy to the talk between them, and in her house at that. She would also have a chance to ask the American Black herself whether it was really so that American women killed their babies with their fingernails. She waited until Gideon had cut his hair with clippers he'd borrowed from the man who sold rum. Waited until great clouds of glittering graphite hair fell to the floor and on the bedspread they had wrapped around the man's neck and the front of his whole body. Waited until Gideon was

150

through with his boasts about when he was in the States, boasts about the nurse he had married, the hospital he had worked in, the hatefulness of that nurse and all American women. Waited until Gideon had lied about all the money he made there and why he returned home. Waited until the stranger who ate chocolate and drank bottled water was properly shorn and his neck dusted with baking soda, and Alma Estée was back and the meat was frying on the two-burner stove. Waited till they ate it and drank coffee loaded with sugar. Waited till they opened the bottle of rum and the chocolate eater had coughed like a juvenile with his first taste of it. Thérèse served the two men but did not eat with them. Instead she stood at the portable stove burning the hair she had swept up from the floor, burning it carefully and methodically with many glances at the chocolate eater to show him she meant him no evil. When they had eaten and Thérèse had grown accustomed to the rhythm of their guest's English, she joined them at the table. Alma Estée sat on the cot by the window.

Son smoked Gideon's cigarettes and poured the rest of the rum into his coffee. He stretched his legs and permitted himself a hearthside feeling, comfortable and free of postures and phony accents. The tough goat meat, the smoked fish, the pepper-hot gravy over the rice settled in him. It had been served all on one plate and he knew what the delicacies had cost them: the sweet, thick cookies, the canned milk and especially the rum. The nakedness of his face and head made him vulnerable, but his hosts gave him adoration to cover it. Alma Estée had taken off her short print dress and returned in her best clothes—a school uniform—but Son knew right away that she had not had school tuition for a long time now. The uniform was soiled and frayed. He could feel her waves of desire washing over him and for the first time in years he felt like a well-heeled man. Thérèse urged him on into a feast of plantain and fried avocado, then leaned toward him in the lamplight, her broken eyes cheerful,

151

and asked him, "Is it true? American women reach into their wombs and kill their babies with their fingernails?"

"Close down your mouth," Gideon said to her, and then to Son, "She's gone stupid as well as blind." He explained to Son that he used to tell her what working in an American hospital was like. About free abortions and D & C's. The scraping of the womb. But that Thérèse had her own views of understanding that had nothing to do with the world's views. That however he tried to explain a blood bank to her, or an eye bank, she always twisted it. The word "bank", he thought, confused her. And it was true. Thérèse said America was where doctors took the stomachs, eyes, umbilical cords, the backs of the neck where the hair grew, blood, sperm, hearts and fingers of the poor and froze them in plastic packages to be sold later to the rich. Where children as well as grown people slept with dogs in their beds. Where women took their children behind trees in the park and sold them to strangers. Where everybody on the television set was naked and that even the priests were women. Where for a bar of gold a doctor could put you into a machine and, in a matter of minutes, would change you from a man to a woman or a woman to a man. Where it was not uncommon or strange to see people with both penises and breasts.

"Both," she said, "a man's parts and a woman's on the same person, yes?"

"Yes," said Son.

"And they grow food in pots to decorate their houses? Avocado and banana and potato and limes?"

Son was laughing. "Right," he said. "Right."

"Don't encourage her, man," said Gideon. "She's a mean one and one of the blind race. You can't tell them nothing. They love lies."

Thérèse said she was not of that race. That the blind race lost their sight around forty and she was into her fifties and her vision had not gone dark until a few years ago.

Gideon started to tease her about being "into her fifties". Sixties, more like, he said, and she had faked sight so long she didn't remember herself when she started to go blind.

Son asked who were the blind race so Gideon told him a story about a race of blind people descended from some slaves who went blind the minute they saw Dominique. A fishermen's tale, he said. The island where the rich Americans lived is named for them, he said. Their ship foundered and sank with Frenchmen, horses and slaves aboard. The blinded slaves could not see how or where to swim so they were at the mercy of the current and the tide. They floated and trod water and ended up on that island along with the horses that had swum ashore. Some of them were only partially blinded and were rescued later by the French, and returned to Queen of France and indenture. The others, totally blind, hid. The ones who came back had children who, as they got on into middle age, went blind too. What they saw, they saw with the eye of the mind, and that, of course, was not to be trusted. Thérèse, he said, was one such. He himself was not, since his mother and Thérèse had different fathers.

Son felt dizzy. The cheap rum and the story together made his head light.

"What happened to the ones who hid on the island? Were they ever caught?"

"No, man, still there," said Gideon. "They ride those horses all over the hills. They learned to ride through the rain forest avoiding all sorts of trees and things. They race each other, and for sport they sleep with the swamp women in Sein de Vieilles. Just before a storm you can hear them screwing way over here. Sounds like thunder," he said, and burst into derisive laughter.

Son laughed too, then asked, "Seriously, did anybody ever see one of them?"

"No, and they can't stand for sighted people to look at them without their permission. No telling what they'll do if they know you saw them."

153

"We thought you was one," said Thérèse.

"She thought," said Gideon. "Not me. Personally I think the blindness comes from second-degree syphilis."

Thérèse ignored this remark. "I was the one made him leave the window that way. So you could get the food," said Thérèse.

"You did that?" Son smiled at her.

Thérèse tapped her chest bone with pride.

"Miss Thérèse, love of my life, I thank you from the bottom of my heart." Son took her hand and kissed the knuckles. Thérèse shrieked and cackled with happiness.

"I said you wouldn't ask machete-hair for anything, so I left food for you in the warehouse. You never came for it."

"Machete-hair? The cook?"

"That one. That devil. The one I almost drown myself for twice a week. No matter what the weather I got to drown myself to get there."

"Don't listen to her. She knows those waters just like the fishermen. She doesn't like the Americans for mean-ness. Just because they a little snooty sometimes. I get along with them okay. When they say to let Thérèse go, I say okay. But I bring her right back and tell them it's a brand-new woman."

"They don't know?"

"Not yet. They don't pay her any attention."

Stimulated by the hand kiss, Thérèse wanted to ask more questions about the women who clawed their wombs, but Gideon grew loud and stopped her. "She was a wet-nurse," he told Son, "and made her living from white babies. Then formula came and she almost starve to death. Fishing kept her alive."

"Enfamil!" said Thérèse, banging her fist on the table. "How can you feed a baby a thing calling itself Enfamil. Sounds like murder and a bad reputation. But my breasts go on giving," she said. "I got milk to this day!"

"Go way, woman, who wants to hear about your wretched teats. Go on out of here." Gideon shooed her

154

and she left the table but not the room. When she was quiet, Gideon waved his arm about the house and told Son, "You welcome here any time you want." His arm took in the cot where Thérèse slept at night, the floor where Alma Estée sometimes slept and the tiny bedroom where he did.

Son nodded. "Thanks."

"I mean it. Any time. Not much life going on over there. Maybe you could find work here. Plenty work here and you young."

Son sipped rum-laced coffee wondering why, if there was plenty work there, Gideon wasn't doing any of it. "How long have you been working over there?"

"Three years steady now. Off and on before. They used to come seasonal."

"Did you become a citizen in the States?"

"Sure. Why you think I marry that crazy nurse woman? Got a passport and everything. But, listen, I don't let on over there that I can read. Too much work they give you. Instructions about how to install this and that. I make out that I can't read at all."

"You've been away so long, you must have lost your citizenship by now."

Gideon shrugged. "The U.S. is a bad place to die in," he said. He didn't regret it. The only thing he regretted was his unemployment insurance. A marvellous, marvellous thing, that was. You had to hand it to the U.S. They knew how to make money and they knew how to give it away. The most generous people on the globe. Now the French were as tight as a virgin, but the Americans, ahhh.

After a while they were quiet. Thérèse was breathing heavily so Son thought she was asleep. He could not see her eyes, but Alma's were bright and on him.

"You going back?" asked Gideon, "to the island?"

"I don't know."

"You want to get in there, don't you, eh? That yalla?" Gideon stroked his chin.

"Man," said Son. "Oh, man." He said it with enthusiasm but he put a period in his voice too. He didn't want her chewed over by Gideon's stone-white teeth. Didn't want her in Gideon's mind, his eye. It unnerved him to think that Gideon had looked at her at all.

The old man heard the period in his voice and turned the conversation to serious advice.

"Your first yalla?" he asked. "Look out. It's hard for them not to be white people. Hard, I'm telling you. Most never make it. Some try, but most don't make it."

"She's not a yalla," said Son. "Just a little light." He didn't want any discussion about shades of black folk.

"Don't fool yourself. You should have seen her two months ago. What you see is tanning from the sun. Yallas don't come to being black natural-like. They have to choose it and most don't choose it. Be careful of the stuff they put down."

"I'll be careful."

"Come on," said Gideon. "Let's go see some of the boys. Let me show you this place. Paradise, boy. Paradise."

They got up to leave and Alma Estée sprang into life. She stood near the door and stretched out her hand. Son stopped and smiled at her.

"You think," she said whispering, "you think you can send to America for me and buy me a wig? I have the picture of it." And she pulled from the pocket of her school blazer a folded picture which she tried her best to show him before Gideon pushed her away.

"TARZAN mind if I use his piano?"

It was incredible what Hickey Freeman and a little Paco Rabanne could do. He held the jacket by his forefinger over his shoulder. With the other hand he struck the keys. Jadine was startled. In a white shirt unbuttoned at the cuffs and throat, and with a gentle homemade haircut, he was gorgeous. He had preserved his moustache but the kinky beard was gone along with the chain-gang hair.

"If I were wearing Tarzan's suit," she said, "I'd show a little respect."

"That's why I asked. I'm showing respect."

"Then ask him yourself," she answered, and turned to leave. She had been sitting in the living room after lunch waiting for Margaret when he entered and stood at the piano. She was impressed and relieved by his looks, but his behaviour in her bedroom was uppermost in her mind.

"Wait," he said. "I want to talk to you—apologize. I'm sorry about yesterday."

"Good," she said, and kept walking.

"You can't forgive me?" he asked.

Jadine stopped and turned around. "Uh-uh."

"Why not?" He stayed near the piano but looked directly at her, the question apparently important to him.

Jadine took a few steps toward him. "I don't have to explain anything to you."

"But I said I'm sorry. You can figure out why I did it, can't you? You were so clean standing in that pretty room, and I was so dirty. I was ashamed kinda so I got mad and tried to dirty you. That's all, and I'm sorry."

"Okay. You're sorry you did it; I'm sorry you did it. Let's just drop it." She turned around once more.

"Wait."

"What for?"

"I want to play you something." He tossed his jacket on the piano lid and sat down on the stool. "Would you believe this is one of the things I used to do for a living?" He played a chord, then another and tried a whole phrase, but his fingers would not go where he directed them. Slowly he took his hands away from the keys and stared at them.

"Couldn't have been much of a living," she said.

"It wasn't. I could barely keep up with the drums when

157

I was cookin my best. Now—" He turned his hands over and looked up at her with a very small smile. "Maybe I'll just do the melody." He tapped out a line.

"I don't like what you did, hear? So don't play any songs for me."

"Hard," he said without looking up. "Hard, hard lady."

"Right."

"Okay. I quit. I just wanted to tell you I was sorry, and that you don't have to be nervous anymore."

"I'm not nervous," she answered. "I was never nervous. I was mad."

"Or mad either."

She walked toward him now and leaned an elbow on the piano, her thumbnail pressed into her bottom teeth. "I suppose Valerian invited you to stay for Christmas?"

"Did he?"

"Didn't he?"

"I don't know. I just got back this minute."

Jadine stepped away from the piano and looked out the sliding glass doors. "He was carrying on this morning about some flower you made bloom."

"Oh, that. He hasn't got enough wind in there. It needed shaking."

"You some sort of farmer?"

"No. Just a country boy."

"Well, listen, country boy, my aunt and uncle are upset. You go and apologize to them. Their name is Childs. Sydney and Ondine Childs. I had to throw the pajamas you left in my bathroom out the window so they wouldn't see them. You don't have to apologize to me; I can take care of myself. But you apologize to them."

"All right," he said, and she sure did look it—like she could take care of herself. He did not know that all the time he tinkled the keys she was holding tight to the reins of dark dogs with silver feet. For she was more frightened of his good looks than she had been by his ugliness the day before. She watched him walk away saying "See you later" and thought that two months in that place with no man at all made even a river rat look good. There was no denying the fact that looking at his face and keeping her voice stern required some concentration. Spaces, mountains, savannas—all those were in his forehead and eyes. Too many art history courses, she thought, had made her not perceptive but simpleminded. She saw planes and angles and missed character. Like the vision in yellow—she should have known that bitch would be the kind to spit at somebody, and now this man with savannas in his eyes was distracting her from the original insult. She wanted to sketch him and get it over with, but when she thought of trying to lay down that space and get the eagle beak of his nose, she got annoyed with herself. And did he have a cleft in his chin? Jadine closed her eyes to see it better, but couldn't remember. She left the room and climbed the stairs quickly. Christmas will be over soon. She had called Air France just as she promised Margaret she would, but she also made a reservation for herself for December 28, standby. Just in case. This winter retreat thing was running out anyway. She had not accomplished anything, was more at loose ends here than anywhere. At least in Paris there was work, excitement. She thought she had better go to New York, do this job, and then return to Paris and Ryk. The idea of starting a business of her own, she thought, was a fumble. Valerian would lend her the money, she knew, but maybe that was a sidestep, too. It was a silly age, twenty-five; too old for teenaged dreaming, too young for settling down. Every corner was a possibility and a dead end. Work? At what? Marriage? Work and marriage? Where? Who? What can I do with this degree? Do I really want to model? It was nothing like she thought it would be: soft and lovely smiles in soft and lovely clothes. It was knife hard and everybody frowned and screamed all the time, and if ever she wanted to paint a predatory jungle scene she would use the faces of the people who bought the clothes. She was bored and no more together than the river rat. She kept calling him that. River rat. Sydney called him swamp nigger. What the hell did he say his name was and even if she could remember it would she say it out loud without reaching for the leash?

SON WENT immediately from the living room piano to the kitchen and, finding it empty, walked down to the lower kitchen which was empty also. He retraced his steps and noticed a door on the landing to the short flight of stairs separating the kitchens. He rapped shortly and a voice said, "Yes?" He opened the door.

"Mrs. Childs?"

Ondine was soaking her feet in a basin. At first she thought it was Yardman. He alone on the island called her that. Even the Filipinos over at the nearest house called her Ondine. But the clean-shaven man in the doorway was not Yardman.

"Jadine said it was all right if I came to see you," he said.

"What you want?"

"To apologize. I didn't mean to scare everybody." Son did not allow himself a smile.

"Well, I'd hate to think what would be the case if you had meant to."

"I was a little off. From not eating. Drove me a little nuts, ma'am."

"You could have asked," Ondine said. "You could have come to the door decent-like and asked."

"Yes, ma'am, but I'm, like, an outlaw. I jumped ship, I couldn't take a chance and I stayed too hungry to think. I was in a little trouble back in the States too. I'm, you know, just out here trying to hang in."

"What kind of trouble?"

"Car trouble. Wrecked a car, and couldn't pay for it. No insurance, no money. You know."

Ondine was watching him closely. Sitting in a chintz rocker, rubbing one foot against the other in an Epsom

160

salt solution. The difference between this room and the rest of the house was marked. Here were second-hand furniture, table scarves, tiny pillows, scatter rugs and the smell of human beings. It had a tacky permanence to it, but closed. Closed to outsiders. No visitors ever came in here. There were no extra chairs; no display of teaset. Just the things they used, Sydney and Ondine, and used well. A stack of Philadelphia *Tribunes* piled neatly on the coffee table. Worn house slippers to the left of the door. Photographs of women with their legs crossed at the ankles and men standing behind wicker chairs, touching them lightly with their fingers. Groups of people standing on stairs. One blue-tinted photograph of a man with magnificent handlebar moustaches. All-dressed-up black people of some earlier day who looked like they had serious business at hand.

Ondine sensed his absorption of her apartment.

"Not as grand, I suppose, as where you sleep."

Now he did smile. "Too grand," he said. "Much too grand for me. I feel out of place there."

"I shouldn't wonder."

"I want to apologize to your husband too. Is he here?"

"He'll be back in a minute."

Son thought she sounded like the single woman who answers the door and wants the caller to think there is a huge, tough male in the next room.

"I'll be gone soon. Mr. Street said he would help me get papers. He has friends in town, he says."

She looked sceptical.

"But even if he doesn't, I've got to make tracks. I just don't want you upset or worried. I didn't come here for no harm."

"Well, I'm more inclined to believe you now that you had a bath. You was one ugly something."

"I know. Don't think I don't know it."

"You went off with Yardman yesterday?"

It bothered him that everybody called Gideon Yardman, as though he had not been mothered. "Yes, ma'am," he said. "Mr. Street told me to. I spent the night there. I started to just stay on there, since that's where I was heading for in the first place. But I didn't want to leave without making peace with you all. My own mama wouldn't forgive me for that."

"Where is your own mama?"

"Dead now. We live in Florida. Just my father, my sister and me. But I don't know if he's alive still."

Ondine saw the orphan in him and rubbed her feet together. "What line of work you in?"

"I've been at sea off and on for eight years. All over. Dry cargo mostly. Wrecks."

"Married?"

"Yes, ma'am, but she's dead, too. It was when she died that I got in that car trouble and had to leave Florida, before they threw me in jail. That's when I started fooling around on docks."

"Huh." ·

"What's the matter with your feet, Mrs. Childs?"

"Tired. Stand on any feet for thirty years and they might talk back."

"You should put banana leaves in your shoes. Better'n Dr. Scholl's."

"Is that so?"

"Yeah. Want me to get you some?"

"I'll get em if I want to. Later on."

"Well, I'll leave you alone now," and he turned to go just as Sydney walked in. His face zigzagged like lightning as soon as he saw who was standing there talking to his wife.

"What are you doing in my place?"

Ondine held up a hand. "He came to apologize, Sydney."

Son moved aside so he would not be standing between them and said, "Yes, sir . . ."

"Anything you got to say to me or my wife, you say it somewhere else. Don't come in here. You are not invited in here."

"It was Jadine," Son began. "She suggested . . ."

"Jadine can't invite you in here, only I can do that. And let me tell you something now. If this was my house, you would have a bullet in your head. Right there." And he pointed to a spot between Son's eyebrows. "You can tell it's not my house because you are still standing upright. But this here is." He pointed a finger at the floor.

"Mr. Childs, you have to understand me. I was surprised as anybody when he told me to stay—"

Sydney interrupted him again. "You have been lurking around here for days, and a suit and a haircut don't change that."

"I'm not trying to change it. I'm trying to explain it. I was in some trouble and left my ship. I couldn't just knock on the door."

"Don't hand me that mess. Save it for people who don't know better. You know what I'm talking about, you was upstairs!"

"I was wrong, okay? I took to stealing food and started wandering around in here. I got caught, okay? I'm guilty of being hungry and I'm guilty of being stupid, but nothing else. He knows that. Your boss knows that, why don't you know it?"

"Because you are not stupid and because Mr. Street don't know nothing about you, and don't care nothing about you. White folks play with Negroes. It entertained *him*, that's all, inviting you to dinner. He don't give a damn what it does to anybody else. You think he cares about his wife? That you scared his wife? If it entertained him, he'd *hand* her to you!"

"Sydney!" Ondine was frowning.

"It's true!"

"You know him all this time and you think that?" she asked him.

"You tell *me*," he answered. "You ever see him worry over her?"

Ondine did not answer.

163

"No. You don't. And he don't worry over us neither. What he wants is for people to do what he says do. Well, it may be his house, but I live here too and I don't want *you* around!" Sydney turned back to Son, pointing at him again.

"Mr. Childs," Son spoke softly, but clearly, "you don't have to be worried over me either."

"But I am. You the kind of man that does worry me. You had a job, you chucked it. You got in some trouble, you say, so you just ran off. You hide, you live in secret, underground, surface when you caught. I know you, but you don't know me. I am a Phil-a-delphia Negro mentioned in the book of the very same name. My people owned drugstores and taught school while yours were still cutting their faces open so as to be able to tell one of you from the other. And if you looking to lounge here and live off the fat of the land, and if you think I'm going to wait on you, think twice! He'll lose interest in you faster than you can blink. You already got about all you can out of this place: a suit and some new shoes. Don't get another idea in your head."

"I'm leaving, Mr. Childs. He said he'd help me get a visa—something—so I can get back home. So . . ."

"You don't need no visa to go home. You a citizen, ain't you?"

"Well, I use another name. I mean I don't want nobody checking me out."

"Take my advice. Clean your life up."

Son sighed. He had told six people in two days all about himself. Had talked more about himself than he had in years and told each of them as much of the truth as he had to. Sydney, he knew from the start, would be the hardest to convince. But he kept calling him Mr. Childs and sir and allowing in gesture as how he was a reprobate, and ended by asking them both if they knew somewhere else he could sleep while he waited for Mr. Street to get the visa and some identification for him. Outside if need be, he said. It would just be one more

164

night, he thought, and he didn't feel comfortable up there on the second floor.

The couple exchanged glances and Sydney said he'd think about it. Maybe on the patio outside the kitchen they could fix something up for him.

"I'd appreciate it," Son said. "And would you do me one more favour? Could you let me eat in the kitchen with you all?"

They nodded, and Son left quickly, pleased, rather, that Sydney thought he was interested in Valerian's generosity.

THE HOUSE locked back together that evening and busied itself for Christmas. In Ondine's kitchen Son ate so much of her food she softened considerably toward him. Sydney was less accommodating than his wife, but he could not doubt the man's hunger and his ways were quiet and respectful, almost erasing the memory of that "Hi". By the time they finished eating and reminiscing about the States, Sydney was calling him Son.

Valerian and Margaret and Jadine had eaten together in the dining room earlier, Sydney serving regally. Margaret was mollified by two telephone calls and a window view of the man who'd been in her closet which made her feel as Jadine apparently did now—that he was harmless. At any rate, he was not sleeping upstairs, she'd been informed by Jadine, nor eating with them, and maybe Michael would enjoy him if he was still on the property then. Especially if B.J. didn't show. The travel agency said the ticket had not been picked up yet. She tried to hang on to her despair about Valerian, but it was hopeless. He was tickled to death by the sight of four cyclamen blossoms, so happy he was considering putting down mirrors for the ants. He'd gone around all morning beating up other plants, especially his miniature orange trees which had come with no blossoms or fruit. He had even drafted a letter to the consulate asking whether a B-

165

class visa could be arranged for a local employee of his. And he spoke of Michael's visit as though it were a reality.

They were amiable that evening. Relaxed. Valerian cracked jokes that were not funny back in the fifties. Margaret chattered and thought up extra niceties for the holidays and ended by insisting that she would cook the Christmas dinner herself. It was to be a really old-fashioned Christmas, and that required the woman of the house to be bustling in the kitchen with an apron roasting turkey and baking apple pies. Valerian should call the consulate. They would have some apples; they always got American produce. Valerian said she'd never made a crust in her life and he wasn't looking forward to an experiment at Christmas. But Margaret wouldn't listen. She was hyper and happy: Michael was on his way. Valerian thought she had gone hog-wild this time — but her cheer cheered him and he encouraged rather than spoiled it.

The quiet amiability lasted the whole evening and there was rest in everybody's sleep that night. Except Son's. He was swinging in a hammock outside in the night wind with that woman on his mind. He had managed a face for everybody but her. The others were seduced by the Hickey Freeman suit and the haircut, but she was not and neither was he. Not seduced at all. He did not always know who he was, but he always knew what he was like.

The soldier ants were not out in the night wind, neither were the bees. But heavy clouds grouped themselves behind the hills as though for a parade. You could almost see the herd assemble but the man swinging in the hammock was not aware of them. He was dwelling on his solitude, rocking in the wind, adrift. A man without human rites: unbaptized, uncircumcised, minus puberty rites or the formal rites of manhood. Unmarried and undivorced. He had attended no funeral, married in no church, raised no child. Propertyless, homeless, sought for but not after. There were no grades given in

166

his school, so how could he know when he had passed? He used to want to go down in blue water, down, down, then to rise and burst from the waves to see before him a single hard surface, a heavy thing, but intricate. He would enclose it, conquer it, for he knew his power then. And it was perhaps because the world knew it too that it did not consider him able. The conflict between knowing his power and the world's opinion of it secluded him, made him unilateral. But he had chosen solitude and the company of other solitary people — opted for it when everybody else had long ago surrendered, because he never wanted to live in the world their way. There was something wrong with the rites. He had wanted another way. Some other way of being in the world that he felt leaving him when he stood in the white towel watching Yardman's — Gideon's — back. But something had come loose in him, like the ball that looped around the roulette wheel, carried as much by its own weight as by the force of the wheel.

In those eight homeless years he had joined that great underclass of undocumented men. And although there were more of his kind in the world than students or soldiers, unlike students or soldiers they were not counted. They were an international legion of day labourers and musclemen, gamblers, sidewalk merchants, migrants, unlicensed crewmen on ships with volatile cargo, part-time mercenaries, full-time gigolos, or kerbside musicians. What distinguished them from other men (aside from their terror of Social Security cards and *cédula de identidad*) was their refusal to equate work with life and an inability to stay anywhere for long. Some were Huck Finns; some Nigger Jims. Others were Calibans, Staggerlees and John Henrys. Anarchic, wandering, they read about their hometowns in the pages of out-of-town newspapers.

Since 1971 Son had been seeing the United States through the international edition of *Time*, by way of shortwave radio and the views of other crewmen. It seemed sticky. Loud, red and sticky. Its fields spongy, its pavements slick with the blood of all the best people. As soon as a man or woman did something generous or said something bold, pictures of their funeral lines appeared in the foreign press. It repelled him and made him suspicious of all knowledge he could not witness or feel in his bones. When he thought of America, he thought of the tongue that the Mexican drew in Uncle Sam's mouth: a map of the U.S. as an ill-shaped tongue ringed by teeth and crammed with the corpses of children. The Mexican had presented it to him with a smile the day Son bashed the snapper's head in, "*Americano*," said the Mexican, and handed him the picture that he'd drawn in prison and kept in his locker. They were close to Argentina and had been fishing off the prow that morning, pulling in snapper so rapidly they seemed to be leaping onto the deck. All but Son. The Swede and the Mexican—the two he was closest to—laughed at his spectacular bad luck. Suddenly a bite and he reeled in a huge glitter of froth and steel. The friends watched admiringly as the fish flopped into death. But when Son bent down to remove the hook, the fish executed a dazzling final arc three feet above the deck and slapped his face. The Mexican and the Swede laughed like children, and Son, holding the tail down with his knee, bashed with his fist the snapper's head. The mouth pulped and a little eye skittered across the deck. The Swede roared but the Mexican was suddenly quiet, and later handed him the drawing saying, "*Americano. Cierto Americano. Es verdad*," and maybe it was so. In any case, if he was punching dying fish in anger, if he was pricked to fury by the outrageous claim of a snapper on its own life, stunned by its refusal to co-operate with his hook, to want, goddamn it, to surrender itself for his pleasure, then perhaps he was *cierto Americano* and it was time to go home. Not to the sticky-red place, but to his home in it. That separate place that was presided over by wide black women in snowy dresses and was ever dry, green and quiet.

There weren't going to be any impalas or water buffalo; no mating dance, no trophies. There was dice instead of tusk; a job when he wanted a journey. And the lion he believed was exclusive to his past — and his alone — was frozen in stone (can you beat it?) in front of the New York Public Library in a city that had laughed at his private's uniform. Like an Indian seeing his profile diminished on a five-cent piece, he saw the things he imagined to be his, including his own reflection, mocked. Appropriated, marketed and trivialized into decor. He could not give up the last thing left to him — fraternity. On the ocean and in lock-ups he had it; in tiny bars and shape-up halls he had it, and if he was becoming *cierto Americano*, he'd better go where he could never be deprived of it — home. He wanted to go home but that woman was on his mind. The one whose dreams he had tried to change and whom he had insulted to keep her unhinging beauty from afflicting him and keeping him away from home.

She is on my mind, he thought, but I am not on hers. What must it be like to be on her mind, and he guessed the only way to know was to find out. The next morning he asked her if she would like to eat lunch with him down on the beach, and she said, "Sure, I want to sketch down there before I go, anyway." It surprised him into awkwardness and the word "go" sent a ripple through him, exacerbating the awkwardness. She was getting ready to leave? Go somewhere?

They took the Willys and she drove, saying almost nothing. She sat quietly under the wheel in an expertly crushed white cotton halter and a wide, wide skirt that rich people called "peasant" and peasants called "wedding", her skin damp and glowing against the Easter white cotton — all temptation and dare.

When they got to the dock and parked, she jumped out with her sketch pad and box of pencils. He followed her with the basket for she was leading the way — making little prints in the hard-packed sand. They walked about

169

half a mile to a bend of good clean sand and a clump of pineapple palms. They sat down and she took off her canvas shoes. It was after they ate that carelessly assembled, hurriedly packed lunch that she seemed really aware of him but only because she was opening her sketch pad and fiddling with the wooden box of pencils. She examined him then with an intent but distant eye and asked him a casual question which he answered by saying, "My original dime. That's all. My original dime." The sun was hiding from them and the mosquitoes were held off by a burning can of commercial repellent. The olives, French bread, uncuttable cheese, ham slices, jar of black mushy cherries and wine left them both as hungry as they were when they started.

It was a deliberately unappetizing lunch which she had literally dumped into a beautiful brown and purple Haitian basket as though to disabuse him of any idea that this was a real picnic or that it was important to her. But they ate it all up and wished for more. It was probably that yearning for more that made Jadine ask him, "What do you want out of life?" A tiresome question of monumental ordinariness, the kind artists ask models while they measure the distance between forehead and chin but one which he had apparently given some thought to. "My original dime," he said. "The one San Francisco gave me for cleaning a tub of sheephead." He was half sitting, half lying, propped upon his elbow facing her with the sky-blue sky of the sky behind him. "Nothing I ever earned since was like that dime," he said. "That was the best money in the world and the only real money I ever had. Even better than the seven hundred and fifty dollars I won one time at craps. Now that felt good, you know what I mean, but not like that original dime did. Want to know what I spent it on? Five cigarettes and a Dr. Pepper."

"Five cigarettes?"

"Yeah. They used to sell them loose in the country. That was my first personal, store-bought purchase. You

170

believe that? Wish you could have seen how it looked in the palm of my hand. Shining there."

"The Dr. Pepper?"

"The dime, girl. The dime. You know I picked up money before. In the street and a quarter once on the riverbank. That was something too, you know. Really great. But nothing, nothing was ever like that sheephead dime. That original dime from Frisco." He paused for a comment from her, but she made none. She just kept busy behind the screen, the wall of her sketch pad. "Just before I left home, I heard he got blown up in a gas explosion. Old Frisco." He murmured the name. "Son of a bitch. I heard about it on my way out of town, and I couldn't wait for the funeral. He worked in the gas field and got blown to bits. I left town crying like a baby. He was a nothing kind of dude, mind you. Treated his wife like a dog and ran other women all over town. But I still cried when he got blown up and I was a full-grown man. It must have been that dime, I mean, no money ever meant much to me after that. I couldn't work just for that—just for money. I like to have it, sure, it feels fine for a while, but there's no magic in it. No sheephead. No Frisco. And nothing to buy worth anything, anyway. I mean nothing like five Chesterfield cigarettes and a Dr. Pepper. Talk about good!" He threw his head back and directed his laughter into the sky. He was beautiful, like that; laughing like that: teeth lips moustache perfect and perfectly disarming. Jadine paused. She could not draw his laughing heaven-raised face. "Well, anyway, I guess that's what I want, all I want, in the money line. Something nice and simple and personal, you know? My original original dime."

Jadine's eyes followed the movements of her charcoal. "Lazy. Really lazy. I never thought I'd hear a black man admit it." She rubbed the line with her thumb and frowned.

"Uh-uh. I'm not admitting any such thing." Son's voice cracked with indignation.

171

"Ah got duh sun in duh mawnin and duh moon at night." Jadine waggled her charcoal stick and rocked her head like "truckin on down". "Oooooo, Ah got plenty of nuffin and nuffin's plenty fo meeeeeee."

Son laughed in spite of himself. "That's not lazy."

"What is it then?"

"It's not being able to get excited about money."

"*Get* able. *Get* excited."

"What for?"

"For you, for yourself, your future. Money isn't what the scramble's all about. It's what money does, can do."

"What can it do?"

"Please. Don't give me that transcendental, Thoreau crap. Money is—"

"Who's that?"

"Who's who?"

"Thoreau."

"Jesus."

"Don't look disgusted. I'm illiterate."

"You're not illiterate. You're stupid."

"So tell me; educate me. Who is he?"

"Another time, okay? Just hold your head still and stop making excuses about not having anything. Not even your original dime. It's not romantic. And it's not being free. It's dumb. You think you're above it, above money, the rat race and all that. But you're not above it, you're just without it. It's a prison, poverty is. Look at what its absence made you do: run, hide, steal, lie."

"Money didn't have anything to do with that."

"Sure it did. If you had some you could have paid a lawyer, a good lawyer, and he would have gotten you off. You think like a kid."

"Maybe I didn't want to get off."

"Then what did you run away for? You told Ondine you got into some trouble with the law and jumped bail."

"I didn't want to go to prison."

"But—"

"That's not the same thing. I didn't want their

172

punishment. I wanted my own."

"Well, you got it."

"Yeah."

"And you might end up with theirs *and* yours."

"No way."

"You're like a baby. A big country baby. Anybody ever tell you that?"

"No. Nobody ever told me that."

"Well, you are. Like you were just born. Where are your family?"

"Home, I guess."

"You don't know?"

"I haven't been back in a long time."

"Where in Florida are you from?"

"Eloe."

"Eloe? What on earth is that? A town?"

"A town, yeah."

"God. I know it already: gas stations, dust, heat, dogs, shacks, general store with ice coolers full of Dr. Pepper."

"No shacks in Eloe."

"Tents, then. Trailer camps."

"Houses. There are ninety houses in Eloe. All black."

"Black houses?"

"Black people. No whites. No white people live in Eloe."

"You're kidding me."

"I'm not."

"Black mayor?"

"No mayor at all, black or white."

"Who runs it?"

"Runs itself."

"Come on. Who pumps the water, hooks up the telephones?"

"Oh, well, white folks do that."

"I'll bet they do."

"But they live in Poncie, Ferris, Sutterfield—off a ways."

"I see. What work do these ninety black people do?"

"Three hundred and eighty-five. Ninety houses, three hundred and eighty-five people."

"Okay. What work do they do?"

"They fish a little."

"Sheephead. Right. Oooooo, Ah got plenty of nuffin
. . ."

"Don't laugh. They work in the gas field too, in Poncie and Sutterfield. And they farm a little."

"God. Eloe."

"Where's your home?"

"Baltimore. Philadelphia. Paris."

"City girl."

"Believe it."

"Oh, I believe it."

"Were you ever in Philly?" She put the pad and pencil down and rubbed her fingers together.

"Never."

"Just as well." Jadine dug her fingers in the sand then brushed them.

"Not so hot?"

"Well, better than Eloe."

"Nothing's better than Eloe."

"Oh, sure. When's the last time you were there?"

"Long time. Eight years."

"Eight, huh. You haven't seen your family in eight years. Even your mother must have forgotten your name by now."

"She's *been* dead. My father raised us."

"He's know your name?"

"He knows it. Sure, he knows it."

"I don't. What is it?"

"I told you already—everybody calls me Son."

"I want to know what's on your birth certificate."

"No birth certificates in Eloe."

"What about your Social Security card. That says Son?"

"No. That says William Green."

"At last."

"One of them anyway. I got another that says Herbert
174

Robinson. And one says Louis Stover. I got a driver's licence that says—"

"Okay. Okay. But I can't call you Son. 'Hi, Son. Come here, Son.' I sound like a grandmother. Give me something else."

"You pick."

"Okay. I will. Let's see. I need something that fits. I know. I'll ask you a question—a question I want to ask anyway and the best name will fit right in. Here I go. 'Why did you have to leave Eloe on the run, leave so fast you couldn't go to Frisco's funeral, uh, uh, Phil?' That's good. That's Anglicized French for son."

"Not Phil. Anything but Phil."

"Well, what then?"

"What about Sugar? 'Why did you have to leave Eloe on the run, Sugar?' "

"All right. 'What did you do to have to leave Eloe on the run, Sugar? So fast, Sugar, you couldn't go to the funeral of the man who gave you your original dime?' "

"I killed somebody."

Actually he didn't look like a baby or even a big old country boy dressed up in a white man's suit. His hair was cut and his nails filed, but he had lived in the house and hid in the closet and pressed his face into her hair and his hips into the back of her skirt and underneath the light cologne was a man with hair like snakes. It was hot. Hazy and hot. A bad day for a picnic.

"Should I be scared?" asked Jadine.

"Not if you have to ask."

"I'm serious."

"So am I."

"Who was he? The man you killed?"

He stood up, untangling himself gracefully but swiftly. They always assume that, he thought. That it was a man. "Let's change the subject," he said. His voice was soft, a little sad, it seemed to her, and he gazed out into the water as he spoke. Fake, she thought. He's faking remorse and he thinks I am impressed by it.

175

"I hate killers," she said. "All killers. Babies. They don't understand anything but they want everybody to understand them. Lotta nerve, don't you think?"

"Killing doesn't take nerve. It takes no nerve, no nerves at all."

"I don't feel sorry for you, you know. I think you ought to be in jail. So you can stop looking pitifully into the sea and thinking how terrible life's been to you."

He glanced at her, briefly, as though she were a distraction from the major work of looking at the sea. "Sorry," he murmured. "I didn't mean to. I wasn't thinking about me. I was thinking about the person I killed. And that *is* pitiful."

"Then why'd you do it?"

"There is no *why*. The reason doesn't hold. I mean it wasn't a good reason; it was a mistake."

"Sure. You didn't mean to, right?"

"Oh, I meant to, but I didn't mean to. I meant the killing but I didn't mean the death. I went too far."

"That's not so smart. Death frequently follows killing. Definitely unhip."

"Yeah."

"Temper, temper, temper," she sang.

He looked down at her again wishing it had been temper. Something simple like that or something forgivable like that. But he knew better and for eight years wherever he looked—in the molten sea, in shape-up halls, in canneries and on flophouse cots he saw that mouth dying before the eyes did when it should have been the other way around and while he could not regret the fact that she was dead, he was ashamed of having been unable to look her in the eyes as she died. She deserved that. Everybody deserves that. That somebody look at them, with them, as they face death—especially the killer. But he had not had the courage or the sympathy and it shamed him.

He looked at Jadine. Now it was her turn to gaze into the sea. "Who'd you kill?" she said.

176

"A woman."

"I should have known. That's all you could think of to do with your life? Kill a woman? Was she black?"

"Yes."

"Of course. Of course she was. What did she do? Cheat on you?" She said it ugly. Cheat. Like "Take away your candy?"

He nodded.

"My my my. And you, I suppose, were the faithful boyfriend who never looked at another girl."

"Never. After I got out of the army, never. I played a little—piano, I mean, at night. Nothing much but okay until I could get on at the gas field. I had this gig in Sutterfield. Off and on for about three months. Then one morning I came home and . . ."

"No," sang Jadine, "don't tell me. You found her with somebody else and shot her."

"No. I mean yes, I found her—that way, but I didn't go in. I left. I got in the car. I was just gonna drive off, you know, and I backed the car out in the road, but I couldn't leave, couldn't leave them there so I turned the car around and drove it through the house."

"You ran over them?" Jadine's upper lip was lifted in disgust.

"No, I just busted up the place. But the car exploded and the bed caught on fire. It was a little place we had, just a little box, and I drove through the bedroom wall. I pulled her out of the fire but she never made it. They booked me after that."

"What about the man?"

"It wasn't a man; it was a boy. Thirteen, I heard. Singed him bald, but nothing more. They had me up for Murder Two."

He was still standing and now he looked down at her and noticed that she had folded her legs under her white cotton skirt. She is scared, he thought. In the company of a killer on an island, far away from the house, she is too scared. Suddenly he liked it. Liked her fear. Basked in it like a cat in steam-pipe heat and it made him feel protective and violent at the same time. She was looking into the horizon and kept her legs hidden under her skirt. Does she think I'll cut them off, or is there something under there she is afraid I will take out and kill? The idea both alarmed and pleased him and he dropped down on one knee and said very softly, "I won't kill you. I love you."

Quick like a doe she turned her head. Her eyes stretched wide with the problem of deciding what to be outraged by: the promise or the confession.

"You better not do either one," she said. "I don't want you loving me, and don't threaten me either. Don't ever threaten me again."

"I wasn't threatening you. I said I won't—wouldn't . . ."

"Why would you even say that? What kind of man are you? People don't say things like that. Nobody says that. Where do you think we are, in some jungle? Why would you say you're not going to kill me?"

"Shhhh."

"I won't shhhhh. You can't just sit here on the sand and say something like that. You trying to scare me?"

She's bolting, he thought. I have disgusted her again. And it was true that she was looking at him as though he were a dwarf with a head lopsided and swollen with water. She's right, he thought. I am crazy. Whenever I try to tell the truth it comes out wrong, or dumb or scary and there was no way to hide his helpless naked face. "No, wait a minute. I . . . I wasn't trying to scare you. I was trying to comfort you."

"Comfort me?"

"Yeah. You tucked your legs in like you were scared of me. You don't have to tuck your legs. I mean . . ."

"What are you talking about?"

"You changed the way you were sitting."

"You thought I sat this way because I was afraid?"

"Okay. I was wrong. But I didn't say it to say, 'maybe I

could but I won't.' I said it so you wouldn't think that I would or . . . I'm not a killer. Just that one time, accidentally when I was fucked-up. I just didn't want to see your legs folded up like that. I wanted you relaxed, like you were before. You were sassy before and rubbing your ankles with your hands."

Jadine looked at him trying to figure out whether he was the man who understood potted plants or the man who drove through houses.

"Honest," he said. "I didn't mean to scare you. Honest. I can live without a lot of things, but I didn't want you to take your feet away from me just because I didn't go to jail like I was supposed to. I don't have a real life like most people, I've missed a lot. Don't take your feet away from me too."

"You are not well," she said.

"Yes, I am."

"No, you're not."

"'Cause I like your feet?"

"You can't have my feet."

"I didn't ask to have them. I just asked to see them."

"I can't carry on a conversation like this. This is not a conversation that anybody has."

"Let me see them."

"Stop it."

"Please?"

"Look, Harvey, Henry, Son, Billy Green, maybe we'd just better pack it up and call it a day."

He sat down on the hard-packed sand in front and a little to the right of her and looked at her steadily. He quit. Quit trying to make an impression.

"I'm not crazy, Jadine. Raw, maybe, but not nuts."

"I'm not convinced."

"A man admires your feet and you want to lock him up?"

"You need professional care."

"Put one foot out. Just one. I prefer two, but if you want, you can show me just one, although two is better.

179

Two feet is a pair. They go together, so to speak. One is just — " he shrugged slightly — "one. Alone. Two is better. I want to see them both."

"I don't know about you."

"Take your time, I'll see them anyway when you stand up, but I'd like it better if you showed them to me yourself."

Jadine's feet were warm under her skirt, each one hidden near a thigh.

"I won't touch," he said, "I promise."

She looked past his face and felt wavy. The sun was still hiding in some fuzz in the sky. Gulls with dark hoods rested beyond the surf. They looked like ducks from where she sat. All the gulls she remembered screeched and dived. She'd never seen them quiet before, sitting still in water as though they were listening.

"Come on," he said. "Show me. Please?"

Slowly she started to unfold one leg, carefully, cautiously as though she was about to do something wild.

"Just a little bit more," he urged her. "Come on."

Quickly then, she straightened both legs and stuck them into the air. He looked at them and did not touch. The waviness travelled from her head to her toes pointing up from the sand. He looked at them, and whispered, "Look at that." He leaned down for a better look. "I said I wouldn't touch and I won't. If you object, that is. But I have to tell you how much I want to. Right there." He pointed to the arch. "If you don't want me to, I won't, though, like I said."

He wants to kiss my feet, she thought. He wants to put his mouth on my foot. If he does I'll kick his teeth out. But she didn't move.

"Can I? Can I touch it right there?"

She didn't answer and he didn't say anything more for several pulse beats. Then he did it. Put his forefinger on her sole and held it and held it and held it there.

"Please stop," she said, and he did, but his forefinger stayed where his finger had been in the valley of her

180

naked foot. Even after she laced up the canvas shoes.

"I've got to get back," she said.

He stood quickly so there would be no mistake, and walked ahead of her, leading the way. He drove this time, while Jadine sat quietly going over in her mind the reasons why she was not going to let him make love to her; the reasons it would be impossible to even consider going to bed with him, fingerprint or no fingerprint, laughing into the sky or not. The most important reason was that he expected her to. As hard as she tried, he did not seem convinced that she was unattracted to him. Second, it would trouble Nanadine and Sydney. Third, he wasn't manageable. Afterward. What would he be like afterward? Stake a claim? Try to trade his room for hers? Drive the jeep into the house if she said no? He was whistling now, driving along whistling through closed teeth like he already had it made. Still, she had been there two whole months with nobody. Jadine sighed and set her jaw. Fifteen more minutes and they would be back at the house where she could put the whole business out of her mind, but the jeep slowed down and she couldn't believe it. He must have done something; did he think she would sit still for something as dumb as that? But it was true; he pumped and pumped the accelerator. Nothing happened. The gauge was securely empty. Jadine looked around: jungle muck on both sides; trees close to the road on the left. An uphill walk to the house was longer than a trek back to the pier. Jadine reached into the glove compartment and took out a key. "It unlocks the pump back at the pier," she said.

"Got something to put it in?" he asked.

"In back under the seat, there's a five-litre bottle. Use that."

"I hope you're right. That there's gas in that pump."

"I hope I am too. If not, get some from the boat. I know there's some there."

He nodded. "Twenty minutes about, to get there and another twenty to get back."

181

She agreed and settled back in the seat crossing her legs.

"You're not coming with me?"

"No," she said, "I'll wait here."

"Alone?"

"Go on, will you? I'll be all right. There's nobody on the island I don't know. If somebody drives down, I'll have them pick you up and bring you back."

He left then and Jadine rummaged around in the basket to see if there was anything left of the awful lunch. Nothing. Nothing at all. She sat for a while under the hateful sun that had come out in full dress when they least needed her. Thank God there were no mosquitoes here, just a funny jungle-rot smell. She waited until the sun burnt a hole in her head. She didn't have a watch on but thought twenty minutes must have passed by. Only twenty more. Then she decided to seek shelter from the sun under the trees to the left of the road, in spite of that unpleasant odour. This was the ugly part of Isle des Chevaliers—the part she averted her eyes from whenever she drove past. Its solitude was heavy and there was something sly about its silence. Her jangled nerves she attributed however to the conversation with Son, the print of his forefinger on her foot, and the silly thoughts she'd had afterward. A fair amount of composure returned quickly once they had gotten back to the jeep where all was familiar, but a tremor had not yet died in her stomach and required the resolutions of a new nun to subdue. It was nothing like the fear-slashed anger she had felt the morning he had held her from behind and pressed into her. Nothing like that. But he was bathed now, clipped and beautiful with spacious tender eyes and a woodsy voice. His smile was always a surprise like a sudden rustle of wind across the savanna of his face. Playful sometimes, sometimes not. Sometimes it made her grab the reins. She took her pad and a stick of charcoal and walked toward the trees, wishing once more that she had had genuine talent in her fingers. She loved to paint and

draw so it was unfair not to be good at it. Still she was
lucky to know it, to know the difference between the fine
and the mediocre, so she'd put that instinct to work and
studied art history—there she was never wrong.

The trees were not as close together as she'd thought.
Tall bushes had made them seem so. She approached the
shade and peeped in between the trees. She almost
laughed at what she saw. Young trees ringed and soared
above a wavy mossy floor. There was hardly any colour;
just greens and browns because there was hardly any light
and what light there was—a sentimental shaft of sunlight
to the left—bunched the brown into deeper shadow. In
the centre under a roof of greens was a lawn of the same
dark green the Dutchmen loved to use. The circle of trees
looked like a standing rib of pork. Jadine tucked her pad
under her arm and clenched the charcoal stick. It was
amazing; the place looked like something by Bruce
White or Fazetta—an elegant comic book illustration.
She stepped through some bushes that looked like rhodo-
dendron and onto the mossy floor. The lawn, the centre
of the place began only a couple of yards ahead. She
walked toward it and sank up to her knees. She dropped
the pad and charcoal and grabbed the waist of a tree
which shivered in her arms and swayed as though it
wished to dance with her. She struggled to lift her feet
and sank an inch or two farther down into the moss-
covered jelly. The pad with Son's face badly sketched
looked up at her and the women hanging in the trees
looked down at her. There is an easy way to get out of
this, she thought, and every Girl Scout knows what it is
but I don't. Movement was not possible. At least not sudden movement. Perhaps she was supposed to lie horizon-
tally. She tightened her arms around the tree and it
swayed as though it wished to dance with her. Count, she
thought. I will count to fifty and then pull, then count
again and pull again. She had only to hang on until Son
returned and shout—fifteen minutes, not more. And she
would spend it edging up the tree that wanted to dance.

No point in looking down at the slime, it would make her think of worms or snakes or crocodiles. Count. Just count. Don't sweat or you'll lose your partner, the tree. Cleave together like lovers. Press together like man and wife. Cling to your partner, hang on to him and never let him go. Creep up on him a millimetre at a time, slower than the slime and cover him like the moss. Caress his bark and finger his ridges. Sway when he sways and shiver with him too. Whisper your numbers from one to fifty into the parts that have been lifted away and left tender skin behind. Love him and trust him with your life because you are up to your kneecaps in rot.

The young tree sighed and swayed. The women looked down from the rafters of the trees and stopped murmuring. They were delighted when first they saw her, thinking a runaway child had been restored to them. But upon looking closer they saw differently. This girl was fighting to get away from them. The women hanging from the trees were quiet now, but arrogant—mindful as they were of their value, their exceptional femaleness; knowing as they did that the first world of the world had been built with their sacred properties; that they alone could hold together the stones of pyramids and the rushes of Moses's crib; knowing their steady consistency, their pace of glaciers, their permanent embrace, they wondered at the girl's desperate struggle down below to be free, to be something other than they were.

Jadine counted to fifty eight times, pulled eight times, then her right knee grazed something hard and she managed to lift her leg and bend it enough to kneel on the hard thing that seemed to be growing out of her partner the tree. It held and she got her other leg up, but the slimy soles of her shoes could find no other footing on the bark. She had to shimmy, using the insides of her knees for leverage. When she was up far enough, she twisted with a giant effort around to the road side of the tree—the part of the trunk that leaned out of solid ground. She slid down on her stomach and when Son

184

came sweating up the hill she was crying a little and cleaning her feet and legs with leaves. The white skirt showed a deep dark and sticky hem and hung over the door of the jeep. She was in halter and panties.

"What the hell happened to you?" He ran to her and put the bottle on the seat. She didn't look up, just wiped her eyes and said, "I took a walk over there and fell in."

"Over where?"

"There. Behind those trees."

"Fell in what? That looks like oil."

"I don't know. Mud I guess, but it felt like jelly while I was in it. But it doesn't come off like jelly. It's drying and sticking."

Son kneeled down and stroked her skin. The black stuff was shiny in places and where it was dry it was like mucilage. Nothing much was happening with her leaves. He shook some drops of the gasoline onto a clean place in her skirt and handed it to her. She took it and continued to clean herself in silence. He poured the gas into the tank and they waited for a few minutes for it to get into the line, and only when the motor finally caught did Jadine hazard a glance back at the place where she'd gone in. She could not identify the tree that had danced with her.

Son drove slowly up the hill to conserve the gas. He glanced at her from time to time, but could see she was not about to be consoled easily. He decided to tease her gently.

"That's where the swamp women live," he said. "You see any?"

She didn't answer.

"They mate with the horsemen up in the hills."

"Oh, shut up. Just shut up."

"I just thought you might have seen one."

"Look," she said. "I might have died. That mess was up to my knees. Don't try to cheer me up; it's not funny! Just drive, will you, and get me home so I can get this shit off me!"

"Okay, okay," he said, and smiled because he liked her sitting next to him in her underwear. Liked it so much it was hard to look serious when they drove up to the house and Margaret, sitting on the living room patio, came round to see who it was.

"An accident," said Jadine before Margaret could shift her stare from the underwear to Son. "I took a walk and fell in the swamp."

"My God," said Margaret. "You poor thing. You must have been scared out of your mind. Where was *he*?" She jutted her chin at Son's back as he drove the jeep to the kitchen side of the house.

"At the dock getting gas. We ran out." Jadine was hurrying into the house. Her legs were burning from the gasoline. "I have to get in the tub."

Margaret followed her. "Soap first. Then alcohol. Jesus, what *is* that stuff? It looks like pitch."

In the bedroom Jadine took off halter and panties and tiptoed into the bathroom.

"He's bad luck, Jade. He really is. Any time anybody gets near him something happens."

"Except Valerian," said Jadine. "He's good luck for Valerian."

"That figures," said Margaret. "Turpentine's better, honey. You have any?"

"No. But it's coming off all right with the soap. I won't be able to wax my legs for a week now. God, it burns."

"He's bad luck, Jade. Really. I just know it."

"Don't worry, Margaret, Michael will show. You'll see."

"I hope so. It's going to be so nice. I'm cooking everything myself, did I tell you?"

"You told me."

"He hasn't been here since he was fourteen. I could like this place if he'd stay. I could like everything about it. He won't spoil it, will he?"

"Who?"

"Him. Willie."

"No. Why would he? He's leaving as soon as Valerian

hears from the consulate. What are you afraid of?"

"Well, Jade, he was in my closet."

"He isn't there now. What's the matter, Margaret? You think he wants your bod?"

"I don't know what I think. I'm all nerves. This place makes me crazy and so does he. Look at you, you go off with him, step out of a car and fall in a mudhole."

"Margaret, I fell in, not you. And it was my fault, not his." Jadine surprised herself; she was defending him against her. She thought it was gone—that mistrust, that stupid game she and Margaret used to play. Any minute now, Margaret would be reaching out her hand and saying "What'd ja do to yer hay-er? What'd ja do to yer hay-er?" like white girls all over the world, or telling her about Dorcus, the one black girl she ever looked in the face. But there was a little bit more in her annoyance now. Maybe she should just say it. He doesn't want you, Margaret. He wants me. He's crazy and beautiful and black and poor and beautiful and he killed a woman but he doesn't want you. He wants me and I have the fingerprint to prove it. But she didn't say any of that; she said she wanted to sleep now. Margaret left but her alarm stayed behind. Jadine got into bed and discovered she was jealous of Margaret of all people. Just because he was in her closet, she thought his sole purpose in life was to seduce her. Naturally her. A white woman no matter how old, how flabby, how totally sexless, believed it and she could have shot him for choosing Margaret's closet and giving her reason to believe it was true.

God. Jadine turned over carefully to protect her raw legs. I am competing with her for rape! She thinks this place is driving her crazy; it's making a moron out of me. Certified.

It took some time before she could fall asleep. The soap had done its job. The little feet he wanted so badly to see were clean again, peachy soft again as though they had never been touched and never themselves had touched the ground.

# 6

CHRISTMAS EVE'S EVE and even the goddamn hydrangea had bloomed!

The whole island was vomiting up colour like a drunk and here in the corner, in plastic filtered light, was one spot of sane, refined mauve. Valerian sprayed it with water and aerated the soil around the stem. "Merry Christmas," he said, and toasted the shy violet buds with his wineglass. Maybe Margaret was right: this would be a warm and memorable Christmas. The black man had brought luck to the greenhouse, maybe he'd bring luck to the whole celebration. Michelin would be there; Michael, Michael's friend; that was just enough. And Margaret was sober and busy and cheerfully preoccupied with something outside herself for a change.

Valerian walked away from the hydrangea and looked out the window toward the washhouse. The washerwoman was there, bless her heart, with the yard boy. He couldn't hear them, but they looked as though they were laughing. A nip, he thought. They're already celebrating and have taken a Christmas nip. He liked that. That was the way a holiday ought to begin and since everything was in its place as it should be—Michael coming, Margaret cooking, hydrangea in bloom—he decided to go out there with the servants and wish them a Merry Christmas too. All that was needed was that holiday bread Grandmother Stadt used to make. Ollieballen.

"Ollieballen?"

"Yes. My grandmother used to make it at New Year."

"The Candy Queen?" asked Margaret. "I never heard of it."

"It's not hard," said Valerian. "It's Dutch."

188

"What's it taste like?"

"Sweet. Like a doughnut."

"We can't serve doughnuts at dinner, Valerian."

"It's not for dinner, it's for afterward. With brandy and coffee."

"This is going to be hard enough without ollieballen."

"Then let's forget the whole thing."

"No. I said I'd do it and I'm going to. Michael will get a kick out of it."

"So will Ondine."

"Maybe. I've never seen her eat anything."

"Nobody ever sees a cook eat anything. Let's go over the menu again. Turkey, mashed potatoes and gravy, green beans—what else?"

"The lemon whip and this ollieballen thing."

"You can use the apples in it. It's easier than pie and it's traditional in our family—or it was. What about something to start? Soup or fish?"

"Valerian."

"Something simple. You can handle it."

"You'll help?"

"I'll be entertaining the guests. I can't do both. And that's not what you said. You said you'd do the whole dinner for everybody."

"So how many is that? Six?"

"Seven. It'll be fun. You'll enjoy it. Don't forget it was your suggestion."

"How do you get seven?"

"B.J. has a girlfriend, doesn't he? So there's me, you and Michael, B.J. and his guest, Jade and Michelin. Seven. The turkey is here—beans, potatoes—nothing to it. You can make the ollieballen ahead of time. Christmas Eve."

"You have the recipe?"

"I have it."

"What do I need?"

"Nothing special: yeast, eggs, milk, sugar, lemon, flour, raisins, apples and butter."

189

"What about the lemon whip?"

"Just lemon-flavoured gelatin beaten to froth and whipped cream on top. Very simple. We can have smoked fish, perhaps, to start. All that needs is parsley. The lemon whip is a light sweet for after a heavy dinner. Then coffee and brandy with the ollieballen." Valerian spread his fingers to show how easy it was. He wanted her occupied the next few days—not sitting around in anxiety about when (or if) Michael would get there.

"Doughnuts and brandy," she said, and shook her head.

"Margaret."

"No: no! It's fine. Just sounded funny that's all."

"They don't have a hole in the middle!"

"Too bad," she said. "It might inspire you."

"I'm sorry about last night. That wasn't why I came. I've been hateful and I know it. I shouldn't have behaved that way when you found Willie up there in your closet."

"We've been through all that. Forget it."

"It worked out okay, didn't it?"

"I suppose."

"You should see the greenhouse now. Black magic."

"Really?"

"Really. You should come and see. And I *am* sorry, Margaret. I liked what you did though."

"Sure. We'll do it again sometime."

"Soon?"

"Soon."

"Now."

"Now?"

"Why not?"

"It doesn't work like that, Valerian. I mean I can't just lie down in the middle of the afternoon."

"I can. I can even kneel. Might need help getting back up, but I can do it."

"No. Wait."

"Margie. Marge."

"WHAT KIND of dinner is that? I wouldn't have it for lunch. Does she think she's doing me a favour?"

"Stop grumbling. It's Christmastime and for once in your life you don't have to cook the dinner."

"But I have to do the dishes, I bet."

"No, you don't."

"Who then? You? No Mary. No Yardman. They decide not to show up without telling anybody. Everything's on me. A pile of laundry a mile high in there. Jadine off playing games with that jailbird; guests coming . . ."

"I told you he already called Dr. Michelin, and Dr. Michelin said he'd get us somebody right away. Maybe not right away because they got Christmas there too, but he thinks his housekeeper can find somebody. We'll just have to make do for a day or two. Let the laundry stay there, and get yourself organized. You are worrying the life out of me."

"You can stop riding me any time you please. And if you expect anything at all to go right, you better quit soon."

"You the one riding people. You been hot for days. Nothing can please you."

"The whole house is upset. Hard to think and be nice in a house that's upset."

"The house is not upset. You are. Everybody else is laughing and having a good time but you. Mr. Street slept with his wife last night. You know how long it's been since he did that? Slept in the same bed with her?"

"Slept is the word all right."

"Don't you believe it. They been cooing all morning."

"I don't care. They ought to sleep together. I never did know how he puts up with that. Whoever heard of married folks sleeping any other way but together. They can sleep anywhere they want. It's where Jadine sleeps that bothers me."

"She slept in her own bed."

"I'm going to bring this basin down on your head. You

know what I'm talking about."

"Well, what you want me to do about it?"

"Talk to somebody."

"Who?"

"Her."

"Get away from me."

"Sydney, listen here. I don't like it. None of it. What she want to mess with him for? He ain't got a dime and no prospect of one."

"She's just playing. Nothing much else to do out here, you know that. Cleaned him up and he looks fine and even acts all right. Look here. They pack a lunch, go off to the beach and swim a little. What is that? Marriage? First you was screaming because you thought she was going to marry some white boy; now she goes swimming with one of us and you still mad. Jadine's not a fool and he's okay."

"He is not okay."

"When he busted in here you were the one trying to get me to calm down. I was ready to shoot him. Now you the one want the gun."

"I just don't like it."

"What you afraid of? She's not going off with him. Just because you foolish, don't think she is. She's worked hard to make something out of herself, and nothing will make her throw it all away on a swamp nigger."

"It ain't what she thinks that worries me. It's what he thinks."

"You know something I don't?"

"No."

"Well then."

"But I've seen his eyes when nobody's looking. At least when he thinks nobody's looking."

"And what did you see in his eyes, Ondine?"

"Wildness. Plain straight-out wildness. He wants her, Sydney. And he'll do what he has to do to get her and what he has to to keep her."

"Takes two, Ondine. He can't kidnap her."

"Wouldn't put it past him."

"Mr. Street likes him."

"He likes him because Jadine likes him."

"No. He helped him with those plants in there. Made something grow that was dying."

"He wants to keep him here so Jade will stay and if Jadine stays then his wife might stay and if Michael does show up maybe she won't want to go running off after him."

"Well. Maybe he's right."

"Don't rely on it. If that boy gets in she'll be out of here like a shot. She's got a lot of cleaning up to do with Michael. It's sitting on her heart and she's never going to have no peace until she cleans it up. She'll trail him to the end of the world and God himself knows that is exactly where she ought to be."

"You hate that woman, and you want her out of here so you can run everything your way."

"I don't hate her; I feel sorry for her, to tell the truth."

"Want some more hot water in there?"

"No, this is fine."

"It's going to be all right, Ondine. She is coming in the kitchen to cook Christmas dinner. And you have to get out of the way. Maybe it'll taste bad, but it's only for one night. We can behave for one night, can't we? Then it'll be over and everything will be back to normal."

"Everything but my feet."

"Your feet too. Put 'em up here. Let me rub them for you."

"They not going to last much longer, you know. I get the littlest cut on them now and it don't seem to heal. I have to stand up to do the work I do, if I can't stand then I can't work."

"When you can't stand, girl, sit down. You don't have to work. I can take care of you, you know that."

"We don't have a place of our own. And the little bit of savings went to Jadine. Not that I regret a penny of it; I don't."

"We got a few stocks and Social Security. Years of it. Remember how I tried to get Mr. Street not to take it out, back when we first started, and he wouldn't listen to me? Now I appreciate the fact that he didn't."

"Such a smart little girl, and so pretty. I never minded not having children after we started taking care of her. I would have stood on my feet all day all night to put her through that school. And when my feet were gone, I would have cooked on my knees."

"I know, baby, I know."

"She crowned me, that girl did. No matter what went wrong or how tired I was, she was my crown."

"He helped too, you know. We never could have done it without him."

"And I'm grateful. You know I am. I've never had no problem with him. He's a nuisance, but he stood by us when we needed him to."

"And she never objected to it, Ondine. A lot of wives would have."

"I suppose."

"Lay back. Put your legs up on this pillow. Rest yourself and don't worry about nothing. Nothing's going to change. Everything's going to be all right."

"She wouldn't up and marry some no-count Negro, would she? I don't care how good-looking and sweet-talking he is. You didn't say nothing about stuffin. Is she going to stuff that bird or just roast him empty?"

"Rest, girl."

"And what the devil is lemon whip?"

NOBODY CAME. At least none of the invited. The emperor butterflies flew in the window, but they were not invited, nor were the bees. They were roused by the six-part singing of the tin-tin birds sitting in formation at the top of the bougainvillea. But the maiden aunts weren't there, thank God, with their wispy maiden aunt hair. Still nobody came. Uninvited and emergency guests shared dinner on Christmas Day. First the telephone operator read off the cable from B. J. Bridges: "Boston weather cannot fly okay postpone New Year." Then Dr. Michelin called with regrets saying the crossing would be too rough. Finally customs *contrôle* reported there was no red trunk on the last flight arriving at nine in the morning from Miami, and there was no Houston flight at all that day. More telephone calls. Michael did not answer his telephone. Margaret would have caved in Christmas Eve except for the busy-ness of confirming the disaster: more placing of calls—forty-five-minute waits until they were connected; more cables with "confirm delivery" instructions; Michael's neighbours were summoned, but the number had changed or the neighbours had; his old girlfriends were asked to go to his house and check. Had he left? When? But it was the day before Christmas and people had other things to do. Then there was the wrappings of gifts, the ollieballen to make, the turkey that was really a goose to prepare. Margaret was too tired to feel her sorrow at its deepest point until Christmas Day dawned bright and secular and nobody at all came to L'Arbe de la Croix, and nobody was in his proper place. Ondine was in the bathtub. Margaret was in the kitchen. Sydney was in the greenhouse cutting flowers for the table. Jadine was in the washhouse waiting for a dryer load to conclude. And Valerian was by the telephone placing incomplete calls. Son, who had no place of his own, got in everybody's way. The exchange of gifts, scheduled for Michael's arrival, took place anywhere, furtively and without fanfare or enthusiasm. When it was certain that no one was coming and the day looked as if it belonged to the tin-tin birds and not to family and friends, Valerian, to raise Margaret's spirits probably or simply to get through the day, said, "Let's all sit down and have the dinner among ourselves. Everybody. Jade, Willie, Ondine, Sydney." They would all have a good time, he said. Margaret nodded, and left the kitchen, where the uses of things now eluded her completely. She was in control the night before—enough to wash the fowl whose legs would not stand up as they ought to. But the ollieballen recipe slipped out of reach entirely. Sydney rescued it and now when Valerian called her away from the kitchen she seemed not to care one way or another. It was just another meal now and the dinner she had planned to cook Ondine had to finish, including the lemon whip. Ondine was persuaded to dress up and join Sydney and the others in the dining room partly because she'd had the foresight to bake a ham and a coconut cake and would not be required to eat Margaret's menu and partly because she'd have to eat alone otherwise, but she was deeply unhappy about being thrown out of her kitchen in the first place and then pushed back in when Margaret abandoned the whole thing halfway through because the guests were different. She was also unhappy because she thought Jadine had secret plans to leave right after Christmas. A few days ago she had the humiliation of Alma Estée handing her a pair of recently worn pajamas that she found in the gardenia bushes underneath Jadine's bedroom. Ondine took them and did not mention the find to anyone, but it worried her. Jadine's scurrilous remarks about Son seemed too pointed, too loud. Sydney took the invitation in stride. The suggestion of a special and intimate relationship with his employer pleased him more than it disconcerted him. And what was unthinkable and undesirable in Philadelphia was not so on that island. In addition, it levelled, in a way, the invitation Mr. Street had extended to Son when everybody thought he was a burglar. More than levelled—this invitation was formal and sober although it was an emergency solution to a rapidly deteriorating holiday.

Jadine was enchanted. Wanted everybody dressed up and gave Ondine and Sydney their presents right after breakfast when she heard the plans, exacting a promise from her aunt that she would wear hers to dinner. It was hard to tell what Son felt. Perhaps he did not know himself. For such a long time a Christmas spent on land for him was an extempore dinner or party with miscellaneous people he never expected to see again. This was another, except that the imminent exit of one of those persons alarmed him. She said "before I go" on the beach. Not "before *you* go". And he had had a brief encounter with Margaret that confirmed it. He was still apologizing all around and saw Margaret lying in a canvas-back chair, sunning herself in the shade and away from the wind too, so she could acquire a tan but not the ageing of skin that would accompany it. Her place for this was on the patio outside the living room where the piano was, sheltered by the bougainvillea bushes. Next to her chair on a small glass-topped table was a box of stationery, Bain de Soleil, tissues and a half-glass of Evian, ice and lime. She was in a bathing suit and Son thought she was like a marshmallow warming but not toasting itself. That inside the white smooth skin was liquid sugar, no bones, no cartilage — just liquid sugar, soft and a little pulley. Quite unlike her tips, where all of her strength was. Direction, focus, aggression, tenacity — all that was tough and survivalist in her lay in the tips of her fingers, the tips of her toes, her nose tip, her chin tip, and he suspected her breast tip were tiny brass knobs like those ornately carved fixtures screwed into the drawers of Jadine's writing table. Even the top of her head was fierce, pulled back as it was into a red foxtail of stamina. She heard him approach and turned her head slowly. The minute she saw him, she reached for her towel. Son picked it up from the flagstones and handed it to her. His gesture was swift and accommodating so she did not fling it over herself as she had probably intended to do but simply held it in her lap.

"I scare you?"

"No. Yes," she said. "I didn't hear you come up."

He did not comment on that so she said, "What is it?"

"Nothing. I just saw you out here and wanted to say hello."

"Hello. Is that all?"

197

"That's all."

"It shouldn't be. You should have more to say after what you did to me."

"What did I do to you?" He was counting on the liquid sugar. Never mind the tips.

"You know what. You sat in my closet and scared the hell out of me."

He smiled. "You scared the hell out of me too."

"Bullshit," she said.

"It's true. Your husband was right; you were wrong. As soon as he saw me he knew I didn't mean no harm."

"He wasn't there. I was. I was in that closet; I saw you."

"What did you see?"

"I saw a big black man sitting in my closet is what I saw."

"I'm not so big. Your husband's bigger—taller—than I am. Besides, I was sitting down. What made you think I was big?"

"There are no small men in a closet. Unless the closet belongs to them. Any stranger in a closet is big. Big and scary. I thought—"

"You thought what?"

She looked at him out of the corner of her eyes and did not answer.

Son finished her sentence. "That I was going to—that if you hadn't come in and turned on the light, I was going to stay there, wait there, until you went to bed and then I would creep out and GETCHA!" He laughed then, laughed like a ten-year-old at a Three Stooges movie. Mouth wide open, bubbly sounds coming from his chest.

"Cut that out. Don't try to make fun of it."

But he kept on laughing, long enough to make a little anger spread inside her. When he could stop laughing he said, "I'm sorry, I wasn't laughing at you. I was laughing at myself. I was seeing myself do it. Or try to do it, and it looked funny. Me, with my raggedy pants down around my ankles trying to get in your bed."

"It's not funny."

198

"No, it's not, but believe me it wouldn't have been much of a rape. Sex is hard when you're starving, but I thank you for the compliment."

"I don't know what you're talking about." Margaret spread the towel across her knees and picked up the iced glass. "And the part I do understand, I don't believe."

"When your son gets here, ask him. He'll explain it."

Margaret stopped sipping the water and looked at him. "How old are you?"

"About as old as your son."

"My son is twenty-nine going on thirty."

"Okay. Almost as old as your son."

"He'll be thirty March tenth."

"Does he favour you or your husband?"

"Favour?"

"Look like. Does he look like you?"

"People say so. Everybody says so. The hair, of course, and his eyes are blue like mine. Everybody says he looks exactly like me. Nothing like his father."

"He must be good-looking."

"He is. He is. But tall like Valerian. Is that true? You're shorter than Valerian?"

Son nodded. "He's got at least two inches on me."

"Huh," she said, "I wouldn't have thought so. Well, Michael is every bit as tall as Valerian, but he does look more like me. Inside though, that's where he's really beautiful. Do you know what he's been doing? for a year now? He's been working on an Indian reservation. With the young people there, teenagers. There's a lot of suicide among Indian teenagers. The conditions are awful, you know. You would not *believe*. I visited him when he was in Arizona. Well, some of the tribesmen have money but they're just—well, they don't really help their own. Most of them live in terrible conditions and they are very proud people, you know. Very. Michael encourages them to keep their own heritage intact. You'd really like Michael. Everybody does."

He listened. She took sips of the Evian and lime as she

199

talked, her knees covered with the towel. She was looking at him now. Relaxed. Interested in what she was saying. Interested in his hearing it, knowing it, knowing that her son was beautiful, wise and kind. That he loved people, was not selfish, was actually self-sacrificing, committed, that he could have lived practically any kind of life he chose, could be dissolute, reckless, trivial, greedy. But he wasn't. He had not turned out that way. He could have been president of the candy company if he had wanted, but he wanted value in his life, not money. He had turned out fine, just fine. "Jade knows him," she said. "They used to see each other during the summers she spent with us. Oh, he'll be thrilled to see her again. She's not leaving till a couple of days after Christmas so they'll have some time together."

Son did not blink—he took it in and nodded his appreciation of Michael into his mother's face. *She was leaving soon*. Margaret was perspiring a little bit on the forehead. A light ʃlisten on the healthy and cared-for skin. Her blue-if-it's-a-boy blue eyes wide open, not squinting in the sun for it could not get to her under the shade of the bougainvillea. Just the heat, and she was warming and marshmallow soft. But her tips were terribly sharp.

THEY SERVED themselves from the sideboard and drank wine in some haste to hurry the dismal affair along. The forced gaiety was helped into some semblance of naturalness by Jadine with much cheery help from Valerian. Sydney was awkward but subdued. Ondine was irritable, her aching feet encased in high heels with zircons up the back.

"The turkey is very tender, Mrs. Street," said Sydney.

Margaret smiled.

"Not bad at all," said Valerian, who had none of it on his plate. "Geese makes excellent turkey." He glanced at Margaret to see if she would be amused. She seemed not to hear.

"Lot of fat in a goose." Ondine was slicing her ham. "It should be cooked on its breast, not on its back."

"Oh, but I like the juices."

"That ain't juice, Jadine, that's grease," Ondine answered.

Valerian lifted his fork like a toastmaster. "Margaret has a surprise for us. Made it last night."

"What?" asked Jadine.

"You'll see. An old family recipe. Right, Margaret? Margaret?"

"Oh. Yes. Right. It wasn't hard."

"Don't be modest."

Sydney looked at Ondine with what he hoped was a stern gaze. They say it's a surprise, his eyes seemed to be saying, let's agree and be surprised. Ondine kept her eyes on her ham.

"Is that the phone?" Margaret was alert.

"Would you get that, Sydney?"

"I'll get it." Margaret was rising from her chair.

"No, let Sydney."

No one spoke as Sydney left the room.

"Dr. Michelin," said Sydney when he returned, "calling to say Merry Christmas. I suggested he call back later."

"I thought it might be the airport," said Margaret.

"Airport, what for? You heard the final news."

"I asked the office to call if there was going to be a break in the weather."

"The weather is in Boston, not California."

"How do you know that?"

"I think," said Jadine, "that the radio said there were storms all over."

"Downed the telephone lines too, I suppose," said Valerian.

"Probably, yes—" Margaret's voice was a bit shrill.

"Well, he'll be sorry," said Valerian. "He's missing some very good food and some very good company. We should have thought of this before. Give Ondine a day

201

off, and you get to show off in the kitchen, Margaret. It's good to have some plain Pennsylvania food for a change. This *is* an old-fashioned Christmas."

"Too bad Gideon couldn't come." Son, who seemed to be the only one genuinely enjoying the food, had been silent until then.

"Who?" asked Valerian.

"Gideon. Yardman."

"His name is Gideon?" asked Jadine.

"What a beautiful name. Gideon." Valerian smiled.

"Well, at least we knew Mary's name. Mary," said Jadine.

"Nope," said Son.

"No?"

"Thérèse."

"Thérèse? Wonderful," said Valerian. "Thérèse the Thief and Gideon the Get Away Man."

Ondine looked up. "They didn't steal that chocolate, Mr. Street. That was this one here." She nodded her head at Son.

"Chocolate? Who's talking about chocolate? They stole the apples." Valerian got up to go to the sideboard for some more mashed potatoes and gravy.

"Gideon stole apples?" asked Son.

"Yep." Valerian's back was to them. "I caught him red-handed, so to speak. Them, rather. She, Mary, had them stuffed in her blouse. He had some in each pocket."

Sydney and Ondine both stopped eating. "What did he say? When you caught him?" Sydney was frowning.

"Said he was going to put them back." Valerian rejoined them and chuckled.

"So that's why they didn't come back to work. Ashamed."

"Oh, more than that," said Valerian. "Much more than that. I fired him. Her too."

"You what?" Ondine almost shouted.

"Ondine," Sydney whispered.

"You didn't tell us," she said to Valerian.

"Beg pardon?" Valerian looked amused.

"I mean . . . Did you know that, Sydney?"

"No. Nobody told me anything."

"Mr. Street, you could have mentioned it."

"I'll get someone else. I've already spoke to Michelin, I told you that."

"But I thought that was temporary help, until they came back after Christmas, I thought."

"Well, Ondine, it isn't temporary help I'm asking for. It's permanent because they are not coming back."

"Please stop bickering," Margaret said softly. "I'm getting a headache."

"I never bicker, Margaret. I am discussing a domestic problem with my help."

"Well, they are guests tonight."

"The problem is still of interest to everybody at the table, except you."

"Certain things I need to know," Ondine was talking into her plate, "if I'm to get work done right. I took on all sorts of extra work because I thought they were just playing hooky. I didn't know they was fired."

"Ondine, what would you have done differently if you had known? You would have grumbled, and tried to make me keep them on. And since they were obviously stealing, and the whole house was upset anyway, I did what I thought was best."

"I wouldn't have tried any such thing, if they stole. I don't condone that."

"Well, they did and I let them go and that's that."

Son's mouth went dry as he watched Valerian chewing a piece of ham, his head-of-a-coin profile content, approving even of the flavour in his mouth although he had been able to dismiss with a flutter of the fingers the people whose sugar and cocoa had allowed him to grow old in regal comfort; although he had taken the sugar and cocoa and paid for it as though it had no value, as though the cutting of cane and picking of beans was child's play and had no value; but he turned it into

203

candy, the invention of which really was child's play, and sold it to other children and made a fortune in order to move near, but not in the midst of, the jungle where the sugar came from and build a palace with more of their labour and then hire them to do more of the work he was not capable of and pay them again according to some scale of value that would outrage Satan himself and when those people wanted a little of what he wanted, some apples for *their* Christmas, and took some, he dismissed them with a flutter of the fingers, because they were thieves, and nobody knew thieves and thievery better than he did and he probably thought he was a law-abiding man, they all did, and they all always did because they had not the dignity of wild animals who did not eat where they defecated but they could defecate over a whole people and come there to live and defecate some more by tearing up the land and that is why they loved property so, because they had killed it soiled it defecated on it and they loved more than anything the places where they shit. Would fight and kill to own the cesspools they made, and although they called it architecture it was in fact elaborately built toilets, decorated toilets, toilets surrounded with and by business and enterprise in order to have something to do in between defecations since waste was the order of the day and the ordering principle of the universe. And especially the Americans who were the worst because they were new at the business of defecation spent their whole lives bathing bathing bathing washing away the stench of the cesspools as though pure soap had anything to do with purity.

That was the sole lesson of their world: how to make waste, how to make machines that made more waste, how to make wasteful products, how to talk waste, how to study waste, how to design waste, how to cure people who were sickened by waste so they could be well enough to endure it, how to mobilize waste, legalize waste and how to despise the culture that lived in cloth houses and shit on the ground far away from where they ate. And it would drown them one day, they would all sink into their own waste and the waste they had made of the world and then, finally they would know true peace and the happiness they had been looking for all along. In the meantime this one here would chew a morsel of ham and drink white wine secure in the knowledge that he had defecated on two people who had dared to want some of his apples.

And Jadine had defended him. Poured his wine, offered him a helping of this, a dab of that and smiled when she did not have to. Soothed down any disturbance that might fluster him; quieted even the mild objections her own aunt raised, and sat next to him more alive and responsive and attentive than even his own wife was, basking in the cold light that came from one of the killers of the world.

Jadine who should know better, who had been to schools and seen some of the world and who ought to know better than any of them because she had been made by them, coached by them and should know by heart the smell of their huge civilized latrines.

Sydney closed his knife and fork and said, "Other folks steal and they get put in the guest room."

Jadine shot a look at Son and said, "Uncle Sydney, please."

"It's true, ain't it? We were slighted by taking in one thief and now we are slighted by letting another go."

"We are quarrelling about apples," said Margaret with surprise. "We are actually quarrelling about apples."

"It is not about apples, Mrs. Street," said Sydney quietly. "I just think we should have been informed. We would have let them go ourselves, probably. This way, well . . ." He looked as if even staying on at the table let alone the job was hopeless.

Valerian, at the head of his Christmas table, looked at the four black people; all but one he knew extremely well, all but one, and even that one was in his debt. Across from him at the bottom of the table sat Son who thought he knew them all very well too, except one and that one was escaping out of his hands, and that one was doing the bidding of her boss and "patron". Keeping the dinner going smoothly, quietly chastising everybody including her own uncle and aunt, soothing Margaret, agreeing with Valerian and calling Gideon Yardman and never taking the trouble to know his name and never calling his own name out loud. He looked at Valerian and Valerian looked back.

The evening eyes met those of the man with savannas in his face. The man who respected industry looked over a gulf at the man who prized fraternity.

So he said to Valerian, in a clear voice, "If they had asked, would you have given them some of the apples?" The whole table looked at Son as if he were crazy.

"Of course," said Valerian. "Some, surely, but they didn't ask; they took. Do you know how many Americans here want special treats and goodies from the consulate? Especially at Christmas. They sent us one crate, and those two, along with that girl they bring, took them, or tried to. I stopped them. Besides, it wasn't the apples alone. It was the way they acted when I caught them. After trying to lie out of it, they didn't even apologize. They got arrogant—the woman called me names I haven't heard since I left the army. So I fired them. Those apples came at great expense and inconvenience from the consulate. I don't see what the problem is."

"Inconvenience for who?" Son asked. "You didn't go and get them. They did. You didn't row eighteen miles to bring them here. They did."

"Surely you don't expect me to explain my actions, defend them to you?"

"You should explain it to somebody. Two people are going to starve so your wife could play American mama and fool around in the kitchen."

"Keep me out of it, please," said Margaret.

"Precisely," said Valerian. His evening eyes had a touch of menace. "You keep my wife out of this. I rather think you have caused her enough mischief." Somewhere

206

in the back of Valerian's mind one hundred French chevaliers were roaming the hills on horses. Their swords were in their scabbards and their epaulettes glittered in the sun. Backs straight, shoulders high — alert but restful in the security of the Napoleonic Code.

Somewhere in the back of Son's mind one hundred black men on one hundred unshod horses rode blind and naked through the hills and had done so for hundreds of years. They knew the rain forest when it was a rain forest, they knew where the river began, where the roots twisted above the ground; they knew all there was to know about the island and had not even seen it. They had floated in strange waters blind, but they were still there racing each other for sport in the hills behind this white man's house. Son folded his hands before his jawline and turned his savanna eyes on those calm head-of-a-coin evening ones. "Whatever mischief I did," he said, "it wasn't enough to make you leave the table to find out about it."

"You will leave this house," said Valerian. "Now."

"I don't think so," said Son.

Margaret raised her hand and touched Valerian on the shoulder. "It's all right, Valerian. Let's just . . ."

"It's not all right! Whose house is this?"

"We got them back," she said. "I made the ollieballen with them." Her voice was limp. Maybe if they all just ignored that "I don't think so", it would disappear. It didn't. It clicked like a key opening a lock.

"That's not the point!"

"Well, what is the point, I'd like to know. It's Christmas . . ."

"I am being questioned by these people, as if, as if I *could* be called into question!"

Jadine spoke. "Valerian, Ondine's feelings were hurt. That's all."

"By what, pray? By my removing a pair of thieves from my house?"

"No, by not telling her," said Margaret.

"So what? All of a sudden I'm beholden to a cook for
207

the welfare of two people she hated anyway? I don't understand."

Ondine had been watching the exchanges with too bright eyes, chagrined by Margaret's defence of her interests. Having caused all the trouble, now she was pretending that Ondine was the source of the dispute. "I may be a cook, Mr. Street, but I'm a person too."

"Mr. Street," said Sydney, "my wife is as important to me as yours is to you and should have the same respect."

"More," said Ondine. "I should have more respect. I am the one who cleans up her shit!"

"Ondine!" Both Sydney and Valerian spoke at once.

"This is impossible!" Valerian was shouting.

"I'll tell it," said Ondine. "Don't push me, I'll tell it."

"Nanadine! Get hold of yourself!" Jadine pushed her chair back as though to rise.

"I'll tell it. She wants to meddle in my kitchen, fooling around with pies. And *my* help gets fired!"

"*Your* kitchen? *Your* help?" Valerian was astonished.

"Yes my kitchen and yes my help. If not mine, whose?"

"You are losing your mind!" shouted Valerian.

Ondine was fuming now. "The first time in her life she tries to boil water and I get slapped in the face. Keep that bitch out of my kitchen. She's not fit to enter it. She's no cook and she's no mother."

Valerian stood up. "If you don't leave this room I'll . . ." It was the second time he ordered a dismissal and the second time it held no force.

"What? You'll what?" asked Ondine.

"Leave!" said Valerian.

"Make me," said Ondine.

"You don't work here anymore," he said.

"Oh, yeah? Who's going to feed you? *Her?*" She pointed uptable at Margaret. "You'll be dead in a week! and lucky to be dead. And away from her."

Margaret picked up her glass and threw it. The Evian splashed on the cloth and some got on Ondine's chiffon dress. As the others jumped up from their seats, Ondine

208

slipped out of her zircon-studded shoes and raced around the table at the target of all her anger. The real target, who would not be riled until now when she got fed up with the name-calling and shot her water glass across the table. "Don't you come near me!" Margaret shouted, but Ondine did and with the back of her hand slapped Margaret across the face.

"Call the harbour!" shouted Valerian, but again there was no one to do his bidding. He had played a silly game, and everyone was out of place.

Margaret touched her flaming cheek and then rose up from her chair like a red-topped geyser and grabbed Ondine's braids, forced her head down to the table where she would have banged it except for the woman's fist blows to her waist.

It was Jadine and Son who managed to separate them. Sydney was shaking and saying, "O Lord O Lord." Valerian was shaking and saying nothing—his evening eyes gone dawn with rage.

Held tightly in the arms of Son, Ondine was shouting wildly, "You white freak! You baby killer! I saw you! I saw you! You think I don't know what that apple pie shit is for?"

Jadine had a hard time holding back Margaret, who was shouting, "Shut up! Shut up! You nigger! You nigger bitch! Shut your big mouth, I'll kill you!"

"You cut him up. You cut your baby up. Made him bleed for you. For fun you did it. Made him scream, you, you freak. You crazy white freak. She did," Ondine addressed the others, still shouting. "She stuck pins in his behind. Burned him with cigarettes. Yes, she did, I saw her, I saw his little behind. She burned him!"

Valerian held on to the table edge as though it were the edge of the earth. His face was truly white and his voice cracked a little as he asked, "Burned . . . who?"

"Your son! Your precious Michael. When he was just a baby. A wee wee little bitty baby." Ondine started to cry. "I used to hold him and pet him. He was so scared!"

209

Her voice was hardly audible under the sobbing. "All the time scared. And he wanted her to stop. He wanted her to stop so bad. And every time she'd stop for a while, but then I'd see him curled up on his side, staring off. After a while—after a while he didn't even cry. And she wants him home . . . for Christmas and apple pie. A little boy who she hurt so much he can't even cry."

She broke down then and said no more. Sydney put his arms around her. Son let her arms go and picked up a table napkin so she could wipe her streaming eyes with it instead of with the backs and the palms of her hands. Sydney led her barefoot, her diadem braids turned into horns, away from the table. Margaret was standing as still and as straight as a pillar. There were tears in her eyes but her beautiful face was serene. They could hear Ondine's cries all the way into the first kitchen and down the stairs to the apartment of second-hand furniture. "Yes my kitchen. Yes my kitchen. I am the woman in this house. None other. As God is my witness there is none other. Not in this house."

Margaret serene and lovely stared ahead at nobody. "I have always loved my son," she said. "I am not one of those women in the *National Enquirer*."


"THAT WAS AWFUL, awful," said Jadine. She was holding Son's hand as they walked up the stairs. There had been no point in staying or even excusing themselves. Valerian was looking at Margaret and she was looking at nobody. So the two of them left as soon as Ondine and Sydney did. Jadine would not admit to herself that she was rattled, but her fingertips were ice-cold in Son's hand. She wanted a little human warmth, some unsullied person to be near, someone to be with, so she took his hand without thinking about it and said, "That was awful!"

"Yes," he said.

"What happened? We all went crazy. Do you think it's

true? What Nanadine said? She wouldn't make up anything like that." They were at Jadine's bedroom door and went in. Still holding hands. In the centre of the room, Jadine stopped, released his hand and turned to face him. She pressed her fingers together in front of her lips. "Awful," she said frowning, looking at the floor.

"Don't think about it. It's over."

Jadine put her head on his chest. "It's not over. They're fired for sure. Tomorrow will be terrible. God, how can I wake up in the morning and face that? I won't be able to sleep at all. Maybe I should go down and see about her?"

"Ondine?"

"Yes."

"Leave her alone with Sydney. You shouldn't bother them now."

"I wish I could figure it out, what got into everybody." Son put his arm around her; she was like a bird in the crook of his arm. "What does it mean?" She closed her eyes.

"It means," he said, talking into her hair, "that white folks and black folks should not sit down and eat together."

"Oh, Son." Jadine looked up at him and smiled a tiny smile.

"It's *true*," he said. "They should work together sometimes, but they should not eat together or live together or sleep together. Do any of those personal things in life."

She put her head back into his shirt front. "What'll we do now?"

"Sleep," he said.

"I can't sleep. It was so ugly. Did you see the faces?"

Son kissed her cheek, bending his neck down low.

"It's true, isn't it? She stuck pins into Michael, and Ondine knew it and didn't tell anybody all this time. Why didn't she tell somebody?"

"She's a good servant, I guess, or maybe she didn't want to lose her job." He kissed the other cheek.

"I always wondered why she hated Margaret so. Every

211

time she could she would jab at her."

"Sleep," he said, and kissed her eyelids. "You need sleep."

"Will you sleep with me?" she asked.

"I will," he said.

"I mean really sleep. I'm not up to anything else."

"I'll sleep."

"You sure? It was terrible, Son. Terrible. I don't want to think about it, but I know I will and I don't want to do it alone."

"I know. I'll stay with you. You sleep and I'll watch you."

Jadine stepped back from him. "Oh, the hell with it. You won't. You'll start something and I'm not up to it."

"Relax. Stop imagining things. You want somebody to be with tonight, so I'll do it. Don't complicate it."

"You start something and I'll throw you out."

"All right. Take off your dress and get in the bed."

Jadine folded her arms behind her and unzipped the top part of her dress. He reached behind her and pulled it the rest of the way down. Jadine stepped out of it and sat down on the bed. "No foolishness, Son. I'm serious." Her voice sounded small and tired.

"So am I," he said, and began unbuttoning his shirt. Jadine sat on the bed and watched him. Then, for the first time, she saw his huge hands. One hand alone was big enough for two. A finger spread that could reach from hither to yon. The first time she had been aware of his hands they were clasped over his head under Sydney's gun, so she had not really seen them. The second time was at the beach when he touched the bottom of her foot with one finger. She had not looked then either, only felt that fingerprint in the arch of her sole. Now she could not help looking, seeing those hands large enough to sit down in. Large enough to hold your whole head. Large enough, maybe, to put your whole self into.

"I hope you are serious," she said. She left her panties on and got under the sheet. Son undressed completely

212

and Jadine shot him a quick look to see if he had an erection.

"Look at you," she said. "You're going to meddle me and all I want is rest."

"Be quiet," he said. "I'm not meddling you. I can't control that, but I can control whether I meddle you." He walked to the bed and got in next to her.

"Well, how am I supposed to sleep with you taking up half the sheet in that tent?"

"Don't think about it and it'll go away."

"I'll bet. You sound like a character in those blue comics."

"Hush."

Jadine turned round on her stomach and then her side, with her back to him. After a silence during which she listened for but could not hear his breathing, she said, "Have you slept with anybody since you jumped ship?"

"Yes."

"You have?" She raised her head. "Who? I mean where?"

"In town."

"Oh *ho*." She put her head back on the pillow. "Who?"

"Can't remember her name."

"Men. Why can't you remember her name? Didn't Yardman tell you her name?"

"Gideon."

"Gideon. Didn't he introduce you?"

"Go to sleep, Jadine."

"I can't. I'm tired, but not sleepy."

"You're agitated. Calm down."

"You won't bother me? I don't want to wrestle."

"I won't bother you. I'll just be here while you sleep, just like I said I would."

"I'm not up to any fucking."

"For somebody who's not up to it, you sure bring it up a lot."

"I know what's going to happen. I'll fall asleep and then I'll feel something cold on my thigh."

213

"Nothing cold is going to be on your thigh."

"I just don't want to fuck, that's all."

"I didn't ask you to, did I? If I wanted to make love, I'd ask you."

"I didn't say make love, I said—"

"I know what you said."

"You don't like me to use that word, do you? Men."

"Go to sleep. Nobody's talking about fucking or making love but you."

"Admit it. You don't like me to say fuck."

"No."

"Hypocrite."

Son thought he must have had this conversation two million times. It never varied, this dance. Except when you paid your money and there was no seduction involved. Free stuff was always a pain in the ass, and it annoyed him that this conversation should be taking place with this sponge-coloured girl with mink eyes whom he was certain he could not live in the world without. He wished she would either fall asleep, throw him out or jump him. "Listen," he said, "I'm not a hypocrite. Whatever you call it, I'm not doing it."

"What do you call it?" Jadine turned over and lay on her back.

"I don't call it anything. I don't have the language for it."

"Why not?"

"I just don't. It's not love-making and it's not fucking."

"If it's not making love, it's because you don't love me and you said at the beach that you did."

"I said that because I don't know how else to say it. If I had another way, I'd have used it. Whatever I want to do to you—that's not it."

"What do you want to do to me? I mean if you had the language what would you do?"

"I'd make you close your eyes," he said, and when he didn't add anything Jadine raised up on her elbows.

"Is that all?"

"Then I'd ask you what you saw."

She lay back down. "I don't see anything."

"Nothing?"

"Nothing."

"Not even the dark?"

"Oh, yes, that."

"Is it all dark? Nothing else? No lights moving around? No stars? No moon?"

"No. Nothing. Just black."

"Imagine something. Something that fits in the dark. Say the dark is the sky at night. Imagine something in it."

"A star?"

"Yes."

"I can't. I can't see it."

"Okay. Don't try to see it. Try to be it. Would you like to know what it's like to be one? Be a star?"

"A movie star?"

"No, a star star. In the sky. Keep your eyes closed, think about what it feels like to be one." He moved over to her and kissed her shoulder. "Imagine yourself in that dark, all alone in the sky at night. Nobody is around you. You are by yourself, just shining there. You know how a star is supposed to twinkle? We say twinkle because that is how it looks, but when a star feels itself, it's not a twinkle, it's more like a throb. Star throbs. Over and over and over. Like this. Stars just throb and throb and throb and sometimes, when they can't throb anymore, when they can't hold it anymore, they fall out of the sky."

# 7

THE BLACK GIRLS in New York City were crying and their men were looking neither to the right nor to the left. Not because they were heedless, or intent on what was before them, but they did not wish to see the crying, crying girls split into two parts by their tight jeans, screaming at the top of their high, high heels, straining against the pull of their braids and the fluorescent combs holding their hair. Oh, their mouths were heavy with plum lipstick and their eyebrows were a thin gay line, but nothing could stop their crying and nothing could persuade their men to look to the right or look to the left. They stoked their cocks into bikini underwear and opened their shirts to their tits. But they walked on tippy-toe through the streets looking straight ahead, and Son looked in vain for children. He couldn't find them anywhere. There were short people and people under twelve years of age, but they had no child's vulnerability, no unstuck laughter. They cracked into the M2 bus like terrified bison running for their lives, for fear the school at their backs would grab them and eat them up one more time. It wasn't until he caught the downtown A that he saw what they had done with their childhood. They had wrapped it in dark cloth, sneaked it underground and thrown it all over the trains. Like blazing jewels, the subway cars burst from the tunnels to the platforms shining with the recognizable artifacts of childhood: fantasy, magic, ego, energy, humour and paint. They had taken it all underground. Pax and Stay High and the Three Yard Boys. Teen, P-Komet and Popeye. He sat on a bench at the Fifty-ninth Street station watching the childhood flash by. Now all he

216

needed to know was where were the old people. Where were the Thérèses and Gideons of New York? They were not on the subways and they were not in the street. Perhaps they were all in kennels. That must be the reason the men walked that way—on tippy-toe looking neither to the right nor to the left. The old people were in kennels and childhood was underground. But why were all the black girls crying on buses, in Red Apple lines, at traffic lights and behind the counters of Chemical Bank? Crying from a grief so stark you would have thought they'd been condemned to death by starvation in the lobby of Alice Tully Hall. Death by starvation in Mikell's, death by starvation on the campus of C.U.N.Y. And death by starvation at the reception desks of large corporations. It depressed him, all that crying, for it was silent and veiled by plum lipstick and the thin gay lines over their eyes. Who did this to you? Who has done this thing to you? he wondered, as he walked down Columbus Avenue looking first to the right and then to the left. The street was choked with beautiful males who had found the whole business of being black and men at the same time too difficult and so they'd dumped it. They had snipped off their testicles and pasted them to their chests; they put the weighty wigs Alma Estée dreamed of on their heads and feathery eyelashes on their eyes. They flung sharp hips away to the right and away to the left and smiled sweetly at the crying girls and the men on tippy-toe. Only the Hilton whores seemed to him quiet and feeling no pain. He had tried a little television that first day, but the black people in whiteface playing black people in blackface unnerved him. Even their skin had changed through the marvel of colour TV. A grey patina covered them all and they were happy. Really happy. Even without looking at their grey, no-colour faces, the sound of their televised laughter was enough to tell him so. Different laughter from what he remembered it to be—without irony or defiance or genuine amusement. Now all he heard were shrieks of satisfaction. It made him shiver. How long had he been gone, anyway? If those were the black folks he was carrying around in his heart all those years, who on earth was he? The trouble he'd had the night he checked in was representative of how estranged he felt from these new people. The Hickey Freeman suit passed muster easily enough, and he wadded Jadine's four hundred dollars in his fist as he approached the desk. The clerk was about to give him a very hard time because no, he would not be paying with a credit card, and no, no cheque either. Cash. Two nights. Cash. Son had chosen that line to wait in because the clerk's little pecan-pie face looked friendly; now he realized the boy was in love with his identification badge. Son was surprised at himself. He seldom misjudged people. He thought the love thing with Jadine must have thrown his sensibilities off, derailed his judgment, so he leaned toward the clerk and whispered, "Brother, do you want to get home tonight? This ain't your fuckin hotel." But now he thought it was less an error in judgment than it was being confronted with a whole new race of people he was once familiar with.

He was heart-weary when he opened the door to his room, and the purple carpet fairly took his breath away. He wanted her in that room with him giving him the balance he was losing, the ballast and counterweight to the stone of sorrow New York City had given him. Jadine would lighten up the purple carpet, soften the tooth-white walls. She'd read the room-service menu as though it were a private message to them both and then choose a corner of the room to make love in. They had spent two whole days following the Christmas dinner in or near each other's arms, and the demoralized house never noticed. But they both understood that Son had to get out fast, so he used Jadine's ticket and Gideon's passport, and split. She was to follow as soon as she could get a flight and had seen what Ondine's and Sydney's situation was—whether they would stay or

218

leave.

He sat down in a plastic tub chair, rested his arms on the windowsill and looked down at Fifty-third Street. How hard this one night's wait would be, shot full already of fallen airplanes and missed connections. Even if he managed to sleep from 6.30 p.m. to 6.30 a.m., what would he do with the morning? Refuse to have breakfast until nine; shave long and shower longer till noon when Air France would glide like a crane into Kennedy. Did she say baggage claim or lobby? Or did she say to wait at the hotel? His mouth went suddenly dry with the possibility of losing her in that city. Was he in the right hotel? Was it the New York Hilton or the Statler Hilton? She just said Hilton. There was no way to call and find out without letting Sydney know. He might answer the phone himself, or Ondine might, and if they knew she was joining him, they both might try to stop her. He could call Gideon. He tried to remember that hillside hut, but all he could summon were the powder pink walls and the record player sitting on a shelf. Gideon had no telephone, but messages got to him via a store halfway down the hill that sold rum and meat pies and lent out hair clippers.

That was foolish. What could Gideon tell him anyway? He was so angry at the Americans, he was actually helping Thérèse prepare all sorts of potions and incantations for their destruction, just in case there was such a thing as magic after all. And he was quite willing to lend his passport to the man who shared his anger at the Americans. He could not understand why Son wanted to return to the country too terrible for dying, but he agreed that one black face would look like another and a difference of twenty years would not be noticed in a black man's five-year-old passport. Thérèse gave Son, as a going-away present, a tiny, dirty bag of good fortune, but he tossed it away—it *looked* like ganja and he didn't want to draw any attention to himself at customs. He took what Jadine gave him and left. Now,

219

on the second day of their separation he would just have to wait and keep on imagining disaster since his emotions were so young that this heavy, grown-up love made him feel fresh-born, unprecedented, surrounded by an extended present loaded with harm.

There was nothing to do; he would have to trust to her city-sense to do the right thing and be in the right places. And this time tomorrow he could smooth back her hair and sweep her eyebrows with his thumb. This time tomorrow the side teeth in her smile would divert him from what she was saying or laughing at. He loved to watch her eyes when she was not watching his. And to listen to the four/four time of her heels. Son sat there wagging his knees back and forth like a schoolboy. Not thinking most of the important things there were to think about: What would they do? Where would they go, live? How would he earn money to take care of her and, later, their children? He smiled at the vigour of his own heartbeat at the thought of her having his baby. Watch her. He would watch her stomach while she slept just the way he had when he'd lived like an animal around the house and spent the hind part of the night at her bedside pressing his dreams into hers. Now those dreams embarrassed him. The mewings of an adolescent brutalized by loneliness for a world he thought he would never see again.

There was a future. A reason for hauling ass in the morning. No more moment to moment play-it-as-it-comes existence. That stomach required planning. Thinking through a move long before it was made. What would he name his son? Son of Son?

He should have thought about that before he left. Perhaps he would have taken things: cash, jewellery and the passport of a stranger instead of a friend. Instead he took the clothes, one piece of luggage and the Bally shoes and his bottle of Paco Rabanne. He saw it all as a rescue: first tearing her mind away from that blinding awe. Then the physical escape from the plantation. His first, hers to follow two days later. Unless . . . he remembered sitting at the foot of the table, gobbling the food, watching her pour *his* wine, listening to her take *his* part, trying to calm Ondine and Sydney to *his* satisfaction. Just as she had done the first night when they found him in the closet. He would not look at her then — refused to lock with those mink-dark eyes that looked at him with more distaste than Valerian's had. The mocking voice, the superior managerial, administrative, clerk-in-a-fucking-loan-office tone she took. Gatekeeper, advance bitch, house-bitch, welfare office torpedo, corporate cunt, tar baby side-of-the-road whore trap, who called a black man old enough to be her father "Yardman" and who couldn't give a shit who he himself was and only wanted his name to file away in her restrung brain so she could remember it when the cops came to fill out the report — five eleven, maybe six feet, black as coal with the breath and table manners of a rhino. But underneath her efficiency and know-it-all sass were wind chimes. Nine rectangles of crystal, rainbowed in the light. Fragile pieces of glass tinkling as long as the breeze was gentle. But in more vigorous weather the thread that held it together would snap. So it would be his duty to keep the climate mild for her, to hold back with his hands if need be thunder, drought and all manner of winterkill, and he would blow with his own lips a gentle enough breeze for her to tinkle in. The bird-like defencelessness he had loved while she slept and saw when she took his hand on the stairs was his to protect. He would have to be alert, feed her with his mouth if he had to, construct a world of steel and down for her to flourish in, for the love thing was already there. He had been looking for her all his life, and even when he thought he had found her, in other ports and other places, he shied away. He stood in her bedroom, a towel wrapped around his waist. Clean as a whistle, having just said the nastiest thing he could think of to her. Staring at a heart-red tree desperately in love

221

with a woman he could not risk loving because he could not afford to lose her. For if he loved and lost this woman whose sleeping face was the limit his eyes could safely behold and whose wakened face threw him into confusion, he would surely lose the world. So he made himself disgusting to her. Insulted and offended her. Gave her sufficient cause to help him keep his love in chains and hoped to God the lock would hold. It snapped like a string.

He stood up, searching for the anger that had shaken him so that first time and again on Christmas Day. But here in this island of crying girls and men on tippy-toe, he could not find it. Even conjuring up that head-of-a-coin profile, the unfleshed skin and evening eyes, was not a vivid enough memory to produce it. He needed the blood-clot heads of the bougainvillea, the simple green rage of the avocado, the fruit of the banana trees puffed up and stiff like the fingers of gouty kings. Here prestressed concrete and steel contained anger, folded it back on itself to become a craving for things rather than vengeance. Still, he thought of it not just as love, but as rescue. He took off his clothes and filled the tub, smiling to think of what the leaden waves of the Atlantic had become in the hands of civilization. The triumph of ingenuity that had transferred the bored treachery of the sea into a playful gush of water that did exactly what it was told. And why not? Wilderness wasn't wild anymore or threatening; wildlife needed human protection to exist at all.

Stretched out in the water, his eyes closed, he thought of this city that he should have remembered. Where was the wavy-seven language on the windows of the butcher shops? The laundries named Hand. What had they done to the Apollo? Where was Michaux's, the awnings on St. Nicholas Avenue? Who were these people on the islands in the middle of Broadway and where were the trees? There used to be trees. Trees coming out of the concrete. But nobody would chop down a tree in New

222

York, so he guessed he must have been wrong. That must have been some other city he had been memorizing.


JADINE sat in the taxi barely able to see over her luggage piled in the seat in front of her. Unlike the anxiety-ridden man in a Hilton bathtub, she wanted to giggle. New York made her feel like giggling, she was so happy to be back in the arms of that barfly with the busted teeth and armpit breath. New York oiled her joints and she moved as though they were oiled. Her legs were longer here, her neck really connected her body to her head. After two months of stingless bees, butterflies and avocado trees, the smart thin trees on Fifty-third Street refreshed her. They were to scale, human-sized, and the buildings did not threaten her like the hills of the island had, for these were full of people whose joints were oiled just like hers. This is home, she thought with an orphan's delig' not Paris, not Baltimore, not Philadelphia. This .. home. The city had gone on to something more interesting to it than the black people who had fascinated it a decade ago, but if ever there was a black woman's town, New York was it. No, no, not over there making land-use decisions, or deciding what was or was not information. But there, there, there and there. Snapping whips behind the tellers' windows, kicking ass at Con Edison offices, barking orders in the record companies, hospitals, public schools. They refused loans at Household Finance, withheld unemployment cheques and drivers' licences, issued parking tickets and summonses. Gave enemas, blood transfusions and please lady don't make me mad. They jacked up meetings in boardrooms, turned out luncheons, energized parties, redefined fashion, tipped scales, removed lids, cracked covers and turned an entire telephone company into such a diamondhead of hostility the company paid you for not talking to their operators.

The manifesto was simple: 'Talk shit. Take none."
Jadine remembered and loved it all. This would be her
city too, her place, the place she spent a whole summer
once in love with Oom. Riding the subways looking for
his name, first as a talisman, then as a friend and finally
as a lover in the tunnels of New York City. And now she
would take it; take it and give it to Son. They would
make it theirs. She would show it, reveal it to him, live it
with him. They would fall out of Max's Kansas City at 4
a.m.; they would promenade Third Avenue from the
Fifties to SoHo; they would fight landlords and drink
coffee in the Village, eat bean pie on 135th Street,
paella on Eighty-first Street; they would laugh in the sex
boutiques, eat yogurt on the steps of the Forty-second
Street library; listen to RVR and BLS, buy mugs in
Azuma's, chocolate chip cookies in Grand Central
Station, drink margaritas at Suggs, and shop Spanish
and West Indian at the Park Avenue Market. She would
look up Dawn and Betty and Aisha and show him off:
her fine frame, her stag, her man.

Jadine was so ruttish by the time she got to the Hilton,
she could barely stand still for the doorman to take her
bags, and when she was checked in, and had gotten his
room number from information, she did not call
him—she took the elevator to his floor and banged on
the door. When he opened it, she jumped on him with
her legs around his waist crashing him into the purple
carpet.

But he insisted on Eloe. In spite of the Gate and
Central Park in the snow. They moved into Dawn's
apartment, available to them for four months while she
was on the Coast shooting her seventh pilot, the one that
was sure to stick. Four months in that apartment of long
and bristling winter days when he slowed her down to
the speed of a tulip. Murky New York days when she
spun him like a top until he slammed into the head-
board. He met her women friends—girls who talked
with their shoulders, and found them less than she; he

224

met her men friends—alight with success, almost rich—and found them less than he. Everybody was ridiculous, maimed or unhappy to them, so satisfied were they with their mutual adoration. He thought he would have to stamp the ground, paw it and butt horns with every male they came in contact with, but he didn't. Her devotion surprised him; she looked only at him and grew her own horns when other men got out of line. She was startled and pleased to discover that his beauty, so sudden and impressive on Isle des Chevaliers, was volcanic in the city. As if waitresses and the eyes of passersby had not already told her, her own friends altered as well in his presence. Dawn went completely Annie Rooney, falling all over herself with helplessness, and generosity. Betty, who had been "into" bisexuality for six months, couldn't get back into the closet fast enough when Son was in the room, and when Jadine told Son about Betty's range of interests, she was angry enough to fight.

Still he insisted on Eloe. Even after she earned $2,500 for four walks and a picture spread all in two weeks and they bought each other pretty things. Even after he worked the bar three afternoons at a fashion show where he got the drinks mixed up, dropped a fifth of gin, and Leonard, the old man who had taken him on as a favour to Jadine, shook his head in disbelief. Son took six bottles of leftover champagne, the $150, and gave it all to her. They got swinging drunk and Jadine laughed in his ear and called him an unskilled sickle-cell-anemia motherfucker.

They were sober too. And he let her be still and cry after she told him about her mother and the awful hat she'd worn to the funeral. Too big and grown-up for a little girl of twelve. She poured her heart out to him and he to her. Dumb things, secret things, sin and heroism. They told each other all of it. Or all they could. He told her what she wished to hear about the war. He could not speak to her or anyone about it coherently so he told

225

her what she wished to hear: no, he never killed anybody "with his hands"; yes, he was wounded and he showed her a burn on his skin from a burst boiler to prove it; yes, he had been afraid, although in truth he had not been, or had not been properly frightened. He had laughed, in fact, laughed all over Vietnam because at eighteen laughter was his only reliable weapon. It was still early in the war, but when trucks sank in mud and grenades exploded too soon or not at all, laughter was always there, almost always; but one day it ran out too, as unreliable as his fucked-up M-14. The silence in his throat where laughter or tears ought to be blew up in his head and he was stockaded, busted and, when he refused to re-up, discharged without honour or humour. He went to Eloe, married Cheyenne, left the set early when a fistfight broke out and found his sleeping wife sleeping with a teenager. He was silent then too as he ran his car through the house and the bed caught on fire. He pulled them both out — the teenager and Cheyenne — but she didn't make it. He watched her wrappings but not her eyes in the hospital and still no sound. It was hearing about Frisco blowing up in a gas field. Old no-good Frisco who used to pay him to clean fish. That did it. His father told him the news when he met him at the bus stop across the state line with money. Told him to hurry; told him to write; and told him about Frisco. In a tiny toilet at the rear of the bus, Son cried like an infant for all the blowings up in Asia.

Jadine kissed his hands and he asked her why she left the States in the first place. She said she always thought she had three choices: marry a dope king or a doctor, model, or teach art at Jackson High. In Europe she thought there might be a fourth choice. They told each other everything. Yet he insisted on Eloe. She listened to him and nodded, thinking anywhere with him would be all right. She was completely happy. After all those sexually efficient men, all those foreplay experts and

226

acrobats, and the nonverbal equipment men, his wildness and fumbling, his corny unself-conscious joy was like blue-sky water. Show me again what it's like to be shining all alone in the sky. And he did that, and he did more. Regarding her whole self as an ear, he whispered into every part of her stories of icecaps and singing fish, The Fox and the Stork, The Monkey and the Lion, The Spider Goes to Market, and so mingled was their sex with adventure and fantasy that to the end of her life she never heard a reference to Little Red Riding Hood without a tremor.

They thought about Isle des Chevaliers sometimes. He would say "ollieballen" and she would scream with laughter. She wrote two misleading postcards to Ondine and Sydney. Got a short, sorrowful, somewhat accusatory letter back which she refused to let sour her happiness. Her leave-taking had been difficult. She was dependent at last on that mulatto with a leer sent by Dr. Michelin as the new yard boy. The Streets seemed not to notice or mind her going. Only Ondine and Sydney were cut up about it. She promised to send for them as soon as they wanted her to, but she had to take this gig, she told them, and she left the two sullen and confused old people at the kitchen table, their hearts steeled against her leaving, even though her New York trip, she said, was vital if she were to arrange things so all three could live together. She couldn't let them know who waited at the Hilton. Son and Jadine discussed their situation in Dawn's apartment. Ondine and Sydney seemed unsure of their jobs, but no steps had been taken to let them go, it seemed. Son was less than sympathetic to Ondine's plight because she had acted too shuffle-footed — keeping her white lady's secret "lak it wuz hern" and loving her white lady's baby "lak it wuz hern, too". And much less sympathetic to Sydney because in thirty years he had not split Valerian's skull. Eighty percent of both Sydney's and Ondine's conversation was the caprice and habits of their master.

"You still like that old man, don't you?" Son asked her.

"Who? Valerian?"

"Yes."

"He put me through school, I told you."

"Nothing in return?"

"No. Nothing. Never made a pass, nothing."

"And Margaret?" he asked. "How did she treat you?"

"Okay. She was more distant than he was, but she was nice to me. Nice enough anyway."

"She wasn't very nice to your folks," he said.

"Actually, she was," Jadine answered. "They both were. At least from what I could see of it. That's why I was so took-out that day. I couldn't believe it. They fought like we did in grade school."

"Wild," he said, thinking of rescue.

"Really wild." Jadine let two of her fingers do the Charleston in the hair of his chest. "We'll get rich and send for them and live happily ever after," she said, and thought it was so, but not right this minute, not today, there was so much nestling to do. They had only two months left in the apartment, but they needed more time. Jadine habitually shaved herself all over like a fourth grade Girl Scout and he finally got around to telling her he wanted some body hair. But they needed time for it to grow. Much more time. Time for her to sketch him right for once. But why sketch when she could touch? Time to make a genuine paella, time for her to finish the macramé plant holder, for him to fix the dishwasher. They must have been in love—they never once turned on the television. They forgot to buy cigarettes or alcohol and they didn't even jog in the park.

There wasn't a permanent adult job in the whole of the city for him, so he did teenager's work on occasion and pieces of a grown man's work. He spoke to the men at the shape-up halls. The black men told him Baltimore. Everybody works on the docks in Baltimore. Or Galveston, or San Diego or New Orleans or Savannah. New York—not a chance. There was a little pilfering

228

money—that was about all. Some small-time truckers gave him brute work, look-out work, and sometimes he dropped payoffs when asked. But none of it could hold his attention and one afternoon while he was helping a trucker unload boxes on Broadway and 101st Street, he heard a commotion in the traffic. A young girl with a shaved head and a small ring in her nostril was cursing a man right in the middle of the street. The man, who looked African or West Indian to Son by the innocent confusion in his face, stood watching her in silence. Two or three of his friends leaned on cars, looking elsewhere but obviously waiting for the finale. The girl was in jeans, platform shoes and a thin sweater. She had the voice of a sergeant and her language was nasty enough to be memorable. Cars honked at them before swerving into parallel lanes; pedestrians glanced and then pretended they weren't there. Only Son and people in second-storey windows gave them their undivided attention. It was beyond embarrassment. The girl's face was as tight and mean as broccoli, her forefinger shot bullets into the pavement. But inside her narrowed angry eyes were many other eyes—some of them hurt, some brave, some just lonely hollow-eyes, and her shaved head reminded Son of his sister. He listened to the abuse, the catalogue of shame and rage until the man felt safe enough (his back-up team still leaned on the cars) to turn his back on her and walk away. None of which dulled the glitter of her nose ring or shut her mouth. She word-whipped him on down the street and probably would have followed him to make it stick except Son, made miserable by the eyes inside her eyes, went over and stood in front of her with his arms wide open. She looked at him with hatred older than lava.

"Come here," he said.

She didn't move, so he put his arms around her to shield her from the eyes of the second-storey people and bank her fire. The girl bucked, but he wouldn't let her go. "You're going to freeze to death," he said. "Let me

229

buy you a drink." She tipped her forehead onto his chest then, and began to cry.

"Come on," he said. "There's a place down the block." Arm around her shoulder, he led the way to a Chinese restaurant and ordered her gin. She drank and began to tell him about the man, but Son shook his head. "Don't," he said. "Don't think about it. You got a place to stay?"

She said, "Not tonight, I don't," so he left the job hauling boxes and took her home.

All three, Nommo, Jadine and Son, went to a delicatessen where, after much discussion, they bought potato chips, A & W root beer, and three Payday candy bars with Son's last ten-dollar bill. They ate it all in the snow. Cold and giggling they trudged back to the apartment where Son and Jadine slept like puppies and Nommo made off with the change.

Yet he insisted on Eloe. She agreed but before they could make plans, she stubbed her big toe on a metal plate bolted to the middle of Sixth Avenue. By the time she got home, her toe was the size of a plum and very painful. Son made a splint for it out of emery boards and the ribbon from a Valentine candy box. All night he woke at half-hour intervals to bathe her toe in an Epsom salt solution. In the morning, the swelling had decreased and he left for work while she slept. When she woke and hobbled to the bathroom she saw that he had drawn a happily obscene picture under the toilet lid. At his coffee break he called.

"How's your toe?"

"Lonely."

"Mine too."

"Come home for lunch."

"I only have thirty minutes for lunch, baby."

"Come anyway."

"I won't be able to get back in time. I'll lose a half-day's pay."

"I'll make it worth your while."

He came home and didn't report to work again until

she could walk effortlessly. In the meantime they ate Chinese food in the tub. She read *True Confessions* stories to him with appropriate "white girl" voices and gestures and he laughed until his chest hurt. She read Césaire to him and he closed his eyes. She read the sexy parts of the Bible and he looked at her.

Gradually she came to feel unorphaned. He cherished and safeguarded her. When she woke in the night from an uneasy dream she had only to turn and there was the stability of his shoulder and his limitless, eternal chest. No part of her was hidden from him. She wondered if she should hold back, keep something in store from him, but he opened the hair on her head with his fingers and drove his tongue through the part. There was nothing to forgive, nothing to win and the future was five minutes away. He unorphaned her completely. Gave her a brandnew childhood. They were the last lovers in New York City—the first in the world—so their passion was inefficient and kept no savings account. They spent it like Texans. When he had a sore throat so bad he could not speak she put him to bed and drew a checker board on the inside of a Bergdorf box. They played the game with M&M's. It didn't work because the crowns wouldn't stay still, so they used her Enovids instead, partly because of their plane surface and partly to keep her from eating the pieces jumped by her kings. She told him straight brandy was good for his throat and made him drink so much so fast, he passed out. She didn't like his being unconscious without her so she drank the rest and passed out with him. He woke first and vomited the strep away. After bathing and dressing, he watched her sleep. She woke unable to see, speak or move and he put his huge hand on her forehead until she could. They didn't go to parties anymore—other people interfered with their view of each other. They stopped going to Suggs and Across 110th Street. They stopped laughing and began to smile at each other. From across the room, across the mattress, across the table. Their language diminished to code at times,

231

and at others ballooned to monologues delivered while cradled in the other's arms. They never looked at the sky or got up early to see a sunrise. They played no music and hadn't the foggiest notion that spring was on its way. Vaguely aware of such things when they were apart, together they could not concentrate on the given world. They reinvented it, remembered it through the other. He looked at her face in the mirror and was reminded of days at sea when water looked like sky. She surveyed his body and thought of oranges, playing jacks, and casks of green wine. He was still life, babies, cut glass, indigo, hand spears, dew, cadmium yellow, Hansa red, moss green and the recollection of a tree that wanted to dance with her. It was difficult to be sober, to take anything other than themselves seriously, but they managed occasionally. She thought about calling her old professor who said he could always find work for her. But maybe May would be a better time to ring him — after exams. They discussed opening a retail flower shop and boutique that they could call Jade and Son; they discussed bank robbery and an agency for black models; they discussed the New School and Empire State and figured out a way to collect Gideon's unemployment cheques.

But Jadine was not worried. She had $1,940 in the bank, $5,000 in Paris and connections. If push came to shove, she'd go permanent with an agency and work her behind off.

The cheque scheme worked, but he had time to pick up just one cheque before they left hand-in-hand for Eloe.

# 8

THE AIR was so charged with pain the angel trumpets could not breathe it. Rows of them wrinkled on the vine and fell unnoticed right in Valerian's sightline. He sat in the greenhouse oblivious to everything but 1950 when he heard for the first time his son's song.

All the years since, he thought she drank, was a not-so-secret alcoholic: the sleeping masks, the clumsiness, the beauty spa vacations, the withdrawals, the hard-to-wake mornings, the night crying, the irritability, the sloppy candy-kisses mother love. He thought she drank —heavily, in private, and that was why she took only wine and sherry in his presence. Non-drinkers take real drinks; only secret drinkers insist on Chablis at every occasion—or so he thought. And he wished it were true. He was devastated knowing that she had never been drunk, had never been "out of her mind", never in a stupor, never hung-over, never manic from being dry too long. Drunkenness he could take, *had* taken, in fact, since he'd always believed it. Anything was better than knowing that a pretty (and pretty nice) sober young woman had loved the bloodying of her own baby. Had loved it dearly. Had once locked herself in the bathroom, a pair of cuticle scissors in her hand, to keep from succumbing to that love. Nothing serious, though. No throwing across the room, or out of the window. No scalding, no fist work. Just a delicious pin-stab in sweet creamy flesh. That was her word, "delicious". "I knew it was wrong, knew it was bad. But something about it was delicious too." She was telling him, saying it aloud at the dinner table after everyone had gone. His knees were trembling and he'd had to sit down again. The Negroes

233

had all gone out of the room, disappeared like bushes, trees, out of his line of vision, and left the two of them in the light of the chandelier. She was standing there next to him, her cheek white again after the blow Ondine had given her, her hair rumpled but lovely. She was serene standing there saying it, and he agreed with that, thought it could be, must be, true—that it was delicious, for at that moment it would have been delicious to him too if he could have picked up the carving knife lying on the platter next to the carcass of the goose and slashed into her lovely Valentine face. Delicious. Conclusive and delicious. But he could not concentrate. His knees were trembling, his fingers shuddering on the tablecloth. He didn't want to see them shaking there, but he did not want to see her face either. He thought about that—how or whether to stop looking at her and look instead at his hands. He couldn't make up his mind and he couldn't shift his gaze. But he thought about it while she was saying it. "It's funny, but I would see the mark and hear him cry but somehow I didn't believe it hurt all that much." "Mark" she called it. She saw the mark. Didn't think it hurt "all that much". Like a laboratory assistant removing the spleen of a cute but comatose mouse.

Suddenly he knew exactly what to do: go to him. Go to Michael. Find him, touch him, rub him, hold him in his arms. Now. He tried to stand but the spastic legs defied him.

"I cannot hear anymore," he said. "I can't."

She stopped then and looked at him with complete understanding and complete patience. Still he could not stand. She understood that too, and without another word walked slowly out of the room, "Later," her footsteps seemed to say, "when you are stronger, I will say it to you. Share it with you. Make it yours as well as mine."

Valerian did not move. I will never be that strong, he thought. I will never be strong enough to hear it. I have to die now or go to him. When I move from this table I

234

will do one or the other, nothing in between. I will never be able to hear it.

It was two in the morning when Sydney returned dressed in robe, slippers and pajama bottoms. Valerian was sitting in the chandelier light—legs and fingers finally at rest.

"You should go on up to bed, Mr. Street."

Valerian gave a small shake of his head. If he went up he might never come down again and if he stood up it would only be to die or go to Michael.

"Get some rest; figure things out in the morning," Sydney said.

Valerian nodded.

The table was precisely as it was when Sydney guided the sobbing Ondine away. No one had moved a thing while he helped Ondine undress, made her lie down and rubbed her feet until she slept. But he could not sleep at all. The sea spread around him and his wife. They were afloat in it and if removed from the island there was nowhere to land. They had no house, no place of their own. Some certificates worth a bit, but no savings. Just the promises of being taken care of in the will of a man whose wife his own wife had slapped. Sydney started to clear the table and stack things on the sideboard. The suspense was too great, so he asked him outright.

"Mr. Street."

Valerian showed him his evening eyes, but did not speak.

"You going to let us go?"

Valerian stared at Sydney trying to focus on, then comprehend, the question.

"What?"

"Me and Ondine. You going to let us go?"

Valerian rested his forehead in his hand. "I don't know. I don't know anything," he said, and Sydney had to be content for now with that answer spoken faintly, remotely, for Valerian, holding on to his head, fell back into the waxen horror Sydney had tried to penetrate. He

235

was still there at six the next morning. His eyes closed at last, his mind slowed to an occasional thud. He woke because nature required him to. Not to die or board an airplane headed for his son, but to go to the bathroom. So he did move from the table and he climbed the stairs on frail new legs. Once attending to that call, it was not unthinkable to attend to another—to rinse his face, clean his teeth, brush back his hair with his hands. He took off his shoes and sat on the bed holding them. The picture of the beautiful boy in the laundry under the sink, singing because he could not speak or cry—because he had no vocabulary for what was happening to him, who sang la la la, la la la instead—that picture had stayed with Valerian all night, through fitful sleep, and was there between his stockinged feet in the morning.

I have to cry about this, Valerian thought. I have got to shed tears about this. But not water, please God, may they be blood. I have to cry blood tears for his wounds. But I will need several lives, life after life after life after life, one for each wound, one for every trickle of blood, for every burn. I will need a lifetime of blood tears for each one of them. And then more. Lives upon lives upon lives for the the the the the. Hurt. The deep-down eternal little boy hurt. The not knowing when, the never knowing why, and never being able to shape the tongue to speak, let alone the mind to cogitate how the one person in the world upon whom he was totally, completely dependent—the one person he could not even choose not to love—could do that to him. Believing at last as a little boy would that he deserved it, must deserve it, otherwise it would not be happening to him. That no world in the world would be imagined, thought up, or even accidentally formed not to say say say say *created* that would permit such a thing to happen. And he is right. No world in the world would allow it. So this is not the world at all. It must be something else. I have lived in it and I will die out of it but it is not the world. This is not life. This is some other thing.

It comforted him a bit, knowing that whatever this was it was not life. He achieved a kind of blank, whited-out, no-feeling-at-all that he hoped would sustain him until the blood tears came. Until his heart, revivified, pumped its way along for a single purpose: to spill out of his eyes throughout the millennia he would have to live. Until then, then.

Margaret awoke very early that morning, having had the dream she ought to have had: it was unspeakable. She rose at once; the wonderful relief of public humiliation, the solid security of the pillory, were upon her. Like the much-sought-after, finally captured, strangler, she wore that look of harmony that in newspaper photos comes across as arrogance, or impenitence at the least. The harmony that comes from the relieved discovery that the jig is up. The parts settle back into their proper places, and the strangler sighs, "Thank God I didn't get away scot-free." She had no idea of what would be next, but that was not a problem to which she had to provide a solution. That was the future, her job at hand was to reveal the past. Right now she had to wash her hair, *hard*. Soap it with mountains of lather, and rinse it over and over again. Then she sat in the sun against every instruction ever given her about the care of her hair, and let it dry.

L'Arbe de la Croix became a house of shadows. Couples locked into each other or away from each other, the murmurings of whose hearts rivalled the dreaming daisy trees. Jadine and Son off together plotting. Sydney and Ondine walking on glass shards, afraid, angry, sullen. Snapping at one another one minute, soothing each other the next. Valerian stayed mostly in his room; the greenhouse remained untended, the mail unread. Silence pressed down on the dahlias and cyclamen — for there was no diet of music anymore. Sydney brought pieces of dinner to the table but no one was there. Jadine and Son foraged in the refrigerator — accomplices. Margaret appeared for breakfast coffee only. Sydney took trays of halfheartedly prepared sandwiches to Valerian's room and brought them back untouched.

Margaret told her husband in pieces. Little by little, she spooned it out to him a sip here a drop there. A fleeting sentence in mid-air as they passed on the stairs: "It was not as often as you think and there were long, long periods of happiness between us in between." But he had stepped inside his bedroom door. Another time she said, "Don't try to persuade yourself that I didn't love him. He was more important to me than my life. Than my life." She had to repeat the phrase for his back was receding fast. He never directed those gloaming eyes her way. She told him in bite-sized pieces, small enough for him to swallow quickly because she did not have the vocabulary to describe what she had come to know, remember. So there was no way or reason to describe those long quiet days when the sun was drained and nobody ever on the street. There were magazines, of course, to look forward to, but neither *Life* nor *Time* could fill a morning. It started on a day like that. Just once she did it, a slip, and then once more, and it became the thing to look forward to, to resist, to succumb to, to plan, to be horrified by, to forget, because out of the doing of it came the reason. And she was outraged by that infant needfulness. There were times when she absolutely had to limit its *being there*; stop its implicit and explicit demand for her best and constant self. She could not describe her loathing of its prodigious appetite for security—the criminal arrogance of an infant's conviction that while he slept, someone is there; that when he wakes, someone is there; that when he is hungry, food will somehow magically be provided. So she told him that part that was palatable: that she could not control herself—which was true, for when she felt hostage to that massive insolence, that stupid trust, she could not help piercing it.

Finally, Margaret entered his room one night and locked the door behind her.

238

"I've just spoken to Michael," she said.

Valerian could not believe it. She could call him? Speak to him? Say his name? Did she think it was business as usual?

"He said he sent two cables telling us he couldn't make it. Two. Neither one was telephoned to us. I asked him to call B. J. Bridges. Obviously we don't need any guests at New Year's."

Valerian was speechless. She was going to go on about it, chatting about things just as if nothing had happened. The blood had not dropped out of his eyes yet, so this still was not life. He could get through it because it was some other thing he was living.

"How dare you call him?" he asked hoarsely. "How do you dare?"

"He isn't damaged, Valerian. He *isn't*."

Valerian said nothing; he only stared at her. She was even lovelier now that her hair had no spray in it, that it was not tortured into Art Deco, now that it hung according to its own will and the shape of her head. And she wore no make-up. Little charming eyebrows instead of styled ones, and the thin top lip was much nicer than the full one she ritually painted.

"How can you know that? How can you know what is damage and what is not? If you don't know the difference between between between between." He stopped, he could not say it. "How do you know the difference between what is damaged and what is healed?"

"I know; I see him; I visit him. Believe me, he's fine. Finer than most."

They were both silent for a few moments and then Margaret said, "You want to ask me why. Don't. I can't answer that. I can tell you that I was more successful in keeping myself from doing it than not. When it did happen, it was out of my control. I thought at first it was because he was crying or wouldn't sleep. But then sometimes it was in order to make him cry, or to wake him from sleep."

239

"I can't hear this, Margaret."

"You can. I have *done* it, lived with it. You can hear it."

She seemed strong to him. He was wasting away, filed to nothing by grief, and she was strong, stronger. Talking about it as though it were a case history, an operation, some surgery that had been performed on her that she had survived and she was describing it to him.

"You are disgusting. You are are are are monstrous. You did it because you are monstrous."

"I did it because I could, Valerian, and I stopped doing it or wanting to do it when I couldn't."

"*Couldn't?*"

"Yes, couldn't. When he was too big, when he could do it back, when he could . . . tell."

"Leave me."

"He's fine, I'm telling you. He's all right."

"Please leave me."

She understood, understood completely, and without another word she unlocked the door and left.

Another time she waited for him at the breakfast table and said, "You are angry because he didn't tell you."

"Why didn't he tell me?" Valerian had not thought of that yet; he had been living with just the picture of the boy under the sink and had only been hearing the la la la, la la la, but now he realized that was part of his anger. "Why didn't he tell me?"

"He was probably too ashamed."

"Oh, God."

"I think he is still ashamed."

Valerian's hands were shuddering again. "Why does he love you?" he asked her over his shuddering fingers. "Why does he love *you*?"

"Because I love him."

Valerian shook his head and asked her a third time, "Why does he love you?"

"He knows I love him," she said, "that I couldn't help it."

240

Valerian shouted then, at the top of his throat, "Why does he love you?"

Margaret closed her blue-if-it's-a-boy blue eyes. "I don't know."

Now the tears came. Not all at once. Not in the rush of blood he anticipated, longed for; rather a twilight glimmer, a little mercury in the eyes that grew brighter and brighter. That was the beginning and he knew there would be more of them. For now he would settle for this bright burning.

Margaret opened her eyes and looked into his. "Hit me," she said softly. "Hit me, Valerian."

His shuddering fingers went wild at the thought of touching her, making physical contact with that skin. His whole body recoiled. "No," he said. "No."

"Please. Please."

"*No.*"

"You have to. Please, you have to."

Now he could see the lines, the ones the make-up had shielded brilliantly. A thread here and there and the roots of her hair were markedly different from the rest. She looked real. Not like a piece of Valerian candy, but like a person on a bus, already formed, fleshed, thick with a life which is not yours and not accessible to you.

"Tomorrow," he said. "Perhaps tomorrow."

Every day she asked him, every day he answered, "Tomorrow, perhaps tomorrow." But he never did and she was hard-pressed to think of a way to ease their mutual sorrow.


ON THE FIRST DAY of the year, Margaret pushed open the kitchen door. Ondine was there as she always was; the braids Margaret had snatched were folded quietly now across her head. Margaret, having had the dream she ought to, felt clean, weightless as she walked through the doors and stood at the oak table. Ondine was napping, her head resting on the back of a chair, her feet resting

241

on another. When she heard the grunt of the door hinges, she woke at once and stood up, alert.

"No, no. Sit back down, Ondine."

Ondine shoved her feet into her moccasins and continued to stand. "Can I get you something?" she asked out of habit and out of a need to do what was wanted of her and get the woman out of the kitchen.

"No. No, thank you." Margaret sat down and did not seem disturbed by the painful silence Ondine was keeping after the refusal. She looked past the black woman's silhouette to a place in the shutters where the sky showed through.

"I knew you knew," she said. "I always knew you knew."

Ondine sat down without answering.

"You loved my son, didn't you?" It was more a statement than a question.

"I love anything small that needs it," said Ondine.

"I suppose I should thank you for not saying anything, but I have to tell you that it would have been better, Ondine, if you had. It's terrible living in the same house with your own witness. But I think I understand it. You wanted me to hate you, didn't you? That's why you never said anything all those years. You wanted me to hate you."

"No, I didn't. You . . . you wasn't a whole lot on my mind."

"Oh, yes I was, and you felt good hating me, didn't you? I could be the mean white lady and you could be the good coloured one. Did that make it easier for you?"

Ondine did not answer.

"Anyway, I came in here to tell you that I'm sorry."

Ondine sighed. "Me too."

"We could have been friends, Ondine. Like at first when I used to come in your kitchen and eat your food and we laughed all the time. Didn't we, Ondine? Didn't we use to laugh and laugh. Didn't we? I have it right, don't I?"

"You got it right."

"But you wanted to hate me, so you didn't tell."

"There was nobody to tell. It was woman stuff. I couldn't tell your husband and I couldn't tell mine."

"Why didn't you tell me? I mean why didn't you scream at me, stop me, something. You knew and you never said a word."

"I guess I thought you would let us go. If I told Sydney he might tell Mr. Street and then we'd be out of a job—a good job. I don't know now what I thought, to tell the truth. But once I started keeping it—then it was like my secret too. Sometimes I thought if you all let me go there won't be anyone around to take the edge off it. I didn't want to leave him there, all by himself."

"You should have stopped me."

"You should have stopped yourself."

"I did. I did stop myself after a while, but you could have stopped me right away, Ondine."

Ondine put the heels of her hands on her eyelids. When she removed them, her eyes were red. She blew out a breath and she was old. "Is that my job too? To stop you?"

"No. It's not your job, Ondine. But I wish it had been your duty. I wish you had liked me enough to help me. I was only nineteen. You were—what—thirty? Thirty-five?"

Ondine tilted her head and looked at her employer sideways. She raised her eyebrows slowly and then squinted. It was as though she saw Margaret for the first time. She shook her head back and forth back and forth in wonder. "No," she said. "I wasn't thirty-five. I was twenty-three. A girl. Just like you."

Margaret put her forehead into her palm. The roots of her sunset hair were brown. She held her head that way for a moment and said, "You have to forgive me for that, Ondine. You have to."

"You forgive you. Don't ask for more."

"You know what, Ondine? You know what? I want to

be a wonderful, wonderful old lady." Margaret laughed a rusty little bark that came from a place seldom used. "Ondine? Let's be wonderful old ladies. You and me."

"Huh," said Ondine, but she smiled a little.

"We're both childless now, Ondine. And we're both stuck here. We should be friends. It's not too late."

Ondine looked out of the window and did not answer.

"Is it too late, Ondine?"

"Almost," she said. "Almost."


AT SOME POINT in life the world's beauty becomes enough. You don't need to photograph, paint or even remember it. It is enough. No record of it needs to be kept and you don't need someone to share it with or tell it to. When that happens—that letting go—you let go because you can. The world will always be there—while you sleep it will be there—when you wake it will be there as well. So you can sleep and there is reason to wake. A dead hydrangea is as intricate and lovely as one in bloom. Bleak sky is as seductive as sunshine, miniature orange trees without blossom or fruit are not defective; they are that. So the windows of the greenhouse can be opened and the weather let in. The latch on the door can be left unhooked, the muslin removed, for the soldier ants are beautiful too and whatever they do will be part of it.

Valerian began going back to his greenhouse. Not as early as before; now he waited until after the breakfast rain. He was still telling Margaret, "Tomorrow. Perhaps tomorrow." But he did not change anything in there. Didn't sow or clip or transpose. Things grew or died where and how they pleased. Isle des Chevaliers filled in the spaces that had been the island's to begin with.

He thought about innocence there in his greenhouse and knew that he was guilty of it because he had lived with a woman who had made something kneel down in him the first time he saw her, but about whom he knew nothing; had watched his son grow and talk but also

244

about whom he had known nothing. And there was something so foul in that, something in the crime of innocence so revolting it paralysed him. He had not known because he had not taken the trouble to know. He was satisfied with what he did know. Knowing more was inconvenient and frightening. Like a bucket of water with no bottom. If you know how to tread, bottomlessness need not concern you. Margaret knew the bottomlessness—she had looked at it, dived in it and pulled herself out—obviously tougher than he. What an awful thing she had done. And how much more awful not to have known it. Which was all he could say in his defence: that he did not know; that the postman passed him by. Perhaps that was why he had never received the message he'd been waiting for: his innocence made him unworthy of it. The instinct of kings was always to slay the messenger, and they were right. A real messenger, a worthy one, is corrupted by the message he brings. And if he is noble he should accept that corruption. Valerian had received no message, but after waiting so long, to receive, know and deliver its contents, imperceptibly he had made it up. Made up the information he was waiting for. Pre-occupied himself with the construction of the world and its inhabitants according to this imagined message. But had chosen not to know the real message that his son had mailed to him from underneath the sink. And all he could say was that he did not know. He was guilty, therefore, of innocence. Was there anything so loathsome as a wilfully innocent man? Hardly. An innocent man is a sin before God. Inhuman and therefore unworthy. No man should live without absorbing the sins of his kind, the foul air of his innocence, even if it did wilt rows of angel trumpets and cause them to fall from their vines.

245

# 9

"THIS IS a town?" Jadine shouted. "It looks like a block. A city block. In Queens."

"Hush up," he said squeezing her waist. "This is not only a town, it's the county seat. We call it the city."

"This is Eloe?"

"No. This is Poncie. Eloe is a little town. We got fourteen miles to go yet."

Now she understood why he wanted to rent a car and drive to Florida. There was no way to fly to Eloe. They had to go to Tallahassee or Pensacola, then get a bus or train to Poncie, *then* bum a ride to Eloe for no buses went out there, and as for taxis—well, he doubted if either one would take them. Bumming a ride didn't seem to be a problem in his mind. Her luggage held all he had and when they got off the bus she saw eight or ten black men lounging there in front of the depot, as Son called it. Son talked to one of them for at least five minutes. They waited another thirty minutes at the candy machine until a black man named Carl appeared driving a four-door Plymouth.

He drove them to Eloe asking pointed questions all the way. Son said he was an army buddy of a man named Soldier—that they were out of Brewton on their way to Gainesville. Thought he'd look in on old Soldier, he said. Carl said he knew of Soldier but had never met him. He had never seen a cashmere sweater with a cowl neckline, or Chacrel boots, and didn't know they could make jeans that tight or if they did who but a child would wear them since no honest work could be done in them. So he looked in the rear-view mirror with disbelief. Nobody dressed like that in Brewton, Alabama, and he suspected they didn't in Montgomery either.

He followed Son's directions and dropped them off in front of a house Jadine supposed was in Eloe since Son paid the man and got out.

"Where are the ninety houses? I see four," asked Jadine, looking around.

"They're here."

"Where?"

"Spread out. Folks don't live all crunched up together in Eloe. Come on, girl." He picked up the luggage and, grinning like a groom, led her up the steps. A frame door was open to the still March morning. They both stood in front of a screen door through which they could see a man sitting at a table with his back to them. Son didn't knock or move, he simply looked at the back of the man's head. Slowly the man turned his head and stared at them. Then he got up from the table. Son opened the screen door and stepped in with Jadine just behind him. He didn't move closer to the man; he just stopped and smiled. The man did not speak and did not smile; he kept on staring. Then he raised his hands, clenching them into fists, and began to jump up and down on both feet, stamping the floor like a kid jumping rope. Son was laughing soundlessly. A woman ran in, but the man kept on jumping—pounding the floor. The woman looked at Son and Jadine with a little confused smile. The man jumped higher and faster. Son kept watching and laughing. The man was still jumping rope, but not smiling or laughing as Son was. Finally when the stamping shook a lamp to the table's edge and a window banged down, and the children were peering in the doorway, the man shouted at the top of his lungs Son! Son! Son! to the beat of his crazy feet, and kept on until Son grabbed his head and pressed it into his chest. "It's me, Soldier. It's me."

Soldier wrenched away, looked him in the face, then ran to the back window. "Wahoo! Wahoo!" he shouted, and came back to march four-step around the room.

Two men came to the front door and looked in at the marcher and then at the visitors.

"Soldier's clownin'," said the woman.

"Soldier's clownin'," said the children.

"Good God a' mighty, that's Son," whispered one of the men. And then it stopped. Son and Soldier hit each other on the head, the hands, the shoulders.

"Who bought you them skinny shoes?"

"Where's your hair, nigger?"

HE ASKED HER if she would mind staying at Soldier's house with his wife, Ellen, while he went to see his father. Jadine demurred; she had run out of conversation with Ellen ten minutes after it started, but Son urged her, saying he had not seen Old Man in eight years and that he didn't want to bring someone his father didn't know into his house the first time they met in all that time. Could she understand that? She said yes, out in Soldier's yard near the mimosa, but she didn't understand at all, no more than she understood the language he was using when he talked to Soldier and Drake and Ellen and the others who stopped by; no more than she could understand (or accept) her being shunted off with Ellen and the children while the men grouped on the porch and, after a greeting, ignored her; or why he seemed so shocked and grateful at the same time by news that some woman named Brown, Sarah or Sally or Sadie—from the way they pronounced it she couldn't tell—was dead. But she agreed. God. Eloe.

He left her there and walked alone to the house he was born in. The yellow brick front looked tiny. It had seemed so large and sturdy compared to the Sutterfield shack he and Cheyenne had—the one he drove a car through. It wasn't as big as Ondine's kitchen. The door was unlocked, but no one was home. In the kitchen a pepper pot was simmering, so he knew Old Man wasn't far and wouldn't be long. His father, Franklin G. Green, had been called Old Man since he was seven years old and when he grew up, got married, had a baby boy, the baby was called Old Man's son until the second child was born and the first became simply Son. They all used to be here—all of them. Horace who lived in Gainesville, Frank G. who died in Korea, his sister Francine who was in a mental home in Jacksonville, and the baby girl Porky Green who still lived in Eloe, so Soldier said, but went to Florida A and M on a track scholarship. They had all been in this house together at one time—with his mother.

Only a few minutes had passed when Old Man climbed the porch steps. Son waited, standing in the middle of the room. The door opened, Old Man looked at Son and dropped his onions on the floor.

"Hey, Old Man, how you been doing?"

"Save me, you got back."

They didn't touch. They didn't know how. They fooled around with the onions and each asked the other about his condition until Old Man said, "Come on in here and let me fix you something to eat. Not much in here but it ain't like I had notice."

"I ate something over to Soldier's."

"You was over there?"

"I wanted to hear about you before I came by," said Son.

"Oh, I ain't dead, Son. I ain't dead," he chuckled.

"I see you ain't."

"Them money orders sure helped."

"You got them?"

"Oh, yeah. Every one. I had to use some of em though."

"*Some* of em? They were all for you. Why didn't you use them all?"

"I couldn't do that. I didn't want to raise no suspicions. I just cashed a few when I couldn't help it."

"Shit, Old Man, don't tell me you still got some?"

"They in there." He nodded toward one of the two bedrooms. "Porky in school, you know. I had to help her out, too."

They went in the bedroom and Old Man took a White Owl cigar box from under his bed and opened it. There was a thin pile of envelopes bound by a rubber band; some postal money orders held together with a paper clip, and a few ten and twenty dollar bills. Eight years of envelopes.

"These were for you, Old Man. To take care of you."

"They did. They did. But you know I didn't want to be going over there to the Post Office every month, cashin em. Might set folks to talkin and turn the law out on account of that other business. So I just took a few in every now and then. Quiet, you know."

"Old Man, you one crazy old man."

"You been to Sutterfield yet?"

"No. Straight here."

"Well, you know Sally Brown died here a while back."

"They told me."

"Be at peace."

"Hope so."

"She slept with a shotgun every night."

"Huh."

"Every night. Well, she burnin up down there now, her and her nasty daughter . . ."

"Don't say it, Old Man."

"Yeah. You right. Shouldn't rile the dead. But you know I was more scared of Sally than the law."

"So was I."

"Law don't care about no dead coloured gal, but Sally Brown, she slept with that shotgun every night waitin for you. Made my skin crinkle to walk past her. And she just about lived in church moanin. Stopped me from vespers altogether. I couldn't sit there listenin to her berate you. Can you feature that? Pray every Sunday and hold on to a shotgun every night?"

"Where's the boy?"

"Gone away from here, his folks too."

"He get his eyebrows back?"

"Never did. Guess his folks figured he couldn't hide

nowhere around here lookin like that. Sally was lookin for him too."

"I didn't see his face. All I saw was his asshole."

"That didn't have no eyebrows either I bet."

"I should have made him some with a razor." They laughed together then and an hour or so passed while Son told what all he'd been doing for the last eight years. It was almost four when Son said, "I didn't come by myself."

"You with a woman?"

"Yeah."

"Where is she?"

"Over to Soldier's. Can she stay here?"

"You all married?"

"No, Old Man."

"Better take her to your Aunt Rosa's then."

"She won't like that."

"I can't help it. You be gone. I have to live here."

"Come on, Old Man."

"Uh-uh. Go see your Aunt Rosa. She be mad anyway you don't stop by."

"Scripture don't say anything about two single people sleeping under the same roof." Son was laughing.

"What you know bout Scripture?"

"I could have lied and said we were married."

"But you didn't lie. You told the truth and so you got to live by the truth."

"Oh, shit."

"That's right. Shit. She's welcome in my house all day in the day. Bring her back so I can meet her."

"She's special, Old Man."

"So am I, Son. So am I."

"All right. All right. I'll go get her and bring her by. Cook up something, then I'll take her by Aunt Rosa. That suit you?"

"Suit me fine."

Son stood up to go, and his father walked him to the door. When Son said, "Be right back," Old Man said,

251

"Wait a minute. Can I ask you somethin?"

"Sure. Ask it."

"How come you never put no note or nothin in them envelopes? I kept on lookin for a note."

Son stopped. How hurried all those money order purchases had been. Most of the time he sent a woman out to both buy and mail them. He'd done it as often as he could and sometimes five would be sent from one city and none from any place for six months. How hurried he had been.

"I guess I didn't want nobody to read em and know where I was . . ." But it was too lame an excuse to continue with. "Is that why you kept the empty envelopes too?"

"Yeah. They had your handwritin on em, you know. You wrote it, that part anyway. 'Franklin Green.' You got a nice handwritin. Pretty. Like your mama."

"See you, Old Man."

"Go by Rosa. Tell her you comin."

JADINE was squatting down in the middle of the road, the afternoon sun at her back. The children were happy to pose, and so were some of the younger women. Only the old folks refused to smile and glared into her camera as though looking at hell with the lid off. The men were enjoying the crease in her behind so clearly defined in the sunlight, click, click. Jadine had remembered her camera just before she thought she would go nuts, trying to keep a conversation going with Ellen and the neighbour women who came in to see Son's Northern girl. They looked at her with outright admiration, each one saying, "I was in Baltimore once," or, "My cousin she live in New York." They did not ask her what they really wanted to know: where did she know Son from and how much did her boots cost. Jadine smiled, drank glasses of water and tried to talk "down home" like Ondine. But their worshipful stares and nonconversation made Son's

252

absence seem much too long. She was getting annoyed when she remembered her camera. Now she was having a ball photographing everybody. Soldier's yard was full. "Beautiful," she said. "Fantastic. Now over here," click click. "Hey, what'd you say your name was? Okay, Beatrice, could you lean up against the tree?" click, click. "This way. Beautiful. Hold it. Hooooold it. Heaven," click click click click.

Son didn't mean to snatch it. Just to end it somehow. Stop the crease, the sunlight, the click click click. And when he did she looked at him with confusion at first, then with evolved anger. "What's the matter with you?"

It wasn't nice. To snatch the camera and then to have to tell her about the sleeping arrangements—it wasn't nice. Not nice at all.

He took her to Old Man's, and after supper there to Rosa's. Drake and Soldier picked them up and drove them to a joint in Poncie called Night Moves, where there was live music, Bar B Que sandwiches and unrestrained dancing under four blue lights that neither flashed or strobed. They even managed some snatch in the car—Jadine under the impression that nobody knew; he aware that everybody did. The back seat turned her volume up, but the beer and the bad whiskey made her so sleepy there was no problem when he left her at Rosa's. She slept like a boulder for three hours, then woke missing him and suffocating in that little bedroom without windows. She sat up naked, for she never wore nightgowns, and held her shoulders. The room had a door to the living room and one that opened to the back yard. She opened the latter and looked out into the blackest nothing she had ever seen. Blacker and bleaker than Isle des Chevaliers, and loud. Loud with the presence of plants and field life. If she was wanting air, there wasn't any. It's not possible, she thought, for anything to be this black. Maybe if she stood there long enough light would come from somewhere, and she could see shadows, the outline of something, a bush, a tree, a

253

line between earth and sky, a heavier darkness to show where this very house stopped and space began. She remembered the blackness she saw when Son told her to close her eyes, and to put a star in it. That would be the only way it would get there, she thought, for the world in the direction of the sky, in that place where the sky ought to be, was starless. Haze, she guessed; there must be haze in the sky. Otherwise there would be a moon, at the least. The loudness of the plants was not audible, but it was strong none the less. She might as well have been in a cave, a grave, the dark womb of the earth, suffocating with the sound of plant life moving, but deprived of its sight. She could see nothing and could not remember what she had seen when it was daylight. A movement behind made her jump and turn around. Rosa was standing in the inner doorway, lit from behind by a lamp.

"Anything the matter? I heard you moving around."

Jadine closed the back door. The lamplight from the other door was weak but it was healthy enough to spotlight her nakedness. Rosa gazed down Jadine's body with a small bowing of her head, and then up again. Her eyes travelled slowly, moving like one of those growing plants Jadine could not see, but whose presence was cracking loud.

"Why didn't you tell me you didn't have no nightclothes. I got somethin I can let you have," Rosa said.

"I . . . I forgot," said Jadine. "I forgot to bring anything."

"I'll get you something."

When Rosa came back, Jadine was in the bed. Rosa handed her a kind of slip, wrinkled but clean-smelling.

"You all right, daughter?"

"Oh, I'm fine. I just got too warm and wanted some air," Jadine answered.

"This used to be a porch. I made it into a extra room, but it does heat up. I didn't feel like buyin no windows."

"Can you leave the back door open?" asked Jadine.

"I wouldn't advise it. Anything at all might come in

here out of those trees. I got a little old electric fan I'll get you."

"No. No. Don't bother."

"You sure?"

"Yes."

"It's beat up, but it stirs the air around."

"It's okay."

"Well, I'll leave this here door open." Rosa propped a wooden slatback chair against the inner door. "Sorry," she said. "That gown ain't much, but it'll cover you."

"Thanks," said Jadine, but it didn't cover her. She lay down in the slip under the sheet and her nakedness before Rosa lay down with her. No man had made her feel that naked, that unclothed. Leerers, lovers, doctors, artists—none of them had made her feel exposed. More than exposed. Obscene.

God. Eloe.

They were leaving Sunday. Surely she could get through a Sunday and then she and Son would be back on the train holding hands, and then on the airplane playing with each other under the Delta Airlines blanket—their faces serene as passengers, their hands devious and directed. She fell asleep on that thought and woke at ten-thirty with Rosa's fingertips tapping her on the shoulder.

"Son's in there," she said. "You all goin to eat with me, ain't you?"

Jadine got up and dressed quickly. He was sitting at the table looking more beautiful than after the first haircut on Isle des Chevaliers, more beautiful than when he stood at the piano with his coat over his shoulder and she saw savannas in his face, more beautiful than on the beach when he touched her foot, than when he opened the door to his room at the Hilton. She wanted to sit in his lap, but Drake and Soldier were at the table too, so she just walked over and put her hand on his head. He smiled up at her and kissed the palm of her other hand. Drake and Soldier looked bathed and glittery. They beamed at Son

255

with the same adoration she did, but they didn't compete. They sat back and enjoyed his presence and his prize woman. They looked at him with love and looked at her like she was a Cadillac he had won, or stolen, or even bought for all they knew.

"YOU ALL gettin hitched?" Soldier asked. They were alone in the house while Son and Drake drove Rosa to church.

"I guess so," Jadine answered. "We haven't talked about it."

"He's good. You ought to snatch him."

She laughed. "Should I?"

"Damn right. You don't, somebody else sure will. He was married before, you know."

"I know."

"Never should have married that woman. That Cheyenne. Every one of us told him that, or tried to. But he did it anyway to his grief and sorrow."

"Was she pretty?" asked Jadine. She didn't want to ask it, but it seemed extremely important to know the answer.

"Naw. I wouldn't say pretty. Not bad-lookin, mind, but nothing like pretty."

"He must have loved her, though."

"That could be what it was." Soldier sounded as though there were some doubts. "Naw," he said. "She wasn't pretty, but you had to hand it to her though. She had the best pussy in Florida, the absolute best," and he turned his eyes on Jadine as if to say Now top that!

It wasn't nice. Not nice at all. Son embarrassed her in the road with the camera; Rosa made her feel like a slut; and now Soldier was trying to make her feel like a virgin competing with . . . She didn't answer him so he went on.

"You ever been married?"

"No," she said, and looked squarely in his face

256

thinking, if he says "Good-lookin woman like you ought to be able . . ." she would smack him in the mouth. But all he said was "Too bad", and that didn't seem definite enough to break his face for.

"Any children?"

"You ask too many questions," she said. "Anything you want to know about me ask Son."

Soldier smiled at that and shook his head. "Son don't talk about his women and don't let nobody else talk about em either."

"I'm glad of that," she said.

"I ain't. Keeps him dumb. He wouldn't know a good woman from a snake and he won't let nobody point out the difference."

"Can he tell the difference between a good man and a snake?"

"Oh, yeah. Son knows people. He just gets confused when it comes to women. With most everything else he thinks with his heart. But when it comes to women he thinks with his dick, you know what I mean?"

"Some people think with their mouths."

"Yeah. I guess you right about that." Soldier smiled. "But maybe it's better'n not thinkin at all."

"How would *you* know?" she asked him.

He laughed. "You a hot one, ain't you?"

"Yes, I'm a hot one."

"Yeah." He ran his fingers over the place on his head where his hair was thinning. "A hot one all right and a live one too."

"Believe it." She got up to pour herself more coffee.

Soldier scanned her hips. "Can I ask you somethin?"

"What?"

"Who's controllin it?"

"Controlling what?"

"The thing. The thing between you two. Who's in control?"

"Nobody. We're together. Nobody controls anybody," she said.

257

"Good," he said. "That's real good. Son, he don't like control. Makes him, you know wildlike."

"We don't have that kind of relationship. I don't like to be controlled either."

"But you like to have it, don't you?"

"Not with him."

"Good. Good."

"Did Cheyenne have control?" She sat down and stirred air into her coffee.

"Cheyenne? Naw. She didn't control nothin. At least not during the day. But good God she sure did run the nights." He laughed and then, since she did not join in, he sobered quickly and asked, "How long you all plannin to stay around?"

Jadine repressed a smile. He'd lost, and wanted her out of town. "We're leaving today."

"Today? You can't leave today."

"Why not?"

"Ernie Paul is coming. We called him up. He left from Montgomery already, be here Monday." Soldier was alarmed.

"Who's Ernie Paul?"

"He's one of us. Grew up with Son and Drake and me. He takin off work to come down and see Son and all of us."

TKO, thought Jadine, but she didn't hang up her gloves. When Son got back she showed him the train schedule.

"One more night, baby," he said.

"I can't. Not in that room. Not alone."

"Come on."

"No, Son. Not unless you stay with me."

"I can't do that."

"Then I'm leaving. I'm long past fourteen."

"Okay. Look. After church, when Rosa gets back, we'll go for a ride."

"Son."

"Listen now. Let me show you this county. Bring your

258

camera. Then tonight you go back to Rosa's . . ."

"Son."

"Wait. Leave the back door open. I'll come in and stay with you all night. And in the morning I'll go round the front like I just got there."

"You promise."

"I promise."

Palaeolithic, she thought. I am stuck here with a pack of Neanderthals who think sex is dirty or strange or something and he is standing here almost thirty years old doing it too. Stupid. "Stupid," she said aloud.

"I know, but that's the way they are. What do you want me to do? You think anything we do is going to change them?"

"I want us to be honest."

"Can't we be gentle first, and honest later?"

Accommodating beyond all belief. Because it was his hometown and his people, she supposed. She photographed everything during the ride until she was out of film. They found sheds and orchards to make love in and an open window of a schoolhouse with a teacher's desk wide enough for two. They got back to Eloe at eight and stayed out as late as they could—when Night Moves closed—then gave everybody a ride home. When Jadine got to Rosa's she put on the wrinkled slip to amuse him when he returned, unlatched the door and got in the bed. Half an hour later he was there. She had been listening carefully so she heard the swing of the door.

"Son?"

"Yeah."

"Hurry up."

He hurried. Something was in his hand as he knelt by the bed, leaves or fern or something. He made her take the slip off and he brushed her all over with the fern and she tried not to moan or laugh or cry out while he was saying Sssh, sssh. He undressed and climbed in. Jadine opened her arms to this man accustomed to the best pussy in Florida. It must have been that thought, put

259

there by Soldier, that made her competitive, made her struggle to outdo Cheyenne and surpass her legendary gifts. She was thinking of her, whipped on by her, and that, perhaps, plus the fact that she had left the door unlatched and Son had opened it on its hinges and after it was open on its hinges it stayed wide open but they had not noticed because they were paying attention only to each other so that must have been why and how Cheyenne got in, and then the rest: Rosa and Thérèse and Son's dead mother and Sally Sarah Sadie Brown and Ondine and Soldier's wife Ellen and Francine from the mental institution and her own dead mother and even the woman in yellow. All there crowding into the room. Some of them she did not know, recognize, but they were all there spoiling her love-making, taking away her sex like succubi, but not his. He fell asleep and didn't see the women in the room and she didn't either but they were there crowding each other and watching her. Pushing each other—nudging for space, they poured out of the dark like ants out of a hive. She shook Son and he woke saying "Huh?" and she said "Shouldn't you close the door" because she didn't want to say there are women in the room; I can't see them, but this room is full of women. He said, "Yeah," and went back to sleep. She just lay there, too frightened to do it herself for then she would have to walk through the crowd of women standing in the pitch-dark room whom she could not see but would have to touch to get through them. And she felt them nudging each other for a better look at her, until finally being frightened was worse then anything they could do to her so she got mad and sat up. Her voice was half as loud as her heart.

"What do you want with me, goddamn it!"

They looked as though they had just been waiting for that question and they each pulled out a breast and showed it to her. Jadine started to tremble. They stood around in the room, jostling each other gently, gently—there wasn't much room—revealing one breast

260

and then two and Jadine was shocked. This was not the dream of hats for in that she was asleep, her eyes closed. Here she was wide-awake, but in total darkness looking at her own mother for God's sake and *Nan*adine!

"I have breasts too," she said or thought or willed, "I have breasts too." But they didn't believe her. They just held their own higher and pushed their own farther out and looked at her. All of them revealing both their breasts except the woman in yellow. She did something more shocking—she stretched out a long arm and showed Jadine her three big eggs. It scared her so, she began to cry. Her back pressed hard, hard into the wall, her right hand in a ball over her stomach, she shook Son and shook him some more. When he stirred and woke she slammed her face into his shoulder crying.

"What is it? What's going on?"

"Tell them to leave me alone."

"What?"

"Hold me."

"Jadine."

"Shut the door. No, don't move. Hold me."

"Those hats again?"

"No."

"What?"

"*Hold* me."

And he did. Till morning. Even while he slept and she didn't and the women finally went away—sighing—he did not let her go.

Nobody was fooled by that little charade. Old Man guessed, the men knew and Rosa heard them as clear as the radio.

She couldn't shake it. Not because Rosa fried eggs in the morning, or even the camera business or Soldier's big mouth or Old Man's phony biblical conversation, or the wrinkled slip and the stuffy room, but the possibility of more plant sounds in the cave and the certainty of the night women kept her nervous. She couldn't shake it. The women in the night had killed the whole weekend.

Eloe was rotten and more boring than ever. A burnt-out place. There was no life there. Maybe a past but definitely no future and finally there was no interest. All that Southern small-town country romanticism was a lie, a joke, kept secret by people who could not function elsewhere. An excuse to fish. Ernie Paul could come to New York—faster, even, if he flew. She needed air, and taxicabs and conversation in a language she understood. She didn't want to have any more discussions in which the silences meant more than the words did. And no, she didn't want to party at Night Moves, Son, please, get me out of here. You know I have things to do. Take me back, or I'll go back and you stay, or go. But Son, I'm not spending another night here.

"I'll come to you again tonight."

"It doesn't help."

"We'll stay out all night."

"No. Just get me to the train on time."

Son closed the eyes inside his eyes to her for a minute—the way he had in the bedroom when he had come in without knocking—closed them without shutting them. She was making him choose. But he opened them again and asked her, "You love me?"

"I love you," she said.

"Will you be there when I get there?"

"I'll be there. Of course I'll be there. Waiting."

"Ernie Paul has a car. I'll go back to Montgomery with him tomorrow and fly from there to New York."

"Okay. No longer?"

"No longer."

"I love you."

"I love you."

They got to the train on time, but he didn't get to New York on time. Four days passed and he still had not come. Jadine was not disturbed—there was so much to do, errands, and lunches, and hair appointments and jobs. She had to call Dawn to see if she was coming back as planned. Did she have to find another place? On the fifth day, she was feeling orphaned again. He could have called. She imagined him carousing with Ernie Paul and Soldier. Then another weekend rolled by and still no Son. Apparently he knew how to call Ernie Paul but not how to call her. She thought of calling Eloe; there was a telephone in Night Moves, but she couldn't remember whether she'd seen one in any of the houses. Now she was biting mad. At his carelessness, his indifference. Then she got desperate. In her heart she knew he would come, sometime, and that he would have either a good excuse or no excuse at all; but she knew that he would come. The desperation came from the sense she had of his being down there with all those women with their breasts and eggs, the bitches. All the women in his life and in hers were down there—well, not *all* the women in her life. Dawn wasn't there, and neither was Aisha, or Felicité, or Betty. They wouldn't have done that to her anyway. They were her friends. They were like her. Not like old Cheyenne with the statewide pussy, or Rosa with the witness eyes, or Nanadine with the tight-fisted braids looking sorrowful at the kitchen table and accusatory in that room. And not like Francine attacked by dogs and driven crazy, or even like her own mother how could you Mama how could you be with them. You left me you died you didn't care enough about me to stay alive you knew Daddy was gone and you went too. But she had re-run that movie so many times its zazz was gone leaving only technique to admire. Of course her mother was with them, showing her boobs; of course she would be there. But what made them think they could all get together to do that to her? They didn't even know each other. What did they have in common even, besides the breasts. She had breasts; so did Dawn, and Aisha and Felicité and Betty. But she couldn't shake it and it kept her angry and the anger was good for the photographers and the agency and the telephone company and the apartment managers. Everybody took notice and got out of the way.

Dawn said May 15, she would be back then. Jadine

263

asked around about another sublet, and found two—one a house for one month, June; another an apartment for six months, but it was way uptown. Then a loft she could share for two weeks and keep for the summer. . . . Every night she went to bed too exhausted to worry, only on waking did it come back—fresher each time, heavier, till finally she sat with a glass of grapefruit juice in her hand in the morning and since she could not shake it, she decided to reel it in. Cut off its head, slice it open and see what lay in its belly. The women had looked awful to her: onion heels, potbellies, hair surrendered to rags and braids. And the breasts they thrust at her like weapons were soft, loose bags closed at the tip with a brunette eye. Then the slithery black arm of the woman in yellow, stretching twelve feet, fifteen, toward her and the fingers that fingered eggs. It hurt, and part of the hurt was in having the vision at all—at being the helpless victim of a dream that chose you. Some was the frontal sorrow of being publicly humiliated by those you had loved or thought kindly toward. A little bitty hurt that was always gleaming when you looked at it. So you covered it over with a lid until the next time. But most of the hurt was dread. The night women were not merely against her (and her alone—not him), not merely looking superior over their sagging breasts and folded stomachs, they seemed somehow in agreement with each other about her, and were all out to get her, tie her, bind her. Grab the person she had worked hard to become and choke it off with their soft loose tits.

Jadine sipped the grapefruit juice. Its clean, light acid dissolved the morning cloud from her tongue. "No, Rosa. I am not your daughter, and he is not your son."

WHEN SON got back, she fought him. In between the sweet times— she fought him. He thought she was fighting him about Ernie Paul and being late and not calling. She thought so too, part of the time—but most of the time she knew she was fighting the night women. The mamas who had seduced him and were trying to lay claim to her. It would be the fight of their lives to get away from that coven that had nothing to show but breasts.

He needed a job, a degree, she said. They should go in business for themselves. He should enrol in business school. He had two semesters of Florida A and M, maybe he could pass the LSAT; he should take the SAT the GRE the CEE. "You can go to law school," she said.

"I don't want to be a lawyer," he said.

"Why?" she asked.

"Think," he said.

"Why?"

"Think."

"Why?"

"I can't hassle nobody that looks like me, or you either."

"Oh, shit. There's other kinds of law."

"No, there isn't. Besides I don't want to know *their* laws; I want to know mine."

"You don't *have* any."

"Then that's the problem with it."

She fought him, but she never mentioned the night women. They fought instead about Valerian Street. He would lend them the money to open a shop or start an agency.

Son said, "No way and I am not about to sit here and argue about that white man."

"Who cares what colour he is?"

"I care. And he cares. He cares what colour he is."

"He's a person, not a white man. He put me through school."

"You have told me that a million times. Why *not* educate you? You did what you were told, didn't you? Ondine and Sydney were obedient, weren't they? White people love obedience—love it! Did he do anything hard for you? Did he give up anything important for you?"

"He wasn't required to. But maybe he would have since

he was not *required* to educate me."

"That was toilet paper, Jadine. He *should* have wiped his ass after he shit all over your uncle and aunt. He *was* required to; he still is. His debt is big, woman. He can't never pay it off!"

"He educated me!" Jadine was shouting, "and you can't make me think that was not an important thing to do. Because nobody else did! No. Body. Else. Did. *You* didn't!"

"What do you mean, *I* didn't?"

"I mean you *didn't! You didn't!*" She slapped him and before he could turn his head back she was choking him with both hands around his neck, screaming all the while, "*You* didn't *you* didn't." He pulled her hair until she let go and when she tried another blow, he dropped her as carefully as he could. She fell back on her behind, turned over and crawled on all fours to jump him again. He held her arms behind her back and she bit him to his teeth. The pain was so powerful he had to put out her light with his fist.

When she came to and touched her jaw he went wild thinking he had loosened one of the side teeth so precious to him. Jadine dressed the bite marks on his face; and they said, "Ollieballen," laughing as best they could with the bruises.

Sometimes they argued about school. Maybe that was the problem.

"It's bullshit, Jadine."

"It is not. When will you listen to the truth?"

"What truth?"

"The truth that while you were playing the piano in the Night Moves Café, I was in school. The truth is that while you were driving your car into your wife's bed I was being educated. While you were hiding from a small-town sheriff or some insurance company, hiding from a rap a two-bit lawyer could have gotten you out of, I was being educated, I was working, I was making something out of my life. I was learning how to make it in *this*

266

world. The one we live in, not the one in your head. Not that dump Eloe; *this* world. And the truth is I could not have done that without the help and care of some poor old white dude who thought I had brains enough to learn something! Stop loving your ignorance—it isn't lovable."

Son picked her up and took her to the window. After a violent struggle he actually held her out of it by her wrists shouting, "The truth is that whatever you learned in those colleges that didn't include me ain't shit. What did they teach you about me? What tests did they give? Did they tell you what I was like, did they tell you what was on my mind? Did they describe me to you? Did they tell you what was in my heart? If they didn't teach you that, then they didn't teach you nothing, because until you know about me, you don't know nothing about yourself. And you don't know anything, anything at all about your children and anything at all about your mama and your papa. You find out about *me*, you educated nitwit!"

It was only ten feet off the ground and she wet her pants, but still she hollered loud enough for him to hear as well as the few people gathered on the sidewalk to watch, "You want to be a yardman all your life?"

"His name is Gideon! Gideon! Not Yardman, and Mary Thérèse Foucault, you hear me! Why don't you ask me to help you buy a house and put your aunt and uncle in it and take that woman off her feet. Her feet are killing her, killing her, and let them live like people for a change, like the people you never studied, like the people you can't photograph. *They* are the ones who put you through school, woman, they are the ones. Not him. They worked for him all their lives. And you left them down there with him not knowing if they had a job or not. You should cook for *them*. What the hell kind of education is it that didn't teach you about Gideon and Old Man and me. Nothing about me!"

When he pulled her back in, her arms were so sore she could not move them. But she was curled up teary-eyed in his lap an hour later when the doorbell rang. Son was massaging her shoulders, and begging forgiveness. They both went to the door and looked so lovey-dovey the police thought they had the wrong apartment, it must have been somebody else throwing a woman out of the window.

Other times they fought about work; surely *that* was the problem.

He mentioned once wanting to go back to the boats.

"You can't; you're blacklisted. You jumped ship, remember?"

"That don't mean nothing."

"You'll be away all the time. Why do you want to leave me?"

"I don't. But we don't have to live here. We can live anywhere."

"You mean Eloe."

"I mean anywhere. I can get good work in other places."

"Where?"

"Houston, Montgomery, Atlanta, San Diego."

"I can't live there."

"Why do you want to *change* me?"

"I want to live, not change. I can't live just for this god-damn city."

"Is it because you're afraid? Because you can't make it in New York?"

"Make it in New York. Make it in New York. I'm tired of hearing that shit. What the fuck is it? If I make it in New York, then that's all I do: 'Make it in New York.' That's not life; that's making it. I don't want to *make* it; I want to *be* it. New York ain't hard, baby. Not really hard. It's just sad, and what you need to make it here is the easy stuff I got rid of a long time ago. I've lived all over the world, Jadine. I can live anywhere."

"You've never lived anywhere."

"And you? Where have you lived? Anybody ask you where you from, you give them five towns. You're not *from* anywhere. I'm from Eloe."

268

"I hate Eloe and Eloe hates me. Never was any feeling more mutual."

She kept him on the defensive; demanded clarity, precision, very specific solutions to open-ended problems, and any furry notion he had in mind of what to do or where to do it matted before her rakelike intellect. He wanted to do things in time—she wanted them done on time. So he let her make private appointments, did take the SAT and scored in the 400s; the LET and was below the 13th percentile; the IRE and ranked above the 80th percentile; the CEE and scored in the 600s. "That proves," he told her, "that I can sit still for three hours at a clip, but I always knew that."

"One of two things," she said finally. "Either you go to school while I work or we ask Valerian to invest in a business."

"Will you marry me?"

"Yes."

"Okay."

"Okay what?"

"I'll go to school."

"Ooo-wee!" She grabbed him around the neck and pulled him to the floor.

"But not here."

"Why?"

"We're living in other people's space. This is not our crib. Let's go someplace else."

"How many times do I have to tell you—I can't work someplace else. You can, but I can't."

"What the hell do you do that's so jive you can't take it out of the city and do it there?"

"I pay the bills is what I do."

It was August. Jadine had sent for applications to C.U.N.Y. and S.U.N.Y. When they came, she sat down and filled them out. She was tired and looking tired. So much so the agency people were skipping her. That twenty-five-year-old face looked twenty-six and she had not been keeping up the regimen that held her at the twenty-year-old peak. Seventeen-year-old girls were getting the jobs. In Europe they liked older-looking black models, but in the U.S. the look was twelve. Soon she would really have to call her old professor. The modelling thing was going bust fast—she'd make all she could as fast as she could since it was seven times what teaching would bring. She sat at the table, perspiring a little, filling out Son's application. You'd think he would at least do *that*.

Son was watching her—she was a model of industry and planning. Every now and then she asked him a question and they agreed on whether to lie or tell the truth. He watched her. There is the power, he thought, right there. That is all the power there is or ever will be and I don't want any of it. She always referred to Eloe as his cradle. As though living there was child's play, easy. As though living anywhere outside the First Cities of the World was kiddy stuff. Well, it hadn't been easy for Francine and it hadn't been easy for Rosa or his mother. Not easy at all. It was hard and he believed it scared her to think of how hard. She thought this was hard, New York. She was scared of being still, of not being busy, scared to have to be quiet, scared to have children alone. He tried to imagine what kind of woman she would be in fifty years. Would she be Thérèse? Or Ondine? Or Rosa or Sally Brown, or maybe even Francine, frail as a pick tearing all her hair out in the state hospital? Bald, bald Francine. Some cradle. It took all the grown-up strength you had to stay there and stay alive and keep a family together. They didn't know about state aid in Eloe; there were no welfare lines in Eloe and unemployment insurance was a year of trouble with no rewards. She kept barking at him about equality, sexual equality, as though he thought women were inferior. He couldn't understand that. Before Francine was attacked by the dogs, she gave him ten points on the court and still beat him. It was her athletic skill that caused her trouble. She was running in the fields and went too far. Some dogs tracking an escaped convict, frustrated at having lost the scent, attacked her. Sixty seconds later the police got them off her and took her home. She stayed nervous after that, well, "nervous" was what they all called it. But God that girl could run. Cheyenne was driving a beat-up old truck at age nine, four years before he could even shift gears, and she could drop a pheasant like an Indian. His mother's memory was kept alive by those who remembered how she roped horses when she was a girl. His grandmother built a whole cowshed with only Rosa to help. In fact the room Jadine had slept in, Rosa built herself which was why it didn't have any windows. Anybody who thought women were inferior didn't come out of north Florida.

ON SEPTEMBER 16, two weeks before registration, a dividend came in the mail, $1,246 from the four municipal bond certificates Valerian had given her one Christmas when she was sixteen. She was delighted; it would take care of the school expenses. Son said no. Valerian educated her, all right; there was nothing to be done about that, but he would not let him finance his own education. Jadine dropped her hands to her side with sheer exhaustion.

"Valerian is not the problem." Her voice was faint, gooey with repetition.

This rescue was not going well. She thought she was rescuing him from the night women who wanted him for themselves, wanted him feeling superior in a cradle, deferring to him; wanted her to settle for wifely competence when she could be almighty, to settle for fertility rather than originality, nurturing instead of building. He thought he was rescuing her from Valerian, meaning *them*, the aliens, the people who in a mere three hundred years had killed a world millions of years old. From Micronesia to Liverpool, from Kentucky to Dresden, they killed everything they touched including their own coast-

271

lines, their own hills and forests. And even when some of them built something nice and human, they grew vicious protecting it from their own predatory children, let alone an outsider. Each was pulling the other away from the maw of hell—its very ridge top. Each knew the world as it was meant or ought to be. One had a past, the other a future and each one bore the culture to save the race in his hands. Mama-spoiled black man, will you mature with me? Culture-bearing black woman, whose culture are you bearing?

"Correct," he said. "The problem is not Valerian. The problem is me. Solve it. With me or without me, but solve it because it ain't going anywhere. You sweep me under the rug and your children will cut your throat. That fucker in Europe, the one you were thinking about marrying? Go have his children. That should suit you. Then you can do exactly what you bitches have always done: take care of white folks' children. Feed, love and care for white people's children. That's what you were born for; that's what you have waited for all your life. So have that white man's baby, that's your job. You have been doing it for two hundred years, you can do it for two hundred more. There are no 'mixed' marriages. It just looks that way. People don't mix races; they abandon them or pick them. But I want to tell you something: if you have a white man's baby, you have *chosen* to be just another mammy only you are the *real* mammy 'cause you had it in your womb and you are still taking care of white folks' children. Fat or skinny, head rag or wig, cook or model, you take care of white folks' babies—that's what you do and when you don't have any white man's baby to take care of you make one—out of the babies black men give you. You turn little black babies into little white ones; you turn your black brothers into white brothers; you turn your men into white men and when a black woman treats me like what I am, what I really am, you say she's spoiling me. You think I won't do all that company shit because I don't know how? I can do anything!
272

Anything! But I'll be goddamn if I'll do that!"

She looked at him and when he saw the sheen gone from her minky eyes and her wonderful mouth fat with disgust, he tore open his shirt, saying, "I got a story for you."

"Get out of my face."

"You'll like it. It's short and to the point."

"Don't touch me. Don't you touch me."

"Once upon a time there was a farmer—a white farmer . . ."

"Quit! Leave me *alone!*"

"And he had this bullshit bullshit bullshit farm. And a rabbit. A rabbit came along and ate a couple of his . . . ow . . . cabbages."

"You better kill me. Because if you don't, when you're through, I'm going to kill you."

"Just a few cabbages, you know what I mean?"

"I am going to kill you. *Kill* you."

"So he got this great idea about how to get him. How to, to trap . . . this rabbit. And you know what he did? He made him a tar baby. He made it, you hear me? He made it!"

"As sure as I live," she said. "I'm going to kill you."

But she didn't. After he banged the bedroom door, she lay in wrinkled sheets, slippery, gutted, not thinking of killing him. Thinking instead that it would soon be Thanksgiving and there was no place to go for dinner. Then she thought of a towering brass beech—the biggest and oldest in the state. It stood on the north side of the campus and near it was a well. In April the girls met their mothers there to sing and hold hands and sway in the afternoon light. Some of the girls hated it—the well, the beech, the mother-daughter day, and sat around in jeans and no shoes smoking herb to show their contempt for bourgeoisie sentiment and alumni hustling. But the girls who did not hate it surrounded the beech and in long pastel shirts swayed in the spring light. Pale sulphur light sprinkled so softly with lilac it made her want to cry.

Jadine joined the barefoot ones, of course, but her tears were not because there was no one to sing with under the biggest beech in the state, but because of the light, pale sulphur sprinkled with lilac.

A piece of her hair was in her mouth and she tried to extricate it with her tongue for her hands weighed a ton apiece. This is familiar, she thought. I know what this is; it's familiar. I am twenty-five and this feeling is too old for me.

Four hours later he was back—repentant, terrified that he had gone too far. But Jadine was solemn—a closed-away orphan in a Cheech and Chong T-shirt with no place to go at Thanksgiving.

Son sat at the foot of the bed and covered his knees with his hands. Jadine spoke very quietly to him.

"I can't let you hurt me again. You stay in that medieval slave basket if you want to. You will stay there by yourself. Don't ask me to do it with you. I won't. There is nothing any of us can do about the past but make our own lives better, that's all I've been trying to help you do. That is the only revenge, for us to get over. *Way* over. But no, you want to talk about white babies; you don't know how to forget the past and do better."

His budding repentance decomposed into a steaming compost.

"If I wanted the editorial page of the Atlanta *Constitution* I would have bought it."

"With what?" Jadine's voice was slick with danger.

"With the money you got from Valerian. The money you fucked your way across Europe for!"

"Well, buy it then. Here, here it is." She picked her wallet up from the night table and opened it. "Here it is. Your original dime. The one you cleaned sheephead for, right? The one you loved? The *only* one you loved. All you want 'in the money line'. Take it. Now you know where it came from, your original dime: some black woman like me fucked a white man for it and then *gave* it to Frisco who made you work your ass off for it. That's

274

your original dime." She threw it on the floor. "Pick it up."

He stared at her. The Cheech and Chong T-shirt was up around her waist and her nakedness below embarrassed him now. He had produced that nakedness and having soiled it, it shamed him.

"Pick it up." She said it again and didn't even sit up. She just lay there, stroking her raw silk thighs the colour of natural honey. There was sealskin in her eyes and the ladies minding the pie table vanished like shadows under a noon gold sun.

He thought it would be hard to do, but it wasn't. He thought it would be cold, too. Cold and hard. But it wasn't. It was warm, almost soft, and quite round.

He put it in his pocket and having no place to put himself left the apartment again. He came back the next night to empty rooms and a door key for each of the several locks. He sat down on the sofa and looked at the keys. A pile of mail was on the coffee table too and in it a heavy yellow envelope. He stared at it awhile and then opened it. Out came the photos she had taken in the middle of the road in Eloe. Beatrice, pretty Beatrice, Soldier's daughter. She looked stupid. Ellen, sweet cookie-faced Ellen, the one he always thought so pretty. She looked stupid. They all looked stupid, backwoodsy, dumb, dead . . .

Son put down the photos. I have to find her, he thought. Whatever she wants, I have to do it, want it. But first I have to find her.

# 10

AFTER THIRTY YEARS of shame the champion daisy
trees were marshalling for war. The wild parrots that had
escaped the guns of Dominique could feel menace in the
creeping of their roots. During the day they tossed their
branches; at night they walked the hills. At
dawn their new formations challenged the wit of the
chevaliers. Their brothers over on Dominique knew
nothing of the battle plans for they were in a rain forest
tamed for tourists that came by bus from the Old Queen
Hotel, gallant and royal since 1927. Now she was dying
from behind. Her front on Rue Madelaine was still sea-
cap white and the columns at her entrance showed no
signs of wear. Yet at her great round-skirted rear among
breadfruit trees and lime, the cells of a motel were growing. A concrete *Y*-shaped thing with patios the size of a
card table extended from the dining room from whose
forty-seven windows diners once gazed at breadfruit trees
and lawn. Now they looked at workmen, concrete and
patios the size of a card table. Beyond that were the hills
of black Dominiques, and beyond that spectacular
mountains of rain forest. The road that cuts through the
mountains is a regular tourist attraction. Breathlessly
steep and winding, without benefit of guardrails, it
offers a view of God's hair, hibiscus, magnolia and
oleander, poinsettia and jacaranda. Away in the distance
under pink immortelles is an occasional dead plantation,
now a hotel with marble dolphins and air conditioning
pumping purity into two-hundred-year-old stone. The
mountain road descends on the other side of the island to
a coastline of cliffs and grottos where fishing villages lay.
No marinas here, no golf courses, for here the winds do

not trade. They are hot and capricious and the fishermen design strange sails to accommodate them so they can sell their grouper, tuna and bonito to the dead plantations, and the Old Queen Hotel where Jadine sat alone at a table for four.

"Crème de menthe," she had said because the words seemed nice and right and she wanted to say them aloud. And when the waiter returned she regretted it immediately and ordered vermouth. She had called L'Arbe de la Croix. Ondine had answered.

"Where are you?"

"Queen of France, but I missed the ferry, Nanadine. Can somebody come?"

"Well, yes, I reckon so. But it might take awhile."

"I'll wait. Tell him to come to the Old Queen. If I'm not in the lobby, ask for me in the dining room."

"You by yourself?"

"Of course. Hurry, please, Nanadine?"

Of course I'm by myself. When haven't I been by myself. She was alone at a table for four, proud of having been so decisive, so expert at the leaving. Of having refused to be broken in the big ugly hands of any man. Now *she* felt lean and male, having left quickly with no peeping back just in case—no explanatory, loophole-laden note. No last supper. New York had agreed with her exit. A cab right at the door, an uncommunicative driver who took her directly to the place she was going to; Raymond at home; his studio available for the night; a short line at Chemical Bank and Air France ready to go. Aloneness tasted good and even at a table set for four she was grateful to be far away from his original-dime ways, his white-folks-black-folks primitivism. How could she make a life with a cultural throw-back, she asked herself, and answered No way. Eloe. No way. Not for all the cadmium yellow and Hansa red in the world. So what if she was alone. So what if when she went away, no one stayed home and remained there all while she was gone and was waiting when she got back.

277

But he had put his finger on the very bottom of her foot. He had opened the hair on her head with his hands and drove his tongue through the part.


THE MULATTO didn't talk, he hummed a Creole hit and drummed a little on the steering wheel. As they passed Sein de Vieilles, Jadine's legs burned with the memory of tar. She could hardly see L'Arbe de la Croix when they got to it, the trees leaned so close to the house. She dashed into Ondine's kitchen, kissed her and said, "Let me get my stuff together first. I'll be right back down and we can talk. Is Margaret here?"

"Upstairs," said Ondine.

No one answered her knock at Margaret's door, but she saw a brighter-than-hallway light falling from Valerian's door and went toward it. Inside, heaped on the twin beds, on the dresser, the chairs and even on the bed table were clothes. Suits, ties, shirts, socks, sweaters and pair after pair of men's shoes.

"Valerian?" she called out.

Margaret stepped from the closet-dressing room, her hands full of empty hangers.

"Well," she said, genuinely surprised. "The prodigal daughter. What did you do to your hair?" Margaret looked flushed and sparkly, her movements directed and sure.

"Something different."

"It's wonderful looking," said Margaret coming toward her, hand outstretched to touch Jadine's hair. Then she stopped and snapped her fingers twice. "We used to call it . . . oh dear . . ." She closed her eyes. "Poodle-cut! That's it. Poodle-cut," and she laughed with such pleasure that Jadine had to smile.

"I'm sorry about leaving you with so little notice. I don't want you to think I didn't appreciate your helping me out last winter."

Margaret waved her hand. "Don't mention it. It was a

lousy time for everybody." She sat down on a cluttered bed and began to unbunch the hangers.

"Are you all leaving?" asked Jadine.

"Leaving? No. Why?"

Jadine looked at the clothes.

"Oh, no. I'm just straightening out this unbelievable mess. You wouldn't believe the things that man has accumulated. Eight shoe trees in his closet and only two of them actually in shoes. And look. Linen slacks. Linen. Never worn and so yellow now they can't be. I never knew what a clothes-horse the man was. See here?" Margaret fingered the garment label. "Silk, and here, virgin wool. Look here, one hundred percent cotton. All his undershirts too. He won't wear nylon or tricot. None of the man-made fibres. Everything he owns has to be made by Mother Nature. But what a mess. It'll take me days to get it all sorted. I can't expect Sydney to do this. It's not his job really. Ondine's either. I really could use you now, Jade, but I don't suppose you're staying."

"No. I'm going back tomorrow."

"France?"

"Yes."

"Will you marry that fellow? Mr. Sealskin?"

Jadine sighed. "No."

"Oh? Why not?" Margaret folded the slacks over padded hangers and laid them carefully on the bed. Now she was sorting shirts, smelling them for mildew, examining them for tears, missing buttons, frayed collars. She didn't seem interested in an answer to her question so Jadine didn't give her one, didn't tell her that she hardly knew what the word meant. Instead she asked how Valerian was.

"Better," said Margaret.

"He's not sick, is he?" asked Jadine.

"He says he isn't, but he trembles sometimes and won't go in to town to see a doctor."

"This is no place to be sick in, Margaret. Maybe you should get him back to Philadelphia."

"Of course I will, if it gets really bad." She looked at Jadine as though hurt that her judgment about what was best for her husband was doubted.

"And Michael, how is he?"

"Oh, you don't know, do you? He got in. Berkeley, I mean. The semester begins next week."

"Then you're not going out there?"

"Oh, no. Michael's an adult, Jade. Thirty. I can't go traipsing around the world looking after him when there's so much to do here. You see the mess these clothes are in." She had finished separating the shirts into three piles and had begun on the sweaters. "Jade," she said; she held a blue *V*-necked sweater to her chest. It was nothing like the blue of her eyes. "Sometimes in the morning he can't do everything he used to. You know: buttons, zippers. I have to tie his shoes even. Yesterday I washed his hair"—she smiled—"with Kirk's Original Castile Soap. He doesn't like Breck."

Jadine stared.

"Sydney's going to teach me how to shave him and maybe together we can get him to let us cut his hair. God, is he stubborn. Worse than a child." She laughed lightly, indulgently, and went on sorting, piling, like a confident curator who knew the names of everything in his museum, while Jadine watched saying to herself, And he thinks Valerian made *me*.

ONDINE picked up a screaming lobster and threw him into a pot of boiling water. She held it down with a wooden ladle to make it die faster for she was in the mood for death. It had been an hour since Jadine had come in and kissed her, all smiles and speed. Ondine didn't like her new hairdo: fluffy, frothy as though it was important to look like a schoolgirl. Now she was back in the kitchen, looking subdued.

"What's come over Margaret?" asked Jadine. "She's working her butt off."

280

"Do her good. Him too."

"But she talks about Valerian like he was a patient, or a baby."

"People do what they have to, I guess, and take payment where they can."

"What's she mad at him for? She's the one who stuck pins in her baby."

Ondine wiped sweat from her forehead with her free hand. "She didn't stick pins in her baby. She stuck em in his baby. Her baby she loved."

"That's a description, maybe, but not a reason. He gave her everything she ever wanted. Remember that little Triumph? And what about—"

"He kept her stupid; kept her idle. That always spells danger."

"Now she's the master, not him?"

"Master, patient, baby—it don't matter. He's still the centre of everything." Ondine withdrew the lobster and got right down to it. "You ran off with him, didn't you?"

"It's over, Nanadine. I don't know what got into me."

"You could have told us."

"Maybe. But everything was so messed up here. I mean that was some Christmas."

"You still could have told us."

"Well, if it will make you any happier, it was a mistake. A mistake of the first order, believe me. You know I never worked so hard in my life to keep something going. I'd never done that before. I never cared whether a relationship worked or not, you know. I mean if it worked, it worked; if it didn't—later. But this time I worked my butt off and all I got for it was a black eye and the rent. So—" Jadine slapped the table with her palm marking the end of the affair. "That's that."

"He hit you?"

"Yes, among other things."

"He actually *hit* you?"

"It's over, Nanadine, besides, I hit him too."

"I should hope so. I should damn well hope so. Oh,

baby, baby, how could you run off with a . . ."

"Let's don't talk about it. I left and that's that. One thing though. If he calls here, you don't know where I am, and if he comes here . . ."

"Comes here?"

"Well, I don't know, he might. Anyhow, don't tell him where I am."

"Where are you?" asked Ondine.

"I'm going to get my stuff and go back to Paris."

Stuff, thought Ondine, meant mainly the fur coat. She wondered if her niece would even have come to say goodbye had it not been that the sealskin coat was there. "Then what?" she asked.

Jadine shrugged and changed the subject. "How's Valerian?"

"Hanging on."

"Did she really do all of that to her baby?"

"She really did."

"Wow. And she's not bugging you anymore?"

"Not at all."

"So what's your situation here?" Jadine's voice was serious, but there was pleading in it too. (Please don't need me now, not now. I can't parent now. I cannot be needed now. Another time, please. I have spent it all. Please don't need me now.)

"Same. They want us to stay. Mrs. Street does anyway, and he don't say much one way or the other. Sits in that greenhouse all day listening to music."

"Do you want to stay?"

"Do we have a choice?" asked Ondine, looking carefully at the ringlets on Jadine's head.

"Sure you have a choice. You can work other places or not at all. You want to come with me to Paris?" Jadine's shoulder ached for a second as she remembered hanging out of a second storey window on Ninety-third Street.

"Girl, don't play with me."

"I'm serious."

"Jadine, we done what we could for you because—well,

282

what I mean to say is you don't owe us nothing. But, well, I never told you nothing. I never told you nothing at all and I take full responsibility for that. But I have to tell you something now."

Jadine lifted her head and looked in her aunt's eyes.

"Jadine, a girl has got to be a daughter first. She have to learn that. And if she never learns how to be a daughter, she can't never learn how to be a woman. I mean a real woman: a woman good enough for a child; good enough for a man—good enough even for the respect of other women. Now you didn't have a mother long enough to learn much about it and I thought I was doing right by sending you to all them schools and so I never told you it and I should have. You don't need your own natural mother to be a daughter. All you need is to feel a certain way, a certain careful way about people older than you are. Don't mistake me now. I don't mean you have to love all kinds of mean old people, and if it's in your mind that I'm begging you for something, get it out. I ain't."

"Yes, you are, Ondine." Jadine's voice was steady. "You are asking me to parent you. Please don't. I can't do that now."

"I am not asking you that. I'm just saying what a daughter is. A daughter is a woman that cares about where she come from and takes care of them that took care of her. No, I don't want you to be what you call a parent. Not me, and not Sydney either. What I want from you is what I want for you. I don't want you to care about me for my sake. I want you to care about me for yours." She reached out to touch her niece's hand, but something made her stop short of it.

When Ondine said, "You didn't have a mother long enough," blood rushed to Jadine's skin the way it always did when her motherlessness was mentioned. But she spoke gently and steadily to Ondine. "No, you don't, Nanadine. You want me to pay you back. You worked for me and put up with me. Now it's my turn to do it for

283

you, that's all you're saying."

"Turn? Turn? This ain't no game a bid whist . . ."

"There are other ways to be a woman, Nanadine," Jadine went on. "Your way is one, I guess it is, but it's not my way. I don't want to be . . . like you. Wait. Don't look at me like that. I'm being honest with you now and you have to listen! I don't want to learn how to be the kind of woman you're talking about because I don't want to be that kind of woman."

"There ain't but one kind. Just one, and if you say another hateful word to me, I'll . . ." She stopped.

"What? Hit me? Would you, Nanadine? You'd hit me too?"

The older woman was quiet. Her niece, her baby, her crown had put her in the same category as that thing she ran off with. And now she was going on talking, explaining, saying, but Ondine never heard anymore. The volume of her heart was up too loud.

When Jadine went off to finish packing, Ondine sat patting the table with her right hand, her chin resting on the fist of her left. She didn't know what she expected. What she was expecting her niece to do or think or feel. But something more than she had seen. Maybe she's right. Maybe I just wanted her to feel sorry for us, she thought, maybe that's what I expected and that's a lowdown wish if ever I had one.

Sydney came in and stopped her thoughts. "That her?" he asked.

"Yes."

"Off again?"

"Yep. Paris."

"Where's he?"

"She dumped him."

"I could have told him that."

"So could I. Go up and say goodbye to her. She's making tracks tomorrow if she can."

Sydney sat down and unclasped his bow tie. "She ask you for any money?"

"Nothing dangerous. Just a few francs for the shuttle. She had a thing full of those what you call travelling cheques. Go on up and see her. I'll take him his tray."

"She wants to say goodbye, she knows where I am."

"Sydney, don't be like that."

"But I *am* like that. She didn't do well by us, Ondine."

"She's young. She'll settle."

"Age ain't got nothing to do with it."

"She's not a savings account, Sydney. You don't get interest back."

"Ought to."

"It's more different for them than it was for us. There's a whole bunch of stuff they can do that we never knew nothing about."

"And a whole bunch they don't know nothing about," he answered.

"Well, maybe you right. Maybe it don't pay to love nothing. I loved that little boy like he was mine, so he wouldn't grow up and kill somebody. And instead of thanks, I get meanness. Disrespect."

"Let's not go into that no more."

"He's okay now. Doin fine. But I'm not responsible for that, no. I'm responsible for not telling nobody. She accused me of not liking her enough to stop her. You go figure that out. Then I take another one in my heart, your brother's baby girl. Another one not from my womb, and I stand on my feet thirty years so she wouldn't have to. And did without so she wouldn't have to. And she couldn't think of nothing better to do than buy me some shoes I can't wear, a dress I shouldn't, and run off with the first pair of pants that steps in the door. Now explain me that."

"I can't explain nothing no more. It didn't used to be this way. Seem like folks used to take care of folks once upon a time. Old black people must be a worrisome thing to the young ones these days."

Ondine went to the oven and removed a baked potato. She put it on a plate and the plate on a tray. Then she

285

went to the refrigerator and removed a wineglass that had been chilling there. Sydney watched her movements.

Ondine got out a napkin. "She said she didn't think he would, but if he did call or come looking for her we shouldn't let him know where she is."

"He better not set foot on this place."

"From what she says he beat her up some."

"Then I hope he does come," said Sydney. "I'll put that bullet in him for sure."

"No, you won't."

"You mistake me if you don't think so. I'll shoot him the same minute I see him and explain later."

"This is not your property, Sydney."

"No, but it's my home. If this ain't my home, then nothing is but the grave."

"Well, we'll be there soon enough."

Sydney thought about that. "You think she'll bury us, Ondine?"

"I think we're going to have to bury ourselves, Sydney."

"Well, in that case the shroud may as well be comfy." He picked up the rattan tray and, since he was a genuine Philadelphia Negro mentioned in the book of that name, he reclasped his bow tie and adjusted his cuff links before he left the kitchen and went to the greenhouse. He noticed that the bricks that edged the courtyard were popping up out of the ground, leaning every which way. Urged, it seemed to him, out of the earth, like they were poked from beneath. Cement, he thought, is all that will keep this earth still. This place dislocates everything. I'll get that mulatto to fix them right this time. And something serious had to be done about the ants. They had already eaten through the loudspeaker wires and he had had to transfer the entire system to the greenhouse: turntable, receiver, records. Sydney was grateful to the ants because he really hated vacuuming or polishing doorknobs while the music boomed through the house. He preferred silence for his work. Now he was free of it and Mr. Street had it all to himself. Still, if ants will eat

286

copper—something serious had to be done. If it's not one thing it's another, he thought, and either he was shrinking in his old age or the trees were jumping up overnight. The roof of the washhouse was completely obscured by a heavy branch. That mulatto may buck if I tell him to cut it down, he thought. Better get somebody from town.

The greenhouse was sunk in violins and Valerian, seated at a seed bench, did not hear Sydney enter. He was drenched in music and although his fingers shuddered occasionally, his head-of-a-coin profile moved accurately to the tempo. Sydney tapped him on the shoulder and he turned.

"Your lunch, Mr. Street."

Valerian motioned for him to put the tray down, his fingers describing a wavy arc in the air.

"You letting this place run down, Mr. Street."

"What's that?" asked Valerian.

Sydney walked over to the record player and lifted the arm away. "I said you letting this place run down. Used to be pretty in here. You letting it go to pieces."

"It's my place," said Valerian. "Turn the music back on."

Sydney did not move, but said, "You don't grow nothing in here anymore."

"I like it this way, Sydney. Put the music back."

"Then you should take care of it."

"That'll do, Sydney. Hand me the mail."

Sydney picked up the stack of letters, circulars and catalogues and held them out to Valerian, but the dancing hands could not receive them. "Want me to open them for you?" asked Sydney.

"No. Yes."

Sydney pulled up a stepping stool and sat down next to Valerian. "You should take care of yourself, too. You need a haircut."

"I prefer it long," said Valerian.

"No, you don't. You just don't want to go into town.

287

The mulatto's here today. If you won't let me cut it, let him take you over."

"What mulatto?"

Sydney slit open a letter with a penknife. "The one Dr. Michelin sent over. A mulatto. Been coming awhile now. He can take you over to get your hair cut."

"Not today," said Valerian. "Not today; later, Sydney." Valerian turned toward the tray and tried to pick up the knife and fork. He succeeded but could not manage to make them do anything else but wave there in his hands. Sydney put aside the mail, and stood up. He took the knife and fork from Valerian, broke open the steaming potato, and scooped out a forkful. He blew on it and then held it in front of Valerian's mouth. Valerian closed his lips and looked into Sydney's eyes. He tried as best he could to see what was there, what was really there. He wasn't sure, but he believed he saw kindness. He opened his lips and swallowed.

"Good," said Sydney. "That's good. It's not too hot, is it?"

Valerian shook his head and opened his mouth for more. He chewed for a little while and then said, "Sydney?"

"Yes, sir?"

"Did you . . . ah . . ."

"No, sir, I didn't. I heard about it same time you did."

"Ondine never told you?"

"Not a word."

"I hear them in the kitchen. Talking, like they used to."

"Yes, sir."

"Remember? How they used to gossip in the kitchen back then?"

"I remember."

"He's all right, isn't he?"

"Michael? Oh, yes, sir. He's fine."

"I'm thinking of going back. I think I should leave this place and go back to Philadelphia."

"What for?"

288

"I don't like it here anymore. No reason to be here now."

"No reason to be anywhere, Mr. Street. But I'd think carefully on it if I was you. Ondine and me, we like it down here. Philadelphia winters can be hard on old people. It's nice and warm down here. Quiet too. We like it fine. Would you like a sip of Chablis now?" He put down the fork and went to the small refrigerator for a bottle of wine.

"No," said Valerian. "Not now."

"I would," said Sydney. "I'd like a glass myself." He worked the screw into the cork. "You sure you don't want any?"

"I said no."

"How are your bunions, Mr. Street?"

"Corns. I don't have bunions. I have corns."

"How are they?"

"Sydney, you are drinking my wine."

"Next time that mulatto comes, I'll tell him to bring you back a pair of huaraches."

"I don't want any huaraches."

"Sure you do. Nice pair of huaraches be good for you. Make your feet feel good. This time next year, you'll thank me for em."

"What do you mean, this time next year? I'm going back."

"I figure we're going to be here a long time, Mr. Street. A good long time."

"What's happening here. Something's happening here."

"Don't agitate yourself. Rest your mind." Sydney put down the wineglass, and went to the record player. He held the arm over the record and turned to Valerian. "We'll give you the best of care. Just like we always done. That's something you ain't never got to worry about." He placed the arm carefully in the groove and turned the volume up high. Valerian smiled then, and his fingers danced lightly in the air.

THE AIRPORT in Dominique is a long building made of pale yellow concrete blocks. If you didn't know you were in the Caribbean, the paper in the ladies' room would tell you. To an American the contempt in which the rest of the world holds toilet paper is incomprehensible. It is treated as though it were, in fact, toilet paper. Jadine stepped out of the stall and stood before the tiny mirror over the sink. She sudsed her hands generously with a piece of her own soap and rinsed them carefully. She wrapped the soap in a piece of wax paper, returned it to her travelling bag, from which she took a tube of hand lotion. She creamed her palms and the backs of her hands, then with tissue wiped away the lotion that had gotten under her fingernails. Unhurried at last, with thirty minutes before flight time. The frantic scampering over with. She had run away from New York City with the same speed she had run toward it. New York was not her home after all. The dogs were leashed in the city but the reins were not always secure. Sometimes walking with their owners they met other dogs and if they were unspayed and unchecked you could see a female standing quietly under the paws of a male who had not even spoken to her, just sniffed for purposes of identification. She thought it could be a shelter for her because there the night women could be beaten, reduced to shadows and confined to the briar patch where they belonged. But she could not beat them alone. There were no shelters anyway; it was adolescent to think that there were. Every orphan knew that and knew also that mothers however beautiful were not fair. No matter what you did, the diaspora mothers with pumping breasts would impugn your character. And an African woman, with a single glance from eyes that had burned away their own lashes, could discredit your elements.

She still had plenty of time to take two Dramamines, comb her hair, check her make-up, but this ladies' lounge was not designed for lingering. She was doing her eyes when a girl came out of the stall next to the one she had used. She had a short mop and a plastic pail of various cleansers in her hands. She wore a green uniform which looked even greener beneath her russet wig. Jadine glanced at the wig in the mirror and then back to her own lashes. The girl stopped dead and did not take her eyes off Jadine, who was flattered but wished she would not stare so. Then the girl approached her.

"You don't remember me?" she asked.

Jadine turned around. The wig was so overwhelming it was awhile before she recognized her.

"L'Arbe de la Croix," said the girl.

"Oh, wow." Jadine smiled. "I didn't recognize you. What are you doing here? You work here now?"

The girl nodded. "You took the chocolate eater away," she said.

Jadine closed her smile and turned back to the mirror. There was nothing like an islander; they never had any chat—or manners for that matter. Conversation with them was always an interrogation and she was not about to explain anything to this child.

"He was going to send me a wig, he said."

"Looks like he did," said Jadine.

"Not this one. I have a picture of the other one. It's at home. Is he coming back? Can you get it for me?"

"No," Jadine answered.

"You kill him?" asked the girl in a very matter-of-fact tone.

Jadine slung the huge, lightweight travelling bag over her shoulder and removed her coat from the top of the stall where it hung. "I have to go now," she said.

"Thérèse said you kill him," the girl insisted.

"Tell Thérèse *she* killed him."

"No," said the girl, perplexed. "Thérèse has magic breasts. They still give milk."

"I bet they do," said Jadine.

"But there is nobody to nurse them."

"She's not looking in the right places," said Jadine. Black pearls of hair were visible at the wig's edge. The girl's eyes were wide, still, the curiosity in them was the only thing that kept them from looking like an animal's. A deer, thought Jadine. She has the eyes of a curious deer. She wished once more that she had had real talent—she'd like to draw her—deer eyes, wig and all. Suddenly she reached into the side pocket of her travelling bag. A few francs were shoved in there and she dropped the whole lot into the girl's plastic pail. "Bye, Mary, I have to go. Good luck." Jadine pushed open the door and was gone.

"Alma," whispered the girl. "Alma Estée."

ABOARD the 707 Jadine had free use of the seat next to her. Not many passengers in first class. She checked her five luggage claim tickets stapled to the envelope that held a copy of her one-way ticket to Orly. Everything was in order. As soon as the plane was airborne, she reached above her head to adjust the air flow. Bringing her hand down she noticed a tiny irregularity in the nail of her forefinger. She opened her purse and took out an emery board. Two swift strokes and it was gone. Her nail was perfect again. She turned her sealskin coat lining side out and folded it carefully into the empty seat beside her. Then she adjusted the headrest. The same sixteen answers to the question What went wrong? kicked like a chorus line. Having sixteen answers meant having none. So none it was. Zero. She would go back to Paris and begin at Go. Let loose the dogs, tangle with the woman in yellow—with her and with all the night women who had *looked* at her. No more shoulders and limitless chests. No more dreams of safety. No more. Perhaps that was the thing—the thing Ondine was saying. A grown woman did not need safety or its dreams. She *was* the safety she longed for.

The plane lifted itself gracefully over the island; its tail of smoke widened, then dispersed. It was evening and the stars were already brilliant. The hills below crouched on

292

all fours under the weight of the rain forest where liana grew and soldier ants marched in formation. Straight ahead they marched, shamelessly single-minded, for soldier ants have no time for dreaming. Almost all of them are women and there is so much to do—the work is literally endless. So many to be born and fed, then found and buried. There is no time for dreaming. The life of their world requires organization so tight and sacrifice so complete there is little need for males and they are seldom produced. When they are needed, it is deliberately done by the queen who surmises, by some four-million-year-old magic she is heiress to, that it is time. So she urges a sperm from the private womb where they were placed when she had her one, first and last copulation. Once in life, this little Amazon trembled in the air waiting for a male to mount her. And when he did, when he joined a cloud of others one evening just before a summer storm, joined colonies from all over the world gathered for the marriage flight, he knew at last what his wings were for. Frenzied, he flies into the humming cloud to fight gravity and time in order to do, just once, the single thing he was born for. Then he drops dead, having emptied his sperm into his lady-love. Sperm which she keeps in a special place to use at her own discretion when there is need for another dark and singing cloud of ant folk mating in the air. Once the lady has collected the sperm, she too falls to the ground, but unless she breaks her back or neck or is eaten by one of a thousand things, she staggers to her legs and looks for a stone to rub on, cracking and shredding the wings she will never need again. Then she begins her journey searching for a suitable place to build her kingdom. She crawls into the hollow of a tree, examines its walls and corners. She seals herself off from all society and eats her own wing muscles until she bears her eggs. When the first larvae appear, there is nothing to feed them so she gives them their unhatched sisters until they are old enough and strong enough to hunt and bring their prey back to the kingdom. That is all. Bearing, hunting, eating, fighting, burying. No time for dreaming, although sometimes, late in life, somewhere between the thirtieth and fortieth generation she might get wind of a summer storm one day. The scent of it will invade her palace and she will recall the rush of wind on her belly—the stretch of fresh wings, the blinding anticipation and herself, there, airborne, suspended, open, trusting, frightened, determined, vulnerable—girlish, even, for an entire second and then another and another. She may lift her head then, and point her wands toward the place where the summer storm is entering her palace and in the weariness that ruling queens alone know, she may wonder whether his death was sudden. Or did he languish? And if so, if there was a bit of time left, did he think how mean the world was, or did he fill that space of time thinking of her? But soldier ants do not have time for dreaming. They are women and have much to do. Still it would be hard. So very hard to forget the man who fucked like a star.

# 11

THE MAN sat on the stone wall that separated Rue
Madelaine from the sea. His legs hung over the ledge
below which were rocks and a thin strip of dirty sand. To
the left a rickety pier extended some two hundred feet
into the water where black boys leaped, splashed,
screamed and climbed back up to leap again. The
garbage on the sand was mostly paper and bottles. No
food garbage down here. Here, away from the tourist
shops, away from the restaurants and offices, was that
part of the boulevard where the sea threw up what it
could not digest. Whatever life there is on the sand is
desperate. A gull negotiated the breeze and swooped
down on a black starfish. The gull pecked it, flew away
and returned to peck again and again until finally the
starfish yielded the magenta string that was its heart. The
man watched the gull tear it out with a great deal of
interest. Then he swung his legs over the wall and stood
up. Shielding his eyes from the sun with his arm, he
looked toward the market crowd: a half-block of cloth
roofs, tables, baskets, pots, boxes and trays. His jacket
was draped across his forearm—both hands in his
pockets—as he started toward the market looking for
Thérèse. Earlier he had taken the shuttle bus from the
airport to the Old Queen Hotel and gone directly from
there up the hill to the powder pink house, climbing
slowly, carefully, keeping to the edge of the road where
the dust gave way to grass. He moved like a man saving
his strength, or one suspicious of trip mines.

No one was in the pink house. The door was latched
although the windows were open; a print skirt ripped
down the back seam hung from one of the front windows

and served it as both curtain and shade. He poked his head through and tossed a piece of hand luggage into the room. Then he walked back down the hill, nodding to a few passersby, and stopped at the house that sold meat pies and rum and sometimes lent hair clippers. He didn't even try the little tin-can French he'd learned in Vietnam, he simply said Gideon? Thérèse? The owner and another man told him something he could not understand about Thérèse, and mentioned Gideon's name in connection with "taxi". He nodded and smiled as though it was all brilliantly clear and continued down the hill. The morning he spent walking the streets, looking at the elegant houses turned into restaurants or offices, and the colonial administration buildings built like castles to last. Away from the town to the north and east were the frightened houses of the whites, hiding on sloped roads behind hedges of tropical flora. South was the business district collected mainly on Rue Madelaine and the tributaries running from it. The Blacks lived in the western hills in shacks and cement-block houses or along narrow streets on the west side of town where the sea spit up what it could not digest. It was unusually cool and his weather eye saw that a rainstorm might be due announcing the hurricane season. He walked the streets of Queen of France, glancing at the drivers of the taxis in case Gideon might be one. Three hours of walking and he was not tired. Had not been tired for days now. Being still was the problem. In the apartment in New York he could not sit for long—except to look again and again at the photographs she had taken in Eloe. A fat yellow envelope of pictures had lain unopened on the coffee table along with the keys. Having nothing quiet to do with his huge hands except finger his original dime, he opened the envelope and looked at the pictures of all the places and people he had loved. Then he could be still. Gazing at the photos one by one trying to find in them what it was that used to comfort him so, used to reside with him, in him like

royalty in his veins. Used to people his dreams, and
anchor his floating days. When danger was most imminent and he fell asleep in spite of himself they were
there—the yellow houses with white doors, the ladies at
the pie table at Good Shepherd—Aunt Rosa; Soldier's
mother May Downing whom they called Mama May;
Drake's grandmother Winnie Boon who switched them
every spring; Miss Tyler who had taught him how to play
piano, and the younger women: Beatrice, Ellen, and the
children who had been born while he was away. The
men: Old Man, Rascal, Turner and Soldier and Drake
and Ernie Paul who left the service a first lieutenant and
now had his own mortuary in Montgomery, Alabama,
and doin fine. There were no photos of them, but they
were there in the pictures of trees behind their houses, the
fields where they worked, the river they fished, the
church where they testified, the joints where they drank.
It all looked miserable in the photographs, sad, poor and
even poor-spirited.

When he was not looking at the pictures, he had telephoned her friends and acquaintances. Her women
friends knew nothing but suggested he come over and
talk about it; the men he would not call. So he paced,
walked the streets, listened to the telephone that did not
ring, waited for the mail and finally made up his mind to
go back to Isle des Chevaliers. Start there in order to find
her. He left the keys with the super and the photos on the
table, and it was hard to sit still on the airplane; hard to
sit still on the sea wall, so he stood up and walked toward
the market. Maybe Thérèse was there.

The afternoon sun had knocked away the earlier chill
and the air was damp and much too warm. A smallish
crowd of local buyers and tourists milled about the stalls
and stands. There were more people selling than buying.
He stopped before a tray of meat tarts thinking to buy
one, but the smell turned his stomach and he moved
away. Farther down he could see crates of bright red
bottles of soda. Something cold to drink, he thought,

297

might be better. As he turned in that direction, he bumped into two young Germans with cameras. Automatically he looked toward where their cameras were focused. There she was, hat intact, mouth moving a mile a minute, her broken eyes cheerfully evil. He stepped in front of the cameras and said No to the Germans. No, and shook his head. The young men looked angry for a second and then, glancing at each other, shrugged and moved on. He stood close to Thérèse for a full minute before she recognized him and shrieked "Chocolate eater! Chocolate eater!" almost knocking her tray of smoked eels to the ground.

"This place is closed," she said to a would-be customer, "*fermé*, madame, *fermé*," and packed up her eels, her folding camp stool and her wooden crate—none of which she would let him carry as they made their way up to the powder pink house. Thérèse laughed and chattered about the weather and her girlhood all the way but once in the house she became shy and formal, making him uncomfortable and unable to sit. To break the awkward atmosphere he initiated a pointed conversation.

"Have you been back over there?" he asked her.

She spit on the floor for an answer and added nothing to it.

He smiled. "What work does Gideon do now?"

"Hires out," she said. "To taxi men."

Drumming up business, he guessed, at airports and hotels for the men who owned their taxis. They would tip him for the fares he got them. Thérèse grew silent and formal again. Like a duenna she avoided his eyes but watched him none the less. Quietly (all she needed was lace in her hands) guarding some virtue that was only in her mind. The atmosphere of starch returned until he remembered something. He'd put his plastic-wrapped airplane snack in his hand luggage: a pastrami on a roll, a tiny packet of pasteurized cheese, one of mustard and an apple. He opened the bag and presented it to Thérèse whose happiness, instead of being cheerful, was so deep

the whole time they walked to the plane. She had seen it, and Son saw it too: the mink-dark eyes staring greedily into blue ones, another hand on the inside of her raw silk knee the colour of honey. Not being able to go further with those pictures, he diverted his mind to the irrelevant. Who was it? Was it Michael who met her, Valerian's son, the one that didn't show up for Christmas, but who came later? Was that the Ryk who sent her the coat? Or was it someone in New York who had come to the island with her? Or was it someone she met in the airport? It was all mixed up, like when he ran out of laughter ammunition and kicked an M.P. in the groin, but the thing that was clear was the thing he knew when he stood wrapped in a towel gazing out of the window at this same man's back: he had not wanted to love her because he could not survive losing her. But it was done. Already done and he was in it; stuck in it and revolted by the possibility of being freed.

Gideon interrupted his questions. "What will you do?"

"Find her. Go to Paris and find her." He pressed his temples with his fingers to stop the drone.

"But if she's with another?"

"I'll take her away from him."

"A woman, man. Just a woman," said Gideon patiently.

"I have to find her."

"How? Paris is a big place."

"I'll get her address."

"Where?"

"From over there."

"They won't give it to you."

"They will. I'll make them. Make them tell me who the man is. Where she went." He was standing now. Nervous. Eager to get going.

"You not going for the address, you going to cause mayhem."

"Let him," said Thérèse. "Kill them, chocolate eater."

"Don't be crazy. It's just a woman, man."

It was true. He wanted to find her but he wanted to

smash something too. Smash the man who took the woman he had loved while she slept, and smash where they had first made love, where she took his hand and was afraid and needed him and they walked up the stairs holding hands, just like she walked to the plane holding somebody else's hand. She should not have done that if she was going to get on an airplane and put her head on another man's shoulder.

"Get me there," he said to Gideon. "Now, while there is still light."

Gideon ran his tongue over his stone-white teeth. "No. I'm not doing that. Take you to smash up the place?"

"I only want her address. That's all."

"You won't be welcome there and neither me."

"I will only talk to them."

"And if they won't talk to you?"

"They will. They'll tell me."

"No, man. That's final."

"All right. I'll take the launch."

"Good," said Gideon. "Take the launch. In two days maybe you'll be cooler."

"Two days?"

"Two, yes. Launch don't go again till Monday. Today is market day. Saturday."

"I can't wait that long."

"Telephone them."

"They won't tell me anything on the telephone. Take me."

"This is crazy-mad shit, man. You can't go there."

"I don't have a choice. There's nothing else for me to do. You think I'd choose this if I had a choice?"

Thérèse turned around and looked at him. Then she looked at the airplane food on the record player. "I can take you," she said.

"You not taking him nowhere. You blind as a bat."

"I can take you," she repeated.

"The sun's going down. You'll drown!" said Gideon. "We'll fish you off the beach in the morning."

"I can see better in the dark and I know that crossing too well."

"Don't trust her, man. Don't. I'm telling you."

Son looked at Thérèse and nodded. "Get me there, Thérèse."

"Two big fools," said Gideon. "One blind, the other gone mad."

"Eat," said Thérèse to Son. "I'll take you when it's time."

Son stood up. "I can't eat," he said. "And I've been awake for days. Sleep won't come and I can't get hungry."

"Come with me then," said Gideon. "Let's go out. Go to Grande Cinq, have a drink and relax a little."

"No," he said. "I don't want a woman."

"Christ!" Gideon was disgusted. He never got over being amazed at that kind of passion, though he had seen it enough. "Well, rum's good anywhere. I resign from the sober world tonight." He went into the bedroom and returned with a pint of rum, the bottle half-full. He poured and passed a cup to Son who took it in tiny sips with much time in between. All three sat at the table, Son alone not eating the fish and rice. Gideon told stories about women he had known: their "wiles" and their "ways" till he settled on the nurse he'd married in the States. His grievances about the lady were trotted out one by one for show: her children by a former marriage; her ailments; her habits of dress; her laugh; her relatives; her food; her looks. He allowed as how she was faithful, but that's all she was. Had she been otherwise he swore he would never have left her out of gratitude. As it was, she was insatiable: mean, arrogant and insatiable. He went to bed fully clothed on that note: the abnormal sexual hunger of black American nurses.

Son lay down on the cot Alma Estée sometimes used while Thérèse got ready and he did not know he slept until she woke him. He sat up relieved that the jaw's harp in his head had stopped. She brought a flashlight, but

305

they did not need it to walk down the hill or to find the *Prix de France*. They checked the gas and agreed there was enough for a round trip. They rowed away from the dock until they were far enough out to start a motor without attracting the attention of any gendarmes who might be on contraband patrol. It was raining a little, getting foggier, but the sea was not high. Thérèse insisted on steering for she knew the way, she said, and could not talk the directions to him. The feel of the current was what she went by. She only prayed no larger boats were out there, as hampered in vision as she was in the fog.

He remembered the trip over as half an hour, forty-five minutes at most, but this trip seemed longer. They'd been out at least an hour. The boat rocked and skipped, rocked and skipped to a regular beat. The jaw's harp was back like a nuthouse lullaby and he dozed a little and woke; dozed a little and woke. Each time his eyes opened they rested on the shadow of Marie Thérèse Foucault. Each time her shoulders and profile grew darker—her outline fainter. Till finally he could barely make her out at all, he simply felt her feet against his. Even her breathing could not be heard over the motor's breath and the insistent harp in his head. The light rain stopped and the clouds descended to examine that party of two. One tranquil, dozing, weakly fighting sleep—the other, head turned landward intent on a horizon she could not possibly see even if she were not as blind as justice. Her hands on the lever were nimble, steady. The upper part of her body leaned forward straining as if to hear fish calling from the sea. Behind the curious clouds, hills crouched on all fours and at their knees were rocks and the permanent sea. Thérèse cut the motor and dropped one oar to guide with. The tide carried them and the little boat seemed to be floating on its own. She held the oar midships until it struck a rock, split and slowed the boat to a half turn and then a rocking on baby waves. Son stirred and opened his eyes. There was nothing to see—not sky or island or Marie Thérèse. The sea was very

306

still as in a lagoon or a cove.

"Here," she said. "We are here."

"Where?" All he could see was mist. "Where's the dock?"

"On the other side. We are at the back of Isle des Chevaliers. You can climb here on the rocks. They are all together here, like a bridge. You can crawl them all the way to shore."

"It's too foggy," he said. "I can't see my way."

"Don't be afraid. This is the place. On the far side."

"I can't see shit. I can hardly see you."

"Don't see; feel," she said. "You can feel your way, but hurry, hurry. I have to get back."

"This doesn't make sense. Why don't you go to the other side, where the dock is?"

"No," she said. "This is the place."

"Isle des Chevaliers?"

"Yes. Yes. The far side."

"Are you sure?"

"Positive."

Son took his tie out of his jacket pocket and began to knot it around the handle of his travelling bag. "I don't get it, Thérèse. You bring me here as a favour, but before I can say thanks, you make it hard for me to land and even harder to get to the house. What'd you do that for?"

"This is the place. Where you can take a choice. Back there you say you don't. Now you do."

"What the hell are you talking about? If I get off these rocks without drowning, I have to stomp all around in those hills to get to the other side. It must be, good God, ten miles. I'll be all night and half the day . . ."

"Hurry! Get out. I have to get away before the water is too small."

He attached the tie to his waist so the bag hung from behind him. Then he moved over to negotiate the rocks.

"It's easy," she said. "Climb to it and the next one is right behind, then another and another like a road. Then the land."

307

"You sure, Thérèse?"

"Yes. Yes," she said, then as he turned toward the rocks she touched his back. "Wait. Tell me. If you cannot find her what will you do? Live in the garden of some other white people house?"

He looked around to tell her to mind her own business, but the inability to see her face in the fog stopped him.

"Small boy," she said, "don't go to L'Arbe de la Croix." Her voice was a calamitous whisper coming out of the darkness toward him like jaws. "Forget her. There is nothing in her parts for you. She has forgotten her ancient properties."

He swallowed and, saying nothing, turned back to the rocks, kneeling, stretching his hand to feel them. He touched one. It was dry above the water line and rough, but large enough, it seemed to him, to hold a grown man.

He leaned out of the boat tipping it so it took a little water. The bag knocked clumsily against his thigh. He sat back down and undid the knot. "Keep it for me," he said. Then he grabbed with both hands the surface of the rock and heaved himself onto it. He lay there for a bit, then stretched his arm again and felt the sister rock at his fingertips. Now he could smell the land.

"Hurry," she urged him. "They are waiting."

"Waiting? Who's waiting?" Suddenly he was alarmed.

"The men. The men are waiting for you." She was pulling the oars now, moving out. "You can choose now. You can get free of her. They are waiting in the hills for you. They are naked and they are blind too. I have seen them; their eyes have no colour in them. But they gallop; they race those horses like angels all over the hills where the rain forest is, where the champion daisy trees still grow. Go there. Choose them." She was far from him now, but her voice was near like skin.

"Thérèse!" he shouted, turning his head around to the place where the urging of her jaws had come from. "Are you sure?"

If she answered, he could not hear it, and he certainly couldn't see her, so he went. First he crawled the rocks one by one, one by one, till his hands touched shore and the nursing sound of the sea was behind him. He felt around, crawled off and then stood up. Breathing heavily with his mouth open he took a few tentative steps. The pebbles made him stumble and so did the roots of trees. He threw out his hands to guide and steady his going. By and by he walked steadier, now steadier. The mist lifted and the trees stepped back a bit as if to make the way easier for a certain kind of man. Then he ran. Lickety-split. Lickety-split. Looking neither to the left nor to the right. Lickety-split. Lickety-split. Lickety-lickety-lickety-split.